DEADLY VISITATION

A faint sound—a metallic clattering—awakened John and he came to semiconsciousness.

His fatigue-weighted mind fought to bring him back to full awareness, but it was too difficult. His upward gaze showed him that the sky above had become extremely dark. Had he slept until nightfall?

He propped himself up to look around. The cloister was plunged in a deeper gloom. Turning his head slowly, he saw a flickering of yet darker shadows on the stone walls of the passages into the cloister.

But it wasn't the benign spirits of the monks that now manifested themselves to him. The forms that came into view were more baleful: men wasted and white, as if from long death. The shreds of long tunics and flowing cloaks fluttered about their bony frames. Teeth showing in rictus smiles gleamed in their skull-like heads, but nothing save blackness showed where their eyes had been.

The ghastly warriors poured into the cloister from all parts of the ruin, forming a solid ring about the still-reclining Milne. The skeletal hands of the figures clutched round shields and swords and spears. Keen-honed blades and points glinted with malevolent light. They lifted to threaten the trapped man.

As one, the ring of beings started to move upon him. . . .

Don't miss any of these exciting titles from
Bantam Spectra!

RHINEGOLD by Stephen Grundy

The Novels of Deverry
by Katharine Kerr
DAGGERSPELL
DARKSPELL
THE BRISTLING WOOD
THE DRAGON REVENANT
A TIME OF EXILE
A TIME OF OMENS
DAYS OF BLOOD AND FIRE
DAYS OF AIR AND DARKNESS

Brian Froud's Faerielands
THE WILD WOOD by Charles de Lint
SOMETHING RICH AND STRANGE by Patricia McKillip

ONCE A HERO by Michael A. Stackpole

The Deathgate Cycle
by Margaret Weis and Tracy Hickman
DRAGON WING
ELVEN STAR
FIRE SEA
SERPENT MAGE
THE HAND OF CHAOS
INTO THE LABYRINTH
THE SEVENTH GATE

LORDS OF THE SKY by Angus Wells

The
Darkening
Flood

Kenneth C. Flint

SPECTRA™ BANTAM BOOKS

NEW YORK TORONTO LONDON SYDNEY AUCKLAND

The Darkening Flood
A Bantam Spectra Book / September 1995

SPECTRA and the portrayal of a boxed "s" are trademarks of Bantam
Books, a division of Bantam Doubleday Dell Publishing Group, Inc.

Yeats poems: Reprinted with permission of Simon & Schuster from THE
POEMS OF W.B. YEATS: A NEW EDITION, edited by Richard J.
Finneran. Copyright 1924, 1928, 1933, 1934 by Macmillan Publishing
Company. Copyrights renewed 1952, 1956, © 1961, 1962 by Bertha
Georgie Yeats. Copyright 1940 by Georgie Yeats, renewed © 1968 by
Bertha Georgie Yeats, Michael Butler Yeats, and Anne Yeats. Copyright
© 1983 by Anne Yeats.

ISBN 0-553-57163-X

Published simultaneously in the United States and Canada

Bantam Books are published by Bantam Books, a division of Bantam Doubleday
Dell Publishing Group, Inc. Its trademark, consisting of the words "Bantam
Books" and the portrayal of a rooster, is Registered in U.S. Patent and
Trademark Office and in other countries. Marca Registrada. Bantam Books,
1540 Broadway, New York, New York 10036.

PRINTED IN THE UNITED STATES OF AMERICA

RAD   0 9 8 7 6 5 4 3 2 1

DEDICATION

This book is for my sixteen-year-old son, Devin Cormac Flint, whose creative and invaluable contributions to my stories show that someday he will become as fine a writer as he hopes to be.

This is also for my son Gavin Donal Flint, whose own ten-year-old's imagination knows no bounds in time or space. He too has made excellent and delightful contributions to my work.

Out-worn heart, in a time out-worn,
Come clear of the nets of wrong and right;
Laugh, heart, again in the grey twilight,
Sigh, heart, again in the dew of the morn.

Your mother Eire is always young,
Dew ever shining and twilight grey;
Though hope fall from you and love decay,
Burning in fires of a slanderous tongue.

Come, heart, where hill is heaped upon hill:
For there the mystical brotherhood
Of sun and moon and hollow and wood
And river and stream work out their will;

And God stands winding His lonely horn,
And time and the world are ever in flight;
And love is less kind than the grey twilight,
And hope is less dear than the dew of the morn.

—WILLIAM BUTLER YEATS: *"Into the Twilight"*

PROLOGUE

✠

The cowled and dark-robed figure stepped out onto the very brink of the high rooftop and stood poised there a moment, staring into the night.

The pastoral countryside of meadows, fields, and groves that stretched away all about the tower showed clearly under the bright moon and brilliant stars of an open sky. Save for the tiny sounds of insects and the faint call of a night bird, a stillness lay upon the land.

The eyes of the figure glinted out from the blackness within the cowl like twin shards of ice as they moved to take in the sleeping world below. They flashed with a sharper, harder glow as they rested upon the small clustered lights of a distant village, flickering through the foliage of the intervening trees.

With its hard gaze fixed, the figure shifted into a new pose. One arm was outstretched to point long, slender fingers toward the sky. One of the gleaming eyes was closed, leaving the single chill orb to stare on with the intensity of full concentration.

From the mouth hidden within the hood a voice now issued. It spoke out in tones deep, resonant, and strongly emphasized, that sounded out in a slow rhythm like the ringing of a great bell. The clanging speech rolled away and lifted toward the sky, each of its words tolled out clearly but still unintelligible. Even so, in its sound it had the force and flavor of a fervently chanted prayer, of an intense exhortation to some power. Clearly the figure was raising an incantation to the sky.

And the sky was answering.

From the far horizon a denser mass of darkness welled up into the night, billowing and spreading like the clouds of a great storm impelled by a tempest wind. In mere seconds it had suffused the sky, snuffing the stars, swallowing the moon.

A wind arose with its coming, sweeping across the countryside, keening in the trees. It tugged at the dark cloak's broad hem, making the garment flutter up like vast bird's wings, causing the figure posed so precariously on the edge to waver slightly. But the being maintained its balance, and it continued the strange litany without a pause.

Darkness rolled in to obscure all sight of the land. It closed in last about the village like a pair of hands clenching tight to throttle life from the place. The tiny nest of lights proclaiming the village's existence winked out.

The rising wind moaned loudly as it swept in to whirl about the village. In one small, thatched-roof cottage, a young girl cried out in her sleep and then sat up in the bed of her little room, staring around her with wide, frightened eyes.

Her mother came swiftly in to her.

"It's all right, child," she said soothingly, sitting down and hugging the girl tight. But the faint tremor in her voice revealed her own fear.

Both looked around them, listening to the sounds. The wind seemed to swirl in a tight vortex around their cottage now. It howled through the door cracks and down the chimney. It blew tree limbs to claw against the walls. It tore savagely at the thatch and shook the roof beams.

Then there came something else. A sound of new movements rose outside. Not sounds of wind, but thuds as of footsteps, rustles as of clothes, sighs and whispers as from human throats. And outside, all around, shadowy figures coalesced from the vaster swirling dark to creep in close about the house.

The bedroom's window rattled in its frame. The woman

and her daughter looked toward it to see faces there. They were ghastly: deathly pale, wasted visages, with eyes red and glowing like the coals of Hell itself. And white teeth glinted bright in death's-head grimaces.

"Mother!" the girl gasped out in horror. "What are they!"

Bony hands appeared to pound against the window glass. The sash rattled louder.

"Come on!" the mother cried.

She got up, grabbing her daughter's hand and pulling her from the bed. They went out of the bedroom and across the floor of a larger room beyond, heading toward the single outside door. But halfway there, the door blew suddenly open, thrown back by an immense blast of wind that spouted into the room.

The darkness too poured in through the open doorway. It spread and divided at once into separate globs of black that rose up, resolving quickly into the forms of more cadaverous beings. Their skeletal forms were clad in ragged tunics and long tattered cloaks. And there was a cold gleam from the sword blades and spear tips of keen-honed weapons clutched in their bony hands.

The nebulous and wavering figures of the dark host, like those of smoke tormented by the wind, suggested that these were not beings of any solid form but phantasms created of the night and clouds. But whether incorporeal beings or not, the mother and daughter still recoiled from their ghastly threat. As the figures advanced upon them, they withdrew, backing into the small and windowless kitchen. The mother slammed its door against the beings, throwing the locking bolt. Then, trapped within the room, the two of them huddled down in a corner, holding tight to one another in their helpless horror.

The door rattled hard. The bolt was torn loose. From the room beyond the armed host surged into the doorway, crowding through to fill the room.

They moved in upon the woman and girl. The mother

pulled her daughter's head tight to her breast in protection and shot a fearful but defiant gaze up at the menacing beings.

Then the dark forms closed in tight about them, the fluttering shreds of their massed cloaks entwining like a web that seemed to engulf the trapped pair.

In an instant the mother and daughter vanished.

CHAPTER
ONE

A man I praise that once in Tara's Halls
Said to the woman on his knees, 'Lie still.
My hundredth year is at an end. I think
That something is about to happen, I think
That the adventure of old age begins.

—W. B. YEATS: *"In Tara's Halls"*

The afternoon skies were gray but not threatening, as is common enough with Irish weather. No hint of the smell of rain was in the air.

So quiet was the village of Ballymurroe that it might well have been abandoned long since. As it was still some hours until the local men would go to their cows for the evening's milking, the only place showing a sign of activity was Ryan's Tavern.

Two of the village men stood in front of the tavern. They looked almost twins with their worn dark coats, wool caps, and thin, weather-lined faces so alike. They stood and sipped at their mugs of stout and gazed across the small village square to the green and gray horizon.

They were gazing at nothing in particular. Nothing had changed in the square for several hours. Nothing had changed on the horizon for a hundred years. Still, they seemed content with their quiet vigil.

A small red car poked into the square from one of the several roads that entered the village to meet there. It swung around the high cross in the center of the square and started down the street running past Ryan's Tavern.

The two men watched it approach with no change of expression. As it passed the tavern, the young man and woman who occupied it raised a hand in greeting. One of the twins raised a hand in reply.

The vehicle moved on a short way and turned in at a gate in a waist-high stone wall. Beyond the wall showed the thatched roofs and whitewashed walls of several low buildings. The red car pulled up by the first and stopped.

With no word at all passed between them, the two men abruptly turned as one and walked into the tavern. It was dim inside and hazy with pipe and cigarette smoke that hung without movement in the stale, stagnant air. A dozen other men sat at tables, talking quietly or dreaming over their glasses of stout.

The pair moved to the bar. Mr. Daniel Ryan—a big, ruddy-faced, soft-looking man—stood behind it. A great collection of just-washed glasses was clustered on the bar before him, and he was busy wiping them off. He picked up the glasses one at a time, worked at them mechanically for a moment with a cloth, then set them away on shelves behind him. The slow, monotonous process seemed almost endless.

The pair of men emptied their mugs and lowered them onto the bar. Ryan looked up from the mugs to the pair of stolid faces.

"Would you be wanting another Guinness, then?" he asked them. He picked up one of the clean glasses and began to wipe it.

"No, thank you, Dan," said one of the men. Then he nodded toward the door. "There's some new ones just come to the cottages."

Ryan carefully finished wiping out the glass, put it away, and picked up another.

"Very nice, Jamie," he said tonelessly, starting to work on the new glass. "But it's nothing very strange, having tourists come to tourist cottages."

"It's not just that, Dan," said Jamie, leaning forward on the bar and speaking gravely. "I think that I've seen these before."

Ryan stopped wiping the glass.

"Oh, you have, have you?" he replied.

He put down the glass and towel and walked around the bar to look out a front window. Across the road the young couple were now out of their car and standing beside it, looking around them with pleased smiles.

Ryan watched them for a moment with narrowed, scrutinizing eyes. Finally he nodded.

"Jamie," he said quietly, "I'm afraid you may just be right."

CHAPTER
TWO

֎

And I shall have some peace there, for peace
    comes dropping slow,
Dropping from the veils of the morning to
    where the cricket sings;
There midnight's all a glimmer, and noon a
    purple glow,
And evening full of the linnet's wings.

—W. B. YEATS: *"The Lake Isle of Innisfree"*

By the small red car, John and Ann Milne stretched themselves and examined their surroundings.

As a face in a crowd, John Milne would not have been noticed. His height and build were medium, his hair a middle brown. At age twenty-eight he had a young, even-featured look that—with the help of a rather bushy mustache and large, dark-rimmed glasses—gave him a certain innocence of appearance.

The innocence effectively masked a character that was both sensitive and intelligent. These were helpful traits to be possessed by a writer and a college instructor of English literature; but if Milne had been asked about them, he would

have denied their existence. He would have labeled himself
a dreamer; a man who worried too much.

Just now, however, he had no worries. He was only concerned with sensual impressions. He was enjoying stretching
muscles cramped from the driving. More importantly, he was
reacquainting himself with the feel and smell of the air, the
look of the village and the surrounding fields. They matched
without variation the clear images that he had carried in his
mind for months. The tourist cottages, evenly spaced about a
small commons, were still neat and new-looking with their
gold thatch and whitewashed walls, their bright gardens and
carefully trimmed lawn.

"It looks the same," John said with satisfaction. "It's like
we never left."

As he gazed about him, his eyes met those of his wife,
Ann, and he smiled at her look of pleasure. Her enjoyment
of the country meant as much to him as did his own impressions. It had been largely for her that he had agreed to come
to Ireland on their first trip, the previous summer. He had
never regretted making that trip.

One look at Ann Milne would have told most people
why she had wanted to come to Ireland. There was little
doubt of her heritage. Her deep red hair flowed down over
her shoulders in a thick, wavy torrent. Her pale skin was
sprinkled with freckles so fine as to be almost invisible, except across her nose and cheeks where the sun darkened
them. She was tall and long-boned, but without seeming frail
or overly thin. Two years younger than her husband, her
clean and strong features still had the freshness of someone
barely out of her teens.

Even without the blazing red hair she would have been a
fine-looking woman; with it she was striking.

Especially, John reflected appreciatively, with the background of this green, green land.

"Very nice," he said with emphasis. "This color scheme is
perfect for you. You ought to carry the country around with
you everywhere you go."

"I imagine that would impress people," she said, trying to visualize this feat.

Her personality ran slightly more to the practical than did his, but their interests and their senses of humor were a match. Between them they struck a good balance.

"Do you think it's a coincidence that red hair ended up in the Emerald Isles?" he asked.

"I like to think my ancestors just had excellent taste," she told him, and they both laughed.

They were cheerful to the point of exuberance. They had been so since they had come back to Ireland.

The summer before had been a honeymoon trip delayed for two years by the need to save the money for it. They had made friends and had regretted leaving, feeling they might never be able to return. But then a charter flight, arranged through the high school where Ann taught English and history, had given them a new chance that they could just afford. They had eagerly taken it.

John took another deep breath of the fragrant air. "Well, shall we see about our cottage?" he asked.

But Ann wasn't listening. She was looking toward the cottages on the far side of the common. Toward one in particular.

She was seeing that cottage in her mind, recalling a vivid memory from a year ago. In it a raven-haired woman of middle age, a tousle-haired girl of twelve, and a yellow-brown dog stood lined up before the door, girl and woman smiling rather shyly for a parting photo.

"John," she said suddenly, "I'd like to go and see the Traherns right away."

She seemed so anxious that her husband didn't hesitate. He'd had that impulse, too.

"Come on, then," he said. He grabbed her hand, and they started across the common toward the cottage the Traherns occupied.

Nancy Trahern and her twelve-year-old daughter, Bridget, were the first and the closest friends they had made the year before. They were exiles of a sort. Mrs. Trahern had brought her daughter from Belfast to the south of Ireland in search of a place free from the violence, hatred, and mistrust. She had told the Milnes that she wanted Bridget to know some peace in her childhood, and had seemed willing to leave a home and husband to find it. Mother and daughter had become year-round residents of the cottages.

The Milnes had corresponded with them steadily since the previous summer, and had written them of their plans to return. On the flight over, John and Ann had talked of nothing but that first trip. On arrival they had rented a car and rushed to Ballymurroe from Shannon Airport, their eagerness to see the village and their friends increasing as they neared.

With the expectation of reunion, broad smiles were in place as they approached the cottage. John looked about him, expecting the Traherns' dog Taffy to appear and investigate these intruders on his sacred space. The big yellow Labrador was allowed to run free most of the day and was usually close by, but today there was no sign of him.

The outer door to the Traherns' was closed. John rapped softly and they waited, braced for the happy shock of greeting. When there was no reply, he rapped again, more loudly, and listened for some movement inside. There was none.

Casually he stepped to a window and peered in.

"Wait! What are you doing?" Ann said, startled by his boldness.

"Just some friendly peeking," he replied affably.

The interior of the cottage was much as John remembered. School drawings by Bridget were taped up on walls around the fireplace. The artist's easel that Nancy Trahern used for her painting was set up by the far window as usual, to take advantage of the light. A sweater cast across a chair arm, cups and teapot on the table indicated that the place was certainly occupied. Still, there was no sign of mother or daughter.

"They seem to be gone," he said, turning to Ann.

"Oh," she said, and the tone of that single word was enough to reflect her disappointment. John felt it as well.

"Where do you suppose they are?" she asked. "In the village?"

"I suppose so," he replied, then brightened. "Hey, why don't we surprise them when they come back? We can hide somewhere and leap out at them and—"

"And scare them to death?" Ann finished. "A nice thing that would be."

"It's the leprechaun that gets into me over here," he said, smiling his best elfish smile.

"Leprechaun?" she repeated with distaste. "That's a pretty clichéd image for a student of Celtic folklore, isn't it? You know they are the—"

But Ann's opinion of leprechauns, intriguing though John was certain it would have been, was cut short by a loud voice.

"Halloo there!" it said.

Both the Milnes turned. They saw a woman coming toward them, bustling across the green with the rapid, shuffling motion of a hard-driving steam engine. They could even hear the puffing.

It was Mrs. Ryan, the caretaker of the tourist cottages. She was a very small woman, a fact that was accentuated by a forward slanted posture that lowered her head and thrust it out ahead of her. Her hair was a cap of tight white curls; and her dress was of the plain, formless kind that many older Irish women considered a badge of maturity.

She was usually a neat woman, but now she was disheveled and a bit out of breath.

"Well, well," she said as she came up to them. "And what have you come for, now?"

Her thickly accented speech had always been difficult for them to understand; but, in this case, her meaning came through clearly; and its directness took them by surprise.

They had naturally assumed that she would know very well who they were, perhaps even welcome them back with a modest but colorful celebration. Instead there was a cool, distant tone to her words.

"Mrs. Ryan," said Ann, "don't you remember us? We're

the Milnes . . . from America. We stayed right here last
summer."

"Really?" she said flatly, with no sign at all of dawning
recognition. She seemed almost disappointed. "But what is it
that you've come here for?"

They had never found Mrs. Ryan to be aware of the
obvious, but this was too much. Ann looked helplessly
toward John, and he took a turn in the attempt to communi-
cate.

"We are here to stay, Mrs. Ryan," he said slowly and with
emphasis. "We booked a cottage here for three weeks.
Through the *Bord Failte*."

"Ah . . . to stay," she said. Again there was that faint
note of disappointment in the words. She shook her head.
"No . . . no, I can't recall the reservation. Perhaps it was at
some other cottages. At Puckane? Or Newbury?"

"We made the booking through the Tourist Board," he
repeated. "*Your* Tourist Board. Didn't they call you to confirm?"

"No. I'm sorry." She shook her head again, more emphatically. "You say you were here before, and I believe you,
although I can't say I recall. But I never got a booking, and I
won't have a room for two weeks. If you like, I'll call the
Shannon office and try to book you elsewhere."

Her suggestion was made just a little too quickly, just a
shade too eagerly, and John became instantly wary. As he
did, his face seemed to become blanker, the eyes behind the
glasses more innocent, as if in camouflage.

"Oh, what a problem," he replied, and his voice expressed confusion and distress. "We were so sure it was here.
I'm afraid we'll have to call the *Bord* ourselves and get it
straight. They did guarantee it"—he looked straight into the
woman's eyes—"and we really couldn't settle for anyplace
else."

Even with John's calm and unthreatening manner, the
implication of his words was clear. There was a silence while
Mrs. Ryan appeared to ponder its significance. Then the

Milnes watched a strange upward stretching of her mouth that they assumed she meant for a smile. Milne was more alarmed than comforted by it.

"No need to call. No need," she said. "Now I'm reminded, it seems I did get a booking cancellation. I can find room for you . . . if you want it."

If they wanted it, he thought; and several rather nasty replies formed in his mind. But he tried to hold back. He had found that sarcasm, like the obvious, was lost on Mrs. Ryan.

Ann saw his jaw tighten and knew the signs of rapidly ending patience. She hastened to answer for him.

"Yes. We would like a cottage here," she said simply.

"Fine. Then I'll take you to the cottage now," Mrs. Ryan told them. "This one is taken."

"We know. We were just about to . . ." John began, lifting a hand toward the Traherns' door.

Abruptly, Mrs. Ryan turned away from him and started across the common.

With open mouth and arm still extended, Milne looked after her for a frozen moment. Ann came close and took him by the arm.

"Oh well, never mind for now," she said, and urged him forward in the little woman's wake.

"Number six is ready," Mrs. Ryan told them when they caught up with her. "I'll put you in there. It will hold seven people, you know."

"Yes," said Ann. "We stayed in number four last year. It was a beautiful cottage."

"Fine," Mrs. Ryan replied noncommittally. "Well, here is number six."

The cottage they'd reached was on the far side of the commons and nearly opposite the Traherns. Mrs. Ryan opened its red-painted outer door with a heavy, old-fashioned key and led them in. The door at the other end of the tiny vestibule was open, and beyond it the large living room opened impressively.

"You go right ahead and settle yourselves in," said Mrs.

Ryan. "You know where everything is, I'm sure. I'll just go and get my receipt book and write you up."

She put the key down on the dining table in the center of the room and bustled out.

The Milnes looked the interior over with contentment. It was immaculate, its floors still damp from a recent scrubbing. Tourists had put little wear on it; but then, there was very little that could wear. The cottage was a typical construction of wood frame and thick concrete block, cemented over and whitewashed, inside and out. Ireland's temperate climate, made insulation unnecessary.

Those who had designed and built the tourist cottages had taken some care to create a look of authenticity. In the main they were of a style that marked an Irish way of life that had existed for generations past. In one such cottage the Irish patriot McAllister had died in the valiant stand of 1799. In another Sean MacDiarmada, martyr of the 1916 Easter rising, had been born.

The furniture was rough but sturdy. The floors were of gray-black slate, a smooth and sturdy stone traditionally given as a gift to brides for flooring their new homes. The huge, open fireplace was equipped with the iron hooks still used for cooking by many Irish families. The concessions to modernity, and ones for which the Milnes were thankful, were limited to an electric kitchen and an up-to-date bathroom.

Altogether it was a tasteful combination of timelessness and changing times. To the Milnes it was a comfortable and convenient place to stay, and it offered one of the most reasonable types of accommodation.

"I'll go bring the car around here," said John. "You pick a bedroom."

"I want the upper one," she replied without hesitation. "You know that it's my favorite."

A cottage of that size had three bedrooms. Two were behind the kitchen. The third was in a loft, above, and reached by an open staircase from the living room.

"What about the Traherns?" she asked.

"We'll unpack. If they're not back by then, we'll wander into town."

After John had gone, Ann went up into the loft bedroom. It was a large, A-shaped room tucked under the cottage's roof. Its ceiling was the line of heavy, wooden support beams.

She went to the window over the bed. It looked out on open pastures that sloped gently away and afforded an unobstructed view of a line of mountains, almost always shrouded in soft, gray mists, but only the more beautiful for that.

The air of the closed room had a faint staleness to it. She knelt on the bed, opened the window wide, and paused to admire the scene.

Behind the cottages a tall man was cutting the grass with a broad, curving scythe that moved rhythmically to mow wide paths in the living green. The fragrant smell of the newly cut grass was strong on the air.

Farther out in the field a few cattle sat, legs folded neatly beneath them, gazing out over the countryside with what seemed to Ann an air of quiet appreciation.

Suddenly, as if by joint agreement, the cattle stood. She was amazed to see the big animals move with such agility. They bunched together and moved to one side and Ann caught a glimpse of what had alarmed them.

Something was moving in the tall grass nearby.

She could follow the passage of a form that was low to the ground. There were quick flashes of what had to be an animal of a fairly large size and a light brownish coloring.

Then the man saw it, too. He turned and charged for the spot, lifting his scythe menacingly. The thing in the grass scuttled away at high speed and disappeared through some shrubs.

He shouted after it in words Ann could hear but not understand. Gaelic profanity, she supposed.

The man turned back toward the cottages and noticed her watching. He stopped abruptly and openly stared back.

Even at that distance she was aware of his eyes.

They were black and set deep behind overhanging brows.

A light sparked and flared in them. It was like the light of a great fire far inside a cavern and only dimly seen from the entrance.

The force of the eyes held her, and she felt a vague alarm that they should do so.

CHAPTER
THREE

✠

Never until this night have I been stirred.
The elaborate starlight throws a reflection
On the dark stream.
Till all the eddies gleam:
And thereupon there comes that scream
From terrified, invisible beast or bird:
Image of poignant recollection.

—W. B. YEATS: *"An Image from a Past Life"*

"Where are you?" John Milne's voice drifted up to his wife from downstairs.

She turned her head at that and the unsettling contact was broken.

"Up here," she called.

"Well, down here I'm being crushed by luggage," came a gasping cry.

"I'm coming."

As she rose to go, she glanced outside again. The man was back at his work, head down, cutting with a slow, effortless rhythm. Just a laborer at his work.

She went downstairs to help John with the luggage. They

had time to bring the bulk of it in and begin unpacking before Mrs. Ryan reappeared, receipt pad and pencil in hand.

Ann remembered that the year before the woman had used any contact with her tenants as an excuse to pump them for news of the world outside the village. This time, however, she seemed intent only on getting away. She scribbled the receipt rapidly, tore off the slip, and thrust it out for Ann to take.

"Thank you for now," she said, moving to the door. "I must rush away. I know you'll be fine. You know where I am if there's anything you need."

"Wait," John called after her. "Please . . . we were wondering about—"

"All the information is in the guidebook on the mantel," she said and, with a wave of farewell, she was gone.

"She comes and goes like the Cheshire Cat," he said with irritation, looking at the doorway where she had vanished.

"She hasn't got the smile," Ann replied humorlessly. Then she shrugged. "In any case, I doubt that her tourist guide is going to tell us where the Traherns are."

"We don't need it to," he answered decisively. "We'll go into the village and try to find them. We can get some food while we're at it."

"Good idea," Ann agreed. "And if we don't see them, somebody'll know where they are."

The two men worked vigorously on the fallen mass of stone and earth with shovels, scooping the rubble back.

They were a strong-looking pair of thick-built men, one middle-aged, one younger. Stripped to the waist for their arduous job, their bodies were darkened with a layer of grime streaked with their streaming sweat.

The room in which they labored was windowless and dank, deeply shadowed save where the focused effect of several large floodlights on tall tripods brightly illuminated the area they worked upon. The residual glow dimly revealed a long, narrow chamber of rough block walls and ceiling.

The room was some dozen feet wide, but the full extent of its length was at present impossible to know. The collapse of the roof at one end had brought a great avalanche of debris down to fill the space, hiding all beyond.

It was this fall that the men were clearing, shoring up the unstable area above with metal jacks and timbers as they went. The work was slow but progressing steadily. The rubble piles behind them and the forest of supports already in place were testament to how far the clearing had gone.

Not far from the two men, just out of the circle of bright glow, a shadowed figure stood watching them. Its already dim outlines were further shrouded by a full cloak, and its features were concealed by a hood. But eyes like shards of ice glinted in the light as their owner intently watched.

A large chunk of ceiling block fallen atop the pile seemed wedged in tight. The older man took up an iron pry bar and shoved at it tentatively. Even that bit of tampering was too much. The block tottered, toppled, slid down the slope of rubble. The remaining ceiling stones above groaned from the new stress and dropped a shower of crushed rock, threatening to fall.

"Careful!" the shadowed figure called in warning.

The younger man swiftly seized a metal jack to shove beneath the stones. The two men feverishly worked to lever it up tight, holding the ceiling in check—for the moment.

"We'll have to get more shoring timbers up there before we go on," the younger man said, examining the temporary support.

The elder man looked around at a small pile of the thick wooden pieces. "Not many left," he said. He squinted out toward the dim figure beyond the light. "We're runnin' short of all the necessaries, Chief."

"I have made arrangements for a new shipment," the figure replied in a low, terse tone. "By tomorrow night we'll have it."

From a doorway behind them—seeming only a black square on the shadowed far wall—another figure appeared.

"Chief!" it called as it moved across the room to them.

The dark figure turned to look. "What is it?" he asked testily. "Why risk coming here now?"

The newcomer stopped just short of the lit area. What light reached him revealed a youngish, fair-haired man in a neat, pale suit.

"I had to come," the newcomer said apologetically. "We've had a call in from the Ryans. Some tourists have come into the village. They're staying at the cottages."

"And what is that to me?" the other demanded.

"It seems they know the Traherns, sir," the man explained. "The Ryans are concerned. They don't know what to do."

The shadowed figure appeared to consider. Then it said slowly: "No need to do anything. No one really knows much about all that. What little they might know . . . or suspect . . . they can simply keep to themselves. Just have the Ryans make that known around."

"And if someone should say a bit too much?" the new man asked.

"Then," said the dark being in a sinister tone, "I'll see to them myself."

When the Milnes had finished unpacking, they left the cottage and walked down the main road that led through the village.

The walk was a pleasant one. It was nearing six o'clock and, as often happened in that land, the afternoon sun finally burned through the overcast to put in a late but brilliant appearance. In its final few hours the cool, gray day became warm and golden.

It was only a short distance from the cottages to the grocery store owned by the Ahernes. It was the best stocked of the three tiny shops in the village. It even had peanut butter and coffee, foods Milne considered necessary for human life.

They entered the shop and found it empty except for Catherine Aherne, the young proprietress. She was deeply absorbed in several pages of scrawled numbers that were spread out on the counter before her. She didn't raise her head even when the small bell over the door announced the entrance of customers.

The Milnes began to pick out the items they needed. The walls of the store had floor-to-ceiling shelves that were filled with a confused assortment of packages and cans. Hunting down the proper items in the jumble was rather like tracking down game in the wild.

Both Milnes considered it to be terrific sport. They found and captured their prey one by one and placed the items on the counter before the silent proprietress. When they had finished, they stood waiting for her to take notice of them.

"Excuse me," Ann ventured when they had waited in vain for some moments, "do you still keep frozen vegetables?"

For the first time the young woman seemed to realize they were there. She lifted her head and examined them. What she saw appeared to affect her very little. No trace of emotion registered in her face.

"Frozen vegetables?" she repeated, pronouncing the words as if they had no meaning.

"Yes. We got them here last year. Mrs. Trahern told us you had them. You remember?"

For a time there was no response. The woman stared at Ann, her face still immobile. Only the fact that she blinked, twice, slowly, assured Ann that she had not in some manner been turned to stone.

"Last summer?" she said finally. "I get so many tourists here. It's very hard to remember them. But, yes, I still have the frozen vegetables. What kind would you be wanting?"

"Peas, I think," Ann told her.

With a curt nod the woman turned and went out through a small doorway at the back of the store.

"The Irish really should learn better control," Milne said gravely. "I've never seen anyone get so excited over a few peas."

"Quiet!" Ann warned, for the proprietress reappeared quickly, a small, frosty box in her hands.

"Is that it, then?" she asked, placing the peas with the rest.

"No. I'd like some peat, too," Milne told her. He wanted a fire that night. "I need that square, pressed kind."

"A bale of briquettes, is it? Well, I'll just add it to the bill here, and you can pick it up outside. It's piled there, by the door."

She pulled a pencil from behind her ear and began to figure on a small pad.

"Oh, by the way, have you seen Mrs. Trahern today?" he asked her conversationally.

"That I have not," she said without pausing in her addition. "Nor will you be likely to. She's gone from town."

If she was aware of the impact this bit of news had on her customers, she was unconcerned by it.

"Gone?" cried Ann. "What about Bridget . . . and Taffy?"

"The three of them are gone."

"But where did they go?" Milne demanded. "Why? When?"

Catherine Aherne finished her totals and looked up to him.

"As to where or why, I can't say for certain. As to when, I've been told it was several days ago. Mrs. Ryan was quite sure of that."

When they made no reply to this, she showed them the figures on her pad.

"Here, then," she said. "Your purchases will be two pounds thirty-five altogether."

Milne paid her, and she put all of their groceries into a small cardboard box.

"There you are," she told them.

"Thanks," said Milne, lifting the box. "You don't happen to know when the Traherns will be back, do you?"

"Not I. Don't be forgetting your briquettes, now. And have a fine day."

She dropped her head back to her page of figures and ended the conversation.

The Milnes had a simple meal that evening. Afterward, to combat the damp chill that was rising, Ann made tea while John kindled a small fire.

Peat fires intrigued him, and he enjoyed the prospect of having them every night. He leaned several of the long, black briquettes against the back wall of the fireplace and started them with tightly rolled tubes of newspaper. The tongues of flame came up, around and between the briquettes. Soon the peat itself began to burn.

It was a slow-burning fire. The pressed peat layered apart as it warmed, slowly turning to a mound of soft white ash with a glowing red heart. It gave off an easy warmth and a pleasant smell of burning wood and autumn leaves combined.

Ann brought in the teapot and cups. She and John sat on rockers before the fire while the tea steeped beneath its cozy.

It was the end of their first, long day, and they were tired.

"It's after nine o'clock," she said, looking at her watch, then to a curtained window. "It's still daylight outside. The time doesn't seem to mean anything. It's all part of one, long dream." She rested her head back, closing her eyes. "Sitting here like this, it does feel as if we've never left. Or . . . maybe we've never really been here."

He smiled. He wasn't surprised that her feelings closely paralleled his own. It was often that way with them.

"I think it's intoxication from the peat smoke," he said. "It opens up the unconscious. Lets all kinds of things out. You'd have enough to dream about forever. Maybe that's why dreaming is such a big pastime here. After all, they've been sniffing this stuff for hundreds of years."

He sat back in his chair and stared into the fire. She uncovered the teapot and poured tea for them both. They were quiet for a time.

For him the warmth and the aroma of the fire were rousing vague but pleasant memories. He relaxed and let them seep over him in a soothing wave. A hazy montage of images from their past visit to Ireland floated through his mind, changing and nebulous as the smoke drifting on the air.

Her mind drifted into warm reverie as well, but, true to her own nature, her thoughts had much more focus. She called up memories of their times with the Traherns, and of one day in particular when they had picnicked together.

The Milnes had discovered that Nancy Trahern and her daughter, without a car of their own and stretched tight for money, had seldom got past the limits of Ballymurroe since coming there. As a treat and to thank the Traherns for befriending them, John and Ann had taken mother, daughter, and dog on an outing.

It had been to Clare Glens, a park area bordering the tumbling rush of the river Clare. On a gold and green gleaming afternoon, the young Americans had hiked and talked and become very close to the exiled woman and her daughter.

Ann especially recalled sitting with Nancy on great boulders above the crashing rapids of the stream to talk on matters great and trivial. The rare chance to get about had made the dark-haired woman quite cheerful that day, dispelling the faint but definite aura of sadness that hung about her. Bridget too had been made exuberant by the escape from the village confines. Ann smiled as she remembered the gangly girl, her wavy brown hair flying as she ran and wrestled with the dog.

They had all been very happy then, in that glowing brief bubble of time.

But the shiny bubble vanished, pricked by a sharp dart of concern for her friends.

"I hope it's nothing serious," John said suddenly.

She had no trouble understanding what he meant. She was not surprised that he had been thinking of them, too.

"Maybe they've gone back to visit Mr. Trahern," she suggested.

"Back to the North? She told us she'd never go back. She left her husband and everything else to bring Bridget here. She never said much about him, but we know he never came here to visit her."

"We don't know the reasons for that," Ann reminded him.

"Because she seemed reluctant to give any. Besides, there wasn't any indication in her letters that she'd even *considered* going back to the North, or anyplace else, for that matter."

"Well, it won't do us any good to guess at it," she said reasonably. "Remember how fast this trip came up. The letter we wrote her that we were coming back here probably didn't reach her in time. She may have gone somewhere to visit friends. She might even have taken Bridget into Limerick to get one of her teeth filled."

John knew that she was right. There was no point in guessing. There was no reason for letting the disappointment cast a shadow across their return. They couldn't do anything but hope that the Traherns would be back soon.

"Why don't we try to make some plans for ourselves, then?" he asked, trying to regain the sense of adventure with which they had arrived.

He gathered their ordinance survey maps, and they pored over them with enthusiasm for some time, discussing travel routes to some of the places they had missed on their previous trip. They talked until darkness came, the fire burned down, and the remaining tea got cold.

It was after taking a great swallow of this tea that John suggested they turn in. Expecting it to be hot and finding it cold was a harsh reminder that they had been up too long.

Some while after they had gone to bed, John was awakened by a sound and a movement. In the faint moonlight from the window he could see that his wife was sitting up in the bed.

"What's the matter?" he asked groggily.

"I heard something crying," she said in an anxious voice.

"You're dreaming," he began. "Lie back down and—"

A long, high wail lifted on the night air, rose to a wavering peak, and died away.

This time he came wide awake. He grabbed Ann's arm.

"I heard it," he said hoarsely.

She shook herself sluggishly. "Heard? What?"

"Your sound. You heard crying. Well, so did I. Listen!"

They waited, holding their breaths, but the sound did not repeat.

"You were dreaming," she said, lying down again. "Go back to sleep."

Feeling he was being wronged somehow, John tried to sleep but found it difficult. He lay awake, listening to the small noises of the night.

He soon became aware that one of those small noises seemed less than natural. It was a faint, intermittent scratching.

He listened to it intently, trying to locate it. Finally he was certain. It was coming from downstairs.

"Why aren't you breathing?" his wife whispered. "Did you die? Or is it something serious?"

"If you really *are* awake this time, listen again. I hear—"

"That scratching noise? I hear it, too."

"I'm glad of that . . . I think. It's from downstairs. I'm going to take a look. I don't want to, but I will."

"Do you want *me* to look?" she offered.

"Yes. But my big, fat male ego forces me to compromise. We'll both go."

She moved to switch on the light, but he shook his head. In the darkness they climbed from the bed, slipping robes on over pajamas and nightdress. They crept quietly out onto the top of the staircase to peer down into the main room. Below

them all was black except for the remains of the fire, glowing
dull red.

The scratching sound came again.

It was loud now, and its point of origin was unmistakable.
Something was scratching against the front door.

Immediately a flood of most unpleasant possibilities presented themselves to John. Foremost were those that concerned Gypsies. Rumor had it that they were often present in
the area and sometimes made "visits" to the cottages. He
had even heard tales of tourists robbed at knifepoint.

They went down the stairs into the main room, fragrant
with the faint smell of the peat fire. He tiptoed to the fireplace and picked up the heavy iron poker.

"Here," he said, handing it to Ann. "You've got a good
arm. I'm going to open the door and check outside. If something unpleasant grabs me, you let 'em have it."

He went through the short vestibule to the outer door,
Ann close behind. It was a Dutch door, latched in the center. He carefully opened the hooks and swung just the top
half back. There was no sign of anything unusual in the
night beyond.

Cautiously he leaned forward over the lower door, cran-
ing out to look up and down the cottage.

The pale moonlight revealed nothing.

He was about to draw back when a strange, throaty
sound came from directly below him. He dropped his head to
look, only to be slapped hard across the face with something
large, long, and very wet.

CHAPTER
FOUR

All the stream that's roaring by
Came out of a needle's eye;
Things unborn, things that are gone,
From needle's eye still goad it on.

—W. B. YEATS: "A Needle's Eye"

With a grunt of surprise and disgust John Milne straightened up.

"What's wrong?" said Ann, advancing with poker at the ready.

Before he could reply, there was a more determined scratching at the lower door, and something appeared over its edge.

It was a head: a strange, furry head with a large nose, hanging ears, and a great, long tongue that drooped from one side of its mouth.

"It's just a dog," said Ann.

"A dog," John repeated with relief. Then he stiffened. "But not *just* a dog."

He fumbled for the vestibule's light switch, snapped on the light, and unlatched the bottom half of the door.

"Be careful," said Ann with some alarm, but he pulled the door open.

A large, tan Labrador trotted calmly into the room, sniffed thoroughly at each of them, then sat down on the floor between.

John looked from the dog to his wife.

"It's Taffy," he said flatly.

"The Traherns must be back," said Ann with excitement. She pulled her shoes from beneath the table and slipped them on.

"It's the middle of the night," he noted as she slipped her raincoat on over her robe.

"I'm still going to check," she insisted.

She ran across the commons to the Traherns' cottage, but there was no one there. It was still dark, still locked tight. Disappointed and unsettled by this, Ann returned to find Milne setting down bowls for the dog. One contained scraps of bread and cheese, the other some water that the animal drank in a few, thirsty laps.

"Well?" he asked.

"No," she said, shaking her head. "They're not there. I don't understand."

She took off her coat and sat down in a chair next to him. Together they looked the dog over curiously while he ate.

"It's no wonder we didn't recognize him at first," Ann said. "What a mess he is!"

That was certainly true. Taffy's yellow-brown coat was darkened by wetness and a matting of dirt. Burrs and thistles spotted his fur. And he appeared much more gaunt than they remembered him.

"It looks like he's been living outside for some time," commented John.

The dog finished eating and walked to him.

"Sit down, Taffy," he said.

Taffy complied readily, and Milne began to pick the burrs from him, tossing them into the fireplace. The dog sniffed briefly at his hands, then sat patiently while he worked.

"But what's he doing here?" Ann said. "Catherine Aherne said they took him with them."

"I don't know," he replied. "Maybe she was wrong. Maybe someone else in the village is taking care of him."

"Taking care? John, he's running loose in the middle of the night!"

"Most dogs run loose in the villages, including Taffy," he reminded her. "If he's lonesome for Bridget, he probably checks the cottages for her all the time."

"It could be," she said doubtfully. Something, some faint image, flickered in a far, dim corner of her mind.

"It could be," he echoed, doubt in his words also. "But if it is, I wonder why he didn't show up here sooner. Maybe when we first arrived."

His words brought Ann's faint image to life.

"Maybe he did," she began cautiously.

"What's that supposed to mean?" he asked.

"I think I saw him once before today," she explained. "At least, I think it was Taffy I saw. He was coming toward the cottages from the field in back."

"You aren't sure it was the dog?" He wasn't quite following her.

"No. It was just a shape moving in the tall grass there. A man who was cutting the grass with a scythe chased it away before I got a good look."

"Chased it? Why?"

"I don't know. I suppose it might have been frightening the cattle," she said without certainty.

"Did you know the man?"

She shook her head. It irritated her that she couldn't be any clearer, and trying to recall the man troubled her even more. There was nothing but those eyes and their odd, flaring light.

"I don't know him," she said. "I'd remember."

"Okay," he said. He sensed her strange distress. "Let it go. It's late. Let's go back to bed. Tomorrow we'll get some answers."

She agreed. Fatigue was making it hard for her to think clearly.

"What about Taffy?"

"He'll be all right down here"—John gave the dog a pat—"won't you, boy?"

Taffy yawned widely in reply.

John turned out the lights and they both said good-night to the dog. He obediently went to the hearth rug and stretched himself out, as calm as if he were in his own home.

"Where do we get our answers?" Ann asked as they started up the stairs.

"Let's ask somebody we know pretty well," he said, yawning himself in anticipation of bed. "Somebody who we know would know about this . . . you know?"

The sentence structure wasn't what it might have been, but she got his meaning, and she supplied the name.

"Father Bonaventure?"

"Why not? We were going up to see him anyway."

She saw it was a good idea. The Father was a monk at the abbey near the village. He was a close friend of the Traherns and had helped them adjust to their new home and new life here.

"Then we'll walk up to the abbey tomorrow morning," she said, taking off her robe.

"'Tomorrow and tomorrow and tomorrow,'" John quoted sleepily as he doffed his own robe and rolled into the bed. "But, for now, good night . . . I hope."

"John," she said, sitting down next to him, "there is one other thing . . . about that man today."

"Your Grim Reaper?" he said, and immediately regretted his choice of imagery. He felt her distress again. "What about him?"

She hesitated longer, then turned suddenly toward him, her voice low and intense, forcing out the words:

"It sounds stupid, but whatever it was I saw out in the field, I think that man would have killed Taffy if he had caught him!"

With that she lay down and pulled the covers over them.

She sidled close to him, and he put an arm around her. She seemed to need the comfort, and he was glad of some himself. Still, something was bothering him.

"There's one other question I have to ask," he said quietly.

"What?" she asked.

"Did you forget to take your shoes off?"

She had.

A scant five hours later the Irish sun of midsummer was already rising again.

The Milnes were not up to meet it. They continued to sleep on until they were finally awakened by a persistent whining and scratching.

"When did we buy a dog?" blurrily asked John. In his half-conscious state he was back home in Nebraska.

"It's not ours," Ann informed him. She was capable of awakening with a clear mind.

"Well, it wants to go out, whoever it belongs to," he said. "Go on. It's your turn." He pulled the covers up tight around his head, leaving only his nose protruding.

"My turn?" she cried. She put a foot up against him and rolled him over. "When did you have *your* turn?" She looked at their travel clock. "Come on. It's time to get up anyway. If you can make it downstairs, you can have some nice, hot coffee to help bring yourself back to life."

The promise of coffee roused him enough to get him on his feet, and together they went downstairs. They found Taffy waiting anxiously by the door.

The dog only wanted to go outside, and for good reasons, but to Ann that presented a problem.

"Can we just let him go loose?" she asked. "He might run away again."

"He's a big dog," John muttered. "He can take care of himself. Besides, I didn't bring a leash along, did you?"

Ann let the dog out with some misgivings, but they were

needless. By the time they had made and eaten breakfast, Taffy was back.

"Once again life shows us that you can't expect your troubles to run away," John said.

Ann was surprised. "Did you *want* him to run away?"

"This is a vacation," he grumbled. "We're not here to mind somebody else's dog." His voice faded and he lowered his head to his coffee cup.

Ann paid little attention to him. She knew his black mood was due to his usual early-morning state. He was slow to awaken and irascible until he did so. Normally she left him alone while he regained a state of at least partial sanity, but today something moved her to prod at him, gently but firmly.

"If it bothers you, why don't we go up to the abbey and get it over with?"

He looked at her bleakly. "You want to walk up now? Why should we have to go the trouble so early in the morning?"

"Early? It's ten o'clock. Come on," she coaxed. "We'll find out who's supposed to be minding the dog, and it'll all be done."

This seemed to make sense to him, and he agreed to go if he could have another cup of coffee first.

She poured it for him and waited while he drank it, impatient without really knowing why.

Finally, when he felt himself sufficiently ready to attempt something so athletic, they set out. Taffy accompanied them, loping ahead or dropping back at times to investigate a new sight or smell, but always returning to them.

"He certainly seems to have adopted us," said John.

"Maybe he can't have children of his own," Ann suggested.

"Why do I feel like a straight man in the morning?" he asked dismally.

"I have an unfair advantage," she said gently, taking pity on him. "My brain is working."

John gave only a grumpy "humpf" at that and plodded on

beside his more sprightly wife. Neither one noted Daniel Ryan peering out the window of his pub at them as they turned into the main road and hiked past it.

Steam from the boiling liquid in the great cauldron hissed upward in a thick white corkscrew to vanish through a hole in the raftered ceiling above.

The cauldron and the fire over which it was suspended by chains from a tripod were in the center of a large, circular room.

Its walls were of stone blocks and rose some twenty feet. Their two-foot thickness was pierced only by a single small door and round-topped, slit windows set high on four sides.

The starkness of this chamber was alleviated by the rich textures of its decor. Plush woven rugs of warm earth hues covered the cold gray slate flags. Tapestries with intricate geometrical designs hung over much of the wall space, while the open areas between were densely arrayed with gleaming displays of ancient weaponry.

There was but one occupant of this room. It was the dark-cloaked being, bent now to work over the steaming vat. From a plank table beside it he took ingredients off plates and out of bowls, sliding them into the thick, bubbling brown mass. They sank into the viscous concoction, sending up fat bubbles that shone with grease.

The small door to the room opened, and the blond-haired, youngish man stepped through. He was clad this time in an impeccable light-gray suit, and looked odd in contrast to the medieval surroundings.

Stepping to the center of the room, he peered past the dark being's shoulder into the vat. He wrinkled his nose at the dun-colored ooze heaving and blurping there.

"What's that awful potion you're brewin', then?" he asked.

"Lamb stew," the being said flatly, lifting a plate of sliced carrots to dump in.

"Stew?" said the other. "Not magical?"

"It will be very much so when I'm done," the dark one said, taking up a long ladle to stir the mass. "It will have that power that only the Old Ones have known, which any man would give all to possess, but which only I, among them all, have learned."

"Is it *that* special power you mean?" said the blond man more excitedly. "And it will work for us, too? As you promised?"

"It will work for you just as it has for me," the other assured. "And when the time comes, you will join my band as reward for your great loyalty." The being put down the ladle and looked around to the man, those icy eyes glinting out sharply from within the hood's shadow. "But why are you here now?"

"It's those tourists again, sir. May be nothing, but Ryan seemed concerned. Seems he saw them go by his place just minutes ago, and the Traherns' dog was with them."

"That dratted Labrador?" the dark one said irritably. "I told you to take care of it."

"It was too slippery to catch," he said defensively. "Still, sir, it may not mean anything to these folks."

"And it *may* rouse their suspicions," the other countered. "Where were they going with it?"

"North," he said. "They seemed very purposeful. But he has no idea where they're going."

The cloaked being sighed. "This is very irritating. But we must be sure. It seems I'll have to discover what they're about myself." He lifted a hand to wave the blond man away from him. "Stand away."

The young man moved off. The dark one lifted his arms, the cloak's folds unfurling like vast wings. In just seconds a shimmering light began to rise about the figure, growing in intensity until the dark shape was hidden from sight.

The blond man stood staring at the eerie manifestation in transfixed awe.

.   .   .

Some quarter mile past the edge of the village, the Milnes turned onto the road that wound in through the abbey grounds.

The morning was cool and fresh, the air clean and scented by the profusion of flowering things that filled the rambling demesne. As they walked, Milne determined that the air and exercise were actually waking him up. His spirits improved, and by the time they had reached the abbey buildings he considered himself almost alert.

Like most products of the eighteenth-century Enlightenment, Glendon Abbey was a neat, clean, carefully symmetrical structure built in the Georgian style. In its cool lines and graceful Grecian columns it bespoke the rational ideal of that age of reason most elegantly. Originally a manor house for its British landlords, it had been donated to the order of monks when the owners had abruptly "departed" during Eire's early years of rebellion. Behind it, modern structures were visible. They were dormitories for the boys' school run by the monks, now empty for the summer holidays.

The Milnes passed through a high archway in the outer battlements and crossed a courtyard to a large front door. There, the ringing of a doorbell produced a young and smiling monk in a black wool habit.

He listened to their request in a friendly manner and promised to find Father Bonaventure. Because of the dog, the Milnes declined his invitation to enter, and he set off on his search.

It was not long before the door opened again, revealing another monk who came eagerly forward when he saw them.

Father Bonaventure was a man of indeterminable years. He was thin and vigorous, and his complexion had the smooth freshness of youth, but his features were mature, strongly masculine, and his hair was a mass of silver-gray.

The Milnes had placed his age between thirty and fifty, but they could guess no closer.

This ambiguousness of appearance echoed the monk's character. Mrs. Trahern had once laughingly called him a druid, not really Christian at all, and he had been pleased and distressed at the same time; Bonaventure was a kind man and a moral one, and he had never doubted the ultimate truth of his faith. Still, he was also a man with an interest in the ancient days of Eire that reached deep into his spirit.

In him, the elements of the two cultures that had blessed and cursed the Irish soul were blended. He was Celt and Christian both, and it was characteristic of his nature that he was not confused by this. Instead he was more clearly understanding of the conflicts of spirit that all humans faced.

Still, as a monk, his contact with those humans was limited, and he had few chances to share his concerns and interests with others. The always perceptive Mrs. Trahern had seen that, and when she had found the Milnes to be students of Celtic lore, she had quickly arranged a meeting. The short time they had all spent together had produced a close friendship.

Now he smiled warmly and shook hands with them both.

"How are you?" he asked in speech so thick with the more guttural pronunciation of the Cork Irish that it added a rich texture to his voice. "I had hoped to be seeing you soon!" Then he saw the dog and his smile broadened. "Ah, and you have Taffy with you. So, the Traherns are back too, are they?"

The Milnes exchanged a glance.

"No, Father," Ann told him slowly. "They aren't."

Bonaventure's smile faltered. He seemed confused.

"But the dog," he said. "I thought . . ." Here he paused at the uncertain looks on their faces.

"We found the dog, Father," Milne explained. "Alone. That's part of why we came."

Bonaventure seemed to find some understanding in that. Quickly he once more assumed a cheerful air.

"Well, never mind that for now," he went on briskly. "We must talk ourselves. It's been a year since I've seen the two of you. Come on, now, and I'll give you a tour of the abbey grounds while we're conversing."

His tone was casual, yet there was a note of strain behind

it. Because the Milnes sensed it, they followed him without argument, but with great curiosity.

He led them across the courtyard and started through the archway, but halted when a tall monk clad in a similar long habit appeared there.

The man walked with eyes down and seemed to be in deep thought, but as he drew near, he took note of them, stopped, and raised his head. Bonaventure introduced him to the Milnes as the Abbot of Glendon Abbey.

He greeted them in a friendly but absent way, blessed them, and went on.

"I wouldn't have guessed he was the abbot," said John, looking after him. "I'd have thought he'd wear something more . . . well . . . aristocratic than peasant."

"Oh, he does have much grander things," Bonaventure explained with a hint of amusement. "But our abbot is a very humble man. He feels more at ease in the everyday robes. That's why it embarrasses him to have the villagers call him Lord Abbot."

"Is that their title for him?" Ann asked.

"Only because he lives in this place," answered Bonaventure. "The people have lived so long with a lord of the manor, it's become a part of the pattern of their lives, you see. These few decades of freedom haven't erased that. Whoever rules the manor becomes the lord to them, I think."

They had left the abbey by now and were climbing a faint path that led up through the fields behind it.

As they walked, the monk began to point out interesting native trees and plants and to recount the abbey's history.

At last they reached an open hilltop. It was a large area, knee-high in grass and bisected by a low stone wall. From its vantage point they could look down on the abbey just below and out across the open country beyond. To the south, the city of Limerick was a flat, gray patch in the green blanket. Away to the west, the haze of the sea edged the horizon.

Bonaventure moved through the field of tall grass, his long robes swishing as he walked, until he reached the stone wall. The Milnes followed. At the wall he turned and looked around him.

"Mrs. Trahern liked to come up here when we talked," he said meditatively. "She said she felt close to the Old Ones in a place like this."

He paused, then he abruptly turned and confronted them squarely.

"Now then, just where did Taffy come from?" he demanded brusquely, dropping the light conversational tone. "What have you two found out?"

CHAPTER
FIVE
ᛉ

This whole day have I followed in the rocks,
And you have changed and flowed from shape to
    shape,
First as a raven on whose ancient wings
Scarcely a feather lingered, then you seemed
A weasel moving on from stone to stone,
And now at last you wear a human shape,
A thin grey man half lost in gathering night.

        —W. B. YEATS: *"Fergus and the Druid"*

The swift change in the monk's attitude caught both the Milnes unprepared. John reacted to it sharply.

"Wait a minute, Father! What's going on? You lead us up here and tell us about the trees and flowers, and then, out of nowhere, you're grilling us about something we brought up fifteen minutes ago. Maybe *you'd* better talk to *us* first!"

His own harsh tones surprised him. He realized that tension had been building up in him and wondered why. He felt guilty for so treating the monk.

But Bonaventure appeared to understand his reaction. He sighed and nodded.

"I am sorry," he replied earnestly. "I should have known that you would be as concerned as I. But she told me you were coming. I hoped that she had written you and that you knew where they had gone. Am I to understand that you don't?"

"*We* don't?" said Ann, emphasizing the pronoun. "Father, we came here hoping *you* did."

A large blackbird soared into view above, the glossy feathers of its broad wingspan glinting with blue highlights as it circled over the little group.

"Can you tell us anything?" John asked the monk.

"Very little, I'm afraid. I went into the village last week to visit them. I hadn't seen them in several days. They were gone with no warning and leaving no word about their going. Of course, I asked after them in the village, but I found out nothing, just that they had left. No one knew why or where or how long they had been gone. It was seeing Taffy that made me think they might have returned."

"Why, Father?" Milne said, feeling he had missed something.

"When I asked about their departure in the village, only Mrs. Ryan would speak to me." He was obviously distressed, but kept careful control and spoke calmly. "She told me that they were to be gone some time and had taken the dog along."

"It's what we heard, too," said Ann, "and we reacted the same way you did when Taffy showed up at our cottage. But couldn't he have stayed behind? Couldn't they have left him?"

"They could," said the monk, watching the golden dog sniffing busily through the grass, "but it's hard to think Bridget would have left him behind by choice, or that he would have left her."

Both Milnes had to agree with this. Mrs. Trahern and the evidence of their own eyes had told them how close the girl and dog were.

Ann again recalled their picnic outing with the Traherns. While she had watched John and the girl in friendly play with the Labrador, Nancy Trahern had explained why a special bond existed between her daughter and the animal.

"In the North of Ireland," the black-haired woman had somberly told her, "the violence and the prejudice have often isolated children from friends, leaving them like captives in their fortress homes. It was so for Bridget especially. Taffy was so often her only companion, my poor girl." She had shaken her head with great regret.

"When we moved to the Republic and became strangers in a new home, their relationship became a vital one," she had gone on. "And even since Bridget has settled in and regained a bit of security, he's remained her closest friend, for he's shared her deepest fears and secrets when it counted most: when there was no one else."

Ann then recalled watching the dog fetching a thrown stick and bounding eagerly back to his laughing mistress. There was no question how crucial such a relationship would be to a lonely child.

"It is hard to think anything could have separated Bridget and Taffy," Ann now said to John and the monk. "But maybe they had no choice. It could have been an emergency. Did Mrs. Trahern tell you anything that might have suggested trouble or some other reason for going?"

"Not for going," Bonaventure told her, "although God knows she had her troubles, and many of those. Separated from her husband, trying to make a home for her daughter. Still, it does seem that she'd heard something these past weeks that had disturbed her."

The huge crow swept down in lazy, seemingly careless circles over them as they spoke on, heedless of it.

"Did she tell you anything about what she'd heard?" asked John.

"No. She said she couldn't tell me. She had to be sure of things first, she said. Even Bridget seemed to know nothing of it. Mrs. Trahern was afraid, I think, but she was angry, too. She was very determined about something."

"Then it could have been some problem," Ann suggested. "Friends? Family?"

"Certainly," he answered. "But then, why will no one in the village talk about her?"

John shrugged. "Maybe they just don't know anything."

"That doesn't explain the fear I feel in them when I go into their shops or talk with them on the street," said the monk.

"You sensed fear?" John asked. "Are you sure?"

"Fear . . . and suspicion, too. It's as if something had gotten at them all. I'm afraid it may even have gotten at me." He hesitated. "I . . . I don't ask you to believe it, but these past days I've been certain that someone was watching. Even here!"

The blackbird fluttered in with a vigorous flapping of its wings to land atop the stone wall some fifty feet from them. It furled the big wings in about itself like a tight-wrapped cloak.

"Here?" John couldn't hide a note of disbelief. "Have you seen anyone?"

"It's a feeling only," said the monk. "But I do feel the eyes when I walk the grounds or work in the gardens." He spoke with conviction and met Milne's eyes levelly.

John looked about the open hilltop. He noted the raven perched atop the wall, pecking in its crannies for insects. He looked out over the surrounding meadow of grasses blowing gently in the fresh wind from the sea. The wind was always fresh from the sea in Ireland. The day was always peaceful. It was hard to consider suspicions or have fears.

"Is that why you brought us on this nature hike?" John guessed. "In case we were watched?"

The monk nodded but said nothing.

From a hole in the wall on the far side of them from the raven, a small rabbit at that moment poked its head out. It looked warily around, then crept along cautiously, slowly, close to the wall. It stopped near them, crouching unnoticed, nose quivering, long ears perked.

"Well, I just don't know, Father," John said doubtfully. "I

mean, people watching? The Traherns leaving without a word or sign? What are you trying to tell us?"

The monk opened his mouth to reply but faltered. He looked from one to the other of them as if unsure of what to say.

"You think something has happened to them," said Ann.

It was a flat statement and, as she made it, she understood that this idea had been in her mind since the dog had appeared. It was fear that had hurried her to the abbey that morning, in hopes that Father Bonaventure would put the fear to rest. Now she knew that he would not.

"I've thought something was wrong since I first found them gone," the monk admitted cheerlessly. "I know in my heart that she'd not leave without some word or some note of explanation to me or to you. I've thought myself a fool, but now that you've found Taffy, my imaginings seem the more real."

John persisted in his skepticism. "It still doesn't make any sense. What could happen to them? What could keep people from talking, or make them afraid?"

The raven hopped fearlessly closer to investigate a new section of wall. It was now within a dozen yards.

"I have no certain idea," Bonaventure replied. "But this is Ireland. You are not Irish. It might be there are many things happening here that you wouldn't understand."

He saw this had confused them, and he pondered some way to explain.

"Here, you see this wall?" he said at last, patting the line of gray rocks. "This is a clear-stone wall. The stones are fitted together without mortar. Strong winds blow across the hilltop, but this wall still stands, because of the gaps left between the stones. They allow the winds through them and around them and are not knocked down by the blasts.

"Well, the truth of it is, many of here have become like these stones." He spoke ruefully now, as if the words gave him some pain. Still he went on, trying to make it as understandable as he could for them. "All the winds of violence and change that have blown over us have taught many to stand aside and let the wind blow past, rather than to stand in the way and perhaps be knocked down."

The wandering Taffy took note of the bird near his friends then. With a bark he bounded toward it. The raven cawed loudly in alarm and lifted off with a frantic pumping of wings, rising out of reach just as Taffy reached the wall.

The three humans looked around to see the dog give a last bark after the ascending bird, then give it up and go back to snuffling through the grass. By the wall base, the little rabbit crouched lower but bravely stayed put, still unnoticed —for the time being—by the dog.

"Are you telling us that this has to do with the troubles this country has had?" John now asked.

"I'm saying it could be many things," said Bonaventure. "The Traherns are from Belfast. They came here as refugees. Even I know little about them. All I do know is that some wind is blowing. I can feel it. I think you can as well."

"It's possible, Father," John conceded, but doubtfully. Still, there had been something, some feeling of wrongness in things. He couldn't deny that.

A few scattered drops of rain began to fall, and they promised to pick up in volume.

"Maybe we'd better start back," Ann suggested.

Father Bonaventure agreed, and they walked back across the field toward the slope, Taffy closing in to follow.

Behind them, the hare also moved away from the wall, hopping through the grasses after them. As it did, the big crow, still circling above, spotted its movement, focusing on the small creature with a glittering black eye.

Without hesitation it pulled back its wings and swept down, shooting in like a cast dart, to vanish in the grass some yards behind the hare. Instantly an intense blue-white glow flared up at the spot, glinting briefly through the waving blades before dying away. Soon afterward a much altered form was slipping away from where the crow had landed.

Only seconds later a whispering sound from its rear brought the hare looking around in alarm. Through the grasses after it was speeding the sinuous long form of a weasel, voracious gaze fixed upon its prey.

Instead of running faster, the rabbit abruptly turned. It waited as if frozen in fear as the predator tore in. The weasel's jaws opened to bite, showing needlelike teeth.

But at the last second, the hare leaped forward. It went right over the attacker's head, rear feet striking down on the weasel's broad, flat head. As the larger animal was sent staggering forward by the blow, the extra push was sending the hare leaping away behind. By the time the surprised predator recovered and wheeled, the hare had a long start.

The weasel put on its best speed in pursuit. Faster than the rabbit, it quickly closed the gap. But it wasn't quick enough. The rabbit reached the wall, diving back into its hole there.

It was a hole too small for the weasel. It tried to force its way in, but could get nothing but its head through the opening, push though it would. It pulled out, giving a low snarl that sounded very like a noise of frustration. Then it sat up on its haunches, stretching the head on its long body above the grasses.

It glanced around, stopping to stare at the figures of the three humans and their dog, now scores of yards away. It tensed. Its slender body began to vibrate. A soft sapphire luminescence rose from the fur, growing swiftly in intensity, surrounding the whole form. And, within that glow, the form began to change.

Bonaventure and his three companions were now just reaching the slope. As they neared the first trees there, the monk picked up his nature lecture again, a cautionary measure that John Milne found slightly absurd.

"There is a fine yew tree," said the monk, pointing out a dark green fir tree.

"A yew," said Ann. "Weren't they sacred trees to the druids?"

"Among others," Bonaventure agreed. He smiled at her with delight at her knowledge. "You know that once the druid priests advised kings and ruled the Celtic lands."

"We know," Ann said, aware of the monk's deep interest in the subject.

"They still exist, you know. At least in name. Just last year I attended a druid meeting in Wales. The meeting was a grand sight. The chief druid convened the ceremonies in his splendid white robes, the gleaming sword of his rank upheld before him . . ."

As Bonaventure went on, he became more and more involved in his story and less and less aware of his surroundings. Finally he walked along, describing the druid ceremonies in glowing color, completely oblivious to the fine, cold rain that had now begun to fall in earnest.

The fact of rain was ever present with the Irish, and they lived with it, largely ignoring it and going on with things irregardless. In Father Bonaventure this talent was expanded by his ability to wrap himself in his subject.

John, who was having trouble ignoring the water trickling down his neck, felt that sleet and hail wouldn't have interrupted the monk.

As they reached the abbey and entered the courtyard, bells began to toll somewhere.

"It's the Angelus bells," said Bonaventure. "I have to go now. So then, just what should we do about all of this?"

John sighed deeply. "I don't know that we should do anything. If you really believe that something has happened, call the police."

"And tell them what, John?" Ann asked. "We don't have one thing to tell them. You don't believe this yourself. Why should they? We've got to have some proof that something really is wrong."

"Maybe," he allowed reluctantly. "But how?"

"We must find out more," said the monk. "And I might give us a place to begin. I've talked with many these past days, and it has just come to me that only one person seemed to know about the Traherns' leaving."

"Mrs. Ryan?" John guessed.

Bonaventure was surprised. "Why, yes. How did you know?"

"Catherine Aherne told us that was her source. Mrs. Ryan gave her the same story she gave you—that mother, daughter, and dog were all gone from town."

"She was wrong about the dog," Ann pointed out.

"She might just have been mistaken," John reasoned. "The point is, whether she's right or wrong, Mrs. Ryan is the only one who acts as if she knows something. I suppose we should ask her where she got her information, if we can get her to talk to us. She hasn't been very anxious to so far."

"I think I can get her to talk to us," said Ann after some consideration.

"It doesn't involve hot irons, I hope," said John. "You know how weak my stomach is."

She laughed. "Not quite, but it will work."

Father Bonaventure still had misgivings.

"Are you certain, now, that you really want to involve yourselves in this?"

"No. But it looks like we're going to anyway," John told him glumly. "Whether I believe your 'imaginings' or not, I won't enjoy my vacation until it's all settled."

The monk eyed the two young people and felt a sorrow rising in him.

"I'm sorry," he said. "You've come for your holiday, and now my fears will bring it to ruin."

"Don't feel sorry," Ann tried to assure him, a little annoyed with her husband's attitude. "John doesn't mean what he says. We're doing this because we *want* to."

John was abashed at this. He hadn't meant to distress the monk.

"She's right, Father," he said, trying to sound hearty and willing. "You're not forcing us into anything. Look, if we get any information, we'll let you know tomorrow."

"All right, then. But it will have to be in the afternoon. I'll be busy here until past my morning offices—around noontime."

"Fair enough," said John. "We'll report to you tomorrow after lunch. In the meantime, you try to keep from worrying yourself."

"I will try to keep from it," he promised. "But for my sake," he added in a more intense, warning tone, "do not take this too lightly. Remember the wind. If it *is* blowing, take care you're not knocked down by it."

The two Americans shook hands with him and started away, Taffy trotting alongside.

None of them noticed that the large blackbird was circling high overhead once again.

CHAPTER
SIX

Sang old Tom the lunatic
That sleeps under the canopy:
'What change has put my thoughts astray
And eyes that had so keen a sight?
What has turned to smoking wick
Nature's pure unchanging light?

—W. B. YEATS: "Tom the Lunatic"

Early that evening, Mrs. Ryan answered a knock on her door and found two smiling Milnes there.

"Yes?" she said uncertainly. "What is it?"

"Mrs. Ryan, we just stopped by to repay all of your friendly visits of last summer," John told her with great enthusiasm.

The term "friendly visits" referred to her barging into their cottage with little excuse and staying to engage them in lengthy conversations. Under the circumstances, however, the Milnes were willing to overlook that.

An expression of anything but happy welcome appeared on the woman's face. She opened her mouth to protest, but Ann acted before she could, thrusting a gayly wrapped box out toward her.

"Here," she said. "We've brought you a present of some biscuits."

The biscuits were Ann's idea, and they were a clever one. Irish visiting customs had definite rules, and one of them concerned the bringing of biscuits to the hostess. Shop-purchased biscuits, because of their expense, were considered a greater gift than home-baked ones. To refuse them was an insult. It wasn't done without a very good reason, and Mrs. Ryan seemed unable to think of one so quickly.

She looked at the box with distaste, but she was trapped, and she knew it.

"Come in, then," she said without cheer and stepped back from the door.

Ann pressed the biscuits into her hands, and she took them with reluctance. They moved past her into a large front room so filled with heavy furniture that it appeared tiny. They sank down into a grossly overstuffed couch and continued to smile politely, but said nothing more. They wanted the next move to be hers.

After staring at them thoughtfully for a moment, Mrs. Ryan spoke.

"Now why is it you're visiting me?" she inquired stiffly.

"Oh, just to talk," John replied affably. "We haven't seen you for a year. We'd like to catch up on things here and . . ."—he paused for emphasis—"we thought *you* might like to hear the news from America."

That got her interest. She perked up visibly, like a small, hungry dog hearing the dinner call. Her thirst for news was insatiable. It gave her a certain status in the village to have access to the kinds of tales the visitors to the cottages provided, and tales of America made better news than most things. Her greed for them overcame her obvious disinclination to talk.

"Well, now, that's very nice," she said with genuine pleasure. "Would you be wanting some tea first?" Tea was always a preliminary to a good, cozy chat.

The Milnes both agreed that tea would be very nice.

"You must excuse me, then, and I'll go make it," she told them and went out of the room.

Casually John got to his feet and followed. Cautiously he peered around the edge of the door through which she had gone. Down a short hall was the kitchen. Its door was half-open, and he could see Mrs. Ryan moving about inside. He signaled to Ann and she, puzzled, stood and walked to his side.

Pointing down the hall, he leaned toward her and put his lips close to her ear.

"Watch her," he whispered.

"What are you going to do?" she whispered in return.

"Poke around," he said. Then he moved away and began a purposeful examination of the room.

Ann saw no reason for what he was doing. She wanted to stop him, but he was paying no attention to her now, and she was afraid to speak out loud. So she stood and kept watch, feeling devious and very uncomfortable.

John made a quick circuit of the room and settled on a small desk as the most promising place to concentrate his search. Luck smiled on him at once. In the first drawer he found what he sought: Mrs. Ryan's record of the cottage rentals.

The cottages were listed by number, and he turned to the page for the Traherns'. A folded slip of paper had been inserted there as if to mark the place, but it contained only a phone number. He ran his eyes down the columns on the page, noting dates and payments. The record for the cottage showed the rent had been paid two weeks before. There was no other notation.

He replaced the slip and turned to the page for their own cottage. The first notification of the booking he had made had reached Mrs. Ryan ten days before. The previous tenants had vacated a week prior to their arrival.

In the same drawer was the official rental form, sent by the *Bord Failte*. It listed their names, the cottage they would have, and the charge for three weeks' rental. Its date indicated that it had been sent to her the day before they had come.

He was so engrossed in all of this that Ann had to hiss at him twice to get his attention. When he looked up, she gestured sharply toward the kitchen, and they both made a dive for the couch as a loud clattering of pottery signaled Mrs. Ryan's return. When she entered the room, carrying an immense tea tray, she found her guests still quietly seated, relaxed, and smiling politely.

She set the tray on a nearby table and began to pour tea from a blue china pot. Ann looked at her husband, uncertain of their next step, but he seemed oblivious, his smile fixed.

Searching for something with which to strike up a conversation, Ann noted a striking decoration on one wall. It was carved of a dark wood to represent what seemed a type of coat of arms. The main feature was a simple round shield with the relief of a winged horse in its center. Atop the shield at either side was a fierce dragon's head, their two flaring tongues intertwined above the middle. Below the shield were fixed the rampant forms of griffins, their batlike wings outstretched. The piece looked very old.

"That's an interesting . . . *thing* you have there, Mrs. Ryan," Ann said, indicating it.

The woman glanced around to it, then nodded, speaking with great pride. "Ah yes. That's the heraldic symbol of the old Earl of Dunraven. Feagh O'Donal he was called. Had a great fortress near here over a thousand years ago. The clan of the Ryans served him then, as they served his ancestors for centuries before that. Back to the most ancient days does our name go," she added with even greater pride, "as those of many others about here. And our love of those old ties is still very strong."

"We know," Ann said. She couldn't think of any way to expand on this. She looked again to John to come in and help. But he said nothing.

With some irritation, Ann was forced to take the lead once more.

"Well, is Mr. Ryan home tonight?" she asked.

"Oh, no. He's gone to work at the pub. With our son at university, he's got to do the work most evenings, now."

Of course, the Milnes well knew that he was gone. They had wanted to catch Mrs. Ryan alone and had waited until they had seen the man leave for the tavern.

Mrs. Ryan finished pouring and handed each of them a cup. She sat down in an easy chair opposite them, ready to begin serious gossiping.

Ann searched for something else conversational to say. Once again she looked at her husband. His vacant smile had taken on alarming proportions. It was clear that he was not going to be of any assistance.

"Well, well," she said. She seemed to be using that word a great deal. She had to say something else. She tried to string something together. "Well, Mrs. Ryan, it really is good to see you again. You were such a help to us last year. It's so nice to see a familiar face in a foreign country. Knowing you was one of our big reasons for wanting to come back here."

Without preamble, John leaned forward on the couch and spoke.

"How do you like my mustache, Mrs. Ryan?" he asked very pleasantly.

The woman, who had been soaking up Ann's flood of lies like a contented sponge, was taken off balance.

"Mustache?" she repeated.

Ann looked at her husband with concern. It occurred to her that he had suddenly lost his mind.

"Yes, my mustache," he said again. He put his hand to his upper lip. "I didn't have it last year. I wondered how you thought I looked with it."

Knowing that her husband's mustache had been a prominent fixture for some years, Ann prepared to correct him. But he had sensed her reaction. He turned his head away from Mrs. Ryan and shot her a warning look that froze her where she sat.

"You didn't have it?" Mrs. Ryan was saying. "I thought surely you did."

"It's easy to forget a thing like that," he told her with great casualness. "It's not a thing to notice, like Ann's hair."

"That's true enough," she agreed. "You see few fine, true redheads like that, even here. You see many more from America, but I trust almost none of them. So many love to dye it, it seems. No, most wouldn't forget hair like hers, and I have a better knack for remembering than most. It's why I'm so certain you had that mustache. You'd have looked much different without it."

"It's not important," he said. "After all, it *has* been a year, and you get so many kinds of people at the cottages."

His tone was still casual, but the challenge to her memory was clear.

"I'm proud of remembering my people," she said defensively. "I could tell you about many of them, even from years ago."

"And you knew us the first minute you saw us, didn't you?" he said, his eyes smiling and innocent behind his glasses.

"Why, a pair like you? Certainly I—"

She stopped abruptly and her face went dead. Her eyes narrowed and snapped a hard, searching glance from one of them to another.

John remained relaxed; and Ann, still bewildered by the exchange, tried to look the same.

"Of course, that was after you had reminded me," Mrs. Ryan finished lamely.

"You just didn't connect us with our name, right?" John asked, but she wasn't following his lead anymore. She only looked at him sullenly.

He stood up and set his teacup down.

"Well, Mrs. Ryan, we've got to be off," he announced cheerfully. "Come on, Ann."

Ann put down her cup and rose. Mrs. Ryan, reduced to silence now, only sat and watched them.

"Sorry we can't stay and tell you more about America, but we have to get home and plan an itinerary for tomorrow," John explained. "Thanks for the tea."

He hustled Ann to the door, opened it, then paused and turned.

"Oh, we were going to ask about Mrs. Trahern," he added, as if in afterthought, "but there's no need. We found out from Father Bonaventure that they went back North to visit for a while. See you later."

He pushed Ann outside and closed the door behind them. His smile disappeared.

"What—" Ann began, but John grabbed her arm.

"Wait," he cautioned, and they moved away from the house.

When Ann felt they were finally at a safe distance, she exploded.

"What did you do to that poor woman? You searched her house, tied her in knots, and then left without even tasting her tea!"

"That 'poor woman,' as you call her, has been lying to us," he said grimly. "I'm sure of it now."

"You're sure of it?" she asked as they walked back toward their cottage. "That's a turnaround, isn't it? This morning you were sure it was nothing."

"Well, it still could be," he said. "I don't know. You said she was wrong about the dog. I figured that if she *wasn't* wrong, then she was covering up. I had to see if she was."

"And you think she was?"

"You look at it. Yesterday, when she saw us for that first time, she couldn't recall our reservations. Not until we insisted that we'd made them. Then she suddenly came up with a convenient cancellation. But it wasn't a cancellation. We were already registered for that cottage."

"She might have forgotten and then was too embarrassed to admit it," Ann reasoned.

"There's more to it," he insisted. "She hadn't forgotten us. The papers in her desk show that she was notified of our coming ten days ago and reminded of it the day before we came. She was expecting us yesterday. She'd just cleaned the place. The floors were still wet, remember? And you know she never cleans until the last minute."

Ann knew. Even the patient Mrs. Trahern had complained about Mrs. Ryan's laxness in caring for the cottages.

"Maybe she'd just cleaned up after the last tenants," she suggested.

"Not a chance. That place was empty for a week before we came. She cleans when she has to, and yesterday she had to. The new tenants were due to arrive. Us."

She was following his line of reasoning now.

"So then, if she *was* expecting guests, why act so surprised when she saw them?"

John nodded. "That's the question, and she just supplied the answer. The minute she saw us, she knew damn well who we were. Until then we were only names, only more tourists. And when she remembered, what did she do? She lied to keep us from staying here. Think back on it. That whole conversation had all the earmarks of a fast, clumsy improvisation."

"Okay, I agree," said Ann as they reached their cottage door. "But does it connect her with the Traherns leaving?"

"It could," he said, pulling out the key. "It's one connection that works. We know the Traherns. We might ask questions about them. So she deliberately tried to get rid of us."

"We *did* ask questions," Ann pointed out. "So did Father Bonaventure. We didn't find out anything."

When John opened the door, he was almost knocked down by Taffy's enthusiastic rush to meet them. The young couple greeted him warmly and entered the cottage.

"Remember what Father Bonaventure said," John told her. "There could be more involved."

"Then you believe him now? You think something has gotten at everyone here?"

"That's still a lot for me, but I'll buy the possibility that *something* funny is going on. So, how about some tea? I really did want some."

He went into the kitchen to make it, and Ann followed.

"What about the Traherns?" she asked. "Did you find anything to tell you where they went?"

"Nope," he said. He filled the kettle and put it on the stove.

"Well, why didn't you ask Mrs. Ryan? That's what we'd planned to do."

"When I decided she'd lied to us, I changed plans," he answered. "Sorry I couldn't warn you." He got out cups and saucers and put tea into the pot. "If she doesn't want us to look, then let her think we're not looking."

"Very clever," she told him, "except it doesn't leave us a way to find out anything."

He didn't respond to that. The kettle began to whistle, and she picked it up from the stove and poured the boiling water into the pot.

"We've still got to prove that Mrs. Trahern and Bridget did something besides just go off on some innocent jaunt before we can talk to the police," she said.

John wasn't listening. He was looking thoughtfully out of the kitchen window.

"It'll be dark in a couple of hours," he said. "We'll have to go soon. You'd better drink some tea to keep you warm."

This time it was distressingly clear to her what he had in mind.

"Do we have to do that?" she asked.

"Where else can we look? We've got to get into their cottage," he said determinedly. "And I know how."

"No. Oh, no!" she said in protest.

His reply was a devious smile.

CHAPTER

SEVEN

✣

On the grey rock of Cashel the mind's eye
Has called up the cold spirits that are born
When the old moon is vanished from the sky
And the new still hides her horn.

—W. B. YEATS: *"The Double Vision
of Michael Robartes"*

A nn was still protesting her husband's intended foray two hours later, when they arrived, by a rather devious route, at the back of the Traherns' cottage.

"We could at least have waited until it got dark," she muttered. It was now after nine o'clock, but still perfectly light.

"How would we look around?" he said. "I forgot to pack my Junior Sherlock Holmes bull's-eye lantern. And I have a feeling that lighting lights inside might just be noticed. Especially with the pub right across the street."

She saw the logic of this. Faintly they could hear the laughter and loud talk of the men gathered for their evening drinking at Ryan's.

The view of the back of the cottage was blocked by high shrubs and afforded the best chance of getting in unobserved. They tested the windows along the back and found them all locked.

John was not dismayed. He had fiddled with the locks on their own cottage before they had left, testing his idea for breaking in. The windows were the traditional slide type with rope pulleys, and they fit together loosely. They had no storm windows and no screens. The latch was a simple one. It was no feat to slip a kitchen-knife blade through the crack between the upper and lower sashes and push the latch open. In a moment he had a window up.

They climbed over the low sill and into the cottage. The air inside was stale and thick with the smell of peat. The Traherns had kept a tiny fire of it going constantly, and the smoke had permeated everything. With windows open the odor wasn't too noticeable. Confined within the cottage, it had grown unpleasantly strong.

The smell was the only sign of a peat fire that remained. The hearth had been emptied of ashes and swept clean. The entire place had been neatened.

"Doesn't look much like a place left in a hurry," said Ann.

John nodded. If the cottage had been policed-up after the fact, their chance of finding anything helpful was greatly reduced.

"Let's check things and get out of here quickly," he said, and they started to search carefully.

John went through a collection of newspapers and magazines that were piled by the fireplace. He found a thick tourist folder on the Republic of Ireland, and thought it a curious thing for her to have. He flipped idly through it and noted that some sections were underlined. Curious, he stuck it in his jacket pocket and kept on looking.

Ann searched through the bedrooms and found nothing unusual. She looked into the closet, but it was impossible to tell if clothing was missing. She grasped the handles of a dresser drawer but then released them. She was already embarrassed by their intrusion, and she couldn't bring herself to invade the Traherns' privacy any more deeply.

Reentering the main room, she noticed Nancy Trahern's paintings, leaning together in a corner beneath her easel. She looked through them. There were a dozen in all. Several of them she remembered having seen the year before. Two of them, however, appeared to be quite recent.

Both of them had the hurried, sketchy look of the first versions Nancy did after seeing something she wanted to paint. Ann knew she worked from memory, feeling it allowed her imagination freer play in the creation.

One of the new pieces was a landscape, typical of the woman's work. The other was quite different and caught Ann's attention. The composition was dominated by a pair of massive, elaborate gateposts flanking a road that disappeared into some trees. The gateposts had received the most attention. The trees and the road were represented by a few rough lines.

She called her husband over and showed him the work. "Does this look like Nancy Trahern?"

"No," he told her. "It looks like a gateway."

"No vaudeville jokes, please. You know what I mean."

He examined it critically.

"All right. It's more like an architect's rendering than an artist's. So what?"

"Nothing," she mused. "I just wanted another opinion."

"Have you found anything important?" he asked.

"I haven't. Have you, O Sleuth?"

He shook his head. "We might as well give up. There's nothing obvious here."

They left the cottage the way they had entered. John pulled the window down and managed to maneuver the latch closed again. They crept back to their cottage, feeling well hidden by the darkness that was, at last, beginning to fall.

"There," John said with self-satisfaction when they reached their door. "We did it, and there's nobody the wiser."

But neither he nor Ann noted a glint-eyed crow that

lifted from a nearby tree to sail away, broad wings flapping, until its black form was swallowed by the dark.

Safely inside, John settled himself into a rocking chair and stared down at the remains of the peat fire on the hearth.

"That's that," he said. He lifted the poker and stirred moodily at the white ash. "There wasn't anything to say they didn't just go off on a trip someplace."

"Nothing to say they did, either," she said, sitting down in the rocker next to him.

"It's still a dead end. There's nothing else we can do."

"We could go back to Mrs. Ryan and you could grill her again," Ann suggested.

"She did lie to us," he reminded her, slightly put out by the remark. "But except for that and some odd bits and pieces, this whole thing could be in Bonaventure's mind."

Ann was certain she heard some disappointment in his voice, and it puzzled her.

"I thought you were sure of that from the start," she said. "Aren't you happy we haven't found anything to make you change your mind?"

He looked at her in surprise, seemed to catch himself, and then smiled.

"You are right. I don't know what I meant. It looks like our vacation won't be brought to ruin after all."

"We'd better tell that to Father Bonaventure. Maybe he'll feel better."

"We can't go up to see him until tomorrow afternoon," John said musingly. Then he brightened with a sudden notion. "Say, why don't we get an early start and do some sightseeing like we planned?"

"I don't know," she said uneasily. "It doesn't seem right to do that while Father Bonaventure's worrying."

He leaned toward her and took both of her hands in his.

"Ann, we can't do anything about that until after lunchtime," he said with solemn earnestness, "so we've got all morning. The time we have on this trip is precious to us. Let's not burn any more of it."

"I suppose," she said, wavering. "Where could we go?"

"To Cashel. That's only fifty miles. We'll drive to Cashel and gawk and take pictures just like any other Americans."

He said it with such vigor and enthusiasm that he won over her mood completely. She knew he was right, and she pushed aside the vague doubts still nagging at her to become a red-blooded American tourist again.

"Okay, partner," she said with a smile. "But I refuse to buy any plastic shamrocks for souvenirs."

"How about a leprechaun to put on the dashboard?" he asked, and then ducked to avoid the tea cozy she shied at him.

The two men labored away in their cavelike room, grunting with their effort, sweat-soaked torsos gleaming in the massed lamps' bright light.

They carefully slid a large chunk of fallen ceiling stone clear of the rest of the pile. But it must have been a key to holding up the steeply sloped debris. Rubble avalanched suddenly down from above, causing them to leap back. They saved themselves from being buried in the fall, but they stood watching apprehensively, waiting for more of the fragile ceiling to collapse.

It held. The avalanche subsided, the dust settled. The two men exchanged looks of relief.

"That was a close one," the beefier man said.

"Hey, wait. Look there!" said the younger one, peering through the last haze of drifting dust.

The other looked, too. "Say. There *is* something," he said excitedly. "Let's get some new shoring up!"

They were working energetically to set new wood rafters and supporting jacks in place when the dark-cloaked figure came into the chamber. He stopped and watched in silence as the two men labored on, not interrupting their concerted efforts.

When they had finished, and were stepping back to take

a breather and wipe the sweat from their dripping brows, the younger one noted him.

"Chief!" he said with elation. "Good news for you. Look here!"

He shifted one of the big work lights around to shine its beam up across the top of the rubble pile. Since the new fall, a gap of some three feet had been opened between the pile's top and the ceiling above. Beyond that gap there showed a section of a stone wall. And something else.

The dark one moved up to examine it searchingly. What seemed to be a wide, smooth beam of smoothly finished stone showed there. And below it, just peeping above the heap of rocks, showed a section of metal that dully gleamed a golden brown.

"You've reached it!" the cloaked being said, a definite note of excitement marking his own usually restrained voice. He looked around to them, eyes flashing. "How long to clear away from it completely?"

"Not long," the bigger man said, but then added regretfully, "if we had supports, that is. Gonna need a lot of shoring before we can get in there safely. 'Fraid those were the last timbers. Sorry, Chief. Looks like we got to wait now."

The figure shrugged. "Only for one more night," he said evenly. "After so long, I can be patient a bit longer." His voice took on a more businesslike tone. "But never mind that now. Listen to me. I may have another need for you two. I might have to call you anytime. You might have to be ready to move with speed."

"What for?" asked the younger man curiously.

"Our American friends' meddling has gotten worse," the being brusquely explained. "They questioned Mrs. Ryan closely tonight. She felt certain they knew something. And they broke into the Traherns' as well. They unfortunately seem both resourceful and clever. That could be very dangerous. I think something more . . . *definite* will have to be done to insure that they can cause no further trouble."

"We can take care of that, all right," the bigger man confidently assured.

"But it must be done carefully," the dark one cautioned. "Nothing can draw outside attention to this place. My plan for dealing with them can only be carried out if it cannot be observed. That's why you must be ready. Should they give us any opportunity, you will have to act at once!"

Arising with the sun the following morning, the Milnes and Taffy were on the road while the sun still hung, like a carelessly draped white scarf, around the shoulders of the hills.

It was fifty-five miles to Cashel, and Milne settled himself for a long trip on the narrow, twisting roads. The tiny Ford Escort was a decent car with more than enough power for their purposes, but it was difficult for him to maintain even forty miles per hour.

John was always tense when he drove in Ireland. Driving on wide, straight, American highways was a relaxed business with a minimum demand on the driver. Irish roads called for constant readiness and sharp reflexes. A curve was always just ahead, and anything—horses, bicycles, sheep, carts—could be waiting around it. The year before he had roared around a bend and nearly tail-ended an entire herd of plodding milk cows.

Irish drivers seemed unimpressed by the dangers and loved to pass, at high speed, even on curves where they had no way of knowing what was ahead. Somehow they seemed to survive. Some special Providence protected them, Milne supposed, and hoped it watched over him, too.

Still, he was more confident of his ability this trip and slightly more relaxed. He found that he was even able to look around at the countryside while he drove.

They were headed south to skirt Lough Derg and turn east, and the changing landscape held much for the admiring eye. Here and there they passed the gray ruins of a church or tower house. Every hilltop seemed to have something on it; something never clearly seen, something always mysterious that invited the curious and delighted the fanciful. Even Taffy, riding contentedly in back, seemed to enjoy the view.

The ancient buildings and the land itself were as much of myth as of reality to John Milne. Many gods and heroes had walked the sod. Many men had fought and died to possess Ireland's strange, ephemeral values.

He wondered if they'd fought for its aesthetic qualities alone. The material ones hardly seemed worth a struggle, save perhaps to lovers of rocks and dairy products.

He remembered W. B. Yeats's comment that the Celtic heroes had fought for the sheer love of fighting. Maybe that was all of it. Ireland demanded strong passions of its people. Everyone who had lived there, everyone who had come, from Norman to Cromwellian, had been infected by that demand.

John realized that in thinking this he was attacking his own skepticism of Bonaventure's ideas. It was a peaceful country on the surface, but it was deeply scored by fissures of great violence that ran very close beneath. Anything could happen here. In the past almost everything had.

While he drove, Ann examined their ordinance survey map. The detailed map was their only sure way of negotiating the maze of highways and of making the right choices at the numerous crossroads.

Without a map, without even the sun to guide them most of the time, they had often found they were going directly opposite to where they had supposed. With the map they made only two wrong turns and were nearing their destination in less than two hours of driving.

Part of this modest success John graciously attributed to the emptiness of the roads. When they pulled in at a lay-by with a view of Cashel, he noted that only one other auto was in sight. It was a blue Volvo with amber foglamps that he had noticed far behind them on the road, and it drove on past them and disappeared, leaving the road totally deserted.

In the distance the Rock of Cashel thrust up jaggedly from the smooth green hills, and they got out of the car to admire and photograph it. It was one of the most spectacular ruins in the country. Called the Acropolis of Ireland, it, like that Greek ruin, filled a rocky hilltop, overshadowing its village and dominating the surrounding countryside.

Like the Acropolis too, it symbolized the social and moral heart of a past era. Even in its semifallen state it evoked the immense spiritual and physical power the medieval church had possessed. It was another of those Irish contradictions—both terrible and beautiful at once.

They drove on in after a time, going through the village and up a narrow way that led to the outer walls of the fortified place. They parked in front of a tiny souvenir shop whose backyard was a rocky cliff rising another fifty feet to the cathedral.

The Milnes and Taffy walked up a pathway that climbed at an angle along the cliffs to the only entrance in the outer works. Here they hiked up rough stairs that led through a crumbling gatehouse to the top. They came out onto a flat, open space; and the walls of Cashel loomed up giantlike ahead of them.

It was a ghostly place in many ways. Abandoned, roofless, empty of any feeling of life, the cathedral was a wasted carcass, thrusting its bare ribs up toward the heavy gray sky which, that day, hung close above. The desolate air was further enhanced by the lack of other sightseers. John, Ann, and Taffy had the rock to themselves.

As they examined the cathedral and wandered the grounds, they felt its atmosphere strongly. Huge blackbirds that inhabited the building's upper portions flew out suddenly at their intrusion, rising upward with a soft flapping like the souls of black-robed monks. John and Ann found they were afraid to turn quickly for fear of seeing one of the spectral figures they felt were lurking just beyond the limits of their vision.

Still, the eerie atmosphere of the place was invigorating for them. They clambered and explored and took photographs while Taffy wandered on his own. In the graveyards that surrounded the cathedral, John stopped to examine some of the mold-spotted headstones. He noted a few with recent dates.

"There are some pretty new graves here," he said. "It's the same in all these places. No matter how old they are, the graveyards are still active."

"I wish you'd use another word," said Ann.

"You know what I mean," he told her with a grin. He looked around him at the impressive stones. "But, boy, what a place to be buried. Think of the company! Bishops, royalty, all kinds of famous people." He lifted his gaze to the country-side spreading out around. "And look at the view!"

"I'm glad you like it," Ann said dryly. "I'll have you shipped over here when you go."

"That's okay," he assured her. "I'm not going. You can go if you want to."

"Look, could we talk about something else?" she begged. "For somebody who used to hate going to bed in the dark, you sure like to talk about morbid things in weird places."

"Funny, Ann," he said sarcastically. "But I quit going to bed with a night-light a long time ago."

"A year, at least," she said.

By this time they had circled the cathedral, and Cormack's Chapel came into their view.

It was an older structure, built in the Hiberno-Roman-esque style of round arch and stone roof. The larger Gothic cathedral had been built around it; and it was now squeezed into a space between nave and south transept, as if it were a puppy trying to hide against its mother.

To get the entire chapel into one photo, John backed away to the low rock wall that edged the hilltop. He snapped a shot, then turned to get a picture of the village below. The cliff there was rocky but not steep. It stair-stepped down to the road and the souvenir shop.

"There's our car," said Ann, pointing.

John nodded. Now another car was parked in the lot, too. A blue Volvo with amber foglamps. There was some-thing significant in that, but he wasn't sure why. He stood for a moment, gazing down.

"Come on," she said. "Let's look inside the chapel."

"Yeah, okay," he murmured, and followed after her in a preoccupied way.

The chapel was an intriguing place, but windowless and damp and difficult to stay in for any length of time. The age and history of it seemed to have concentrated themselves into an almost physical presence that pressed in on them. They soon retreated to the relative cheerfulness of the outdoors.

As they came out of the door, they nearly collided with a young man. He was short, stocky, with thick features and a tousled mass of brown hair. He wore a dark suit and a bulky turtleneck sweater with a rather worn look about them.

He muttered something that might have been an apology and stepped aside to let them pass; but as they walked on, he remained where he was, looking after them.

The Milnes rounded the end of the chapel and found themselves back at the cathedral's main entrance. There they found a second man who sat on a stone by the gateway in the outer works. He was older and heavier, also dressed in a worn suit. When he saw them, he stood immediately and started in their direction.

John glanced back and noted that the first man was also moving toward them. At that moment he came to a rather disturbing realization. That Volvo in the parking area was the one he had noted behind them on the road, and these two men had to be its passengers.

"I think these men want us," he said, trying to keep his voice calm.

Ann had already formed that opinion independently.

"What do they want?" she asked.

"Should we ask?" he suggested.

The man ahead of them reached into his coat and produced a rather large revolver. Taffy bristled and growled deep in his throat.

John changed his mind. "We'll ask later. Let's run now!"

But they were already cut off in two directions.

CHAPTER
EIGHT

Who will go drive with Fergus now,
And pierce the deep wood's woven shade,
And dance upon the level shore?
Young man, lift up your russet brow,
And lift your tender eyelids, maid,
And brood on hopes and fear no more.

—W. B. YEATS: *"Who Goes with Fergus?"*

John looked desperately around. The only way open was toward the cathedral entrance.

"Inside," he said, and they charged for the doorway, Taffy close behind them.

Their sudden movement caught the gunmen by surprise, and the three made it through the entrance far ahead of them.

Inside, the young couple paused at the sight of the vast, roofless space, uncertain of where to go next. The only promising place lay across the wide nave, where a jumble of rock filled the north transept. They made for it at full speed, but it was too far. They had yards to go when one of the men stepped into the doorway and raised his gun toward them.

A bullet screamed off the far wall. The explosion echoed

through the ruins, and every bird there took flight at once. The sky above was suddenly filled with them as they soared away, cawing loudly in alarm. The din they made was eerie and disconcerting, and the gunman looked up with surprise.

This unexpected diversion gave the Milnes and their dog enough time to get around the corner and into the shelter of the transept. They stopped there, simply because they didn't know where else to go. The cathedral only had one way in and out, and that way was now most uncomfortably crowded.

Afraid to move, afraid even to breathe, they stood for some time listening, hoping the gunmen had not seen where they had gone. In the great silence that fell, John could feel his heart beating loudly. His hands and knees shook with reaction to the adrenaline surge that had taken him this far. He grasped Ann's hand and found that it was shaking, too. But Taffy sat quietly beside them, calm and alert and waiting.

Then the silence was broken by a distant voice.

"Where are they? Did you see?" it said breathlessly.

"They've gone into the walls somewhere," another, younger voice answered. "I don't know quite where. Over toward there, I think."

"What'll we do, then?" said the first voice. Its accent was so heavy with the country that the Milnes could barely understand.

"We ferret them out," the younger voice responded. Its tones were casual, its volume high. Its owner was not concerned if anyone heard. He must have known, as the Milnes did, that they were alone on the hilltop.

"And just how can only the two of us do that?" the first one complained, still wheezing. "They could be anywhere."

"There's only the one entrance," the other said impatiently. "You stay near it. I'll do the looking. And mind you, don't breathe so loudly. You can't be that much out of condition."

The older man gave a faint curse in reply, and the voices ceased.

The Milnes looked searchingly around them for some

way to move. The side wall of the transept behind them offered the only likely outlet in a dark, narrow doorway.

They knew that beyond it was a staircase to the second floor of the cathedral's central tower. In their earlier examination of the interior, they had decided against going up. Now there was no hesitation.

Moving very quietly, they went in through the doorway and started up the small, circular stairway. It led them to a narrow landing whose open side hung out over the floor of the cathedral. Another doorway there gave access to the base of the great tower that sat over the crossing of nave and transept. Their choice of avenues was not expanding.

They moved through the tower, trying not to trip over fallen stones in the darkness, wondering if the gunman was close behind them. In a short time they were out again, finding themselves at the top of another landing with a staircase that led right back down into the cathedral.

John peeked over the edge of the landing to see if the way below was open, but drew back quickly in despair. They were trapped. The older gunman was pacing directly beneath, watching both the transepts and the nave while also staying within sight of the main door.

John knew they had little time left before the other man would find one of the stairways to the tower and come up after them. He looked about for any other means of escape and noted a loose block of stone, some two feet square, lying near the edge of the landing. He went to it and peered over again. The gunman's pacing took him right under it. John smiled with grim satisfaction.

He signaled Ann to come help and took a grip on the stone.

Ann started forward but, suddenly grasping his intention, stopped in horror.

He looked up at her, and she saw the cold determination in the look. It had transformed the pleasant, mild lines of his face so that, for an instant, she looked at someone she did not know.

Milne pointed emphatically at the rock and then at the man below.

She shook her head with equal emphasis. She would not help in such an act, no matter what the danger.

His eyes narrowed in puzzlement. Then he shrugged. They were going to have to act quickly. They were in no position for a discussion of ethics.

He squatted by the stone, wrapped both arms around it, and, with an effort, got it off the ground. He moved carefully to the edge and peered over. The gunman was walking back from the corner, moving slowly toward a point just below.

John held the stone, arms clenching it tightly and vibrating with the strain. He felt his muscles cramping into knots and willed himself to hold, hold, until the man was directly under him.

But he never released the stone. Taffy acted first. Without a sound the dog leaped over the edge.

Something, perhaps some extra sense of his own, must have warned the man below. He stepped back against the wall and almost saved himself, but not quite. The big animal's solid weight slammed into his back, and the two went down heavily.

"Let's go!" said John, and they raced down the stairs into the cathedral.

They ran past Taffy and the gunman. The dog had a firm grip on the man's gun hand. He had already shaken the weapon loose, and his victim was thrashing wildly, trying to get away.

Ann stopped, staring, but her husband grabbed her arm and pulled.

"Come on!" he cried urgently.

"We can't leave Taffy," she argued.

"The other man will come any second," he told her. "We've got to get away!"

He hauled her off toward the door. As they went through it, they heard the struggling man begin to call for help.

Outside they stopped and looked toward the gateway in the outer works. To gain it meant a long run in the open.

Staying out of sight and range seemed much preferable, so they made for the nearest corner of the building instead.

Once there they stopped again, heatedly discussing their next move in whispers.

"We can't leave Taffy," Ann said adamantly.

"He made his own choice to help us," John reasoned. "Getting ourselves caught won't help him any. He'll be all right. Let's worry about us. Look, if we can get to that east wall, I think we can climb down to the car. Are you ready?"

"Okay," she said reluctantly.

They moved away from the cathedral through the cemetery, dodging between headstones and moving as fast as they could.

When they reached the outer wall, they helped each other across it. Below them were the town and the road. Their own car and the Volvo still sat alone by the souvenir shop. The climb, though rugged, seemed one that they could manage, and they started down.

Within minutes they reached the parking lot. They were just getting into the car when Taffy trotted casually up to them.

"Taffy!" cried Ann, stooping to hug the animal. "How did you get here?"

"I knew he could take care of himself," John said, not admitting his own relief. "Now let's get out of here!"

They were in the car and had it turned around in the road before the men appeared again. The pair emerged from the gatehouse and started down toward the Milnes at a run.

John stepped on the gas and the little Ford took off, leaving the gunmen in its dusty wake.

"How do we get to the police?" John asked.

"Just drive through the village and look," she advised. "There must be a *Garda* station somewhere."

He wheeled the car around a tight corner and up an avenue that squeezed between two buildings. He glanced in the rearview mirror. No Volvo appeared from the cathedral road.

The narrow road reached the main street through the village. He stopped at the intersection and looked both ways.

"Right or left?" he asked.

"It depends on where the police are," she told him.

"I don't need logic," he said, "I need help." He looked in his mirror again.

This time the Volvo was there, turning the corner and coming on fast.

"Left," he decided and turned the car onto the main road.

It took only seconds to see that was a mistake. The buildings stopped and they were abruptly in the country.

"We missed the town," he pointed out unnecessarily.

"Turn around," she suggested, unaware of the close pursuit.

"I think we'd better go on," he said, jerking a thumb back over his shoulder.

She looked. The Volvo was a hundred yards back and beginning to close.

They raced up the highway. It was the main Dublin road and unusually straight for Ireland. John pushed the accelerator to the floor, but the Volvo continued to gain.

"That car is faster than ours," he said. "On this kind of road they'll catch us soon."

A side road came up on their left. He geared down suddenly and swung the Ford into it without braking. The little car responded and they were onto the secondary road with a minimum of sliding.

"I'm hoping the curves will slow them down," he told her. "We can keep them behind us until we hit another town."

"If we don't hit something else first," Ann said.

She watched him drive and knew he had to be under tremendous pressure as he kept up speed and piloted the car down the twisting lanes. To make it worse, the inevitable stone walls closed in on either side, turning the road into a narrow alley and making a mistake a certain collision.

"I think you should slow down," said Ann, watching the walls flash past only inches from her face.

"I think I'm getting the hang of it," John replied in a voice so well controlled that she looked at him more closely.

As he drove, his mind had forced his body to act in response to the situation. He found that he was able to handle the car more naturally, more easily. He relaxed and began to guide rather than wrench the car around the curves. The more simple this became, the more he realized that he was actually enjoying himself.

She could see the change in him now. She noted the easy movements and the odd, tight smile. For the second time that day, she got the momentary impression that she viewed a stranger.

"Where are we?" he asked abruptly. "We've come quite a way."

Ann fumbled with the map, turning her attention from the road ahead to the maze of tiny lines.

"We're headed for Tipperary," she said, tracing their route.

"How far?"

"It's hard to say," she told him. Under the circumstances, time and distance were somewhat hard to measure. "But we should be close."

"I think we've arrived," said John, for suddenly they had.

There were no outskirts. The town just began, plunging them instantly into the traffic nightmare of Tipperary.

Irish villages were most definitely not built with the modern world in mind. In many places the buildings edged close to what had been paths for carts in older times. And, since ancient buildings meant more to the Irish than speed and convenience, these paths had never been widened. The result was a funnel effect, forcing several converging streams of two-way traffic through what was often a single-lane street.

This situation was especially true of Tipperary. As the Milnes plunged deeper into the town, the traffic pressure built, slowing them to a cautious crawl. The Volvo, by recklessly ignoring pedestrians and other autos, began to gain on them once again.

"They don't seem to be put off by the town," John said.

"What can they do here?" she asked, looking back with anxiety.

"Maybe anything they want," he answered grimly.

He concentrated on trying to put more distance between them and the Volvo. Accelerating up a low hill, he saw that the way ahead was blocked by a parked ale truck, large even by American standards. Two thirds of the narrow street was obstructed by it, and a flow of traffic from the other direction was squeezing itself through the small opening left.

"Prepare to abandon ship," John said as the Volvo closed in.

At that moment, Providence seemed to take a hand. The line of oncoming cars abruptly stopped. A hole appeared and, without hesitation, he ran the Ford into it, praying it was open at the other end.

It was. In fact, it was too open. The next car in the approaching stream was half a block away. There was time for another car to get through the narrow gap behind them. And the driver of the Volvo clearly saw this, for that car leaped forward after the Milnes with a sudden burst of speed.

It didn't make it.

From nowhere a square brown auto cut it off, jamming itself into the hole just ahead of the Volvo and forcing the other car to brake to a sliding stop, its horns blaring in loud anger.

The brown car paid no heed. It squeezed through behind the Milnes, getting past the truck just as the oncoming traffic reached the gap and plugged it again, leaving the Volvo trapped on the other side.

John turned up the only side street within sight and pulled into a parking lot. They sat there, watching through the driver's window to see if the Volvo would follow them. They waited for tense, long moments, but it didn't appear.

"Hey there! You folks!" a voice suddenly called loudly.

The unexpected voice, coming from the opposite side of the car, startled them. The Milnes snapped around while Taffy, in the rear seat, crouched back, bristling, making a sharp, angry sound.

ChAPTER
NINE

❦

'Though logic-choppers rule the town,
And every man and maid and boy
Has marked a distant object down,
An aimless joy is a pure joy,'
Or so did Tom O'Roughley say
That saw the surges running by,
'And wisdom is a butterfly
And not a gloomy bird of prey.'

—W. B. YEATS: *"Tom O'Roughley"*

Through Ann's side window a lean, sun-darkened face smiled pleasantly in at them.

"I saw that car chasing you," the man said in a casual American drawl. "You need some help?"

They examined him suspiciously. He was a large man, so tall he was doubled almost in half to lean in at the small car's window. He looked a well-conditioned fifty years of age, with graying hair and a ruggedly lined face. In John's mind flashed an image of cowboys and wide-open prairies.

Then he saw the brown car parked behind the man, and he relaxed a little.

"You're the one who cut them off!" he said.

The man's smile grew wider. "And you're fellow Americans," he said heartily. "I knew you were when I saw you close up. It's the clothes. I can always tell by the clothes. But what was that all about?"

There was something about the man's personality that seemed to envelop them with its forcefulness. Without question they found themselves believing that he was capable of taking charge in any situation. So strong was this feeling that John almost poured out their problem to him right there.

But then some reluctance to ask for help stopped him. He didn't know the exact reason why, except that they just couldn't be too cautious.

So, instead, he said, "It wasn't anything, really." He tried to sound as casual as he could. "I think it was just some local kids trying to race with us on the road. It was kind of a stupid thing to do in town, wasn't it?"

The man's calm blue eyes appraised them carefully. His voice turned grave.

"Now, I know trouble when I see it, and you two are scared. It's your business, not mine, but I hate to see fellow Americans go without help when they need it."

"We're okay, really," John insisted, although Ann threw him a puzzled look at that.

"If you say so," the man said, though he was obviously still dubious. "Do you live around here?"

John would have dodged the question, but Ann spoke before he could stop her.

"We're staying in Ballymurroe."

"Well, no kidding!" the tall man said with pleasure. "I live pretty close to there myself. Look here, if you decide you do need help, you can look me up. My name's Butler . . . Douglas Butler. Most of the folks around these parts know me."

"Douglas Butler, the director?" John said, suddenly struck with open awe.

"Have you heard of me?" the man replied with a modesty John didn't believe.

Of course they had heard of him. Most of the civilized world had. Butler had dominated the movie-making realm for nearly forty years, producing and directing scores of films, many of them classics. But if this was that same man, Milne had another reason to be impressed. This hardy figure who looked fifty at most had to be more like seventy years of age!

Again some inner sense of caution overcame John's awe. As calmly as he could, he said, "We're really glad we met you, Mr. Butler. But we've got to get going. Maybe we'll see you again. Okay?"

Butler seemed perplexed, as if he'd expected a warmer response. He stood up from the car.

"Okay, then," he said, then added, "and who might you be?"

"Maybe you've heard of us," John said with a smile. "I'm John Milne, and this is my wife, Ann."

Butler chuckled and said, "I'm afraid I haven't, but I'll be looking for you."

John put the car in gear and pulled away. Ann looked back at the tall man who remained standing there, gazing after them.

"John, are you crazy?" she asked with deep sincerity. "Why didn't you tell him what happened? He wanted to help."

"We don't know him," her husband replied. "He could be anybody. I'm not trusting anyone—even the *Gardai*—until we've talked to Father Bonaventure about all this."

Ann was too worn to argue. She got out the map and helped John set a twisting course back to Ballymurroe that would hopefully throw off any chance of pursuit.

But they didn't see the Volvo again.

When Father Bonaventure finished reciting his noon office, he found the Milnes and Taffy waiting for him in the visitors' room.

The gray morning had by now given way to a bright and pleasant afternoon, so they went into the gardens to talk.

Once the flowers for a grand lady had been grown there, but now the monks kept them up for their pleasure and that of their guests. John wondered if the flowers were pleased or disappointed by the change in admirers.

The three sat down on stone seats in a little arbor thickly covered over with bright rhododendrons. While Taffy amused himself, the Milnes took turns telling Bonaventure what had happened since they had seen him last.

The incident at Cashel disturbed the monk, as they had guessed it would. He interrupted the balance of their story several times for reassurances that they had not been hurt.

"You should never have come into this," he told them, much aggrieved. "And I feel the cause of it, filling you up with fears for the Traherns. Perhaps the hunt after them should be given up."

It was a difficult thing for the monk to suggest. He knew that the Milnes' withdrawal would end any chance of finding the mother and daughter.

"Father, what are you saying?" asked John in surprise. "You think we should quit just when we've discovered your fears are founded on some pretty hard ground? No," he added decisively, "we're *sure* not giving this up!"

Ann eyed him curiously at that, but said nothing.

"That's decided, then," said the monk, less anxious now that his guilt had been lifted from his shoulders. "But what will we do?"

"We're not really sure," Ann told him. "I got John to stop at the policeman's house in the village, but his wife told us he was gone."

"And I'm afraid he will be for some time now," Bonaventure said. "He's been called to the border. Poor lad. Only married a week and gone off already."

"What for?" asked Ann.

"Ah, there's some rumor of trouble again, in the North. They call up *Gardai* from the villages and send them up to man checkpoints and the like. Sometimes they are gone for days. Each time it happens I hope it will be the last. It never is."

"What if something happens in the villages when the law is gone?" asked John. He found the logic of this kind of strategy hard to comprehend.

Bonaventure shrugged. "One can always find the *Gardai* in the larger towns," he said with casual indifference. "They would be of no help to us in any case. There's little enough that you could tell them, and less that you could prove." He thought a moment and then asked, "Did you get the license plate number?"

"It was covered in mud. Maybe we could describe the men and the car," said Ann.

"Both types much too common in this country, I'm afraid. And there's really nothing to link them to the Traherns but our poor imaginations. What happened to you happened some way from here."

"That's true," Ann agreed. "We *don't* know for sure there's a connection. I mean, what's to say those men had anything to do with this? They could've just been trying to rob us or something. We were tourists in an isolated place."

"First of all, I doubt that robbers would have been persistent enough to chase us all over the place," John told her. "Second, I can't buy that that was some coincidence. Not unless they chase all the tourist trade."

"That would be a fine sport," Bonaventure mused, "but, no, it's surely not done. Not even the worst IRA terrorists would be so mad as to act against innocents, most especially Americans, in the Republic. It would lose sympathy for them here, and in your own country, where they get so much of their backing. No, it would take something very important, something important about you two, to make someone go after you that way."

"That's what I say," said John. "We've stepped on some sensitive toes, and the only unusual thing we've done since we got here is to try to find out what happened to our friends. My gut tells me that something is really going on."

Ann sighed. "None of this matters anyway," she said tiredly. "We're still left on our own, still without anything more than we knew before."

"So, you found nothing at all in the cottage?" the monk asked.

"No. Well . . . just a tourist brochure," said John, remembering. He searched in his jacket pocket, finally pulling out the crumpled folder. "Here. I thought it was an odd thing for Nancy to have, until it occurred to me that she's really a tourist in the South, too."

"I've never seen it before," said Bonaventure. "Might I look at it?"

John handed him the folder and he examined it carefully, noting the underlined sections.

"The *Teac* . . ." he said thoughtfully.

"Chock?" John repeated. "What's that?"

"*Teac an Ceoil*," Bonaventure told him, and spelled it out. It's Gaelic for 'House of Music.' There are only references to it that she's underlined in here. There's a new *Teac* nearby, you know."

"Oh?" said Ann. "We didn't see it."

"It's in Conlish, actually. Some two miles from here. Just a tiny spot with a victualler and a few houses."

"That probably explains why she was interested," said Ann. "But what is it? A music school?"

"It's a great deal more than that," the monk replied absently. He was still pondering something. Suddenly he stood up. "There is one here who could tell you more about it than I," he said. "I'll go find him, if you'll excuse me."

John tried to tell him not to bother, but the monk was strangely adamant.

"No, no. I'd like to know more of this myself," he said, and hurried away before John could say more.

So the young man tried to settle himself more comfortably on the stone seat for the wait. Failing in this, he turned toward his wife and found her watching him with a bemused expression.

"What's the matter?" he asked.

"It looks like we're just going right ahead with it?" she said, as if it were a question, and that perplexed him.

"I thought that was what we just decided," he said.

"It's what *you* just decided," she pointed out.

"What do you mean? You don't want to stay involved in this?"

"I'm really not sure," she said truthfully. "John, weren't you afraid today?"

"I . . . I don't know," he told her, uncertain of her direction. "I hadn't really thought about it." He considered. "Yeah, I suppose I was."

"Were you?" she said. "I couldn't tell. You . . . well . . . surprised me. That's pretty unusual for us. Anyway, if you were, it sure didn't affect your decision to go on. I mean, that was enough to make most people stop and think. And you of *all* people. But it didn't. You were sure. You knew you'd go ahead before we ever talked about it. That surprised me, too. I really don't like the feeling."

His first impulse was to deny what she suggested. But when he examined his behavior, he found truth in what she had said. The John Milne who worried about his faults, analyzed his actions, and examined his character constantly had been acting without hesitation, making decisions without question. What had happened seemed to have awakened a sense of adventure in him. There was fear there, certainly, but it was only a minor check and balance to an impulsive, all-out involvement.

"I guess I'm surprised myself," he said. "It all just seemed natural at the time."

Besides, he told himself, having always been a man of thought rather than action, in a way it was pleasant to realize that the second quality came forward on its own when needed. It gave him a confidence in his abilities he hadn't known before.

"I could say the same thing about you, though," he told Ann. "You've gone right along. I haven't been alone in any of this, partner."

"No," she admitted. "And I suppose I do agree with you now. We have to do something. *I* just don't like it much."

He wanted to try to explain his new feeling further to her, but Father Bonaventure reappeared, accompanied by a man of about the Milnes' age. He was a square, solid-looking individual, dressed in worn blue jeans and work shirt.

"This is Brother Coleman," Bonaventure said. "He's our tradition and folklore expert."

As the young monk shook hands with them both, he noted a look of surprise in John's eyes.

"Did you expect someone older?" he asked with a smile.

John was abashed by this reference to what he felt was bad manners. He wasn't sure how to respond.

"My husband isn't used to someone like you," Ann explained with good humor. "His knowledge of the church is mostly medieval and very romanticized. I think he expected you to be in a habit."

"Oh," said Coleman with a laugh. "Well, they are very nice. We wear them for public occasions, and they are fine in cold weather, but they are rather in the way for working. I've been cleaning some bits from the Lough Gur area. Neolithic pottery and such."

John's fingers still tingled from the monk's powerful handshake. He looked at the thick, square hands with their blunt fingers and tried to imagine Brother Coleman piecing tiny shards together.

"Brother Coleman is also a friend of the Traherns," said Bonaventure. "He knows all that I do and is anxious to help."

"That I am," Coleman agreed. "What is it you wish to know?"

"About this *Teac* place, I suppose. I'm not really sure," said John. "Father Bonaventure seemed more interested than we were."

"It's true," said the older monk. "I had some remembrance of Mrs. Trahern mentioning the *Teac an Ceoil*."

"What is it, exactly?" asked Ann.

"Now, there's a fine place to start," said Coleman, sitting down on the ground and crossing his legs. "The *Teac an Ceoil* is a House of Music. That means it's a place to keep music alive and well. Most of it is traditional Irish, but all types are played, and welcome. The gatherings are held weekly in the warmer months. Entertainers from all over come to dance, sing, and play. Many others come to listen. There are quite a number of music houses on the western coast, and there's a new one here, you know."

"Father Bonaventure told us," said John. "Was Mrs. Trahern interested in these gatherings?"

The young monk thought a time, his brow furrowed in concentration. Absently, but with delicacy, his large fingers explored the petals of a rhododendron blossom. John watched him with fascination and found it easier to imagine his pottery work.

"She was interested, you know," he said finally. "Now you've brought it back to me, it seems we did have a talk much like this one."

"That was it!" Father Bonaventure abruptly declared. "I recall now, too. She asked me what I knew about the *Teacs*, and it was then I told her Brother Coleman would be the one to ask. It was her impatience at the time that made me wonder, for I never heard any more about it from her afterward."

"Well, it was surely very little she got from me," said Brother Coleman. "It was quite common things mostly: where the other *Teacs* were, how they were run, what musicians came to play . . ."

"Was that all of it?" asked John.

"No," he said, more slowly now. "Come to think on it further, I do recall one thing more. She was interested in just who came to the nights. She was especially keen about knowing if there were *strangers* there."

CHAPTER
TEN
✠

Surely among a rich man's flowering lawns,
Amid the rustle of his planted hills,
Life overflows without ambitious pains;
And rains down life until the basin spills,
And mounts more dizzy high the more it rains
As though to choose whatever shape it wills
And never stoop to a mechanical
Or servile shape, at other's beck and call.

—W. B. YEATS: *"Ancestral Houses"*

"Strangers?" John repeated with aroused interest. "Do many show up there?"

"I've not noticed any," Brother Coleman replied. "A great number of people come from the surrounding villages. She was still a new arrival here. Perhaps she hadn't seen some of them before."

"Maybe," said John, but uncertainly.

"Why was it you never told me about this?" asked Bonaventure, his tone slightly reproving.

"It seemed to have no importance at the time," the younger monk said simply. "We talked often about my work.

She and Bridget were always interested. They both hold great affection for the Old Ones. Although I believe I agree with you, Father. She was . . . impatient . . . or something else."

"Could we talk to someone at the *Teac?*" asked John. "Maybe someone there could tell us why she was so impatient."

"The *Teac* is nothing more than a hall," said Coleman. "We'll find no one there now. It's only open for the music nights."

"But that might be the perfect thing," said Father Bonaventure thoughtfully. "There's a gathering every Friday. That's tonight. There would be many there then. People you might not see otherwise." He spoke with more excitement as he continued, and a ruddy glow began to suffuse his pale face. He seemed to have become infected with the adventurous spirit of the thing. "I think we should all go down."

"All of us, Father?" said John.

"You two and I. You see, I might be able to find out things there that you couldn't."

John understood what he meant. Any reluctance on the part of the villagers to talk would be even greater with outsiders. Still, he felt a strange unwillingness to have the monk along. He had no chance to protest, however. Ann, grateful for the offer, took the decision out of his hands.

"That's a great idea," she said with evident relief. She looked at her husband. "Don't you think so?"

"Yes," he agreed, slowly. "But . . . you know, we aren't sure what kind of risks we're running here."

"But *you* are still going to run them," Bonaventure pointed out. "Let me remind you that Mrs. Trahern and her daughter are our friends, too. We'll have a part in this."

"Okay, Father," John said, capitulating with good grace. "How do we work it?"

"I'll pick you up well before the playing starts," Bonaventure said. "We'll drive down to the *Teac* early and talk to those involved."

"Good idea," said Coleman. "You can talk to the Kileys.

They organize the music nights, and many visiting musicians stay with them."

"You'll drive?" John asked, surprised.

"We do have an auto or two here," said Coleman. "Even monks have to travel about."

"I warned you John's views were archaic," Ann said with a smile. "He probably thought you rode around on asses."

John turned an affronted eye on his wife. "Any comeback I could make to that—and there are one or two obvious ones—would be entirely out of place here."

During this exchange, Bonaventure had been considering another avenue, and he now presented it.

"There is something else that might be done in the meantime," he said. "This Butler you met was spinning you no tale. He's bought and restored a grand old estate nearby called Dunraven. He's a respected man about here. It was even he who helped open the *Teac an Ceoil* in Conlish. Near to a year ago that was."

"You think he could be helpful?" asked John.

"He did offer his aid," Bonaventure replied. "Perhaps you should go tell him what you suspect."

"I'm not sure what good that would do," said Ann.

"Well, he does have what I think you call clout," the monk explained. "If he believes there is something wrong, he might be able to bring more official powers into this."

"I don't like it," John said. "We don't know him, and talking to him might just make things more complicated."

"I'm afraid there's little choice," said Bonaventure. "You can't ignore the danger we may be facing. If there's a chance of gaining help in this, we must take it." He paused and took a deep breath before going on resolutely. "You've risked yourselves alone too much already. If you refuse to see him, I'll not be a party to involving you any longer."

"That's blackmail!" John cried. "You can't do that!"

"And why not?" Bonaventure replied defiantly.

"Because you're a monk! A man of the church!"

"A very poor reason, both ethically and historically," the monk told him. "This is for your own good."

"That's a lousy excuse," John said gloomily.

"And I support it," Ann said with more cheer.

"Okay. Okay," her husband agreed. "We'll go and see him. But, no matter what he says, you'll still go with us to the *Teac?*"

"I promise that I will. Go and see Mr. Butler now. Leave Taffy here with us, and we'll look after him. We'll meet tonight. With luck we'll find help somewhere this day."

Bonaventure gave the Milnes careful directions for finding Butler's estate. Then the two Americans returned to their cottage to eat some lunch and change clothes. By that time it was midafternoon, and the day had turned into one of the first truly sunny ones they had seen.

Because of that, and because Dunraven was little more than a mile from Ballymurroe, they decided to walk over.

When they reached the entrance to the estate and began to walk along its drive, they realized that no one was ever going to drop in on Mr. Butler by chance. The way from his gate to his front door was nearly as long as the road from town had been.

Once past a thick line of trees that screened the estate from the public road, the grounds opened up and revealed their extent. The gravel lane turned to run parallel with a rushing stream, and on either side broad meadows swept away to distant woods.

They passed some ruins on the stream's far bank that were little more than a huge, jumbled mass of rock, half-hidden by vines and bushes. Farther on, the roofless shell of an ancient monastery jutted starkly from the center of a meadow. And the road led them further and further, deep into the heart of the demesne.

"This is getting to be a habit," he said. "I hope we're not going to end up in Oz this way." But after a moment's thought, he added, "Or maybe I hope we are."

He had spoken too soon, however, for in another moment they passed another line of trees and came within sight of the manor house.

Like Glendon Abbey, Dunraven was the home of a departed English aristocrat. The two estates contrasted sharply, however. From its appearance, Dunraven had been built in the middle eighteen-hundreds, during the height of the famines, when labor could be had for a few meals, and the neo-Gothic style of architecture was rampant. So, where Glendon well exemplified the age of reason, Dunraven fully embodied the spirit of Romanticism.

The result was an immense stone edifice, castellated to resemble something from a medieval fairy tale. And even in the reality of the present, its sudden appearance afforded the Milnes the momentary impression of having stepped into an Arthurian fantasy.

They crossed the graveled yard to a massive front door. Milne searched about fruitlessly for a doorbell, then reached for a heavy iron knocker. He raised and dropped the circle of metal against the wood, and a deep boom echoed hollowly inside. Almost immediately the door was swung open, and a young man looked out at them with surprise.

"Well, hello!" he said brightly. "You must be the Milnes. We were told that we might see you. Though maybe not quite so soon. But the Old Man said two Americans, so I expected middle-aged with fat bellies, not young, flaming-haired beauties."

His manner was casually masculine, and the Irish charm flowed like electric current lighting a crystal chandelier.

Only in this case, John told himself, the fixture was probably only glass. The man had raked his gaze up and down Ann's body in frank appraisal, and had roused an urge in John to punch the man's long, straight nose, perhaps spreading it out a little. He tried to convince himself that he could actually do it.

But Ann hadn't liked this look-over either, and she handled things in her own way.

"And I didn't expect the butler to be a classy blond," she said with a broad but humorless smile.

The man's assuredness failed him suddenly, as if his electric current had been switched off. She had hit him directly in his manner of relating to women, and she could see that her unexpected comeback had thrown him off balance.

It was only a momentary reaction, however. He laughed to cover himself and stepped aside to let them enter.

"Actually, I'm a production assistant to the Old Man," he said. "My name is Padraic O'Gadhra."

Ann noticed that this was directed to her husband, not to both of them, and she smiled to herself. The man was steering clear of her now.

O'Gadhra led them into an entry hall that was both broad and high, its ceiling soaring up to pointed arches two stories above. Though it was a bright day, this windowless place was plunged in gloom, crisscrossed by twisting shadows flung various ways by the few, scattered lights.

John decided the advent of electricity hadn't hurt the Gothic atmosphere. He doubted that the bulbs in the shaded wall lamps provided any more light than the more primitive forms of illumination had.

From the entry, O'Gadhra led them through an archway into a main hall even larger than the Milnes expected from their previous visits to Irish manor houses. It was an immense room with a groin-vaulted ceiling suitable for a modest cathedral. A broad staircase on the far side led up to a gallery that ran along one wall.

The quarter-acre-sized room was furnished with massive pieces of dark wood, unpolished except by the wear of years. Some of it Ann identified as bog oak, the steel-hard wood half petrified by long immersion in the peat bogs. The floors too were wood, formed of wide-cut planks and largely uncovered save for a few "tiny" rugs that she estimated would have fit wall-to-wall in an average American living room. The paneled walls were hung with ancient tapestries and decorated with displays of antique weaponry.

The effect of it all was strongly medieval, the room's heavy somberness lessened only by the fine textures of the metal, wood, and cloth.

O'Gadhra was not giving any tours, however, and there was no stopping to admire anything as they moved quickly through the room. As they went, the young man continued to display friendship, at least to the male Milne, speaking to him in an intimate way.

"I suppose I actually am funcitoning as butler now," he said, "but for a short time only. Himself can't abide servants, even in a great barn like this. He does it all on his own, or as nearly as he can. Says he's always done it that way. He only has a few of us here to help him."

On the far side of the room they entered a hallway that led behind the main stairs. O'Gadhra stopped by the first door.

"*He's* working in the front study," he said, suddenly lowering his voice and giving the personal pronoun a peculiar importance.

He knocked, opened the door, and disappeared inside for a moment. Then the door was opened wide, and he ushered them into the Presence.

Butler was standing at a massive desk at which he had evidently been working; at what, John and Ann could not be sure. The desk top was clear of papers. But Dunraven's master made an impressive first sight there, his large form silhouetted against the light.

The room was full of light. Quite a change from the gloom of the main hall. Its outer wall was a double row of windows giving out onto a formal garden. The room itself was furnished in a different style, medieval ponderousness giving way to a lighter, Enlightenment elegance. In contrast with Butler's bulk, it was made to seem almost fragile, giving the man a look of dominance.

In spite of his awe, John found himself wondering cynically just how much of the effect was accidental. The man was, after all, a master filmmaker. Staging dramatic effects was his life.

"Well, I hoped to be seeing you again," the man said heartily. "You met Paddy? He's a good production man, a fine pilot, and a fair cook, but a lousy butler." He looked toward the young man. "Thanks, Paddy. See you later."

O'Gadhra nodded in acknowledgment and withdrew, closing the door after him.

"Are you sure we're not bothering you?" John asked.

"No, no," he assured them. "Just finishing some work. Sit down."

He waited while they seated themselves before the desk and then sat down himself. John was surprised to see the fragile-appearing chair take his weight without a protesting squeak. It added to his impression that the man would be more in his element amidst the giant scale of the main hall.

"I'm happy you accepted my invitation," Butler said. "I'm guessing you decided you might need help after all."

"Yes, sir," John agreed. "A friend of ours convinced us we should talk to you." He didn't add the "Or else!" that he was thinking.

"I'm glad of it. I knew right off there was some trouble. I had half a mind to check up on you two anyway. I wasn't joking when I said I'd help. What's it about?"

John found himself hesitating again. It puzzled him that he should. As before, he was aware that Butler actually seemed to project an aura of confidence and strength. No one could doubt that he could solve any problem. Yet John simply didn't want him involved in this. He couldn't bring himself to begin.

Ann didn't have that problem. She jumped right in, telling their whole story from the first suspicion of the Traherns' disappearance to the attack at Cashel. At its conclusion, Butler leaned back in his chair and whistled.

"Well, you've had quite a time of it," he said. "And I can see your problem. You haven't got a stick of proof for any of it. I'd doubt you myself except that I saw that car after you, and I've got a feeling you're not the type to spin a line like that."

His voice was a friendly, casual drawl, and his smile was warm in the leathery brown face. The teeth were gleaming, the eyes bright gray-blue and piercing. Again John thought of cowboy heroes and the old Wild West. It seemed a strange image in the setting of the carefully civilized room.

Butler appeared to consider their story for some moments, and the two waited patiently. Then he nodded as if he'd made a decision.

"All right," he said briskly. "I don't know your Traherns, but I sure do think a lot of all the people around here. Since I came back and restored this place, they've sort of looked to me as if I'd taken on the lord-of-the-manor job along with it." He smiled broadly again. "It sounds conceited, but I *like* playing the lord. I've even helped some of the locals fix things up and get a music hall going."

"We know," said John. "We saw it listed in the tourist brochures."

"I didn't do it for the tourists," Butler said, dismissing the faceless herd of them with a wave of the hand. "They want museums and ruins and antiques. Old, dead things, not live-and-kicking ones. No, I did it because I wanted to keep something alive for the people here."

"Does that mean you'll help us?" Ann asked hopefully.

He looked at her and smiled in a warm and fatherly way.

"Well, good lady," he said expansively, "I'd be a poor sort of lord if I didn't, now wouldn't I?"

chapter
eleven

❧

Many times man lives and dies
Between his two eternities
That of race and that of soul,
And ancient Ireland knew it all.
Whether man die in his bed
Or the rifle knocks him dead,
A brief parting from those dear
Is the worst man has to fear.

—W. B. YEATS: *"Under*
Ben Bulben"

"Look here," Butler said, leaning toward the two and assuming a brisk, confident air, "there are sure some things I can do. Why, I know people all over Ireland. If I can't find out what happened to your friends, I can stir up somebody who can!"

"That's fabulous, Mr. Butler," Ann said, beaming with pleasure. "We hoped for that kind of help."

"Yeah, that's great," her husband said flatly. "We'll be glad to know anything you find out." He climbed to his feet. "But we don't want to bother you any more than we already have. We'd better get back to town."

"No, wait," Butler protested. "While you're here, let me show off my place. I don't get many chances."

Ann was thrilled with the idea. "I'd love to see it! Wouldn't you, John?"

"Sure," John agreed. He couldn't ignore the fact that he was curious about the place, too. "If you're sure it won't be an imposition."

"It'd be a pleasure," said Butler, getting up. "Come on. We can start on the grounds. Let's just go right out through these doors."

He opened some French doors, and they followed him onto a wide stone veranda.

"It's a pretty complicated place," the man said. "This main structure is neo-Gothic and fairly new, but it was built right on top of an older Georgian manor. That was done in the 1840's by a Welshman who was fair as a landlord but damn rotten as an architect." He pointed out past the formal gardens to a neatly mowed lawn that stretched away for a hundred yards. "If you want to walk out there a bit, you can get a good perspective on the place. But I'm warning you, it's pretty much a sprawling pile of gray rock."

The Milnes didn't agree with this assessment. At the very least the building was an intriguing and intricately ornamented pile of rock, with complex designs on the windows and chimneys and gargoyles at all the corners. Still, it was quite a walk to the end of that lawn, and they politely declined to make it.

"Very smart," said Butler. "Besides, there's something more interesting over this way."

He led them down to the north end of the manor. The stream that they had followed on their walk into the grounds passed along this side, at points coming up almost to the building's base. They walked onto a stone quay that jutted out over the water and ran along a portion of the wall. They stopped there, and Butler pointed toward the northwest corner of the building.

"There . . . there's the real heart of it all," he said with a ring of pride.

The object of his attention took some finding on the Milnes' part. They saw only the rather plain corner of a large, stone manor house, ending in a rounded tower whose bottom blocks were washed by the flowing stream.

Then Ann realized that the tower was of a different style entirely. Instead of the arched casement windows of the rest, it had only narrow slits spaced widely around it. Its stone was heavier and its effect sterner. The exterior was devoid of the decorative work. The rest of the building was fitted neatly against it, but there was no doubt of its separate identity.

"A tower house?" she asked.

"Tenth century," Butler told her. "The earliest stone structure here, most likely. They incorporated the thing right into the house. Hell, they never tear anything down here."

"I'd love to go into it," Ann told him earnestly.

"It's just a hollow shell now," Butler told her. "I've sealed it off until I can restore it. A lotta work, time, and money it's gonna take to do that. But someday I'm figuring it'll be my private quarters. That just seems right somehow."

Past the tower, far along the stream to the west and almost lost in the trees, the Milnes could see parts of another stone structure.

"What is that building downstream?" asked John, pointing.

"There? Oh, that's a monastery from the fourteenth century. It's pretty much a ruin."

"Oh, right," John recalled. "We passed it on the way in."

"The grounds are filled with ruins. There's a church ruin of the same period, too. There's a hill fort, and even some ogham stones in the garden. Quite a cross section of Irish history here."

"It's like a time machine," said Ann.

"A time machine?" Butler repeated, seemingly delighted by the image. "That's an interesting way to look at it. I'd like to think we can escape time, if we try." He examined his watch. "Say, it's getting pretty late. Nearly five. That's time for my dinner. Why don't you stay and join me?"

He addressed Ann directly, and she felt the choice was hers.

"We'll be happy to join you. But we'll have to start back soon after. We're meeting a friend later."

"I'll keep an eye on the time," Butler assured her. "I'm warning you, though, it'll be a pretty plain meal. I don't have much help here. I bring in some hired hands when we have guests, but the rest of the time I like to rough it. Paddy does the cooking."

"We're used to simple cooking," Ann told him. "We always prefer it when we're traveling."

"Anyway," John added, "nothing you served in this setting could help but be elegant."

Butler's and John's statements both proved themselves to be true. The meal was simple, the surroundings anything but. The three of them sat at one end of a twenty-foot-long table of polished oak six inches thick. Around them the glassware and silver of generations of diners glowed richly in the soft light.

The Milnes faced each other across the table, and Butler sat between them on the end, serving them himself from plates of beef and vegetables that O'Gadhra brought to him. Following the meal they sat on at the table, sipping a fine Irish whiskey from Waterford crystal tumblers while Butler recounted the manor's history to them.

"The original tower was built by a Celtic warlord," he said, "right on the site of an even older fortress. Guess the boy's own clansmen had controlled all this country for centuries before. That appealed to me a lot. I've got strong Irish roots myself. Not Celt, of course. The Butlers were Normans first. Didn't come here till the eleventh century. But they changed. Became just as much part of this land as the ones already here. Fiercely loyal to the sod. Lots of their blood's soaked into it, that's for sure."

"But they still left?" said Ann.

"The famines did that. Drove millions away. My own great-grandparents went from Ireland to Virginia then, built up a good plantation, and lost it all again in the Civil War.

Their kids went on west and built right up once more in Texas. I guess fighting to build something and hold it has always been a part of things for us."

"But after *you'd* built something in America, you came back here," commented John.

"Don't get me wrong there," Butler said. "I'm really not one of those snooty rich fellas come back to lord it over the folks. At least, not by choice. No, I still think of myself as just a plain ol' wrangler who wanted to come back to where he felt his real roots were. The spirit of this place has a real strong hold on me. All I want to find is that plain and simple life my ancestors had."

"Plain and simple," John repeated with a certain note of sarcasm in his voice as he looked around at the splendor of the room.

Hearing the tone, Ann hastened to shift subjects. "So, Mr. Butler, you said the first part of this house was built by a Celtic warlord?"

"Oh, right," Butler said, clearly relishing the chance to talk about it. "Well, the stories I've picked up here say he was an earl named Feagh O'Donal. I guess that's his clan coat of arms over there."

They looked where he pointed. The device—a massive piece sculpted in stone—dominated the center of one wall. The details of the shield—dragon heads, flying horse and griffins—were carefully chiseled in high relief.

"We saw one like it," said John. "At Mrs. Ryan's house. She said the Ryans used to serve the earl."

"And lots more," said Butler. "He was a warlord with quite a reputation. Last of the great fighters against the British control. Last real Celtic war chieftain in Ireland, some said. Refused to change with the times. Even denied the church and stayed Celtic in religion. Didn't give one inch. Sort of a cross between Robin Hood and King Arthur, I suppose. Helped folks against their oppressors, supported hopeless causes. When the other Irish kings and chiefs gave up, he attracted a big following. Great champions from all over came to join and keep on fighting."

"What happened to him?" asked John.

"Well, I guess the outside forces pushing in finally got too overpowering even for him. He fought off a last major attack on this stronghold here. But it was only a matter of time. Ireland had been the only corner of his world—of the old Celtic world—left. And now his little earldom was its last bastion, the last holdout of tough-minded and independent people. They couldn't hold out forever against an entire changed world."

The power of Butler's voice had grown as he talked. The Western drawl had receded, replaced by a strong, forceful style fitting the dramatic tale. John envisioned him using the same style to sell the story line for some new film project to his backers.

"So, was he finally defeated?" asked a clearly enthralled Ann.

Butler shrugged. "Not exactly. From what I heard he just up and vanished one day, and took his whole army with him, too. No one knows where. Like some big fog just rolled in and swallowed them up. And then there was nothing at all left to keep a newer, colder, more organized world from coming in and 'civilizing' Ireland."

"He wasn't killed, then?" said Ann.

"Might have been just as well if he had been, rather than live to see what the world became," Butler answered, a definite tinge of bitterness about that kind of world in his voice.

For all its starkness, the simple story held John and Ann. In their minds they could see the ancient tower and feel the forces that had swirled about it so long ago.

"What did the warlord want?" Ann asked. "To keep Ireland free?"

"Or maybe just to keep his own power," John suggested more cynically.

"I think maybe he just wanted to stop time," Butler said thoughtfully. He looked at them intently. "I think I can understand that. The pull of the past is pretty damn strong here. In fact, the whole country pulls at you. It tries to get into your skin, into your mind. I can feel it when I'm here. Even when I'm a long way from here."

"I've felt it, too," said Ann.

"You have?" Butler responded with interest. "Was that your reason for coming here? That's one of the things I was meaning to ask you."

"I guess it is," she began. She had made the first remark impulsively, because Butler had put words to a feeling she'd never identified herself before. Now she tried to analyze it more closely. "I've wanted to come as long as I can remember. Not for any reason. No one told me about it or told me I should go. It was just something I needed to do. Once I was here I felt . . . well . . . content. I wanted to belong here. It was like I had to come home."

Her husband began to grow impatient. This exchange of mystical experiences between his wife and Butler had only served to further delay their departure.

"Look, Mr. Butler," he put in, "I'm sorry, but we're really going to have to get going now. It's a long walk back, and it's getting late."

"Hold on just one more minute," Butler said. "Before you go, I want to suggest something I've been considering. Now, you've been attacked once, and I don't much like the idea of your staying alone at those little cottages. Why don't you two move in here with me for a while? Just till I've checked things out."

"Oh, there's no way," John protested. "We can't impose on you that way. And we're paid up at the cottages for three weeks."

"I've certainly got the rooms," Butler argued, "and I'm sure we could make some arrangements about your rent at the cottage. It's only got to be for a couple of days, just until I can find out something about your friends. It'd make me feel easier—and you too, I'd bet.

"I just don't know, Mr. Butler," John said.

"John, why not?" Ann asked, not believing her husband's reluctance. "You know you'd love to stay here. So would I. What's wrong with it?"

He wasn't sure. He only knew that moving in here would mean the whole thing was being taken out of his hands. But that was such a foolish reason that he couldn't say it aloud.

"Okay," he agreed, trying to cover his reluctance. "But can we come tomorrow? We've got to meet Father Bonaventure tonight and then get our stuff together."

"That's fine," said Butler, flashing his warm smile. "I'll be looking forward to talking with fellow Americans who love this country as much as I do."

"So will we," John assured him. "Come on, Ann. Let's get going."

Butler showed them out through the house, and they made their farewells at the door. Once the two were well down the drive, Ann turned to her husband in irritation.

"Why did you hustle me out of there? And why wait until tomorrow to move in? He wants to help us. He could solve all our problems!"

"I know," he replied. "But there's still something we can do ourselves, and I want to do it before *he* takes over. We did decide to go to the *Teac* with Bonaventure, didn't we?"

"We did," she had to admit. "I don't know what good it will do us."

"Who knows? Maybe we'll see this mysterious stranger and have something more solid for Butler to use. At least I'd feel like I was doing *something*."

"Maybe." She looked at him intently for a long time as they walked on. Something else was bothering her. "You don't like Mr. Butler much, do you?" she asked finally.

He thought about it. "I don't know. He's just so *much*! He sort of overpowers everything. In a way he reminds me of your grandfather." He smiled at the idea. "I guess that's not really bad, is it? I should just think of him as a concerned grandpa."

Ann laughed at that, and he looked curiously at her.

"What's so funny?"

"Well, I know what you mean, and I know how old Butler is supposed to be, but I can't think of anybody who seems less like a grandfather than he does."

CHAPTER
TWELVE

✤

Time drops in decay,
Like a candle burnt out,
And the mountains and woods
Have their day, have their day;
What one in the rout
Of the fire-born moods
Has fallen away?

—W. B. YEATS: *"The Moods"*

Two hours later, John Milne was tightening his grip on the bouncing seat beneath him and praying that Father Bonaventure really did know how to drive.

The monk sped the Morris Minor along the twisting road with a lighthearted abandon that verged on the suicidal. The tiny auto, filled near to capacity with just the three of them, was sure on its wheels. Still, John felt that Bonaventure was asking more of it than any sane man could reasonably expect.

John had volunteered for the back seat, and he was now regretting it. The lurching and swaying of the auto was giving him a feeling of car sickness that he hadn't known since childhood. As nostalgia, however, its value was entirely lost on him.

Ann, seated in the passenger seat next to the monk, seemed perfectly relaxed, but he wondered if she was covering up her own distress. He leaned forward and put his head close to hers.

"Is the ride bothering you?" he murmured.

"I think I'm getting the hang of it," she replied airily. "How are you?"

"I'm sorry they really *don't* ride asses," he told her sincerely.

The trip was mercifully short. They were in Conlish in minutes, and Bonaventure was pulling up before a modern-looking, two-story house.

"Here it is," said the monk. "Brother Coleman said they would be expecting us."

John couldn't have cared less at that point. He only wanted his feet on solid ground again. He clambered out of the car and looked around him.

He and Ann had driven through Conlish once or twice the previous year without paying it any attention. There were a number of tiny hamlets like it scattered around, all served by the village of Ballymurroe, where the parish church and the largest tavern were located. It was little more than a shop or two, a dozen homes, and some other odd buildings, strung out for a hundred yards along both sides of the road. Directly across the road from them was a victualler's shop with cattle and pig carcasses hung up in its windows to attract the flies.

"It's odd how human they look, hung up that way," the monk commented casually, looking toward the shop.

John looked quickly away from them, his stomach heaving.

"Where . . . where's the *Teac?*" he asked, trying to get his mind on something else.

"It's up the street. You'll see it later. How do you like Conlish?"

John shrugged noncommittally. Then, as he looked the

place over again, he paused to consider it more carefully. Something about it bothered him.

He couldn't identify what it was at first. Conlish was typical of a thousand other Irish communities: simple . . . neat . . . tidy.

And then he realized that this was exactly what was bothering him. It lacked the uneven kind of wear that a village would ordinarily show. It was too uniformly neat, as if it had been painted and patched in one fell swoop. The thatched buildings all sported new roofs and clean, pastel-colored walls. Similar gardens of brilliant flowers embellished all the homes. It had the atmosphere of a museum exhibit.

They walked up to the Kileys' door, and Father Bonaventure knocked. Almost at once it was answered by a large, cheerful woman of middle years whose red hair color rivaled Ann's.

"Mrs. Kiley," said the monk. "It's good to see you. Sorry to be descending upon you this way."

"No, it's no trouble at all," she assured them. "Brother Coleman called to tell me you were interested in our *Teac*, and I would never deny any who were after knowing about that!"

She led them into a large, comfortably furnished living room where two men and a woman rose from their seats to give the newcomers greeting.

Mrs. Kiley introduced the young woman as her daughter, Megan, but that relationship the Milnes had already guessed. The looks, build, and deep red hair of the two left little doubt of it.

"Well, now," said Father Bonaventure, looking around at the three women, "if I'm to be blinded by other than the Glory of Heaven, I wouldn't mind it coming from three such red blazes of Irish glory together."

"Why, Father, I didn't know you had such charm in you," said Megan, smiling broadly, and Ann felt real pleasure at being included with the other two.

"It's aesthetics, purely," said the monk with a wink, and

then turned to the two men who stood quietly by. "And these must be the musicians I've heard about."

"Right, Father," said Mrs. Kiley. "Brian O'Phelan and Donal Kirwan. They're from Mowbry, just southwest of Londonderry. I don't think even you have met them before, have you, Father?"

"No. Sad to say, but I've only been able to get to one of the gatherings this year. So it's good to meet you both now."

They shook hands all around, and John found himself giving the musicians a rather critical appraisal. He wondered if his quick judgment was based on surface appearance or something in their manner. They wore longer hair, beards, and the studied carelessness of dress that demonstrated a lack of concern with social convention rather than poverty. But that look had become a uniform for certain elements of youth in all cultures, all about the world, and he had never before been one to make character assessments just from looks.

They sat and began to exchange small talk that focused largely on the Milnes at first. The Americans fielded questions about their trip over and the times at home, and they all compared automobiles and houses and television programs.

As they talked, John tried to identify something in the musicians, some radical comment or subtle hostility, to support the negative impression that stayed with him. After a short time, however, he gave it up. The two were a little withdrawn, but anyone would have seemed so in contrast with the buoyancy and straightforwardness of the Kiley women. When they did talk, they evidenced intelligence and good cheer.

Everyone but Ann and Meg Kiley smoked constantly as they conversed, and none more than Father Bonaventure. Away from the abbey he revealed an insatiable desire for Sweet Aftons, that very strong Irish cigarette. John normally smoked very little, but the custom seemed to be to offer packs around when anyone lit up, and he found himself smoking one after another. Ann, who had never smoked, had no desire to take it up now, and found the hazy atmosphere a bit hard to take.

"What are you down here for?" John asked the musicians, trying to steer the conversation toward the real object of their visit. "Are you on a vacation?"

"No," answered Donal with a smile. "No vacations for us. We're working. We use this as a center. Sort of a safe house. We travel here and there and play our music, but we come back to Conlish to rest between. The Kileys are kind to let us stay."

"Kindness is only a part of it," Megan assured the guests. "They play at our *Teac* too when they can. They're playing tonight."

"We'll be there to hear them," said Father Bonaventure. Then he added casually, "We hear another friend of ours has been at the gatherings, too. Nancy Trahern, it was. Have you seen her?"

Mrs. Kiley seemed genuinely surprised. "Seen her here? Well, I've met the woman, but we're not really friends. Didn't she and her daughter leave the village?"

"That's what we *heard*," Ann said cryptically. "But we were wondering if you had seen her at the music nights before that."

"No." The woman shook her head. "Not unless it was some time ago, and I've forgotten it."

"Mother, of course!" Megan exclaimed. "It was three weeks ago. The last time Brian and Donal played the *Teac*." She looked toward those two. "She talked to you, didn't she?"

Milne saw the young men stiffen at this. It was only for a moment, and then they relaxed again, but he was certain that he had seen it, as when a flicker of lightning illuminates a scene, freezing it for an instant.

"Nancy Trahern?" Donal said then in a casual way. "Oh, it's possible we saw her. I don't really remember her, do you, Brian?"

"I might at that. She asked about some song, is all. A

very old one. Wondered if we knew it. 'Never Go More,' I think it was."

"You're right," Donal agreed emphatically. "We did sing it here . . . three weeks ago, was it?"

They lied, Ann told herself. There was no concrete reason for her sudden judgment, but she was as certain they weren't speaking the truth as if they had openly told her so.

"It doesn't matter," John said with apparent indifference. "We're just friends of hers. We're more curious about this *Teac an Ceoil*. We hadn't heard about it before. How long has it been here?"

"Ah, about eight months," said Mrs. Kiley, a ring of pride in her words. "It's an old cottage made over, thanks to Mr. Butler."

"We know," said Ann. "We met him. Does he do a lot of things around here?"

"He does, but there are few who know how many," Megan told her. "He's kept it that way. He's a very modest man, and one who likes time to be off by himself, and we all respect his right to that. He loves it here, and he's done much to help the area."

To help the area, John repeated in his mind. Now he understood why the village of Conlish looked the way it did. It had a patron.

"Sounds like Butler really does like playing lord of the manor for you," he said.

There was a noticeable pause, as if everyone had caught their breaths at once. Then Donal leaned stiffly toward John, his face setting itself in hard lines.

"Mr. Butler is not one you should be making light of," he said coldly. "You know nothing about him or what he's done for us . . . for all of us. He has a deep affection for Ireland."

The intensity of his reaction stunned John to silence. Had his note of sarcasm been so much greater than he had intended?

"Now Donal, please," Mrs. Kiley began in a soothing tone.

"Don't make him apologize," Ann told her with a glance

of annoyance at her husband. "John asked for that. He says things without thinking."

"Attacked from my own quarter," said Milne, trying to sound amused when all he felt was foolish. "I'm raked, stem to stern. I surrender."

"No, Mr. Milne," Mrs. Kiley insisted. "You are strangers in our country, and guests in my house. Donal was wrong to speak so. Still, you should know that we all have great respect for Mr. Butler. Our little place had much gone to wrack and ruin before he came. We're much beholden to him for saving it."

"I'm sorry," said John, truly regretting his snap opinion of the man. "A lot of Americans with money have come over here to buy themselves a position and return to the Old Sod. I just ranked him with them. I suppose I see them all the way your ancestors saw all their old invaders."

"Not all who came here were evil," said Megan. "Many great Irish names came from Anglo-Saxons and Normans and Romans, and those of Spain as well. And you'll find that even many of the English landlords helped us when we were sorely in need of help."

"I'd be much doubting the truth of that today," said Brian with conviction. "There seems to be a gap now between us that can never be closed. But Mr. Butler is Irish in his heart. He understands."

"He certainly is an interesting man," Ann remarked.

"You may see him tonight," Mrs. Kiley told her. "He comes often to visit the *Teac*."

"What about other visitors?" John ventured. "Do you get many strangers at these folk nights?"

"Strangers?" Megan appeared perplexed. "Like yourselves, you mean?"

"Or Irish," John pressed. "Do you know anyone who drives a Volvo?"

If he expected some reaction to this question, he was disappointed. It was greeted by blank looks from the company.

Brian took advantage of this pause in the talk to get to his feet.

"Excuse me," he told them apologetically. "I've remembered a call I was to make before. I'll only be a moment."

"Certainly, Brian," said Mrs. Kiley. When he had gone, she turned her attention back to John's inquiry. "Now, as to your Volvo, I'm afraid I've seen none. And I've seen few at our gatherings I didn't know. That's to be expected, of course. The entertainment is little advertised outside the nearby villages."

"Well, then, how do the musicians find out about it?" Ann asked. "Brother Coleman told us they come here from all over."

"Ah, musicians are a race apart," said Donal with a small smile. "They have their own ways of finding out. They hear the music floating on the wind, and they follow it—"

"—and they pass word of the new *Teacs* from one to another when they meet," Megan added. "You should be grateful Donal didn't tell you of the talks he has with the fairies. He mustn't take you for such fools as he does most tourists."

"There are some things even tourists won't swallow," said John. His tone was light and friendly, but he met Donal's eye squarely as he said it. "Anyway, I'm sure the invading hordes of them would love to know about your Houses of Music."

"We do try to save some things for ourselves," said Megan. "It's another reason this *Teac* is here rather than in Ballymurroe itself. It's a little away from the tourist cottages. Not that you aren't welcome."

"I'm glad you save it," said Ann. "Although it looks like it would be safe this year in any case. Mrs. Ryan told us the cottages were all booked, but we haven't seen anyone else there yet."

"The first of June is very early in the season for most," Mrs. Kiley assured her. "They should be filled soon enough."

"I'm in no hurry," Ann told her. "I know these two particular tourists would like to thank you for your warm welcome. It's one of the first friendly ones we've had since we came back."

At this point Brian reappeared and addressed himself to his fellow musician.

"Donal, we must be getting up to the house to prepare. The playing will begin soon."

"Go on ahead, then," Mrs. Kiley said. "And you get along too, Meg. We'll come along in a bit, after it's begun."

She went to the door with the three and, while she was gone, Father Bonaventure leaned toward the Milnes.

"Do you think those lads really talked with Mrs. Trahern about music?" he asked.

"You're wondering, too?" said John.

"It's unanimous," said Ann. "There was something they weren't comfortable about."

Bonaventure nodded. "I think our two young friends might just be worth keeping an eye upon."

CHAPTER
THIRTEEN

'The fiddlers are all thumbs,
Or the fiddle-string accursed,
The drums and the kettledrums
And the trumpets all are burst,
And the trombone,' cried he,
'The trumpet and trombone,'
And cocked a malicious eye,
'But time runs on, runs on.'

—W. B. YEATS: "I Am
of Ireland"

Mrs. Kiley and her guests stayed on and talked a bit longer. Then she announced that it was time they were all heading down to the *Teac an Ceoil.*

They left her house and found that the street of the tiny hamlet was now quite full of cars lining both curbs and stretching away out of sight in both directions. As they walked up the street toward the House of Music, the sound of it came out to greet them, voices and instruments both in one immense swell of sound.

When they reached the doorway, they discovered a place

packed tight with humanity. They worked their way through a wall of people and finally made it inside.

The interior was one long room in traditional style, with stone floors, open beams, and a great fireplace at one end. Scores of people filled it. They sat on benches along the walls or stood grouped in the corners to keep the center of the floor clear.

Some young women moved down and gave Ann a seat on a bench. John and the monk stood in a tiny, open space just inside the door. No one in the crowd gave the new arrivals as much as a curious glance. All their attention was turned on the entertainment.

The musicians were gathered before the fireplace at the far end of the room. John counted more than fifteen of them, including Mrs. Kiley's daughter and the two young men from the North. They were of all types and ages, and with instruments as varied as they were.

Fiddles predominated with half a dozen players, from a boy of ten to a white-haired ancient. Meg Kiley played her own with power and skill, her thick mane of hair swinging and rippling with red-gold light. Next to her an aging priest worked his bow with like abandon.

Others played flutes, guitars, accordions, and a variety of rhythm instruments that included bones, fire tongs, spoons, and strange, tambourinelike drums. Two young men played the Irish bagpipes, their thin, high skreel rising in an eerie wail above the rest.

"Cigarette?" Father Bonaventure asked during a lull between pieces.

John turned his attention from the entertainment to the pack the monk offered him. Smoking was allowed here, as in most public buildings, and many were taking advantage of it. The room was filled with a drifting, blue-white haze.

He accepted a cigarette, largely to be polite, and the monk lit it for him. He leaned back against his little section of wall, relaxed, and listened to the music.

The musicians played all kinds of songs from the ancient Irish ballad to the modern folk song; but the fast, loud pieces were what everyone enjoyed the most. All the players joined in on those, working together with verve and vitality to produce a joyous harmony.

After a few numbers, several couples organized themselves in the center of the floor and the musicians began to play dance music for them. Ann noted that teenagers in jeans and adults in their best clothing danced the traditional dances together, and she sensed that no differences, no gaps separated them here. They were one age, one spirit, united by something deeply rooted and timeless.

Ann let her gaze roam over the room across the watching crowd. In a large knot of people across the floor from her, was a man, far back in the group, watching her. His eyes held a dim flame that flickered deep within.

"John," she said, grabbing her husband's arm, "I've just seen him!"

"What?" he said, turning toward her and straining to hear above the music.

"The stranger! I've just seen him!" she said again more loudly.

"Across a crowded room?" he replied with a smile. He thought she was joking.

"Damn it, I saw him!" she flared. "The man at the cottages. Over there." She pointed, and John looked toward the crowd opposite.

"Which one?" he asked, still not understanding.

"The tall one. Can't you see?" she demanded. It seemed impossible to her that her husband could miss him. Then she realized that the spot at which she pointed was empty.

"He's gone," she said with dismay. "But he was there."

"Who was it? One of the men from Cashel?"

"No. The man I saw at the cottages. The one who chased Taffy. He was staring at me."

"Oh," said John with disappointment. "Just your Grim Reaper. I'd forgotten about him."

"John, could he be involved in this?" She looked intently at him, concern growing in her.

"Why? Because he visits the *Teac*? We can't suspect everyone who's a stranger to us." Her agitation over this man was inexplicable to him. She had seen him only once before, and John not at all. "Are you even sure it was the same man? Where did he vanish to?"

"I'm sure. I couldn't forget those eyes. But I don't know where he went. He just disappeared." She noted her husband's skeptical expression. "And he's *not* some figment of my imagination. *You* have the figments. I'm far too practical."

"Well, if you see your nonfigment again, let me know," he told her.

He was aware of her taking up a close scrutiny of the crowd again. He tried to do the same, but soon found his attention refocusing on the music. It had, he felt, a mesmerizing effect. It was pulling him in, filling his mind, enveloping his thoughts and carrying them away into another realm.

The haze seemed to grow thicker as he watched. Within it, the now soft and glowing images of the dancers transformed. He realized in a slow, pleasantly musing way that they seemed rather differently dressed now. The men looked to be in short tunics and trousers with full, flowing cloaks of brilliant hues about their shoulders. And the women were in long gowns of deep colors and rich texture, their skirts flying about in the wheeling dances, sweeping together with the men's swirling cloaks, creating dizzying patterns like those of a spinning kaleidoscope.

But the movement and music stopped abruptly when the door beside him flew open suddenly. A huge figure pushed through into the room, and everyone there ceased dancing and playing and talking to gaze toward it with expressions of mingled fear and awe.

He turned also to see the figure, and found an imposing man towering above him. He was clad in a brilliant white tunic edged in gold. Over this was draped a fine cloak of deep green wool, fastened at the throat by a brooch of winking-bright silver wrought into the shape of a flying horse. Long hair of a glowing silver-gray hung about the shoulders in neat plaits threaded with colored beads, and a long, slender golden-hilted sword in a scabbard bound with bronze hung at one high hip.

This splendidly adorned fellow stopped and stood looking majestically about while an astonished John just stared.

"My chieftain," came the voice of Mrs. Kiley from behind him.

But it wasn't any chieftain, thought John. He knew this figure's lean and weathered face. It was Douglas Butler's.

He blinked. And in that instant of dark and then light again, it was Butler who stood before him, clad in a modern outfit of slacks and Aran-knit sweater, a wool cap on his head.

"Good evening, Mr. Butler," Mrs. Kiley greeted him graciously. "We all welcome you to the hall."

A bit bewildered, John looked around him. The odd little reverie that had momentarily overlaid reality for him was wholly gone, vanished like a burst bubble. Everyone was back in present-day dress.

He looked back toward Butler as the tall man came on into the room, apparently not noting him or Ann in the crowd.

Watching the man there, John was not surprised that his fancy had put the filmmaker into a chieftain's dress. The young American felt that he would have guessed Douglas Butler was a man of some high position even if he had never met or heard of him. The stamp of long-time authority was clearly present in him. It was in the erect carriage, the lift of the head, the directness of the gaze.

In the crowd Butler seemed huge and bearlike, dominating the others physically as well, and once again John marveled at how little Butler's age showed in him. There was no evidence at all of that shrinking process associated with age, no stoop to the square shoulders, no stiffness to the movements of the long arms and legs. Only the few bold lines that creased his massive features attested to the amount of wear that face must have survived.

The gathering grew silent and parted obediently as he entered, and in John's mind appeared the image of a liege lord visiting the huts of his vassals. Reality and fancy became one for a brief moment. In some ways he found the comparison understandable. Butler was one of a special brand of two-fisted filmmakers who, like ancient warlords, had shaped a powerful empire with hard work, ruthlessness, and an almost mystical insight into what the public wanted. He was one of the last survivors of his type and his time.

Still, there was something too deferential in the crowd's reaction, a pulling-of-the-forelock sort of attitude that annoyed John. These proud Irish with their strong identity were playing to the famous American. Regardless of how *they* felt, John didn't like it.

Butler pushed forward to the center of the floor, those around him giving ground to leave a way for him. At the center he was joined by Mrs. Kiley, who was serving as mistress of ceremonies. Butler shook hands with her, and they talked together while the crowd waited, expectant, murmuring amongst themselves. Then Mrs. Kiley raised her voice to address the others:

"My friends, we have here tonight Donal Kirwan and Brian O'Phelan from Mowbry in the North, and . . ." Scattered applause caused her to pause a moment before continuing. "And because of Mr. Butler's known sympathy for what sadness the people there have endured these long years, they would like to do a song they have dedicated to him."

The two musicians, beaming proudly, stood up amidst the crowd, readied their instruments, and waited.

Everyone waited, John noted. Even Butler waited, until all the talk had stopped and all the eyes were turned to him.

He nodded then, and the singers began.

Their song was in a modern folk style, its lyrics bitter, attacking the British and enumerating past injuries to Eire. It raised memories of oppressed Irish, both past and present, and scraped at old wounds that had never really healed. John was reminded of Vietnam War protest songs.

It was well sung, and the audience seemed to enjoy it immensely. Butler listened with sober concentration, and when it ended, he led the audience in enthusiastic applause.

Then he moved forward to congratulate the young men, and the crowd closed in around him.

In the renewal of general talk, Father Bonaventure leaned toward the Milnes.

"I believe that is the most anti-British song I've ever heard sung anywhere about here," he said.

John looked at him in astonishment. He had supposed open expression of such sentiments to be common.

"This is unusual?" he asked.

"Oh, yes," the monk replied. "The North has had the troubles, of course, and the Republic has had opinions of them, but we're more removed from it here than you might think. Seeing it in the papers and on the telly isn't the same as its being in the next street. The IRA is outlawed, of course, and the radicals stay pretty well close to the cities and universities . . . until lately, at least. I've heard from Brother Coleman that such types have been coming here more often these past months. It seems Mr. Butler is quite interested in it all. He always comes when those from the North are down."

"Maybe he thinks the Republic should be more involved," Ann suggested.

"I'd say that wasn't any of his—" John began loudly, but stopped as Bonaventure grabbed his arm.

"Quiet now," the monk said cautioningly. "Remember, that man is very popular here."

"He is also coming this way," Ann warned.

John looked up and found that Butler was moving toward them in a purposeful way, stopping only to say a word here, to shake a hand there. Clearly he had finally spotted them.

He came up to them and the crowd fell away, leaving the Milnes suddenly in a clearing and feeling very self-conscious.

"Didn't know I'd be seeing the two of you here," he said, shaking hands with them both. "You didn't tell me you knew about the *Teac*."

"We didn't know we were coming until the last minute," John genially lied. "A friend brought us."

He introduced the monk, who had been waiting quietly beside them.

"I've seen Father Bonaventure in the village before," said Butler, also shaking his hand. "You're quite an expert on the country, I've heard."

"A lover more than an expert," the monk assured modestly.

Butler wanted to talk further, but things had been held up long enough. The people around them were growing restless, and the musicians were making small noises with their instruments.

"Well, I think the show has to go on," he told them. He nodded at Mrs. Kiley; the players began and again the hall was filled with sound.

Butler continued to stand with the Milnes, listening to the music and watching the traditional dances. The room was crowded and hot and filled with smoke, but it didn't faze the big man. He stood for nearly an hour, watching and applauding and enjoying it all with enthusiasm.

Finally, when they called a rest, he turned to address the Milnes again.

"I'll have to go and talk with the musicians now. They always expect a good pat on the back for their work. Just like actors. You two have a good time, and I'll get back to you later. Right?"

They both agreed and watched him move across the room toward the far end, offering many greetings on his way.

"I think it's time to be getting about what we came here for," Bonaventure reminded them as some of the women began passing tea and biscuits through the crowd.

"Good," said John. "Let's ask some questions. Ann may have one stranger spotted already. Be careful who and what you ask. We'll—"

He stopped. As he was talking, a peculiar sensation had begun to creep over him. It wasn't a dreamy, drifting-away feeling as before. This time it was more physical, and more unpleasant. The thick atmosphere of the room and the effect of the last cigarette he had smoked had gotten to him. The feeling had been growing slowly on him for some time, but he had fought it off. Now it had suddenly reached a point where it was intolerable to him. He began to feel dizzy and to perspire heavily. He was certain that unless he acted quickly he might faint.

"I've got to go outside," he told Ann. "The smoke's gotten to me."

She noted the shakiness in his voice. "Do you want me to come along?" she asked with concern.

"No," he said quickly. He felt weak and foolish and wanted to go alone. "Stay here with Father Bonaventure. I just need some air."

He left them and went quickly outside. The cooling night air swept over him in a refreshing wave. He took a deep breath and leaned back against the wall of the music hall, fighting off the faintness and nausea.

After a few more breaths the distress subsided somewhat. He looked around for a place to sit and recuperate for a while. The most likely spot was a bench on the far side of the street. He crossed, walking gingerly, and sat down there.

He felt the cool breeze across his sweat-soaked shirt. It made him shiver, but he didn't mind. The shivering helped to alleviate the feeling of illness.

As he recovered further, he began to examine his surroundings: the sounds of the night, the music once more drifting from the *Teac*. A woman with a fine, high voice like a strand of silver wire was singing an Irish ballad that sounded very, very old.

Then something else intruded.

John felt he was not alone in the night, and he turned his head. A man stood only a few feet away, in the shadows behind a neatly trimmed hedge that edged the street.

The man was watching and, while John could not see his face, he could see his eyes. They seemed like blacker holes in the blackness, like bottomless shafts sunk into the earth.

But far, far down within those pits flared a light like a distant hot core.

CHAPTER FOURTEEN

❧

One man, one man alone
In that outlandish gear,
One solitary man
Of all that rambled there
Had turned his stately head.
'That is a long way off,
And time runs on,' he said,
'And the night grows rough.'

—W. B. YEATS: "I Am
of Ireland"

"Hello," said the man in a surprisingly soft and gentle voice. It had an odd, faraway quality, like the ballad drifting from the music house. "I didn't mean to alarm you."

John stood quickly. "What do you want?" he asked as he began to move forward.

"Please, sit back down," the man implored. "I don't want to be seen. I'm Keith Trahern . . . Nancy's husband."

John stopped moving, more disconcerted by the man's revelation than by his strange request.

"You're Mr. Trahern?" he said. "What are you doing here?"

"If you mean in Ballymurroe, I'd think you'd know well enough yourself," the man replied. "If you mean here, to-night, why, I followed you from your cottage. I've followed you these past days. I've got to talk with you. But, please, sit back down first."

John felt his brain knotting tightly, like a fist closing. He knew that the sudden tension was a warning. Things were moving too fast for him. He had to slow them down, give himself time to sort them out.

Without turning away from the man, he moved back to the bench and seated himself before he spoke again.

"How do I know who you are?"

He felt that was a reasonable first question to ask. He had never seen Trahern, and he could see very little of the man in the shadows. The figure was tall and spare, and the face thin, but the features were masked by the brim of a cap pulled low on the head. A single street lamp lit small patches of a worn gray coat. The rest was in darkness.

The man seemed to read his thoughts and understand.

"It's a fair enough thing you wish to know," said the soft voice.

An arm and hand appeared from the shadows, and the man reached into his coat. John's backbone tickled with a sudden chill, but the hand pulled forth nothing more deadly than a wallet.

The man fumbled in the wallet for a moment, then held two scraps of paper out at arm's length.

"Take these, please, but go back to the bench to look at them," the man advised. "Someone may be watching."

John did as he was asked, still disturbed by the man's fearfulness. He examined the two objects in the light. One was a driver's license issued in Northern Ireland to one Keith Trahern. The other was a photograph showing a younger Mrs. Trahern, holding a baby, standing beside a man.

He was a tall man, with a hard, wiry thinness and an easy, athletic stance. His face was long and angular, the features sharply, broadly hewn. Most significant were the eyes, set back within their sockets, further overhung with bushy brows that matched a head of thick, curling hair.

John studied the photo a long moment. Then he looked up toward the figure in the darkness.

"Let me see your face," he said.

The man moved slightly forward, pulling the cap from his head. The revealed features were the same. The hair was graying, the lines of the face a little more pronounced, but it was the face in the photo. John stared into the deep-set eyes, searching for that odd flare of light he had seen before, but there was nothing now. The eyes were only black holes in the face.

"All right, Mr. Trahern," he said. He stretched out from the bench and handed the objects back. "Sorry to do that, but it's a surprise finding you here."

"I can see where it might be so," Trahern replied, replacing the cap and moving back into the shelter of the bushes.

"There are things I don't see," John told him. "Like, why the caution?"

"As I told you, I've been following you. I found out what you've been doing. I—"

"John?" said a voice.

Both men looked toward it. Ann stood outside the door of the hall, looking across to her husband with a puzzled expression.

"What's the matter?" she asked, and John saw at once that she had sensed something was wrong. Her manner was stiff, her body tense.

"Be careful," the man in the bushes warned quietly. "Don't draw notice here. Just ask her to come on across the street."

"It's fine, Ann," her husband called to her. "Come on over. I'm just getting some air."

She crossed the street to him, still not reassured, still wary.

"John," she said as she reached the bench, "what's happening? Who are you talk—"

"Just getting some air," he interrupted. "Sit down."

He took her hand and pulled her down, gently but firmly, to the bench beside him.

"Nice night," he said conversationally. Then, in the same tone, he added, "Don't look around too quickly, but there's a man right behind us in the . . . wait, wait!" He grabbed her elbow as she started to turn. "It's all right! It's Mr. Trahern."

"Mr. Trahern?" she repeated with astonishment.

She turned her head slowly until she could see the man. Even though he was in the shadows, she knew him at once. She knew he was the man she had seen inside the hall, the man from the cottages. When she realized that, her astonishment turned to anger. She shook loose John's restraining hand, jumped to her feet, and turned to confront the dim figure.

"Why are you here?" she demanded. "Where are Mrs. Trahern and Bridget?"

The door of the music hall opened.

"Quickly, look away from me!" Trahern commanded. "For God's sake!"

The imperative in the voice caused Ann to obey. She sat down on the bench and turned toward John, who had lounged back casually.

Across from them two women left the gathering and walked up the far side of the street until they disappeared into the darkness.

"There are too many coming and going here," said Trahern. "Go down the road, to your left. There's a hurling field there. We can talk inside."

"I don't think . . ." John began, turning toward him. But he was too late. The figure was gone, the shadows empty.

"Well, shall we walk?" he said to Ann.

"I don't know," she answered. "Can we trust him?"

"He *is* Mr. Trahern," John assured her. "He showed me proof."

"He is also my mysterious stranger. The one you weren't sure existed."

"I guessed that much," said John. "It doesn't mean anything. He may have reasons to be suspicious of us, too. He is her husband, so we can at least hear what he has to say."

"If he's looking for his family, or knows where they are, why is he hiding?" Ann persisted. "We don't know anything about him."

"In case you haven't noticed, we don't know anything about *anything* yet. If he can help us, we have to take a chance and talk to him."

She knew he was right. She wasn't sure why she felt such reluctance. She wanted their questions answered as much as he did.

"Let's go, then," she said.

They walked up the street. The sounds of the *Teac* faded, and the darkness of the street gathered about them. They passed two small houses and came to the iron gates of the hurling field. Beyond the gates was a vast black space.

"Into the valley of shadows," he said. They moved through the gates and stopped.

"Now what?" she asked.

"Over here," said Trahern's voice. "This way."

It came from their right. They could see the skeleton of metal bleachers, barely lighter than their surroundings. They walked toward them, and a tall figure appeared ahead.

"Thank you for coming," said Trahern. "I'm afraid it would be bad for us to be seen together."

"Then I don't think we have to worry," said John. "*I* can't even see us."

"But why?" said Ann. "Why are we sneaking around in the dark to meet you?"

"You have good reasons to mistrust me, Mrs. Milne," he told her in a voice that she was surprised to find gentle and unruffled. "I'm sorry for this, but I'm sure that it's concern for my wife and daughter that moves us all."

"Ann and I are moved by it anyway," John said curtly. He had a more pressing question. "Mr. Trahern, just where is your family?"

"Where *are* they?" said Trahern, caution creeping into his tones. "I don't know."

"You don't know? What's happened to them?"

"Why, they've disappeared." He seemed disconcerted by these questions. "I thought you knew as well as I. It's why I've come to you."

John felt like laughing. "Oh, that's fine. Blind meets blind. Would you care to lead?"

"I don't understand," said Trahern.

"Mr. Trahern, why come to us this way?" said Ann. "What are you afraid of?"

"I need your help to find them. I thought you knew where they had gone. As to my fear, you should know the why of that as well as I. Or did Cashel teach you nothing?"

"You know about Cashel?" John asked with surprise.

"I knew you were coming. I've watched you since before you broke into the cottage. I knew then you were after the same thing as I. When I followed you to Cashel, I saw that others knew it, too."

"You followed us to Cashel?" said John.

"You've become important to me," Trahern answered simply.

It still wasn't enough for Ann.

"Okay, so we've been careful since Cashel," she said. "But you knew there was something wrong before that. You were in the village before we were."

"Of course," he said. "I was about to tell you."

His voice never wavered, never hurried. It only moved on placidly, smoothly from point to point. It made Ann feel as if she were inordinately impatient, even unreasonable. When he sat down on the lower step of the bleachers and pulled off his cap, she saw that his face, faintly visible in the darkness, was impassive, too.

"I haven't seen my wife and daughter in over a year," he explained. "My only real contact was the letters they wrote me. They wrote at least weekly, until a fortnight ago. When a week went by and no letter came, I feared something had happened."

"Why did you think that?" said John. "They could have

just gone visiting without telling you. They must have said something in their letters to make you afraid."

"Mr. Milne, when my wife first came here, she loved this place. I couldn't hear enough about its peace and openness. But suddenly that changed. She talked of something strange that was happening here. When I wrote and asked her what it was, she only said that she wasn't sure . . . that she had to find out more. Then she and Bridget disappeared."

"You have no idea what she was concerned about?" John asked.

"No. I think she wanted to tell me, but something kept her from saying it right out. I know this, though: it must have been a real fear to disturb my wife. She is a knowing woman, and a hard one. Years of seeing death and trouble have done it to her, and that I'm sorry for."

"If you were so certain something was wrong, why didn't you come and ask after them openly?" said Ann.

"And gotten exactly what, Mrs. Milne? No, I've learned some myself, over the years. I've learned to take no risks. Until I know more of what's happened, I'll do nothing to risk my family. It's for that reason I took the clothes of a worker. I came into the village three days ago and stayed about, hoping to find some sign, some trace. I watched the cottages and the people in the village, without luck, until you came."

"I saw you," said Ann, an image still nagging at her. "You chased Taffy away."

"I didn't want to drive the dog off," he told her evenly. "It was I who got him for Bridget. But he knew me. He would have come to me, and I couldn't chance his exposing me. I had to be rid of him."

It was a hard explanation, and it was that very fact that led Ann to accept it. Still, the calm directness of the man was harder for her to accept. She kept asking herself why she felt this way. What did she expect? Fear perhaps? Or agitation?

"How did you finally get onto us, Mr. Trahern?" asked John.

"By strange chance it was Taffy who led me to you. When I saw he had gone to you and trusted you, I began to watch. When you broke into the cottage, I knew you had to be searching, too."

"Why didn't you meet with us then?" said Ann.

"I couldn't be seen with you. I couldn't chance showing myself, and after Cashel, it was even more of a risk to meet. I followed you here tonight, hoping for a chance that might be safe."

"Lucky for you I have a weak stomach," John told him, "or you might not have had your chance."

"Mr. Trahern," said Ann, "could this have anything to do with the troubles in the North? Could something from there have . . . found them here?"

"Found them here . . ." Trahern repeated, and an edge appeared in his voice for the first time. "You know, there is much irony in what you say. I sent them here to keep them safe from the troubles. But I should have known. There is no safe place, here or in the North. There could always be something . . . but exactly what it might be, I have no way of knowing."

"The North," said John, half to himself. Then, to Trahern: "You don't know the two musicians who are playing in the hall, do you?"

He shook his head. "Why? What makes you ask?"

"Nothing solid. Your wife just had some extra interest in this place that she kept to herself. She talked to those two here. They're from the North, too."

"You think they are involved?" Trahern asked.

"There's nothing to really say they are. It's just a feeling. A very vague feeling."

"Look, do we have to go on doing this by ourselves?" put in Ann. "We didn't go to the police because we didn't have any proof. But you can declare your wife missing, can't you? They must have better ways to handle things like this."

"I've not made it clear yet, have I?" Trahern responded. "My Ireland is at war. I've watched it going on for my whole life. I know the signs of strife. There are changes. People stop speaking, to friends or to strangers. Everyone withdraws inside themselves, and the walls go up. You may not see it happening here, but it *is* here. Something sinister and secret is going on. The walls may not be stone, but they're no less real. Tell me, haven't you felt it yourselves? Haven't you felt that tightness, that suspicion that infects them all here?"

"Bonaventure feels it," said John. He looked at Ann. "After last night, I guess we do, too."

"Bonaventure?" said Trahern. "The monk? Ah, yes, my wife has spoken of him. He is a clever man, and he is right. It's like a blinded man you are. You must be aware of every move. Anything could be a danger."

"Including the police?" said Ann.

"Anything, I say. In my own country, they're the ones you trust the least. So until we're sure of what's happening, I can see no other way but that we keep this to ourselves. But I'm fully beaten in doing that unless you agree to help." He fixed a searching gaze on them. A certain anxiousness came into his voice as he asked, "Do you agree?"

John looked to his wife. His own gaze was sure. Hers held a strong doubt, but the apparent necessity forced it away. She nodded her head.

John nodded too and looked to Trahern. "Okay," he told the man with conviction. "We agree."

CHAPTER
FIFTEEN

A shadow of cloud on the stream
Changes minute by minute;
A horse-hoof slides on the brim,
And a horse plashes within it;
The long-legged moor-hens dive,
And hens to moor-cocks call;
Minute by minute they live:
The stone's in the midst of all.

—W. B. YEATS: "*Easter 1916*"

"Hold on, Mr. Trahern," Ann said in a firm way. "It's your family and you know the country, so we agree. But only for now. If we decide we don't like what's happening, or we get some solid evidence, the deal's off. We go to the police right away. Understand?"

"Of course," he said calmly. "I'd expect nothing else."

"All right," she said, more satisfied. "Then just what should we do?"

"I suppose that for now you should continue as you are," he said. "You've acted already, and you've clearly drawn attention to yourselves. Even so, anyone watching you must believe you're innocents, come in by chance. You can go on acting in the open. That's something I have a fear of doing."

"What will you do?" asked John.

"I'll continue to stay in the shadows. I've a few matters of my own I must attend to. I'll stay as near as I can, but don't look for me. If you find something, or if you need help that I can give, I have a safe place where we might meet."

He pulled the photo he had shown John from his pocket, tore it across the middle, and handed half of it to the American.

"Here, take this. When you need to see me, go to O'Brien's Tower at Moher Cliffs. It's only a few miles west from here. Give this to the man in the shop. I know him. I can trust him that much. I'll come then and meet you."

John looked at the scrap of photo. It was the half with Nancy Trahern and Bridget. He slipped it into his own pocket.

"I hope you have a lot more luck than we've had," he told Trahern. "We're going to need all the help we can get."

"Some help you might just not want," the older man said. He got to his feet and settled his cap firmly on his head. "I must leave you now. We've been far too long here."

"Mr. Trahern," said Ann, "please tell me, do you really think you can find out where they went?"

"I will," he said, slowly and deliberately. "It was my own stubbornness about staying in the North that brought them to come here, far from me, far from my help. I believed that at least they would be safe here. I was wrong. You can believe that I will find them."

There was another man revealed to Ann in these fiercely spoken words: a man whose cold deliberation was only part of the tight rein he held on his fears for his family and his anger for his own failure to support and protect them. She thought that she understood him better now, and she felt sorry for her harsh treatment of him.

"You didn't have any way of knowing there might be danger here," she told him. "It's not your fault."

"Well, that's of little enough value now," he replied shortly. "Good luck to you both, and good-bye."

He backed away into the shadows and, again, he was gone.

The two walked out of the hurling field and back up the street toward the music hall. They were surprised to find Bonaventure standing outside the door.

When he saw them coming, he went toward them, relief evident in his face.

"At last," he said. "I'd begun to worry. Where were you?"

"On a walk," said John. "We'll tell you about it later. Why are you out here? What about the party?"

"It's going on strongly, as you can hear," Bonaventure replied. "But your two musicians are gone."

"Gone?" said John. "Where?"

"They left soon after you. Got in their little car and headed toward Ballymurroe. A bit strange it seemed to me for them to rush away in the middle of playing." He smiled with a certain self-satisfaction. "So I followed them. They went straight to Ryan's Tavern."

"They may have been thirsty," Ann reasoned. "Or someone may have asked them to go for a drink."

"It might be," said Bonaventure. "Or it might be more."

"Now you sound like John," Ann told him. "You're both too suspicious, and I'm too tired."

"I think we should see what they're doing," John said. "We all agreed they knew more than they were saying. Let's get back to Ballymurroe."

"Wait," said the monk. "What about your Mr. Butler? He's still inside there, trapped by his duty and the adoring throng. He asked me before where you'd got to. Seemed quite frustrated that you'd gone out while he had to stay. I believe he was expecting to talk to you again tonight."

"We'll see him tomorrow," John said dismissively. "We can talk plenty then. Right now, let's not waste more time."

They were soon roaring out of Conlish. As Father Bonaventure wheeled the Morris into the first turn, John concentrated on keeping his stomach in line.

They came into Ballymurroe soon and passed Ryan's Tavern. Bonaventure pulled up by the wall in front of the cottages and looked back across toward the pub. At Ryan's the evening business was at its height. The street in front was lined with bicycles and autos, and the monk pointed out amongst them the battered Volkswagen beetle belonging to the two musicians.

John forgot his queasiness and the weight of the fatigue that had begun to drag at him. He followed Ann out of the Morris and stood gazing across at the pub.

"Look, why don't you two go ahead?" said Ann. "I'll go to bed. I'll leave a lump of peat burning in the window to guide you home."

"I think it'd look more natural if we all go," John persisted. "I know how tired you are, but fifteen minutes more won't make any difference now."

"All right, all right," she agreed. "But if I fall asleep, don't let me fall face first into my beer like some kind of pub dormouse."

"The dormouse didn't fall," John reminded her as they started across the road. "He was pushed by the Mad Hatter and the March Hare."

She eyed her two companions critically.

"Then I'm in more trouble than I thought," she said.

John had assumed no one would notice them stopping for a drink at the pub. When they entered, however, something told him he had miscalculated. He felt as if he had just pushed open the doors of a B Western movie saloon. If there had been a piano playing, he was certain it would have stopped.

The impression was another fleeting one: a slowing of the ripple of conversation, turned heads, quick glances, and then things were normal again. Or, John considered, were things just a little louder than before, just a little more animated, as if to cover some slipping of the mask?

He told himself to go slowly. He was getting conspiracy on the brain, and that strange, twisted beast called paranoia was creeping in around the dark corners, waiting to leap into the light.

He and Ann followed Bonaventure around and between tables crowded with men and reached a small empty one in the center of the room. The monk politely greeted men here and there, John noted, but they, themselves, got little notice. Father Bonaventure might have been alone.

Dan Ryan had been watching them from behind the bar since they had first entered. As they seated themselves, he came around the bar and approached them, his big, florid face impassive.

"What is it you and your . . . uh . . . 'friends' want, Father?" he asked the monk.

"What will it be?" Bonaventure said to the Milnes. "Ale?"

"Sounds fine," John replied.

"Just a small one for me," said Ann.

"Good, then," said the monk. "Two ales, Mr. Ryan, and a Powers for me."

Ryan went for the drinks, and the monk leaned toward his companions.

"Did you see our musicians?" he asked quietly.

"Where?" said Ann.

"To the back. Go ahead and look. It's the tourist's right to gape about."

The Milnes glanced around the room with open curiosity. They picked out the two men, seated at a small table in the back corner of the room. They were alone, facing one another across their mugs of beer, silent and immobile.

"A lively pair," said John. "They haven't seen us?"

"They have, I think," said the monk. "One of them looked up when we came in, I'm certain. They're avoiding it now, though. They've gone as stiff as frightened rabbits, hoping it makes them invisible. But why are they here, I wonder? They've surely not come for a bit of carousing. They *must* be meeting someone."

Ryan returned with their drinks, and John paid for them,

over Bonaventure's protestations. The pubkeeper was about to turn away when something else occurred to him.

"Oh, I would just like to say that if you want to be asking any more of your questions, you can ask them of me instead of my wife. But you may not be liking my answers so much."

"We haven't liked any we've gotten in this town so far," said John, smiling his most amiable smile.

"There's nothing anyone can tell you," Ryan responded emphatically.

"I don't know about that." John was deliberately offhand. "Your wife managed to tell us quite a lot."

"She did, did she?" Ryan sounded disconcerted, not wanting to confirm, unable to deny. John pressed the advantage.

"You have too, Mr. Ryan."

"I? How have I?" He looked around him and seemed to realize that many eyes had gradually been turning toward him. He glared about savagely, and those who had been watching looked hastily away. "I've told you nothing it wasn't your business to know," he said vehemently. It was more an announcement delivered to the house than a statement to the Milnes. His public declaration of innocence.

"You're afraid of us, aren't you, Ryan?" said John. "You wouldn't be so hostile if you weren't afraid. Why is that, now?"

The conversation had turned against Ryan, and he knew it. He chose to get in no deeper. With a snort he turned away and went back to the bar. The life of the pub resumed again.

"So, both of the Ryans are involved," said Father Bonaventure.

"We thought that was possible," said John. "I wonder how many of these others are."

It was an uncomfortable thought and, to Bonaventure, a particularly painful one. He knew all of these people and was well acquainted with many. It was hard for him to accept the notion that they could be involved in such ominous circumstances.

They had taken only a sip or two of their drinks when a man entered the tavern. He was the only new arrival since they had come, and they watched him expectantly.

He didn't keep them in suspense for long. He moved purposefully through the room to the musicians' table. The young men greeted him, and he sat down with them.

"Who is that?" Ann wondered.

"I don't know," said the monk. The newcomer, a short, bulky man in his forties, wasn't a villager or anyone else Bonaventure had ever seen before.

"That's it, then," said Ann with resignation. "He's the one they were waiting for, and you don't know him, so let's give it up."

"Ah, but just wait," Bonaventure replied, getting to his feet. "I'd like to find out who he is."

"What difference does it make?" she asked.

"Because . . . he's a stranger!" he told her simply, and moved away.

He worked his way to a bar that was lined solidly with men. He tapped the shoulder of one he knew quite well: Jamie Farron, dairyman for the monastery's cows.

Jamie turned from the bar with a smile of greeting, but the smile died as he saw who he faced.

"Hello, Jamie," said the monk. "And how are you tonight?"

"Just fine, Father," the man said. "I haven't seen you in here much."

"I'm with some friends, Jamie. But, say, you're about the village more than I. Tell me, that man in the back with the two lads from the North. Do you know him?"

Jamie hesitated. The maze of lines in his weathered face spread and deepened with tension. He seemed caught on the horns of a very painful dilemma. He moved back slightly as if to give himself room to breathe.

Bonaventure knew the look. The man didn't want to talk to him, but he couldn't deny a man of the church. The conditioning of sixty years as a Catholic was too strong in him.

"I . . . I'm not sure who it is, Father," he hedged.

"Come now, Jamie. Are you certain you've not seen him before?"

Jamie was growing more uncomfortable, but Bonaventure had him trapped against the bar and was determined not to let the dairyman escape until he got an answer.

But he had reckoned without Daniel Ryan. The pub-keeper's attention was caught by the exchange and, in an instant, he had descended upon them, his ruddy complexion deepening to red with indignation.

"What is it you're doing now, Father?" he demanded. "Are you going over to your Americans' ways? It's not bad enough they're poking and prying into everything. Now you've got to be doing it, too."

The monk turned to face Ryan across the bar. Rescued by the interruption, Jamie slid away.

"I've got good enough reasons for what I do," Bonaventure said quietly.

"Not that I can see, and you'll do none of it in my tavern. Go back to your friends, have your drink, and be done now."

"I'll be done . . . but *only* for now," the monk returned, shooting a parting glare at Jamie Farron, who was now re-established a safe distance up the bar. The dairyman felt the hellfire heat of the look licking at him and gulped at his stout nervously.

Bonaventure reluctantly went back to the table.

"I'll get nothing from him. Not here, at least," he told them.

"Maybe we should just get out of here," said Ann. An acute sense of discomfort had taken hold of her.

Bonaventure considered a moment, then he shrugged.

"Oh, well, I suppose it will do us little good to stay." He took a final sip of his whiskey. "Are you ready?"

"We're ready," said Ann with relief.

"I hope Ryan realizes he's ruined his chances for a tip," John observed as they got up.

"I think our departure is reward enough for him," the

monk replied and waved gayly at the barman, who watched them closely as they crossed to the door.

They went out of the pub into the cool night. John breathed deeply of the air to clear the stale pub atmosphere from his lungs.

"Whew. What a place," he said. "Like a neighborhood bar back home, but with a chilly reception. Twenty degrees colder inside without air-conditioning."

"Nancy Trahern was right after all," said Ann. "We didn't miss anything last year."

"Hey, that truck must be what our new stranger came in," John noted with interest.

This really wasn't much of a guess. The medium-sized van now parked along the curb had not been there when they went in. It was the only truck, and too large for them to have missed.

"I know that lorry," said Bonaventure. "I've seen it passing through the village. Five times at least in these past months."

"You know what it hauls?" John asked.

Bonaventure shook his head. He walked up to the truck and examined it more closely. It was a plain, boxlike vehicle, painted a dull brown. It had no identifying marks, no company name or logo.

Curious, the monk stepped to the truck's rear and boldly lifted the canvas curtain covering its opening. In the darkness beyond he could see the dim outlines of a few crates and some stacked long objects piled upon its floor. Otherwise the truck was empty.

Suddenly a hand fell heavily upon his shoulder. He was yanked around and shoved back hard against the truck.

CHAPTER
SIXTEEN

When beak and claw their work began
What horror stirred in the roots of my hair?
Sang the bride of the Herne, and the Great Herne's Bride.
But who lay there in the cold dawn,
When all that terror had come and gone?
Was I the woman lying there?

— W. B. YEATS: *[When beak and claw their work began]*

A powerful hand gripped one of Bonaventure's arms while the new stranger from inside the pub thrust his face close to the monk's.

"What are you doing in there?" the man demanded.

"I'm not after stealing anything, I assure you," said Bonaventure soothingly.

"Be careful," said John, moving forward. "This is Father Bonaventure."

"It's nothing to me if he's the Bishop of Loughrea," the truck's driver growled. "Nothing gives him rights to peer into other's matters. You understand what I'm saying?"

"I understand," said the monk. Calmly he lifted his hand and, with a sudden twist on the man's arm, he released the hold, stepping away to join the Milnes on the sidewalk.

The trucker was a heavy man, thick and hard, and he was surprised by the ease with which the monk had escaped him. He stood glaring at them a moment, but seemed to decide against any further action.

"Just stay away, I'm telling you," he said. He walked around the truck and climbed in.

"Where did he spring from?" the monk asked placidly, apparently unruffled by the encounter.

"He came out of the pub and shot past us full ahead when he saw you," John supplied. "He moved too fast for me to do anything to stop him."

"I'm glad you didn't get to try," Ann said gratefully. "He was pretty big . . . and mean."

"This is more and more wrong," Bonaventure told them. "We've got to know who he is."

"We can try to find out where he goes," John suggested.

"All right," the monk agreed. "But you two go." He held his keys out to John. "Take my auto. I'll stay to keep watch on our musicians, in case there's something else."

"Good idea," said John, taking the keys. "C'mon, Ann."

He headed for the monk's little Morris as the truck started up. Ann followed him, tired but past argument.

"Be careful, though," Bonaventure called after them. "Go with God!"

The two reached the Morris as the truck was pulling away. They climbed in hurriedly. John started the car and drove them down the main street in time to see the truck turning into one of the roads leading from the town center.

They pursued the truck southwest out of the village, following the red taillights bouncing far ahead of them on the road. John kept far back, fearing they would be seen. He tried to drive without headlights, but realized at once that the twisting black lanes made them a necessity.

Then the red lights disappeared. They flashed out of existence and did not reappear. John stepped on the accelerator and bore down full speed on the last spot they had been.

It was an intersection.

He slammed on the brakes and they slid through it to a

stop. He backed up to its center, and they looked up the roads that radiated from there. No taillights showed on any of them.

"Shall we guess or shall we give up?" he asked.

"We've taken too long," she said. "It could be anywhere now. Let's go back."

"Okay," he agreed. But instead of turning the car around, some sudden, strong impulse seized him. He turned onto a road that angled sharply to the right.

"Where are we going?" she asked.

"This goes north. It'll take us back."

"How can you be sure it's north in the dark?"

"A really acute sense of direction," he told her. "Anyhow, I just want to go this way, okay?"

He said this so firmly that she didn't protest. He headed up a road that led them through an area thick with trees that edged the way without break for some hundreds of yards. When they did abruptly break, it was at a narrow side avenue marked by gateposts that gleamed whitely in the light from the car's headlights.

"Hold it!" cried Ann.

Once more John slammed on the brakes and brought the car to a sliding halt. He tried to peer ahead of the beam of the lights, searching for the animal he supposed she had seen.

"No. Back there," she said, pointing through the rear window toward the gates they had passed.

"Those are stone posts," he explained, looking them over. "There isn't much chance that they would have leaped recklessly into the path of our car." He tried to sound reasonable, but this second and, to him, unnecessary stop had unnerved him.

She ignored this. Her concern was with her discovery.

"Take a good look at the posts," she insisted. "Aren't they the ones in Mrs. Trahern's painting?"

He pushed his slipped-down glasses firmly back on his nose and examined the posts closely. They were very clear in the moonlight, glowing palely with the layer of inevitable white mold that covered them. Their similarity to those in the painting was unmistakable.

"I think you're right," he told her. "So what? We can't be more than a mile or two from the cottages. So why couldn't she have painted them?"

"That doesn't tell me *why* she painted them," said Ann. "Not with all the beautiful countryside around. She liked landscapes. This was different. I think it meant something special."

John looked up the lane between the stone pillars. It was extremely narrow and thickly overgrown; and it disappeared into a black, endless hole in the trees.

"I wonder where that road leads," he said.

"Drive in," Ann said simply.

"Come on, Ann!" her husband said irritably.

"Hey, I've been humoring you all evening," she retorted. "You humor me a little."

"Okay," he agreed. "I guess we don't have much to lose. Down the rabbit hole we go."

He drove in through the stone posts. They rode on slowly and in silence for a time. The roadside was so thick with trees that they could see nothing but the white cones of the headlamps projected ahead.

"This is ridiculous," John said at last. "That truck probably didn't even come in here."

"Wait!" Ann said suddenly.

They had come out of the trees. Ahead of them the country was largely open to the horizon. The road and the broad meadows were coldly lit by the nearly full silver moon. And there, against the lighter background of the night sky, a familiar silhouette was starkly clear.

"Dunraven," John said quietly, staring.

"Turn around. Quick!" said Ann.

Something rattled outside the small door of heavy planks. Nancy Trahern and her daughter, Bridget, seated on the pallet bed opposite the door, looked up toward the noise with expressions of anxiety.

Until this noise, the two had been sitting rather forlornly together, the black-haired woman with a comforting arm about the thin, sandy-haired girl.

Their surroundings looked equally as forlorn. The circular space had a rough stone wall and a floor without adornment. There were small slit windows set near the top of the twelve-foot-high wall, but only night's blackness showed beyond them.

Besides the bed the room was sparsely furnished. There were a second pallet, a plank table, a few chairs, and a large plastic cooler. A stack of magazines sat on the table along with plates and cups holding the remnants of a meal. The room was illuminated by the light of a shaded brass kerosene lamp, which was the gloomy cell's only source of light.

There came a loud click from the door now, and the thick panel creaked open on its heavy hinges. The mother and daughter pulled tighter together as two figures came through the doorway.

First came a middle-sized man's form clad in a gray suit, wearing a black executioner-style hood over his head. He held a revolver. Behind him followed the tall figure of the black-cloaked being. He clutched a short, gold-tipped staff with a cut-crystal sphere glinting at its head.

The first man stepped to one side, where he could keep the pistol trained with what seemed unnecessary caution on the two helpless-appearing women. The black-gowned one strode toward them, stopping in mid-room.

"Why is it you're coming to bother us now, you black demon?" the older woman said heatedly. Clearly she was not intimidated by the ominous figure. "Isn't it enough that you've stolen my poor daughter and me from our home to lock up here?"

"It was necessary," sounded the being's voice from the depths of the hood, "and you know why. Your unfortunate insights had brought you too close. And they are helping to bring others close now, too. That's why I'm here."

"What do you mean?" she demanded. "You're speaking riddles to me."

"Don't play with me, woman," he answered tersely. "You know I am speaking about your young American friends, the Milnes. I believe you left more clues behind for them than you've told me. They seem to know a disturbingly great deal. They keep turning up in most unexpected places."

"I've told you what I know," she told him stubbornly. "I can tell you no more."

"You might try just a bit harder, for their sakes as well as your own," the being urged. "They can't really be such innocents as you said they were. There is more to them."

"More?"

"Something to account for their persistence. And for their sleuthing skills."

"If there was something, I wouldn't tell the likes of you," she retorted boldly. "But I can say the truth when I tell you again: there's nothing else I know of."

"I must be sure," the dark-cloaked one said. "I hate doing this, but you are a stubborn woman. You will speak the full truth to me now, if not for yourself, then for your daughter."

He lifted the staff before him. The crystal sphere began to glow with a blue-white light.

"What is that?" the woman asked, eyeing the thing uncertainly.

"The Serpent's Egg, it's called. The druid's most valuable tool, and a most prized possession to me. It has unusual powers. See here."

He pointed it out toward them. The crystal blazed out with a brilliant sapphire glare.

In moments, out from under the pallet on all sides, things began to writhe forward into view.

Flat heads with glinting ruby dots for eyes and long fangs gleaming in opened, hissing mouths emerged first. They wriggled out, drawing the glittering, scaled lengths of their bodies forth, lifting their heads high on waving stalks to fill the air with darting forked tongues.

One score, two score, three, and more of the serpents

crawled out, surrounding the two women. Bridget gasped in her terror and pulled tighter to her mother, drawing her legs in. The movement drew the attention of all the creatures to the pair at once. The forest of weaving heads turned toward them in concert. Then the snakes moved in, coiling and twining in a seething mass as they found their way up over the edges of the bed on all sides.

As they closed in upon the two, their sinuous bodies interwove to form a living ring, like some awful crown of evil spiked with the upthrust heads. The heads were all within striking distance now, one here, one there, continually darting to within a few inches of the pair.

"Keep them away," Nancy Trahern said, the tremor in her voice betraying her attempt to put up a courageous front.

"Only you can do that," said the cloaked man. "Your last chance now. Tell me all you know."

"I already have!" the woman all but screamed at him. "By God, why don't you believe me?"

"I do now," the being said calmly. He lowered his rod. The blue-white light within the crystal instantly died. And in that same instant, the serpents faded away, vanishing like smoke dispelled by a breeze. "It was no more than an illusion. You wouldn't have been harmed."

The girl buried her face in her mother's breast and sobbed uncontrollably. Nancy Trahern looked toward their captor in rising outrage.

"Not harmed? You call frightening my daughter near to death not harming her? It's enough terrible things she's seen in her few years not to be so frightened by such a monster as you."

"I am sorry, dear lady," the being said with true regret audible in his tone. "I have no wish to make an enemy of you. We should be friends. All of Ireland should be a friend to me. If you could only understand."

"I understand that no one who treats us in this way can ever be my friend," she shot back. "So if you're done with your torturing of us now, leave us alone."

The being only nodded in reply to this. He signaled to

the hooded man and both withdrew, leaving mother to soothe crying child.

They stopped on the landing of a circular stairway outside while the guard relocked the door.

"She knows nothing. I'm convinced," the dark one said.

"It doesn't mean the Milnes aren't dangerous," the other commented. "Something should be done."

"No, there's no need yet. They can still be controlled. Perhaps they did see the truck. Still, what real connections can they make?"

It was past midnight when the Milnes and Bonaventure returned to Glendon Abbey. Over tea in the monastery visitor's room, the three discussed the night's strange developments with a fascinated Brother Coleman.

"Before, we didn't have enough information," John said irritably. "Now, we've got almost too much. Mrs. Trahern's interest in the *Teac*, the musicians, and some stranger. So we find the musicians, and we find a stranger, and what happens? We end up in Butler's backyard."

"You can't be sure that they're connected," said Ann. "We don't know that the stranger in the pub is the one she meant."

"Look, one of those boys went off to the phone right after I asked about strangers at the music hall. I'll bet he was warned not to show up there because we'd see him. That's why they had to sneak off early and meet him somewhere else as soon as they thought we were gone. They sure weren't happy to see us show up at Ryan's. They must've figured they were safe there."

"Even if he is the one, we can't be certain his truck went into Dunraven," she argued. "We didn't see it turn in there, and we didn't see it again after we turned in."

John was becoming irritated. "Why are you playing devil's advocate? No, we didn't see it. But where else could it have disappeared to so quickly? We checked the other roads. I didn't see another way it could have lost us so fast. And we've got another thing to link Butler to the Traherns, don't we, Ann? We've got that painting. You pointed that out, remember?"

"I remember. I remember!" she said sharply, irked by the harping note in his voice. But she didn't give up. "I still can't see how Mr. Butler could be involved in this."

"What about that truck, Father?" John asked him. "You looked inside. Was there any clue to what that guy was doing? Anything to connect him to Butler's place?"

Bonaventure shrugged. "I saw some kind of equipment. Mostly indistinguishable in the shadows. But there did seem to be some kind of working tools: shovels, picks, things like that. Butler did do a lot of restoration at the place. Though none's supposedly been done since he moved in. Still, there could be a link somehow."

"What do we really know about Dunraven, anyway?" asked John.

"Well, not much besides what Butler said about that old warlord character," said Ann.

"What, do you mean Earl Feagh O'Donal?" said Brother Coleman.

"You know about him?" said John.

"Well, some, of course. He was quite the local legend hereabouts once, as is not surprising. Seems that if the British were after putting some new wrong on the country, it was he who stood up against it. Quite a leader in the fight, and a master of weapons too, they say."

"Yeah, that's the one Butler talked about," said John. "He didn't say much more, except that the guy supposedly vanished somehow."

"Well, I can tell you a bit more about that," said Brother Coleman. "There was said to be something quite mysterious about the event. Lots of storm clouds and lightning about the tower the night O'Donal and his army vanished away. Some called it the trickery of the British, sneaking in to massacre the earl's host by treachery and covering up their evil deed that way. Others claimed O'Donal had made a pact with the devil for his power, then had been whisked away by the Dark One along with all the rest. Anyway, there were tales of him being seen after."

"Tales?" said Ann, spellbound by Coleman's story.

"There was a legend that every twenty years the earl reappeared to ride about the whole county on a great black steed whose silver shoes were only half an inch thick when he disappeared. When those shoes were worn thin as a cat's ear, said the tale, he would be restored to the society of living men, fight a great battle with the English, and reign as king of Ireland for two score years. This legend is a very old one, though," he added. "I've not heard of a claim that the earl's been seen for the past hundred or more years."

"What about his warriors?" asked John.

"There's nothing said for certain of them, but there is another vague old legend of an enchanted host sleeping in a long cavern hidden somewhere about here. A man of the village seeking a lost lamb supposedly came upon the place many centuries ago. He saw a long table running through the middle of the cave with great men in their full armor sitting along both sides, their heads down and resting upon it. He saw a great gold horn there too, and blew a note on it. There was a faint stirring amongst the men, and one lifted his head and said in a deep, hoarse voice, 'Is it the time yet?'

"The frightened man had enough wit to say 'Not yet, but soon will be.' And when the warrior settled down again, he ran from the place and never went back."

"Most interesting," said Bonaventure. "Unfortunately it doesn't tell us anything about the present Dunraven or its occupants."

"We need to know more, and fast," John said. "We're scheduled to become Butler's adopted children tomorrow."

"How do we find out?" Ann asked. "Nobody around here is going to tell us anything about him or that truck or that manor, even if they know anything."

"Well now, I may just have an idea about that," Coleman said in his quiet, reasonable way. "There might just be one man who might be of help. He's a tinker who works about the county. One Cian O'Teague by name. A very skilled and a very curious sort of man. He did much work on the manor when they were restoring it. He's said to be a master at duplicating ruined wood and stonework. I'd say he'd be the only one who might know much about Dunraven and this stranger with the truck."

"Why should he talk to us any more readily than the rest?" wondered Ann.

"He's not of here, as I said. O'Teague is a wanderer, owing allegiance to no one. A most congenial fellow too, who loves to help out. A much better chance you'll have getting something from him."

"Better chance, maybe. It's still another long shot, though," said John. But then he sighed. "Even so, I suppose we might as well try talking to him. Maybe we could see him in the morning, before we're supposed to head for Butler's. Where is he?"

"Ah, well, that's the real problem," Coleman said. "Tinkers seldom stay put for long. They're moving about almost from day to day. All I can tell you is that I saw him headed north on the main Gort road maybe a week ago."

"Could we find him there?"

"Not very likely now," said the monk. "That way is only a start. But you should be able to trace him from village to village. He'll ask for work in each one, and people are certain to take notice. He travels only a short distance at a time, and he stays mostly in our county, as I said. In your car, finding him might not take but an hour or two."

"Why are you so sure he'll be noticed?" asked Ann.

"Because, my dear young woman, very few can overlook a large, brightly painted caravan pulled by horses. But," he cautioned, "you must be careful. Don't go too far astray in your hunt, or I'll fear losing you, too."

"Who could try anything now?" John answered casually. "They must all realize that you and a whole abbey full of monks will know everything we do. I mean, they might shut us up, but they couldn't shut up all of you, could they?"

"Could they not?" said Bonaventure grimly. "I thought you understood our history better by this time. Doing away with interfering clergy has been a favored pastime here since Patrick lit his bonfire on Slane Hill and brought Christianity to Eire. Those ruined churches and abbeys that dot the countryside . . . did you think it was the *Sidhe*—the fairy people—who knocked them down?"

"I love the Irish sense of humor," John said dryly.

"It was not meant to be humorous," the monk replied.

chapter
seventeen
✢

Here, traveller, scholar, poet, take your stand
When all those rooms and passages are gone,
When nettles wave upon a shapeless mound,
And saplings root among the broken stone,
And dedicate—eyes bent upon the ground,
Back turned upon the brightness of the sun
And all the sensuality of the shade—
A moment's memory to that laurelled head.

—W. B. YEATS: *"Coole Park, 1929"*

Early the next day, the Milnes left Taffy at the abbey and began tracing the route of the tinker's wagon north from Ballymurroe. Stopping, asking questions here and there, and taking wrong turns in some places consumed most of the morning.

Each place they asked after him, they found themselves closer to him. When they finally reached Gort, they felt they had almost caught him. He had been there only the day before.

They traveled north eight miles more to Ardrahan, but found no trace of him. They tried other roads that ran west and east from the hub of Gort with no better luck. Finally tiring of the fruitless driving, John pulled up along the road.

"It's after one o'clock," he said. "Let's stop for lunch."

Ann had been looking over the map as they moved from village to village. Now a point of interest marked on it caught her eye.

"Say, Coole Park is only about a mile from here," she said, feeling a sudden sharp desire to see the noted place. "Want to stop there? Maybe they have a place to picnic."

"I won't mind seeing Lady Gregory's home," he said, feeling a tug toward the place himself. Still, there was a note of doubt in his voice. "But can we really afford the time to stop?"

"No, I suppose not," she had to agree.

"We haven't seen much on our romantic holiday, have we?" he asked, sensing her disappointment. He hadn't given it much thought in the last hectic days, but it was true.

"I'm not complaining," she assured him. "How many people get involved in intrigue and adventure and violence? In a weird way that's even more romantic."

"Sure it is," he said, unconvinced. Then, with sudden enthusiasm, he said, "Hell, let's stop! We ought to have our lunch hour free at least."

"Don't do it just because you think I want to," she said.

"What better reason could I have?"

She smiled. "In that case, all right."

He followed her directions and turned off the road onto a lane that led up an arching tunnel of huge, ancient trees. It took them to a small car-park, and there they decided to leave the car and stroll along the paths that led through the area.

It was a cloudy day, and they donned raincoats. John stuffed his cloth cap into a pocket and picked up the sack of lunch they'd brought.

"Too bad we don't have some wine," he said. "But it probably wouldn't go with peanut butter anyway."

They locked the car and started off, choosing a path that soon brought them to the gateway of the estate's walled gardens.

The gardens inside the walls were large and well kept,

with broad gravel walks and neat beds of flowers spotted amongst neatly trimmed hedges. They stopped to look at the massive old Autograph Tree in the garden's center, pointing through its protective iron fence to trace the initials of famous visitors, carved there fifty years before.

"Look at the G.B.S." said Milne, tracing the broad sweep of the letters carved by Ireland's most famous playwright. "Shaw, Yeats, and all those others walked these same paths," he went on with awe in his voice, looking around. "Think what it must have been like here then."

"Less quiet," said Ann. "Less empty."

They walked on, more slowly this time. They carried with them a faraway, mystic feeling, as if at any moment someone—a lady in rustling silk or a gentleman with waistcoat and gold watch chain—would appear and invite them to tea.

This spirit of the place stayed with them as they went out of the garden and up the road to Coole House. The feeling of timelessness lingered so strongly that the scattered ruins they came upon were a shock.

The famous house should have been there, John strongly felt. Perhaps it *had* been there, shimmering in the gray, uncertain light until they had come into sight of it and broken the spell.

There were some ruined stone structures and a wall to one side of the road. They identified these as the remains of outbuildings. Nearby was a square of grass with a sunken wall around it. Beyond that was an open meadow.

"Is this really where the house was?" he said.

From farther up the road an old man on a bicycle appeared, a scruffy brown dog trotting after him. He peddled up to the Milnes, stopped by them, and removed his cloth cap. He smiled and uncountable small wrinkles turned upward.

"It was the house here, you know," he announced to them cheerfully.

John found himself accepting this unexpected source of information without question.

"What happened to it?" he asked.

"It was sold years ago to a contractor from Galway, and he took it all for the stone. The heirs, they had no money, you know."

The old man seemed saddened as he said this. Then he smiled again.

"Oh, the road leads to the lake," he added, replacing his cap. "It's just a short way. A good day to you."

With that he rode off, the dog trotting contentedly behind.

Still seeking a place for their lunch, the Milnes decided to take the road he'd indicated. As they walked along, they noted that the first part of it had been recently cleared of brush and fallen limbs and had its stone walls repaired.

"Here and in the garden it looks like someone's made an effort to save what's left," Milne said. "Too bad it's so late."

They continued walking and began to wonder what measure of distance the old man had used. The way seemed far from short to them. It seemed to go on and on and on.

The farther they walked, the more the trees closed in, crowding the road and cutting off light from above until they walked in a green semidarkness. Always they expected to see the road open just ahead, but it didn't. They began to fear that they had taken a wrong way and become lost.

Then, far down the green tunnel, there appeared a bright sparkling between the leaves. They came out of the trees and found themselves on the shore of a small, wild lake.

As they stood looking out over the placid waters, a poem began to come back to John and, as he remembered it, he spoke the lines aloud:

"The trees are in their autumn beauty,
    The woodland paths are dry,
    Under the October twilight the water
    Mirrors a still sky;
    Upon the brimming water among the stones
    Are nine-and-fifty swans."

"Where did that come from?" she asked him.

"That was William Butler Yeats," he told her. He was slightly surprised at himself. Reciting poetry aloud usually embarrassed him. Here, it had seemed quite natural. "Yeats was writing about this lake," he went on. "The swans seem to be gone now, though."

"Hauled away by contractors?" Ann asked without humor.

"The swans are still there . . . for the patient," said a voice.

They turned and saw a man only a few feet away.

He was a tiny, compact man, perhaps in late middle age, dressed in the typical Irish wool jacket and cap. His face was dark from the sun, but soft and free of lines. It seemed capable of much expression.

"Hello," said Ann brightly. Their new companion gave off a friendly aura. "Do you work here?"

"Only visiting," he said in a warm burr of voice. "I like to take my rests at this place, even more than Mr. Yeats did, I'd say."

He continued to stand there, smiling broadly and watching them. John felt he was waiting for them to continue the conversation.

"You like Yeats?" the young man asked, not really certain what to say.

"Synge is really more to my liking," was the reply. "That other was just a bit too British for me. Still, he did say some fine things, and I won't argue it. That bit from 'The Second Coming,' now. 'Turning and turning in a widening gyre, / The falcon cannot hear the falconer.' Quite a one with the birds, he was."

"You come here a lot?" asked Ann.

"Oh, yes. Whenever I'm by. There are many places I'm fond of visiting. But what about yourselves? Not many of the tourists bother with the hike down here."

"We almost didn't," said John. "We thought we were lost."

"Ah, but you did make it, and that's what matters," he

said philosophically. He seemed then to take notice of the
sack Milne carried. "I see you have your midday meal along.
Would you like some tea to go with it?"

"Tea?" said Ann, looking around at the wild scene.
"Where?"

"Please step this way," the man said with an elaborate
bow; and then he led them off on a path that edged the lake.

"I always make extra tea," he said. "Being prepared for
unexpected company is the measure of a good host."

"Very true," Ann agreed. She looked at her husband
quizzically, and he shrugged in reply. He didn't know where
they were going, either.

What they finally did reach was a wide, flat area by the
lake shore. As the Milnes approached it, they both stopped
in astonishment. In the center of the clearing sat a large,
covered caravan wagon, painted in blue and green. Two
stocky draught horses were nearby, hobbled and browsing on
tufts of grass.

When he realized they were no longer following, the
man stopped and looked back at them.

"What is the trouble?" he asked. "Here we are."

"You're Cian O'Teague," said John, so certain of it that
he said it as a statement, not a question.

"I am, for a fact," the other replied, not seeming surprised at the young man's knowledge. "And you have been
looking for me?"

John could only nod in reply.

"Well, well," said the unflappable little man. "Come,
have some tea and tell me about it."

They followed him to a modest turf fire built on the
ground by the wagon. A battered kettle sat over it on a small
grill.

"I must get a pot and cups," he said, opening the back
door of the wagon. "Sit down and talk to me."

They seated themselves on a clear spot of earth while he
climbed inside.

"I don't know where to begin," John said uncertainly.

"At the beginning, as Humpty Dumpty told Alice," came

a muffled voice from inside. "Go on to the end. Then stop. So, for a beginning, who are you, and where have you come from?"

"I'm Ann Milne and this is my husband, John," she said. "We came here from Ballymurroe. Well, I mean, we're from America, but we're staying in Ballymurroe."

"America. And Ballymurroe," O'Teague repeated, sounding impressed. "A long way to come to find the likes of me." He reappeared at the door with a pot and mugs in his hands. "How did you find me here?"

"By the purest, purest coincidence," John told him, still a little amazed by it.

"Life is mostly coincidence, have you noticed?" said O'Teague calmly. "You don't think, sometimes, there's really no such thing as chance?"

He set the pot and cups down by the fire, lifted the kettle gingerly using a corner of his coat for a pot holder, and poured the steaming water into the pot.

"That sounds like a contradiction," John said, considering it.

"Not really. This land of mine has some very old ways of explaining what you would call coincidence. There are many living here, like myself, who still say it's the *Sidhe* who lie behind such happenings."

"The *Sidhe*?" said Ann, surprised. "We've read about them, in Irish folklore books. But I thought that no one who believed in them ever used their name aloud."

He grinned and winked knowingly at her. "Ah, but it's their friend I am. I've nothing to fear from them. And it's well known they seldom act directly in the affairs of men. They gave that up hundreds of years ago and retired to their hidden places when the mortal races took over the rule of Eire." He leaned toward them then, and his voice dropped low, as if he were confiding some great secret of his own. "Of course, they'll still guide men or warn them if there's need. They'd never stand to see certain kinds of troubles plaguing their country."

"Oh, really?" John said carefully, not sure whether he

was supposed to nod gravely or laugh aloud at this. "Do you really think that's true?"

"Don't you?" O'Teague countered, holding John's eye soberly for a moment. Then, abruptly, he laughed. "Well, all of that aside, now. Why is it that you wanted to see me?"

"We want to know something about Douglas Butler's manor, Dunraven. We heard that you had helped to restore it. Ann and I are interested in studying that kind of thing."

"Oh, are you now?" the tinker said. "Well, I'll be delighted to help you. But have your lunch. We'll talk while you two eat."

John obediently opened his paper bag and took out their simple lunch. Ann wanted only the apple they'd brought, and he took the peanut butter sandwich for himself. An orange remained, and he offered it to the tinker.

"Why, thank you," the man said with pleasure. He took the orange and carefully began to peel it. "You know, it's still a bit difficult for me to understand why you'd seek out a wandering mender of other's broken things to speak to," he went on thoughtfully. "It's a fair trade I have, and honest of course. Not like the dealings of some others I've often been confused with."

"You mean the Gypsies?" John asked.

"Some of them only," the man corrected. "I'm not condemning the lot, mind you. Here . . . take a cup." He handed them both mugs and poured out strong, dark tea from the pot. "The difference is, their kind are wanderers by blood, and mine from necessity. It was the famines took the homes and lands of the tinkers and made them follow the roads. I myself don't mind it. I could have gone back to staying in one spot, but it's a free life I have."

"Was your father a tinker, too?" John asked out of curiosity.

"No. He farmed the Golden Vale. He never saw that life go, the fates be blessed for that. He was deep under a rich green sod before the famines turned it to barren dust."

"Before?" said John. "But when was—"

"Ah, but we're getting away from your purpose again,"

O'Teague said, changing the subject. "You say you wish to talk of Dunraven's restoration. How was it you knew of my part in that? Who sent you after me?"

"A friend of ours in Ballymurroe told us about you," John said, cautiously hedging.

"I see. And what was it you wished to know?"

"Well, just anything you can tell us about it. You did work there, didn't you?"

"Oh, yes. I patched a great deal of the stonework. Why, there are a hundred chimneys for a start, all with different designs. The most difficult thing was a great wooden screen. Medieval, that was. One of a pair. Got itself burned up ages ago. I copied the one left. Quite pleased with that, I was. Can't be told apart, the new and old."

"Have you done anything there lately?" asked Ann.

"Not for some months."

"So you wouldn't know if any work is going on now?"

"I'd be surprised if there was," he answered. His head was down now, and he seemed fully involved in the delicate work of peeling the orange. "I'd think I'd know of it. Mr. Butler told me he was all finished with the place, at least for the time being."

"When you were working there," put in John, "you didn't see a gray truck driven by a thick, tough-looking guy, did you?"

"I think that now you're coming to the real reason you've sought me out," he said casually, still working at the orange. "It's not about your interest in restoring at all, is it?"

"Well . . ." said John, not quite certain how to respond to this.

"It was a friend told you of me, was it?" the tinker said, suddenly looking up and meeting John's eye squarely. "And could this friend have been a Mrs. Nancy Trahern?"

CHAPTER
EIGHTEEN
❦

Some violent bitter man, some powerful man
Called architect and artist in, that they,
Bitter and violent men, might rear in stone
The sweetness that all longed for night and day,
The gentleness none there had ever known;
But when the master's buried mice can play,
And maybe the great-grandson of that house,
For all its bronze and marble, 's but a mouse.

—W. B. YEATS: *"Ancestral Houses"*

John Milne almost choked on a bite of his peanut butter sandwich. He took a swig of tea to get it down and scalded his mouth on the hot liquid. While he recovered, Ann answered for him.

"Not exactly. But it's about her," she openly admitted. "We've known her for a year."

O'Teague looked up at her. His eyes expressed his concern. "I'm wondering then, why isn't she here herself? Tell me, has anything happened to her?"

The look in his eyes went to the heart of them both. He

wanted a truthful answer, and they saw that he would know another at once.

"She's missing," John said simply. "We're trying to find out what happened to her. We think it might have had something to do with Butler."

The news distressed the tinker. He shook his head sadly.

"It's what I was afraid of. No, I've not read your thoughts. I guessed that somehow she'd led you to me, for she talked with me of Dunraven herself not two weeks ago. She's a wise and a fine woman, and I tried to aid her, but I warned her that she went into greater danger than she knew."

"What do you mean?" Ann asked. "From Butler?"

"Of that I can't be sure. There's little I could tell her about him. It's true I worked restoring the manor, but I saw very little of him."

"Did you see that truck or its driver?" John asked.

"She asked me about them as well," he replied. "I'm afraid I wasn't of much help there, either. Many trucks and many men came and went while the work went on. Yours may have been among them, or they may not. I know of nothing since that work was done."

"At least we know for sure that she was looking for them, too," said John. "We must be on the right track."

"But what made you believe Mrs. Trahern was going into danger?" Ann asked the tinker.

"Because of what I've felt lately. She'd felt it, too. I know. I think it's what began her searching. She wanted to know if there was truth behind it."

"Behind what?" said John.

"The rising sense of . . . of *something* happening. It's been growing stronger in me steadily. There's some force growing there, about Ballymurroe. A dark power, like something from our ancient tales. It's spreading its shadow out now over the country round, growing and growing, as if it were a great cloud drawing over the sun. The winds are colder than they were before. I've not felt the like in many, many years."

"What is it?" asked Ann.

"That I don't know. Some are afraid to speak about it much. Others seem to be hiding some great thing, as if from pride or loyalty. The why of that hasn't touched me yet. I do know that it's something I want no part of."

"How do you know that?"

"Because its end lies in chaos," he said with a tone of anger rising in his voice for the first time. "For long years Ireland has struggled for peace and freedom, to become part of a world of reason and order where it might thrive. I'll not see anything take that. The old times are gone, and should stay so. There's no place for them in the world if we're to survive. Once I may have believed something else, but my long years of seeing life have taught me different."

"Are you saying that the IRA or someone like that is behind this?" said John, trying to interpret the man's cryptic speech.

"Or someone much worse," said O'Teague grimly. Then he turned a determined but more kindly eye upon the young couple. "That's why I'm wishing to help you in this. If that fine woman's searching has brought her to some trouble, I mean to know what it was she found."

"Thanks," said John, "but I don't know what you can do."

"I might go back myself and see what I can find," he suggested. "I know more of the area than you."

Ann thought that was a fine idea, but her husband was doubtful.

"I think we'd better do it, Mr. O'Teague." Again John was aware of a feeling of reluctance to bring anyone else into this.

"You said we'd take all the help we could get," Ann reminded him. "Mr. O'Teague would be perfect for getting information from the villagers."

"I suppose," John admitted, seeing the logic of it and wondering why it was so hard to accept. "How soon can you get there, Mr. O'Teague?"

"Tomorrow late, for a certainty."

"Good," he said. "If you need to talk to us, call Father

Bonaventure at Glendon Abbey." He pulled out a pen and scribbled on a scrap torn from his sack. "Here's the phone number." He crumpled the rest of the sack and threw it into the fire, then got to his feet. "We're going to be staying at Dunraven for a while."

Ann, taken off guard by this, looked up to her husband in shock. "John, how can we do that now? How can we go and act like he's our friend if we don't trust him?"

"Because it might be the only way to find out if he is our friend or not."

She sensed his determination and knew it would do no good to argue. She sighed and got to her feet, too.

"Okay, I'll go," she said, "but I'm going to feel funny about it the whole time."

"Thanks for the tea," John told the tinker. "We've got to get going. Butler is expecting us today."

But before they left, Ann had another question.

"Mr. O'Teague, I was wondering, why do you keep on traveling? You seem to be an educated man. There are lots of other things you could probably do. Why have you continued wandering like this?"

"Why, I was waiting to meet you, of course," he replied, smiling. "Don't you know it's all one grand scheme we're in?"

She laughed. "If you say so. I hope we'll see you again."

"Of course you will," he answered with certainty. He shook hands with them both. "Good-bye, now, and good spirits go with you."

As the Milnes walked back around the lake, John considered their talk with the tinker.

"The famines were back in the eighteen-hundreds, weren't they?" he asked his wife.

"Yes, I guess so," she answered. "Why?"

"I just wondered," he said thoughtfully.

They walked back up the road, arriving again at the site of Coole House. Here they stopped a final moment, trying to regain a feel of what it had been like.

"Yeats wrote another poem about this place," John recalled, looking over the lonely, grass-covered mound. "He said in it that he and the others who came to visit here were the last romantics. At the end of the poem he said:

> But all is changed, that high horse riderless,
> Though mounted in that saddle Homer rode
> Where the swan drifts upon a darkening flood."

"Maybe he knew what would happen to the house," said Ann.

"Or to the world," said John.

By that evening, when Butler's guided tour of Dunraven Manor's many rooms had concluded, it was raining. A gray curtain had dropped around the house, leaving the Milnes feeling uncomfortably isolated.

The afternoon spent with the old filmmaker, the dinner, and the tour had been pleasant enough. They had talked about America, about movies, about the dreams of the two young people. Butler continued to show a real interest in them and their feelings about Ireland. In spite of their suspicions, they found themselves still fascinated by him, and his confidence and strength seemed to wrap around them like a cloak.

When it was time for bed, he took them to their room. It was clean and cheerful, restored to a new look but with the feel of a hundred years past. Once Butler had gone, John began to nervously prowl the place while Ann turned down the covers on a massive four-poster bed.

"What about this?" he said. He had opened a door, revealing a full bathroom with shower. "Look here. They must have made over the original dressing room. Half the hotels in the country don't have baths in the rooms, and it would cost us fifty pounds a day to stay in one that did. Here, we've even got a built-in celebrity to boot."

"Careful," she warned him. "Your cynicism is showing."

He turned and faced her. "Oh, really? You think he's doing this for us because we're Americans or because he likes rescuing people in distress? He's just so damn helpful. He even got Mrs. Ryan not to charge for the days we don't use the cottage. I wonder what other little services he gets from her. Did you know she has his phone number? I saw it on a slip of paper in her desk when I was searching her place."

"How did you find out that it was Butler's?"

"I checked his number to give to Bonaventure so he could contact us here. I'll bet Butler's been using her to keep tabs on us." He looked around him. "'Course, he doesn't need her now. He's got us where he can keep an eye on us himself."

"You've really got him into this, haven't you?" she said, sitting down on the bed. "What can he be hiding? He showed us the house. He let us wander around on our own. And he's done everything to help us."

"Has he? Look, we could wander around here forever and not see it all. I saw so many rooms in this maze of a mansion that I can't even be sure I didn't see some twice. Ann, he's been a champion filmmaker for years. I mean, the guy's a master of special effects. It's what made him so big. He can make people believe anything he wants. Hell, he's already got you under his spell."

"What's that supposed to mean?" she asked sharply. "You seemed to be enjoying him pretty well yourself."

His answer was heavy with sarcasm: "Maybe, but you were sure soaking up all that snake oil about how Irish you looked and how strong the 'spirit of the country' was in you. I was waiting for him to ask you to star in his next movie. Probably a remake of *The Quiet Man*. No wonder you want to trust him so much."

That made her angry. "You're not being fair. Sure, I was flattered, and he might have been making it up, but I think he really does have some strong feelings for Ireland. He loves the past, and he wants to know what it was like then, the same way we do. You'd see that if you weren't trying so hard to dislike him. I keep wondering just why it is you *can't* trust him."

"I'll go over it again," he said patiently, as if he were explaining things to a small child. "Something is going on here, and the Traherns disappearing is only part of it. We don't know what it is, but everything we've found—that *Teac*, the musicians, the tinker, Mrs. Trahern's painting, Mrs. Ryan, that guy with the truck, the whole village he plays lord to—leads us right back to this manor and to Butler!"

Ann jumped from the bed, her eyes bright with anger. She faced her husband stiffly, hands on hips, and scorched him with the heat of her voice.

"Don't talk to me that way! You're the one acting like a child here, not me. Of course you think it all leads here. You want to see everything lead to Mr. Butler so you can keep on playing detective! Well, I'm not so sure that it leads anywhere."

He opened his mouth to protest further, but she held up a staying hand.

"No, no," she told him firmly. "I don't want to argue anymore. I don't like it. I think we should just drop it and go to sleep."

John was determined not to let her succeed in getting the last word. He said tersely, "No matter what you think, I came to find out if he's involved, and I will."

His attempt failed. Ann looked at him coldly and said, "I don't know how you will. There's just nothing else to do."

He sighed and gave up.

In the dark hours of early morning, Ann shook her husband to wakefulness.

"John, get up. I hear something."

"What?" he said groggily. Then he pulled his pillow up around his ears. "Oh, no. I don't want to know about it. Probably just the rain."

She yanked the pillow away. "The rain's stopped. It was a screaming sound. Outside."

"Not again," he moaned. "Last time you were dreaming."

"This time I'm awake," she said emphatically, "and I'm going to look."

She got out of bed and went to the window. Unable to sleep now, John rose, too.

The night was very black. The only light came from the droplets of water that clung to the trees and bushes and shimmered like tiny bulbs of light under the pale moon.

"I told you there was nothing," he said. "Nothing to see except the light at that house way out there."

"Light?" she said peering. "Where?"

He pointed off to the right. "There. Back in the trees."

"John, there's no house out there. We're looking into the grounds. It's just woods and meadows."

"How do you know?"

"We're facing west. There's nothing ahead of us but a mile of the manor's land."

"I thought we were facing south."

"No. Look at the building." She pointed out the window toward the left. "See, that's the main turret over the front door. You can just see it." She pointed the other way. "And that mass down there to the right is the tower." She pointed forward. "Straight ahead is the road we walked up on."

He peered intently out along the line of her finger. "Well, if you're right, we'd best be calling in a psychic investigator on this, 'cause I'd estimate that light must be around the old monastery."

As if the object of their scrutiny had suddenly sensed them, the light wavered and then was extinguished.

"Well, that's nice," said John. He went back to the bed and lay down upon it. "The spirits have settled back into their crypts. We can do the same."

"John!" said Ann with astonishment. "Don't you wonder what that was?"

"Let's put it this way," he answered calmly. "If it was ghosts, I'm not going out in the dark to find them. If it was something physical, we'd need light to see it. We don't have any lights, do we?"

"No," she admitted.

"And we don't want to go out confronting the Great Unknown in the dark, do we?"

"No," she admitted again, but more reluctantly.

"So I say we plan to just get up a little earlier in the morning and take a casual little stroll through the grounds."

"Earlier?" she repeated suspiciously. "How much earlier?"

For all practical purposes, it was actually still dark when the Milnes dressed and left the manor.

As they started down the gravel road, the dawn light was only just beginning to brighten the tips of the highest trees. Only when John felt that they were a safe distance from the house did he venture to speak.

"Too bad Mr. Butler couldn't join us."

"And what a surprise he didn't, considering we just snuck out so nobody would see us," Ann replied dryly.

He looked back toward the manor, now only a gray mass against the lightening sky. It showed no signs of life as yet.

"Well, if you sleep late, you just miss out," said John and yawned widely. "Anyway, that monastery is across the stream from this road. I hope there's some way to get over."

There was. A narrow side trail led off through low shrubs to a stone bridge that spanned the water. Once past the screen of trees that lined the stream's far side, they could see the monastery clearly. It sat, abandoned and dead, in the center of a broad meadow. Like most such ruins, it was roofless, but its walls were largely intact.

They approached it by the curving trail, here faint and overgrown from lack of use. It was also muddy from the rain, and their shoes grew quickly thick with the dark, gooey stuff. They tried walking in the tall grass along the roadside, but found the blades heavy with droplets of water that rubbed off on their clothing as they passed.

"I'd rather have muddy shoes than damp kneecaps," said Ann, accepting the inevitable and stepping back into the road.

Her husband only shrugged and strode stoically on.

When they reached the monastery, John paused before its gaping entrance and regarded it uncertainly.

"Plunge ahead," Ann prompted.

"Go ahead," said John, stooping. "I have to squeeze out my knees first."

"Quit stalling," she told him. "It's daylight now."

"No. After you," John insisted. "Don't be afraid. Butler gave us permission to look around."

"Afraid? I'm not afraid. You're the one who's just rooted to the spot."

"Don't argue. Go on in. You're the Catholic here." John himself was a quasi-indifferent agnostic.

"Oh? And is my religion supposed to give me some kind of immunity?"

"Yes. At least to Catholic ghosts."

"That makes it kind of a risk to buddy up with you then, heathen."

"I detect a definite sneering tone there," he said with dignity. "And I'm deeply hurt. To show you how wrong you are, I'll . . . go in with you."

"Fair enough," said Ann with a smile and, together, they entered the ruins.

It was forbidding inside, thanks to the long shadows cast by the early morning sun, but the Milnes made a quick canvass of all the rooms, except for the cloisters.

That central courtyard had once been open to the sky. It was there the monks had gone to be outside for fresh air and sunshine without leaving the monastery, their separate world. Now, by an ironic twist of nature, it was the only part of the structure that was roofed. Trees, flowers, and vines growing within the court and on the rocks above had interwoven to form a solid cover, creating a dark enclosure beneath.

The Milnes felt a reluctance to go into this court, and stood looking down the gloomy entrance passage. An almost physical oppressiveness welled out, as if the spirits of those

who had once walked there were asking not to be disturbed.
The Milnes easily decided to let them have their way.

"You can see that it's empty," said John. "No sign of
life."

"Did you expect to find any?" she asked.

He shrugged. "There could have been rooms still intact.
Rooms where things could be kept."

"Things?" she asked.

"Or people," he added. "Let's get out of here."

Once outside, they walked around the monastery. Behind it the faint trail continued on across the meadow to the
small church Butler had mentioned to them. It sat with its
back against some trees and its graveyard spread out in front
of it. Like the monastery, it was roofless, overgrown, and
long deserted.

"No point in checking there," said John with disappointment. "They couldn't hide a truck in it."

"Why should the truck be hidden?" she asked.

"Who knows? We haven't seen it anywhere else. I
thought that might have been its headlights we saw last
night. This has got to be the road we drove in on from the
back gateway. But if that truck did come in again last night,
there's sure no sign of it now. I guess it *was* ghosts."

"John, I could believe that you might see things that
don't exist, but I saw it, too." She smiled. "And you know I
only see solid, practical sorts of things."

"Yeah, right," he said, laughing. "Thanks for the support.
Maybe we were just wrong about the direction. Let's go back
and dry out."

They plodded back along the muddy trail, across the
bridge, and up the gravel road toward the manor.

"It might even just have been some trick of the light," he
mused as they walked. "You were probably right about there
not being anything else here."

This was something that she was glad to finally hear him
say.

But close to the manor, they came to a point where the
road divided, and John stopped to examine the two ways.

One led back to the manor's main entrance. The other turned left toward the river side of the building, disappearing down a slope.

Milne started along the left-hand road.

"Where are you going now?" Ann asked.

"We didn't see this lower front part of the house yesterday. I want to take a look now."

"Aren't you ever satisfied?" she said with exasperation as she moved after him.

"With what?" he replied.

"Never mind," she said, falling into step beside him.

The road they followed this time sloped down to river level. On this lower, northwest corner of the manor a graveled yard had been created in the space between river and manor walls. To their left was the water. Ahead, the way was blocked by the looming tower. On the right a flat, spliced-on wall of one of the manor's newer sections was broken by a row of wide doorways.

"These must have been the old manor's stable or coachhouse," Ann guessed.

New-appearing doors suggested it had a contemporary use.

"I'd say it's the garages now," said John. "I was figuring this was the only place they could be. They sure are tucked away down here, aren't they? Very conveniently out of sight?"

"You could just *ask* our host if he's got the truck," said Ann, having guessed her husband's intentions.

"I can see for myself," he told her. "Besides, I'm curious about the parts of this place he didn't show us."

He went to the first of the doors and pulled it back far enough to peer in. He was met with a distinctive odor and a deep, snorting sound. Two pairs of large eyes stared back at him.

"There are horses in there," he said, "and a whole row of stalls. So it's still partly a stable at least."

Ann looked over his shoulder. "Very handy, if you like horses."

"He's got enough room for a cavalry troop's worth," said John. "I wonder who takes care of them."

"Never mind," she said with some urgency. "Let's hurry. He'll have to be getting up for breakfast soon."

"All right," John agreed. He slid the door closed and moved on to the next one.

He opened the second door a bit, and his eye caught the glint of light against metallic surfaces.

"There's a car in this one," he announced, and slid the door all the way back.

They were looking at a blue Volvo whose amber foglamps met their startled gaze like two blank eyes.

CHAPTER
NINETEEN

✣

(*Scene:* room in castle on cliffs of Clare. Window looking out on the sea and LADY O'CONNOR at it. O'CONNOR looking intently at a shrine or sacred picture in the corner.)

LADY O'CONNOR (looking eagerly from window): Was that a cry?

O'CONNOR: Some scald crow straying on the northern clift or lonesome seal this tide has washed adrift. (He looks out.)

LADY O'CONNOR: If even birds and fish are lonesome here, it's I'm in dread what we'll grow year by year, where scarce a person comes save tinkers only.

O'CONNOR: Where God is, Lady, no soul is truly lonely.

—JOHN MILLINGTON SYNGE: *The Lady O'Connor*

B oth Milnes stared at the Volvo in shock.

"My God," gasped Ann. She looked at Milne. "What do we do?"

He slid the door closed. "We get out of here, quick!"

But even as they began to move, they stopped again in

alarm when the rhythmic crunching of gravel told them someone was descending the road to the garages.

The footsteps were already close. Instinctively John seized the nearest place of concealment. He pulled the door open again and signaled Ann inside. He followed her in, pulling the door shut, leaving only a small crack through which he peered apprehensively.

"How do you know they're not coming for the car?" Ann whispered.

"Not much choice anyway," he replied. He glanced around the large space, stacked with boxes, barrels, bits and pieces accumulated over the years. "Pick a place in here to hide . . . in case," he said, and put his eye back to the opening.

Around the corner of the building Butler himself suddenly appeared. He was dressed in work pants and a thick wool sweater, and he wore leather gloves. He moved quickly and purposefully, his face set in lines of concentration.

John held his breath as the man approached.

Butler stopped at the door to the stable, slid it back and disappeared inside.

Exhaling with relief, John turned to signal Ann that it was safe and found her missing.

"Hey!" he called in as loud a whisper as he dared.

There was a movement behind a broken stone grave marker propped against the back wall of the room, and Ann was visible again. She moved to him. He gave her a sign to be quiet, then slowly, carefully pulled the garage door open.

It squealed as it moved, very faintly, but enough to make Milne wince as he pulled. When it was open a foot, he stopped. They slipped out through the opening and edged cautiously up to the open stable door. Inside they could hear Butler moving around and talking to the horses. Milne chanced a peek and saw him pitchforking hay from a pile into one of the stalls. He was working his way back to the door, so John took Ann's hand and they tiptoed by.

They stopped again at the corner of the building while John checked the road going up to the front of the manor.

"It's clear," he said. "Walk fast."

They were almost running when they reached the main road again, and they stopped there to consider the situation and regain their breath.

"What about that?" said John. "Would you call that suspicious? Would you say that's proof?"

"Now wait," she said, trying to think calmly. "We don't know for certain that's the same car."

"Gimme a break, Ann!" he said with conviction. "I looked at that car in my rearview mirror for a long time. I know it was the same!"

"That doesn't mean it's his or that he knows anything about what happened," she insisted stubbornly.

"I don't believe you!" he cried in exasperation. "You *still* don't think that he's involved?"

"No. It's possible he is, somehow," she grudgingly conceded. "I just can't think of a logical reason why he should be."

"To hell with reasons. Right now let's just think about getting our little selves out of here."

"Shall we start back for town?"

"Not now. We don't want his suspicions aroused. He doesn't know what we've seen. Let him think we just went for a walk. Then we'll make an excuse and leave . . . all friends together."

"Where should we go now?"

"We'll just have to go inside and wait for him to come back."

"Maybe not," Ann said and nodded toward the road to the garages.

A man on a horse had appeared there suddenly. The animal was tall and elegant and black, and its rider sat proudly in the saddle like some noble figure from the manor's far past.

The horse came up to them, prancing, its great energy tightly controlled by the rider. It came up next to them and stopped, and Butler leaned forward to address them.

"I was going to look for you," he said. "You got up early."

"It was such a nice morning," John explained. "We just took a walk around."

"I didn't know you had horses!" said Ann with inspiration and with as much girlish excitement as she could muster.

"Yep. Always have horses around," he told her with genuine pleasure, patting the animal's neck. "You know, my first job with the movies was wranglin' mounts for Westerns. But they were short, hard-nosed ponies, not aristocrats like this fella here. Tell me, Ann," he said to her, "have you ever ridden by the ocean, in the sand, where you can feel their muscles really working and understand the power in those long legs?"

There was a sensual intimacy in the question that obviously excluded John, and it embarrassed her somehow. She answered as plainly as she could.

"I've never really been riding."

"Then we'll have to go," he said decisively. "You'd be fine on a horse. I can tell."

"Ah, where do you keep the horses?" asked John, feeling a sudden desire to step closer to his wife.

"Down below there," Butler casually replied. "I didn't show you before. I can show you later, if you want."

John caught Ann's sidelong glance at him and knew what she was thinking: that Butler wasn't trying to cover up. But he was willing to bet that if they did go "later," they wouldn't see any car there.

Aloud he said, "Maybe this afternoon. But Father Bonaventure asked if we could stop by the abbey this morning. Is that all right?"

"Whatever you want!" Butler said, beaming genially. "Don't you want to have some breakfast first?"

"Sorry," said John, "but he asked us to eat with him. In fact, we'll have to start now if we're going to get there in time."

"Good enough," the rider agreed. "I'll see you to your car."

They went around to the parking area in front where

their car was. John forced himself to walk slowly, trying to avoid appearing too anxious to leave.

As they were getting into the car, Butler said, "Have a good time, then. Maybe by the time you get back I'll have some word about your Traherns."

"I hope so," John said enthusiastically, not really believing it.

With a wave of good-bye, they drove off, away from Dunraven. Ann looked back to see Butler still sitting astride his horse, motionless, staring after them.

The last of the metal support jacks was cranked up tightly into place, forcing the last of the heavy shoring timbers tightly against the ceiling.

With the jack in place, the ragged hole and unstable sections of ceiling stone about it were firmly upheld by a new, solid layer of thick wood. The two laborers set about clearing the final rubble away, at last fully revealing what had been hidden in the wall behind.

It was a massive panel of red-gold bronze streaked with deep brown by the tarnish of great age and the corrosion of the damp debris so long piled against it. The surface of the panel was deeply incised by complex curvilinear patterns weaving inward from each corner. The four separate patterns ended in tight spirals that touched at the center. A great, thick ring of metal was affixed there. The whole piece was set in a wide frame of carefully cut and polished stone and displayed massive hinges down one side.

The bronze panel was not a decorative artwork. It was a door.

The dark-cloaked being came into the chamber as the two were scooping the last of the rubble away.

"Ah, Chief!" the older man greeted, tossing down his shovel. "Just finishing the last of it. Way clear. All secured. We can make the try at openin' her up whenever you're ready."

"Something more urgent has come up," the being said

brusquely. "Our friends have done something very foolish, I'm afraid. This time it's made them most dangerous to us. There's no choice now. Something must be done, and quickly."

"Something?" said the younger man, tossing a last scoop of rubble aside and throwing down his own shovel.

"Something unpleasant," the being said darkly. "Something permanent."

The red Ford sped out of Ballymurroe, making the turn onto the road that would take it to the coast. Inside, John sat intently behind the wheel while Ann unfolded the highway maps.

"We could have stopped at Glendon first, and told Father B.," she said reasonably.

"No," he replied uncompromisingly. "You wanted to tell Mr. Trahern about this. That's what we're going to do. He said he'd meet us at the Moher Cliffs."

"Well, we did tell him we'd let him know right away," she said. "It seems the best way. He can decide what to do then."

"Yeah, yeah. I suppose," he agreed reluctantly. "But there's probably more we could find out."

"We've found out enough already."

"I just hope we can meet with him right away. It's tough to delay things now that we've finally started to get at this."

"Maybe you and I are almost finished with it," she suggested hopefully.

"Finished?" He sounded surprised by that. "Not by a long shot. There's too much we don't know."

"That doesn't mean we have to be the ones to keep going with it. Somebody else can now. The police can now."

"We'll see," he said doubtfully. "Keep an eye on the map. I don't want to get lost today."

It was only a few miles to the coast and the place called Lahinch. They motored on through the resort town past the magnificent beaches and found the road that would take them to O'Brien's Tower. To the north they could see the beginning of the cliffs, rising steeply from the sea around the Hag's Head peninsula.

The road ran away from the sea for a time, cutting across the neck of the peninsula some way inland, and they didn't realize how close to the cliffs' high point they were until the land ahead just ended, and they were abruptly at the top of a seven-hundred-foot drop with the sea far below them.

Leaving the car in a tiny lot, they walked a path that climbed along the very brink, separated from it only by large, flat slabs of gray slate set upright in a row to form a barrier.

The path ascended to an even higher point of the cliffs where the squat, round tower of O'Brien sat.

It seemed to be a fortification, built long ago here in this wild, protected place so that someone might live safely and watch the sea, or meditate securely and hide from the world. Instead, it was only a romantic's dream of such past things, constructed for a nineteenth-century tourist trade.

The wind was very strong here. It kept a large white gull suspended motionless in space, wings extended, so close above the trail that when the Milnes passed beneath it they might have jumped up and brushed its belly with their fingertips. Finally it gave up the struggle, lifted, turned, and swooped down toward the water in wide, lazy circles.

The Milnes battled their own way to the tower and entered it, grateful to be out of the punishing blast. They found that the main floor was given over to a small, neat shop for the selling of souvenirs. Behind a counter a young man with a thin face and absurdly large glasses watched them with a cheerful smile.

"Well, hello," he said. "You're very early. Would you be wanting anything?"

The Milnes looked around uncertainly. Besides this shopkeeper, the place was empty.

"We were told to come and meet a man in this shop," Ann told him.

She wasn't quite sure how to ask him if he was that man, but he saved her the trouble.

"Were you now?" he said. "And might you have something for me?"

"We have something for *him*," answered John. He took the half of the photo from his billfold and handed it to the man.

"Very good," he said, examining it critically. "Could you please stay?"

Without waiting for a reply, he left them, going out through a door at the back. The Milnes tried to entertain themselves by looking around the shop, but found it difficult. Fortunately for their nerves, the man was not gone long. He came back into the room, still smiling broadly.

"Well, well, there's no one else about here yet," he said affably, "but I'm sure they will be soon. You're welcome to wait."

"I guess we'll have to," said John, and Ann nodded in agreement.

"Would you like something for the wait?" the man asked.

"I think we might as well," Ann suggested. "We came away without any breakfast." She shot her husband a look. "Some of us were in a hurry."

"No kidding," said John, ignoring the criticism. "You don't happen to have any coffee, do you?"

"I have that," said the young man with enthusiasm. "And biscuits too, if you're wanting something to eat."

They took both. Sitting at the counter, they sipped at the hot coffee with satisfaction. The morning wind off the sea had chilled them through. They held the steaming mugs in both their hands to warm them.

"It's a beautiful place to work," John said to the young man.

"I think so. You can't mind the wind, of course, to stay here long. But I have the birds, and that's my love. You know, there are actually puffins here, right down in the cliffs."

The man spoke with such reverence that John tried to express proper amazement. His own knowledge of puffins was limited to comical images from a childhood story.

"What was the tower built for?" he asked. "Did someone live in it?"

"Oh, no," the man assured him. "It was always for tourists. These cliffs have been a tourist spot as far back as the Middle Ages. People traveled from the Continent to see them. And even before that, in the very ancient days, the men of Ireland's clans came on Midsummer Eve to watch the setting of the midnight sun."

"There aren't many tourists here now," Ann observed. "There haven't been many anywhere we've gone. Even the cottages where we're staying are empty."

"Ah, that is a bit unusual," the man agreed. "But I suppose it's rumors of more trouble that've frightened them away. Not just in the North, mind you, but now all over Europe, too. Before it was only the fighting up there that seemed to bring fear to those visiting. But lately the whole world seems to be caught up in killing and terror. It's as if things were breaking down everywhere, don't you think? Countries and rules and beliefs that have been around for centuries. I mean—" He stopped abruptly and turned his head. "Wait. Listen . . . did you hear that?"

They both shook their heads.

"It was just the wind," said John.

"No," said the man, rushing around the counter. "It was a falcon's cry, I'm sure."

He disappeared outside, leaving his customers staring after him in surprise. After a moment he returned, shaking his head.

"Nothing there," he said, walking back around the counter. "And yet, I'm certain it was the cry of the peregrine falcon I heard. They've become very rare hereabouts."

"You really are a bird fancier," said Ann.

"Oh, that and I like to meet the folk who come here from all over," he said, and Ann noted with amusement that he ranked the people second to the birds.

"Well, I've finished my coffee," John said pointedly.

"Me, too," said Ann. "Now what?"

"There'd be no point in not waiting a bit longer," the

man replied. "Why don't you go up to the top of the tower for a look round? The stairs are straight back. If someone comes looking for you, why I'll just send them up."

They took this as a hint. They paid him, thanked him, and went through the door he indicated. A circular iron staircase wound up through the building's open shell. They climbed it carefully until they reached a low door, held so tightly closed by the pressure of the wind rushing past that they both had to pull to get it open.

They stepped out onto the top of the tower and stood at an embrasure to look out across the deep blue sea that stretched away to the edge of the world.

CHAPTER
TWENTY

✦

Bolt and bar the shutter,
For the foul winds blow:
Our minds are at their best this night,
And I seem to know
That everything outside us is
Mad as the mist and snow.

—W. B. YEATS: *"Mad as the
Mist and Snow"*

Due west, John and Ann could just make out the hazy
outline of two of the three Aran Islands. One behind
the other they lay, looking like floating patches on the sea.

Away to the right and left stretched the cliffs, dropping
away sheerly for hundreds of feet. Far away to the south,
Hag's Head was visible at the end of its peninsula, the dark
mound of some other man-made structure showing atop the
crown of its craggy profile.

They mounted a small platform to look down over the
parapet. Far below the waves crashed against the rocks in
solid white piles, and hundreds of gulls, some only tiny spots
at that distance, wheeled above the spray.

The wind was stronger without the protection of the parapet. It pushed at them, tugging at their clothes. Ann's hair streamed out like some torrent of red-gold liquid.

John felt that if he raised his arms and just let himself go, the wind would lift and hold him suspended as it had that gull. He looked down from the height, and the rocks below held no terror for him. For an instant he felt as if he couldn't fall.

"Easy," said Ann, catching at his arm; and he realized he had been leaning far forward, over the edge.

"Sorry," he said with a laugh. "The wind and the height do tend to carry one away."

"You were almost carried away bodily," she said. "But I know what you mean. I still haven't gotten used to the effect that seeing the ocean has on me."

"It's quite a jump from the Great Plains," he said. "There couldn't be many better places than this to experience what the sea is."

"To look at the sea is not to experience it," said a voice behind them.

They whirled. Mr. Trahern stood beside the door, watching them expressionlessly.

"The sea is never really known to us," he went on. "It's too broad, too deep, too violent."

"Then it's a lot like this country, isn't it?" John replied. "And like this country, it hides many things."

"What do you mean?" Trahern said. "Have you found them?"

"That's not for sure. But we did find enough to bring us here."

Trahern moved forward, his eyes flashing a hard, cold light. "Don't play with me, man. What is it?"

"We might have found someone who's involved in this. I mean, the one who had us chased at Cashel."

"We think," Ann qualified.

"You 'might' and you 'think'?" Trahern repeated impatiently. "Will you just tell me who? Who is it?"

"Butler. Douglas Butler," John told him. "He owns an

estate near Ballymurroe. We visited him and found the car that chased us hidden in his garage."

"The American," Trahern mused. "I know about him. Yes, it could be. He's a powerful man. He could be capable of anything."

"We thought you should know about it," Ann explained, "so you could decide what to do next. You can talk to the police now."

Trahern shook his head. "I'm not sure of that. It's his word to yours, and he is better known here than you. Is there nothing to tie him to my wife?"

"Not really," John answered.

"Then, the thing of it is, we can't act against the man until we can prove he's got to do with her disappearing, or is up to something else illegal."

"Something else?" said Ann.

"Yes, surely. The man surely must have something to hide. Something large to judge by the trouble he's gone to."

He said this with so much conviction that John grew suddenly wary.

"Mr. Trahern, do you know more about this than you've told us?" he asked.

"I've told you everything I could," the other replied.

John didn't believe him. "If that's true, maybe it is time to bring in the police," he said heatedly.

"No!" Trahern protested. "I warned you they can't be trusted. No one can."

"That's what you say," countered John. "But I think it's time you tell us all you know, or we'll walk away from this."

Trahern eyed them a moment. Then he nodded. "I will tell you," he said heavily, "but that might be what makes you walk away."

"What do you mean?" said Ann.

"I do know more about this. Only a little, but it is an uncomforting little. You see, my wife not only told me her fears, she also told me her suspicions. She felt something was happening in Ballymurroe. Something quite large and dangerous. I think you've had some hint of that already."

"We've heard some rumors," John replied. "Forces gathering, winds rising, things like that. They sounded like a fairy tale."

"There's truth behind them, believe me," Trahern said. He sat down on the edge of the tower parapet and removed his cap. The wind ruffled his thick iron-gray hair. "I told you that Nancy wrote me of the change in the village and the people about there. But she felt that more was happening beyond that. She said there was something growing there like a dark power out of the ancient myths. She's always been a sensitive woman, you know. Always feeling things of an otherworldly nature, if you understand what I mean."

"I know she said she's had premonitions," Ann put in. "And she told us she felt very close to the old spirits of Ireland."

"Well, she told me that she felt those very spirits closing in. She felt that, somehow, the time was turning back. The people were returning to a way of thinking they'd had hundreds of years ago. The old ways and beliefs are very close beneath the surface here anyway, you realize. It takes little to scratch away that thin veneer of modern ways to expose them. The past is clung to tightly, like the old buildings and the old traditions. Especially in country places like Ballymurroe."

"I'm not sure what you mean," said John. "Just what did she think was happening?"

"It's hard to say. Somehow the past was . . ."—he stopped, searching for a way to express the idea—"was being brought alive again. Someone was regenerating in the people's hearts the powerful beliefs and loyalties of those days when chieftains and high druids ruled from their fortresses."

"That's ridiculous," Ann said with force. "That couldn't happen again."

"Oh, and couldn't it?" he challenged. "Haven't I seen it happen myself, in the North? It was ancient hatreds that caused the troubles there. As they've continued, the walls have gone up. Cities have been divided into walled citadels. Clans have gathered about the strongest warlords. And now

the warriors strut amongst us again, just like the heroes of
the legends."

"Maybe that has happened," Ann admitted. "But that's
in Northern Ireland. What could happen here?"

"The past holds tight to all of Ireland. Remember, it's
not been so many years since rule by force was the normal
way of things here, too. There are still many living who
remember those brutal days. It's very hard to change down
deep, no matter what the surface seems. From what I've
heard and seen since I came, I'd say that some influence was
already very strong in Ballymurroe. Some fear it, and some
hold it a strange fealty, but none will challenge it. Worse yet,
Nancy felt that some physical force was gathering."

"Physical force?" Milne repeated. "What kind?"

Trahern shrugged. "I don't know. It might be some kind
of new underground army, or a terrorist faction. Those
strange men you've encountered may be only a part of it.
Understand, the troubles have bred many men who only
know the rule of the gun. A great number have broken from
the old IRA, and many of them are drifting now or hiding in
villages all over Ireland. It may be that this new power is
drawing them together with money or promises of glory.
This Butler could surely offer them both."

"But there's just no sense in Butler's being involved that
way," Ann argued. "Why would he do it? He's rich, and his
reputation is international . . ."

"Some can never have enough," Trahern said, "and some
act out of their own private loves and hates. The fact is that
something is happening, and he seems to be in it deep
enough."

"That isn't fact, it's speculation," Ann said. "Butler may
be in this without choice or even real knowledge. We've
worked up a whole conspiracy around him without any solid
proof."

Trahern sighed. "It's right enough you are. You've just
stated the other reason why we can't go to the police.
There's nothing they'll believe about a man like him without
serious proof. And if we did convince them something was

wrong, they might go charging in on him blindly. Who knows then what might happen to my wife and daughter?"

"He's right," John agreed. "We don't know if Butler or someone else is holding them, or where they might be, or even if—" He broke off there, seeing the look of horror dawn in his wife's face as she realized what he was about to say.

"—if they're still alive?" Trahern supplied. "Of course I've considered that. If it's true, it only makes finding the one behind this more important."

The quiet, mechanical way he said this chilled Ann more than the fresh sea air. His words had the coldness of death in them. She turned away to look out at the beauty of the cliffs. Suddenly she only wanted this all to be over.

"Our real task now is to try to find them," Trahern went on. "If it *was* Butler Nancy was interested in, it's likely through Butler we'll have a chance of finding them."

"So, what can we do?" John asked. "It's still your show."

"We've got to stay near him. Use any means to discover where he might have them or what he's about."

"What he's about?" echoed John. "What good would that do?"

"It would insure the help of the authorities, once we needed it, and it could give us some lever to use against him, if need be. If we can't release them safely any other way, we might force him to release them by threatening to expose him."

"We can't do that," protested Ann. "If we find out he's doing something illegal, we've got to tell the police. We can't deal with him."

Trahern turned his gaze full on her and, once again, she saw that strange flicker of hot light deep within his eyes. When he spoke again, his voice was calm, reasonable, and very brutal.

"Understand me: I don't much care about what he's doing or why at this point. I only care about my family. If dealing with him is the only way I can get them back, then

I'll deal. Once I have them safe, Butler will be taken care of. I promise that."

She tried to meet his gaze, but failed. She turned away from him again, and John spoke up.

"I guess it's up to us, then," he said calmly. "We can go back to Dunraven and try to find out where they are."

Ann looked at him in disbelief. "What are you saying? How many chances can we take?"

"We're the only ones who can do it, don't you see?" he told her reasonably. "We can search the place for them or for anything else Butler might be hiding there."

She didn't reply. She couldn't argue with him anymore. She couldn't understand why he was becoming so impossible to talk to.

"Just keep in mind he knows you're my wife's friends," said Trahern. "I'm certain he's asked you there to keep a watch on you."

"What can he do to us?" John said lightly. "Bonaventure and the other monks at Glendon know we're there. If we disappeared, it'd point a finger right at him. Hell, being at his manor's the safest place to be now."

"That may be true," the man agreed. "Still, I'll not let you go without some help nearby. I'll return to Ballymurroe and stay close to the manor. If you find anything of help, meet me at once. Where can we safely meet?"

"The abbey," John suggested.

"Agreed," said Trahern. He looked out from the tower toward the parking area. "We'd best be parted now. It's nearly mid-morning. Others might be coming to see the view. Why don't you go first? I'll follow after."

"Fine," said John. "We'll see you soon, I hope."

The Milnes went back down the winding stairs into the shop. The young man there greeted them as if they were old friends.

"Leaving, are you? Where are you headed?"

"Back to Ballymurroe," Ann told him. "It's southeast."

"Well, if you're looking for a fine way to drive, go

through the Burren," he suggested. "Just take the left turning on the road to Lisdonvarna. It's a fine, wild place, and flowers grow there the like of which you'll see nowhere else: sea lavender, bloody cranesbill, fairy foxglove . . . even the Burren's own orchid."

"It sounds beautiful," Ann agreed.

"Well, sad to say, some of the tourists do pick them," he said with regret. "I normally don't direct people there. They don't realize the fragile nature of it all. They don't understand that the beauty of it is in where it is, growing freely, to be seen living. They pick the flowers and take them home to save. Of course, the flowers dry and become only poor brown things." He smiled at them. "But I can feel you'll not do that, and so I tell you . . . and with pleasure."

"That's quite a compliment," Ann told him sincerely. "Thank you for it."

"You're most welcome."

The Milnes said good-bye to him and went out of the tower. The sharp wind caught at them again, trying to whirl them away into the clouds.

"That man scares me," Ann said as they started down the long path toward their car.

"Who, the birdman?" John asked. "Or do you mean Butler?"

"I mean Mr. Trahern. I can feel the violence held deep inside him."

"He's angry and frightened. He has good reasons for the way he feels."

"Does he?" she said. "I'm beginning to wonder. The hatred seems to feed on itself too much."

They stopped then and looked back toward the tower, pulled by a common impulse.

They saw the figure there on top, alone against the sky. Even at a distance they felt his gaze and were aware of the strange light flaring deep within it, intimation of some latent energy.

Then, abruptly, he was gone, vanishing while they

looked at him, and they realized they had never asked how he had come here.

From the tower's top, John's eye was then drawn upward to something drifting high above. It was the shape of a black bird circling over the cliffs.

"Hey, look at that," he said, pointing it out to her. "Could that be the birdman's 'whatever' falcon?"

"Peregrine," she amended, squinting up at it. "No, I don't think so. That just looks like a crow."

"Pretty damn big for a crow," he said. The bird's wing-spread did seem quite wide, but it was hard to judge how far away it was.

"You know how big they get over here," she reminded him. "Like chickens." She shuddered then and pulled her coat tighter about her. "Come on. Let's get to the car. I'm freezing."

He nodded and they headed on. Neither saw the second bird that abruptly appeared to join the first. And neither was aware that the black pair now began to sweep down toward the cliff . . . and them.

The Milnes were only halfway down the long, narrow trail to the car when they had a first inkling of anything behind them.

It was a rising whoosh of sound that alerted John. He looked around, stared an instant in shock, then crouched, grabbed Ann's arm, and hauled her down as a form shot just feet above their heads.

They looked up as the form lifted away, cawing loudly. It was one of the blackbirds that had dived upon them, and it was indeed big.

The body of the animal was larger than a man's. Its vast wings spread out ten feet on either side. And the curved, sharp rapier of its massive beak was nearly a yard long.

"My God!" said Ann, staring after the creature as it began to lift on the huge, flapping wings. "What kind of bird is that?"

"I don't know," said a dumbfounded John. "I've never heard of anything so large."

They had no time to consider it further. Another loud caw from behind brought both their gazes jerking around.

A second giant blackbird was sweeping in toward the two, its long and keenly taloned claws outstretched to snatch at them.

CHAPTER
TWENTY-ONE
✠

You ask what I have found, and far and wide I go:
Nothing but Cromwell's house and Cromwell's
    murderous crew,
The lovers and the dancers are beaten into the clay,
And the tall men and the swordsmen and the
    horsemen, where are they?
And there is an old beggar wandering in his pride—
His fathers served their fathers before Christ was
    crucified.
    O what of that, O what of that,
        What is there left to say?

—W. B. YEATS: *"The Curse of Cromwell"*

The bird shot over them just inches above their heads,
claws nearly raking them. The two huddled back into
the partial cover of the slate wall lining the cliff's edge.

John peered over the top edge of the stones to see the
creature headed out to sea.

"It's gone," he announced to her. "Quick, head for the
car!"

They rose and headed down the pathway at a run. The
parking lot and car were just in their sight when one of the

birds appeared below and swept up toward them, cutting off their route.

"Damn!" said John. "Back to the tower!"

They turned back, heading upward for the only other place of safety on the open cliff top. But the second giant crow swooped in above to hover in their path with a furious flapping of wings. They were cut off both ways.

"Let's keep heading for the tower," said John. "We'll dodge around that thing."

They charged boldly toward it. It seemed at first nonplussed by the move, continuing to hang in place. Only when they were nearly under it did it act. It dropped down, striking out with its beak to drive them back. But they didn't retreat this time. They ducked around the thrusting curve of beak, ran beneath the bird, then headed on.

It cawed angrily and wheeled after them, arrowing in like a fighter on a strafing run. The time it took the bird to turn had given the Milnes a fair lead, however, and the tower was now not so far.

"Just keep running," he urged his wife, looking back at the pursuing bird.

They put their best effort into it as the creature closed in. They looked to be winners in the desperate race until Ann tripped on a stone. She went down hard.

John stopped to help her up. The speeding bird, in its single-minded attempt to stop them, dived in very close this time. Its sharp talons all but grazed the top of John's head.

He jerked sharply away to save himself. His body slammed against the waist-high wall of stones and he fell back, overbalanced, his upper body bent over the top of the wall an instant and teetering there, literally on the brink.

Still on the ground, Ann looked up to see her husband topple over the wall and disappear.

"John!" she cried in horror.

She scrambled up and looked over the wall of slates. Relief flooded her. He had not gone over the cliff. Not completely. For the moment. Instead he was partly on a narrow space between wall and edge. His lower body had somersaulted on over and was hanging out over the sheer drop. His upper body was stretched out on the ledge, his hand holding tight to some dried tufts of grass.

But the tufts were pulling loose.

She clambered over swiftly, grabbed his arm, and hauled back, giving him support. He crawled a bit higher, then got a knee up and levered himself back over the edge. They lay together on the narrow strip between cliff and wall, panting heavily.

He peered down the seven-hundred-foot cliff to the crashing sea and pulled back quickly, shuddering.

"I will never believe that I can't fall again," he said wholeheartedly.

One of the black birds screamed low overhead. The other came into view out at sea, gliding in broad circles and watching them.

Crouched in the narrow space between the slates and the drop, the Milnes watched their attackers anxiously.

"What do they want?" asked Ann.

John shrugged. "Food? We're just big rabbits to them."

"That's awful!" she replied. "What can we do?"

He shrugged again. "Looks like we're trapped here."

From somewhere inland, another bird shot suddenly into view.

It was a graceful brown bird with a white belly. Though a good size, it was still much smaller than the crows. It was quicker and more agile, however, and it was very brave as well. Without hesitation it dove upon one of the giant birds.

The Milnes watched with amazement as a sort of dogfight occurred in the sky above. The larger bird was clearly afraid of the smaller one. It turned, climbed, and dived frantically to shake off pursuit. In vain. The brown bird caught the black and sailed right into it.

The effect was a strange one. The smaller bird slashed through the larger like a keen saber tearing through gauze. It blasted out the other side of the black mass, trailing a streamer along behind like a dark contrail.

The crow seemed stricken, its movements growing

slower, more ponderous. Its wings pumped with great effort, and it began to sink earthward.

The brown bird swept around and struck in again. Its helpless prey put up no more defense. The attacker ripped through over and over with relentless force, and with each stroke the form of the black bird lost more integrity. The Milnes stared upward as the crow dissolved into ragged black shreds that swiftly dissolved and drifted upward like fog wisps, dissipating into the gray sky.

In moments, not a tatter of the giant bird remained.

The brown bird wasted no time there, but went after the other crow still circling at sea. It gave a frightened squawk and wheeled away, the small bird in pursuit. They were soon both out of sight.

The Milnes climbed up and looked around them. There was no more sign of any birds. They looked upward. The first crow had evaporated as if it had never been.

"Rescued," said a disbelieving John, "by a bloody miracle. What was that other bird?"

"I think it was the peregrine falcon," said Ann. "The tower man was right. But what were those two things it attacked, John? They weren't birds, were they? I mean, they couldn't have been real and disappear that way, could they?"

"Never mind," he said, shaking off the rather mind-numbing idea for the time. "Let's just get out of here while we can."

She agreed. They quickly climbed back across the wall and headed for their car.

Some minutes later, they were riding down the coast highway from the cliffs at a good speed.

"This is too strange," Ann was saying in a troubled way as her husband steered their course. "Being chased by men is one thing. Being chased by . . . by magic birds . . ." She shook her head and looked to him. "John, what's going on here anyway?"

"I wish I knew," he said.

He raced the car on down a relatively straight stretch of road that the road sign proclaimed as the way to Lisdonvarna. A fork came up ahead, a secondary branch heading off sharply to the left. John peered intently up the main branch as they approached, then yanked the car around onto the side road.

"Why did you do that?" she asked.

"Whaddaya mean?" he asked testily. "There was a sign for Lisdonvarna and Ballymurroe. Pointing this way. Didn't you see?"

She looked back toward the disappearing fork. She hadn't really seen anything even like a sign.

But John drove on, for the moment intent only on putting more distance between them and the tower. Still, he couldn't help but be aware that his wife had become withdrawn and silent. He tried to start a conversation several times, but she only answered with nods or short sentences and nothing more.

His attempts to discover a way of getting at what was bothering her came to an end, however, when he began to note the change in the countryside.

Trees and pastures were giving way to more rocky areas. The road began corkscrewing up some rather steep slopes from whose highest points the glimmer of sea could be seen in the west. The way brought them up, finally, onto a higher, flatter plain.

"This is really strange," he said. "This can't be the way back to town. I don't recognize anything. Check the map, will you?"

She did, but even the detailed chart didn't help them. The oddly meandering road that they followed didn't seem to match anything marked down.

"Can you even tell generally where we are?" John asked his frustrated wife.

"Well, if that left you took back there was really *off* the Lisdonvarna road," she said, "and we're heading sort of east-southeast now, then I'd say this was the Burren."

"Burren?"

"The place that the man at the tower talked about."

Though they had not planned to take the young man's advice, John's turn apparently *had* put them on the secondary road. It had taken them in from the coast to plunge them into the very heart of that area.

John slowed and they looked out on the scene as he drove. The Barony of the Burren was the full geographical title for the area, and it was an apt descriptive name as well. It was a limestone desert that covered many square miles of land with colorless rock that stretched away to the horizon in an overwhelmingly empty vista.

It reminded John of nothing so much as the sea bottom, thrust rudely up into the air, ripped from its own environment and forced into another one strange to it. And, like any alien in a strange world, it lay separate and hostile and waiting.

By its look it would have prevented any flowers from growing on it, so much did they manage to compromise its somberness. The man at the tower had not understated their beauty. The gray land was alive with a riot of colors that filled holes and crannies everywhere amongst the rocks. It was a startling example of those Irish contrasts—vibrant life in a barren setting.

They saw no sign of homes or inhabitants as they drove, passing only a few goats grazing on the scattered patches of grass. Then, quite suddenly, the road came to a dead end.

It terminated at a small parking area labeled as a "Lough-By—scenic outlook." It seemed the little rest stop was intended as a place to view this section of the Burren and a structure that sat in the center of the vista.

This odd gray construction of stone looked rather like a vast mushroom at a distance. It sat in a wide plain of the same rock and would have been invisible had it not stuck up so starkly from the flat surroundings.

"Hey, look at that!" he said, stopping the car.

"What is it?" she asked with curiosity, peering toward the thing.

"It's a dolmen," he said. "And a big one. Got to be a landmark."

He took their guidebook from the glovebox and found the area in it. A photograph matched the object on the plain.

"Right," he announced. "It's Poulnabrone. That's one of the most famous. It says here that the dolmens were traditionally thought to be shelters built by Diarmund when he and Grania were fleeing the wrath of Finn. Now they know that dolmens were megalithic tombs."

"I think I'd rather believe the traditions," she said tonelessly. "Look, if we know where we are now, just turn around and let's get away from here. I—"

She stopped abruptly, her gaze fixing on the dolmen. Then she threw open the door and climbed hurriedly out.

"What are you doing?" asked a surprised John.

She didn't answer at once. She was staring intently out toward the structure. She had seen a face there, peering from behind it toward the car. She *knew* she had.

And there it was again. A figure lifted up into view above the dolmen's stone top. A head, shoulders, a torso. The figure of a young girl. A young girl that Ann knew very well.

Bridget Trahern.

The girl smiled, waved, then vanished behind the stone.

"Bridget!" shouted Ann, and began to run toward the dolmen.

"Wait a minute!" cried John, climbing from the car to stare after her. "Where are you going?"

"She's there!" Ann excitedly shouted back, pointing toward the stones. "Bridget! I saw her! There!"

"There?" echoed an astounded John. "You couldn't have. Ann!"

But she was unheeding, impulsively carried away by her discovery, running on. He shook his head and started after her.

They made their way out across the field of rocks toward the ancient structure. Their movement was difficult. The surface rocks were rounded, polished by wind and rain. They were split by long, wide cracks that all seemed to run in one direction, and the Milnes were often forced to jump from one spot to another and watch their footing carefully.

As they neared the dolmen, they could see its construction clearly. It was simply two flat slabs of rock upended, with a third, massive piece laid across the top. A crude, primitive structure, and appropriate to the land.

Ann reached it first, searching frantically around it. No one was there.

The light of hope faded, replaced by a look of frustration and concern.

"I saw her," she told her husband stubbornly when he reached her. "I know I did."

He shook his head. "You couldn't have. It was wishful thinking and some trick of the light."

"I did," she repeated testily. "There was *something*. *Not* light!"

"It doesn't make sense," he insisted.

"Just how much has lately?" she countered.

"Okay," he soothed. "We'll take a good look around."

It was quiet in the Burren, with not even the sound of breezes or insects to disturb the air. It was an oppressive silence, and so complete that they found themselves reluctant to disturb it.

They moved around the dolmen, examining it from different angles, looking searchingly at the ground around it. Ann gave up after some moments in defeat.

"Nothing here," she said. "I guess it *was* just wishful thinking. Wishing hard that this could be over. That we'd just find Bridget and Nancy and it would be ended." She looked toward him, the thing that had been troubling her since leaving O'Brien's Tower coming back to the fore. "John," she said, "just why are we going ahead with this? Haven't we had enough proof it's over our heads yet? Are you sure we shouldn't go to the police?"

He looked up from his examination of the empty hollow within the tomb. "You heard what Trahern said. We don't have anything to tell the police. Anyway, who's going to believe us over the Great Producer? Especially if we tell them what happened today. They'll think we're just nuts!"

"But that isn't true. We do have something more concrete now. We can tell them about the car. And we have what the tinker said. Why didn't you tell Mr. Trahern about the tinker?"

"I don't know," he said evasively, apparently intent on thoroughly examining the rock. "Trahern held back from us, so I guess I did the same to him. Childish, maybe, but as he said, it wouldn't have helped much."

"That's right," she said, realizing he had put his finger on exactly what was disturbing her. "You did it just the way he did. You're like him, in a way. He seems to have some need, some drive to act himself. So do you. That's what's wrong. You didn't tell him because you wanted to keep it for yourself. You didn't want Bonaventure and the tinker in because you wanted to do it yourself. It's been growing and growing, ever since Cashel. You *like* this!"

He looked at her closely and saw how intent, how serious she was. He tried to laugh, but it was a shallow sound. The dead air swallowed it up.

He considered the idea of letting the police take over and encountered a stiff inner resistance, a deep reluctance, as if he would be losing something very close to him. He realized that this was an absurd attitude. He applied reason to the idea, and reason told him it was the logical thing to do. If he was acting against reason, maybe he *was* being a fool.

"I just don't understand you," Ann went on. "That's not normal for us. I think this has gone too far."

"You may be right," he admitted. "It was so easy to get caught up in it . . . almost as if it were natural. Maybe it *is* this country, after all. Too much about fate and legends. It pulls at you. I can feel it. Things happen like they were meant to be that way, and we have no choice about it."

"We have a choice," she said. "But don't decide now. We'll talk to Bonaventure about it when we get back. I just wanted you to stop and think."

"I'll think," he assured her, "about a lot of this."

Ann suddenly turned from him and lifted her head.

"Listen . . ." she said. "Listen. Do you hear it?"

She seemed so concerned, so grave, that John obeyed. He heard nothing.

"What was it?"

"I . . ." She hesitated. "You'll think I'm crazy, but I heard a baby cry."

A chill ran through his body at her words. For no reason he felt afraid.

He looked around them. The land was empty of human life, or any evidence of life, as far as he could see. Nothing but the dolmen.

"Maybe it was a bird," he said, looking up to the sky with some apprehension. He almost wanted to believe that it was. He wanted to shake off the irrational feeling that the cry had come to her across time, across a hundred lifetimes.

But there was something about this place, something detached from the real world, that made him wonder if they had walked into a rent in the weave of time and were close, very close, to things incredibly ancient.

He had a strong desire to look back toward the car, to reassure himself; but he found it difficult to do so. He was afraid that he would find it and the narrow road gone, and themselves somehow lost, forever lost in this alien place.

He forced himself to look, battling the superstition he felt welling out from his own subconscious. The car was there. Their link with reality still existed.

"I think we'd better just get going," he said with relief.

"Yes," she said simply. Her own sense of ease had gone. More than anything else that had happened, that cry had disturbed something deep and basic in her.

They started back toward the car. Motivated by some sense of urgency, they moved as quickly as they could.

"What a setup, though," he said as they neared the car. "Another great place to be laid to rest."

He turned his head to look back toward the dolmen.

From the corner of his eye he saw the form rising up out of the ground.

CHAPTER
TWENTY-TWO
✣

Nor dread nor hope attend
A dying animal;
A man awaits his end
Dreading and hoping all;
Many times he died,
Many times rose again.
A great man in his pride
Confronting murderous men
Casts derision upon
Supersession of breath;
He knows death to the bone—
Man has created death.

—W. B. YEATS: *"Death"*

"Look out!" he cried and swung around, striking forward with his foot.

An arm holding a gun came up as the man, who had been lying hidden in a deep crevice in the rocks, struggled to climb to his feet. The gun struck John a glancing blow on the side of his head, but the young American's foot connected solidly with the man's stomach.

As John staggered back, the man doubled up and went down, falling backward into the crevice. Through a bright haze John saw a second man—the younger of those who had chased them at Cashel—coming toward them from the road in a rush.

Ann grabbed her husband's hand, and they started to run, John fighting the dizziness that threatened his balance.

Behind them the first man—the older and stouter of those from their previous encounter—fought to pull himself from the crevice, but he'd become wedged into the narrow space, and his arms and legs flapped uselessly. The younger man was forced to stop and pull him out. This gave the Milnes time to reach a distant line of rocks.

Beyond this line the ground sloped sharply off into a lower area jumbled with larger rocks. They moved down into it and slid into a sheltered spot to rest.

"You're bleeding," Ann whispered hoarsely, and touched his temple where a ragged cut poured a thin stream of blood over the left side of his face.

He shook his head angrily to clear it of a faint buzzing.

"I'm okay," he assured her in a barely audible whisper. "They're the ones from Cashel. Butler's stopped playing."

"What do we do?" she asked.

"We can make it tougher for them if we separate. They can't catch us both. Give me a minute to lead them off, then you go for the car. Get help."

"They may shoot you."

"No. They'd have done it right away. They want us alive."

"What will you do?"

"I may not have to do anything. If you get away, they'll probably give it up." He pulled the car keys from his pocket and pressed them into her hand. "Here. Be careful driving on the left. We don't want to lose you."

"What if you get caught?"

"It doesn't matter," he assured her. "If you get away, you can go for the police. They'll know that. It won't help them then to do anything to me." He himself wasn't sure of the real logic of this, but it was all they had. "Just focus yourself on getting away from here!"

She tried to smile to assure him she understood. She couldn't think of anything to say.

"Give me a couple of minutes, then," he said. He gave her hand a hard squeeze and leaned forward to kiss her hard on the lips. "Good luck."

John got up cautiously and moved carefully through the rocks away from her. He went some distance, then climbed to a higher point to try to locate the men.

He saw them, still on the plain of rock near the dolmen. They had apparently just concluded planning strategy, for now they started walking toward the last point where they had seen the Milnes, spreading apart as they went.

John was glad to see the gunmen were making the same mistake as they had at Cashel. Both were following their quarry into a large, confusing area, and were neglecting to cover their rear. Ann could easily flank them, if he led them far enough away.

He took a deep breath and got to his feet.

"Let's go!" he cried loudly and paused in view long enough to be quite certain they had seen him. Then he took off.

He realized at once what a task he'd undertaken. His ears were ringing and his balance was poor. He stumbled often and scraped his knees several times. He told himself he had to keep going long enough to allow her time to get clear.

Ann, meantime, had continued waiting in her hiding spot, holding her breath, after he had left. She had heard John shout and, moments afterward, she had heard the men scrambling across the rocks in pursuit.

For some time longer she waited to insure they had gone on. Only then did she leave the cover. She climbed over the rise and, with the large rocks now between her and the gunmen, stood upright and ran for the car with a desperation that pushed her on, lifting her over bumps and crevices.

Nearer and nearer she drew to the car, not looking back,

expecting at every step to hear the crack of a shot. But no sound broke the quiet except for her own labored breathing.

She reached the car, her relief filling her with sudden exhilaration. She climbed in and shoved the key into the ignition.

"Please don't start the car, Mrs. Milne," said a voice beside her.

She turned her head and looked at the muzzle of a revolver thrust in the window. Behind it the face of Padraic O'Gadhra smiled broadly at her.

This time there had been three of them.

John continued to run, to crawl, to force himself on, unaware of the futility of his gambit. He reached another rise of ground and made it to the top, but there his legs failed him, and he rolled forward.

The other side was a steep incline, and he tried to catch himself, but the rock was smooth, and he found no grip. He slid and rolled down the slope, landing in a heap at the bottom. He tried to rise, but his head pounded. He fell back. He couldn't go any further.

There was a deep crevice in the rock near him, and he crawled into it. He lay still, both hoping the men would not see him and not really caring if they did. When he heard sounds of movement, he raised his head and peered out from his hole. The two men, worn and dirty themselves, were on top of the little rise not twenty feet above him. If they descended from where they were, they would land at Milne's feet.

Suddenly they stiffened and turned in attitudes of listening. John listened too and heard what they heard: a distant shouting.

"Boys," it said, "come on back!"

"That was Paddy," said one of the men. "It must be he has them."

"I hope to God he does," said the other, wiping his brow. They turned back and disappeared from the top of the rise. For a moment John lay in the crevice, stunned by what this meant. Then, in fear and anger, he crawled from the rocks and started back toward the car, his aching muscles forgotten.

He didn't see the gunmen again until he topped the rise that overlooked the plain and the dolmen. By the time he reached that point they were far ahead, passing the stone burial marker, headed for the car.

And beside that car stood his wife with Padraic O'Gadhra.

John ducked back into the shelter of the rocks, cursing himself for underestimating these men and for separating from his wife.

When the two men reached the Ford, O'Gadhra talked with them a moment, then walked out to the dolmen. From there he shouted up into the rocks.

"Milne! Please give it up. There's nothing you can do now. We won't harm you. We only want to talk."

John said nothing. Once Butler had them both, he could do anything he liked. One of them had to stay free, he told himself.

"All right, Milne," said O'Gadhra when a few silent minutes had passed. "It matters little enough. You're not much good alone, and you can't hide forever. Not in our country."

John still waited silently.

"It's your pain and your choosing, then," the man went on. "Just be remembering, the only way your wife will come to harm is if the authorities are brought into this. You keep that in your head while you run, John Milne."

He walked back to the car and talked again with the two gunmen. Then he gestured to Ann with his gun, and she climbed in behind the Escort's wheel. As he walked around and got into the passenger seat, the other two started back into the wilderness of rocks, guns out, preparing to carry on the search.

In an agony of helpless frustration, John watched Ann start their car and drive it off. Then the approach of the gunmen forced him to turn his attention back to them. If he was going to stay free, he was going to have to run again.

He turned and headed away from them, plunging into the depths of the eerie wilderness.

Back in their Escort, Ann piloted the car away under O'Gadhra's direction, her agonized look going often to the dolmen shrinking away behind her.

"Well, well, and very neat that was," said the gloating man. "Worked out just as neat as planned, misleading you way out here."

"Planned?" she said with surprise. "You mean you *got* us to come out here?"

"How else could we have been waiting for you that way?" he said, smirking. "Didn't know how truly amazing our talents were, did you, you so-clever Americans?"

She remembered her husband's wrong turn, their bewilderment in the Burren, her own vision of Bridget. Still, she fought against the idea.

"It's impossible," she told him stoutly. "How could you have done that to us?"

He gave her a broad, mischievous grin. "Magic!" he said cryptically.

Meantime, behind them, John Milne was continuing to run. He headed eastward through the Burren, going as fast as he could, trying to ignore the complaints of his mind and body.

He had no way of telling whether his hunters could even guess which way he had gone, so he changed course often and zigzagged through the rocks, stopping occasionally to see if anyone was visible behind him. There never was.

He had walked for what seemed to him miles when he rounded a rocky knoll and found another dolmen. It was somewhat smaller than Poulnabrone, but the hollow space beneath its covering slab was still large enough to shelter him.

In his exhausted condition, it looked like a secure, inviting place to rest. He crawled in and curled himself up where the ashes of some ancient chief or champion had once been laid to a last sleep.

In the vast silence that fell about him there, he began to hear a soft humming sound rise.

It grew stronger, resolving into the soft, steady murmur of many people gathering around him. They came to mourn his passing and begin the rituals that would prepare him for his last rest.

Rising clear of the murmur and twining through the voices of the rest now came the rhythmic chanting of the druid priests and the low keening of the *Sidhe* women. The melodic and melancholy sounds echoed faintly in his ears.

He opened his eyes and looked over the black-cloaked ranks that closed respectfully around his funeral pyre. He lay stretched atop it, clad in the gold-edged white gown of a slain champion, draped in mistletoe. A single figure stood close at his side, a burning brand in his hands. He saw without surprise that it was Douglas Butler, clad in a deep green druid's robe. The man stood giantly silhouetted against the fiery disk of the midsummer's midnight sun, just settling to the horizon. The flare of the torch seemed drawn from the flaring orb.

The man lowered the brand toward the brush and timber piled beneath the bier. The cremation would soon begin.

There was only one trouble. Milne was still alive!

He tried to cry out, but his mouth wouldn't move. The words stuck in his mind. He tried struggling, but his body was frozen. He lay helpless while the flaming torch moved to ignite the tinder.

Smoke soon billowed up around him. The haze of heat blurred his view. He cast a wild gaze about him as the crowd moved back. Beyond them, squatting by the nearby dolmen, he glimpsed a rabbit watching him.

But through the haze, its image seemed to waver. As the flames rose to momentarily obscure it, it seemed suddenly to lift and swell. And in an instant it was the form of the little tinker named Cian O'Teague who stood there.

The little man lifted arms and called out in a deep, rolling language Milne couldn't understand. The flames lapping up around the bier instantly died.

From beyond the man, other forms appeared, rushing forward. They were clad in long tunics and bright-hued cloaks, carrying swords and spears and shields. The crowd about the bier scattered before them.

Bonaventure himself led the host, a great silver sword uplifted before him and flashing the last crimson rays of the midsummer's midnight sun. He charged upon Butler and swung the weapon as the green-robed man drew his own huge sword to parry the assault.

Iron struck iron over John's recumbent form with the din of lightning crashing to the earth, and the glinting sparks flew.

John started violently and opened one eye.

The other eye was stuck closed with clotted blood. He looked blankly at the rock above him. Slowly his confused brain sifted reality from dream. He realized that he had fallen asleep in the hollow of the dolmen. Butler, Bonaventure, the tinker—none of it was real. Or was it?

He rubbed at his eye and managed to open it. He shifted slightly, and his muscles screamed in protest. He lay still again. The pain had decided him to lie there and rest longer . . . possibly forever.

It wouldn't matter if he didn't go on. It wouldn't do anyone any good if he did. Who had he thought he was, anyway, playing his little game, proud of his supposed new-found talent for adventuring?

Ann had been right. He'd acted without thinking, and his so-called talent had failed him utterly, leading them to be trapped in an empty place like this. He'd been so fixed on the need to go on, so oblivious to the dangers, so certain nothing could happen to them.

And now?

Now, he was finished. He was as helpless as he'd been in the dream. There was no more bravado or cleverness left. Someone else would have to do the thinking and make the decisions. Someone else would have to take the responsibility. Ann's life was too important to depend on his lousy judgments.

Father Bonaventure could do it from now on, he decided. The man was clever. A clever warrior. He would know what to do.

But Milne knew that this meant he was going to have to tell the monk what had happened, and he would have to go back to Ballymurroe to do it. He wouldn't be able to stay in his cozy den, curled up like an infant who knew what the world was like and had no desire to be born into it.

With a sigh of both resignation and weariness, he climbed out of the dolmen and got to his feet. That made his head throb harder, and he rested for a moment against one of the cold stone slabs.

There was no sign of any pursuer on the circle of the horizon. He prayed that they had lost his trail for good. That would mean he only had to worry about getting back to the village.

With a determined effort he stepped away from the dolmen and started off toward the southeast.

Since O'Gadhra had returned Ann to Dunraven Manor she had been alone, locked in one of the bedrooms.

She had been asked no questions and given no information. The young Irishman had taken her directly to the room, wished her a pleasant stay and left her. Through the agonizingly long hour that followed, she saw no one but O'Gadhra again when he brought her food and drink and magazines to read.

She had grown steadily more nervous as the day had progressed. What was Butler going to do? What had happened to John? What was going on in this place?

She had no way to answer her own questions. She could only imagine possibilities that grew wilder and wilder as the minutes passed. It was actually a relief to her when, after what seemed hours, the door of the room opened, and Butler entered.

"Mrs. Milne," he said, smiling warmly. "I'm sorry about keeping you here this way. I hope you've been comfortable."

"I've been comfortable," she said, trying to keep her voice even and calm. She was determined to be careful and move as slowly as she could, feeling her way through whatever turns events were going to take. She had no other strategies.

"Well, I didn't want to do it this way," he said, "but I was hoping your husband would turn up by now."

"You haven't found John?" she asked, not certain whether to be cheered or distressed.

"I'm afraid that's the problem," Butler said, pacing the room. "I was planning to get you and your husband here and talk this out."

"Talk it out?" She couldn't believe what he was saying. "Is that why you had your men chase us through the Burren with guns?"

"Be logical, Mrs. Milne. After you left, I found out you'd seen the car in my garage. One of my men was watching you. I figured you'd connect it with Cashel. I didn't know what you were thinking. I didn't want you to go to the police, so I asked my men to bring you back."

"They could have been more polite about it," Ann said without humor.

"Tell me the truth," he said, stopping and facing her squarely. "Would you have come if they had asked?"

"Not after Cashel."

"I'm sorry about that," he said with apparent sincerity. "But I assure you, they weren't meaning to harm you. See, I set that little incident up myself. Of course, you forced me to."

"We did?" she said with surprise. "How?"

"Well, of course we knew you were checking around for your friends from the very start. We didn't think you'd find much until Mrs. Ryan called up, nearly hysterical, saying you'd been after her. And then you went into the cottage.

Paddy was all for your having an 'accident' . . ." He paused a moment, gazing at Ann, letting that sink in. "But I was set against harming anyone. Always have been." His voice took on a greater earnestness. "That's what I really want you to see. That I mean no harm. So I decided the best thing was just to keep close tabs on you. And the easiest way to do that was to make friends."

Ann saw what he meant. The truth of the whole Cashel incident dawned on her. "So you had those men chase us at Cashel just so you could rescue us? Sure. Naturally. We'd have to trust a friend. Especially a fellow American!" She was angry at herself now. Angry for having trusted Butler and not her husband. "Damn! John said you'd invited us here just so you could keep an eye on us. He was right!"

"A bright young man," said Butler. "Of course, that's only helped you get more involved with this. You just *had* to keep at it. Keep digging. Nosing around. In the end, you didn't leave me much choice."

"Except to kidnap us and drag us here," she said angrily.

"I can explain," he said in that still assuring, still friendly tone. "I can convince you that I'm right, I think, if I've read your hearts clearly. You've got to give me a chance."

"All right," she challenged, hands on hips. "I'm ready. Convince me."

"It won't be much good unless your husband's here, too," he said. He glanced at his watch. "And time's flying by. I've got to go now, Mrs. Milne. See if I can't make some arrangements to get your husband rounded up soon."

"You'd better not hurt him," she said fiercely.

"I told you I wouldn't," he said, but added grimly, "unless he doesn't give us any choice. Best pray that he does, Mrs. Milne."

chapter
twenty-three

✦

I have walked and prayed for this young child an hour
And heard the sea-wind scream upon the tower,
And under the arches of the bridge, and scream
In the elms above the flooded stream;
Imagining in excited reverie
That the future years had come,
Dancing to a frenzied drum,
Out of the murderous innocence of the sea.

—W. B. YEATS: "A Prayer for My Daughter"

As John Milne felt his way slowly through the Burren, a fine rain began to fall. He had put his cloth cap in his jacket pocket, but decided against putting it on. The cool wet felt too good against the throbbing heat of his wound. The slight bleeding seemed to have stopped, but he was afraid to touch the spot and find out.

Shortly he came upon a road and was able to move along with a little more speed. It was not too much longer before he saw the buildings of a little village, so colorless as to seem a natural feature of the land around them.

It occurred to him that he could call Father Bonaventure

from here and have the monk come and get him. With that in mind, he slipped on the cap to somewhat hide his wound and walked boldly into the place, looking around for a likely spot to phone.

It was a very small place with half a dozen houses on either side of the road and one or two small shops. He saw no one on the streets as he moved along, but after passing one of the shops he heard footsteps behind him and felt a hand close on his arm.

"Excuse me, sir?" said a nervous voice, and he turned to find a short, round-faced man beside him, looking anxiously into his face.

"What is it?" he asked in an abrupt way. He tried to pull his arm loose, but it was tightly held, and the effort caused him to stagger slightly.

"Are you all right, sir?"

"Yes, I'm all right. I'm just looking for a phone."

"You're hurt, sir," said the man, looking at the dried blood visible below the brim of the cap. "Let me help you."

"Just a slight accident," John explained. "I'm not really hurt. I only need to find a phone."

"Certainly," the man agreed. "Just come along with me."

He led John back and into the tiny shop he had passed. It was a chemist's shop, John noted without interest, its shelves and counters filled with medicines for both man and beast.

"I saw you go by, and you seemed not to be walking well," the chemist explained as he eased John down into a chair. "Can I get you something?"

"No, no," John assured him, relaxing gratefully. "I just need someone to pick me up. Where's your phone?"

"Right here." The man pointed to the instrument on a desk at the back. "But let me make the call for you. You seem tired. Stay there and rest."

John agreed, thankful for the chance to rest and still content to let it all be taken out of his hands. He gave the man the abbey's number, his own name, and the name of whom to ask for there. Then he rested his head back and closed his eyes.

Vaguely he was aware of the man dialing, of the faint clicks of the old-fashioned rotary dial turning and running back. Then some unconscious warning snapped his eyes open again.

Something was very wrong. The first digit of the abbey's number was three. The dial had been turned too far for that . . . hadn't it?

Quietly John got to his feet and walked up behind the chemist, who had now finished dialing and was waiting while the phone rang. Over the man's shoulder John glimpsed a notepad lying by the phone. When the chemist realized how near he was, the man moved a hand to cover it, but not before John saw the number scrawled there.

It was the number of Dunraven Manor.

"Hello?" said the man when the phone was answered. "I have a Mr. Milne here. He's needing a ride and told me to call you. Ah, you'll pick him up then? Fine. I'm the chemist in Midhir. And he should wait here? Yes, I'll tell him."

But when he hung up the phone and turned around, there was no one there to tell.

John was racing down the street as if some demon pursued him. He turned in between two houses and stopped there, fighting for breath, head pounding again.

Was every village around there owned by Butler, he wondered? And now the man had been alerted to his presence here. Somehow he would have to get very far away, and very quickly.

The man from the chemist's shop did not seem to be pursuing him so, after a moment's rest, he continued up the street. At the sight of an old bicycle propped against a wall by the local pub, he stopped again and looked around. There was no sign of anyone. The bicycle was quite unprotected.

"No time for scruples," John told himself. He lifted the bike, got casually on, and rode out of the village, picking up speed as he went.

Soon he was wheeling along the narrow lanes, a fair breeze blowing the fine rain in his face. He kept himself headed toward the south as much as possible on the winding ways, pedaling as fast as he could and wishing he had stolen a bicycle with gears instead of the ancient collection of rusty pipes he was now riding. He'd been almost done in before he started, and he wasn't sure how long he could push himself on.

The nature of the country changed as he rode. The Burren landscape was slowly replaced by green meadows and low, forested hills. Thick vegetation closed in along the road, and stone walls appeared to mark the grazing pastures.

If he were coming out of the Burren, John prayed it was on the south side. If he remembered the map correctly, that would mean he was only a few miles from Ballymurroe.

When he first noticed the sound of an engine on the road behind him, he ignored it, until it slowly dawned upon his fatigue-befuddled brain that anyone guessing his direction of flight could have followed him from that last village. He had just time to stop and pull the bicycle into the cover of a thicket before an auto rounded a bend he had just passed and came into his view.

It was the blue Volvo.

It came up the road and went by his hiding place without slowing. The two men in it were intent only on the road ahead. John watched it until it was out of sight, then sat down and looked at his bicycle in despair.

His ill luck was holding. His only means of transportation was now useless to him. Butler's men could easily patrol the roads he would have to travel. Plus, who knew how many more of the local folks would be helping watch for him. He couldn't move in the open anymore, knowing his pursuers might appear ahead or behind at any moment. He would have to abandon the bike and go on foot, across country, avoiding the roads as much as possible.

Wishing the ancient vehicle good luck, he left it and went through the thicket into a large field. He crossed it at a jog, pushing his way through a herd of cattle that sat placidly unconcerned. Beyond them he found a narrow lane that pointed generally southward, and he began to walk parallel to it, stumbling through the underbrush that edged it, concentrating only on closing the distance between himself and Ballymurroe.

Ann Milne heard a key turn in the lock of her bedroom door. The door opened and O'Gadhra gestured sharply to her.

"Come on, then," he said brusquely. "The Old Man wants you moved elsewhere."

"Where?" she asked.

"Someplace a bit more comfortable," he said. "Someplace he can explain things better to you. And he thought you might just be lonely."

"I'm fine here," she said stubbornly.

He sighed. "Come along, Mrs. Milne," he coaxed her. "Be a good girl now. I can guarantee you you'll find the new place agreeable."

She hadn't much to lose, and there was no point fighting. Any change might be an improvement anyway. She nodded acceptance and got up.

O'Gadhra ushered her into the hall and stayed close beside her. He guided her along the corridors of the manor. She accompanied him without argument, unable to see any clear means of escape. They went through the main hall, up the central staircase, and along the gallery. At the far end he stopped. They faced a doorway boarded over with thick planks. It looked unmovable until he produced a key and turned a hidden lock. Then it opened outward like a door.

"Where are we going?" she asked uncertainly.

"Into the old tower. This is the only way into it from the house."

Inside, a small vestibule contained a second door and a narrow, circular staircase. He led on up the staircase to another door, unlocked this too, and ushered her in ahead of him.

She stepped through, expecting to find a gutted ruin. Instead, she found herself in a vast room, vaulted and hung with draperies. But her first impression of it was fleeting. Her attention was focused on the two figures seated at a table across the room from them, looking toward them in amazement.

They were Nancy Trahern and her daughter, Bridget.

"Have a nice reunion," O'Gadhra told her. He slammed the heavy wood door closed behind her, and another key grated in its lock.

But Ann didn't care at the moment about being locked in again. She was fully taken by her unexpected reunion with the missing woman and girl.

The three of them exclaimed their joy and surprise together. The Traherns rose from the table and came to meet Ann, each grasping one of her hands in a tight grip.

"Well, I'm certainly glad to finally find you," Ann said. "But I can't say I'm too happy about the way I did it."

"For my part, I hoped never to see you here," said Nancy Trahern. "How did this happen?"

"The same way it probably happened to you, I'm afraid," said Ann. "We got too close to something to be let go."

"I'm sorry for that," Nancy Trahern said regretfully. "But you said 'we.' Where's John?"

"John is still on the loose . . . I think," said Ann. "They missed catching him."

"A great pity that may be for Mr. Butler," Nancy said with obvious pleasure. Then, more anxiously, she said to Ann, "And are you all right? You aren't hurt?"

"No, no," Ann assured her. "How about you two?"

"We've been comfortable enough. Mr. Butler has provided us with necessities and books and even games for Bridget. But come, let's sit down now."

They all went to the massive table at which the Traherns had been sitting and took chairs there. A silver bowl of fruit, a crystal decanter of water, and fine cut-glass goblets sat on its polished surface.

For the first time, Ann made an assessment of her surroundings. They impressed her. This was a place from another time. The open room rose up a full two stories to an arched ceiling roofed with heavy, age-blackened beams. A fire burned in a pit in the floor's center, its smoke floating up to disappear through a hole in the roof. Gleaming black slate floored the room, and richly colored tapestries covered the curved walls. Open areas of wall between them were mounted with displays of medieval armor and weapons, and the giant skeleton of a prehistoric reindeer stood at one side, its antlers reaching up six feet above its skull.

At the room's far end was a heavy, curtained, four-poster bed and a writing desk. The rest of the room was sparsely furnished. Benches lined the walls and several chairs sat around the fire. It was at once a spartan and exotic decor, fit for a warlord's lair.

"Just what is this place?" she asked.

"Butler's real living quarters, we think," said Nancy. "The whole tower's closed off secretly from the rest."

"He said he hadn't restored it," said Ann.

"Another of his little mysteries," Nancy replied. "Oh, he's got plenty of those, that one has. But now, about you." She leaned toward Ann and spoke earnestly. "You should never have come into this, my dear. It has nothing to do with you."

"It involved you," said Ann. "You're our friends. That's enough."

"You did as you wished, I suppose, but you *were* taking much too great a chance to come to this place on a visit."

"You knew we were here?" Ann asked.

"Of course we did. Once Butler knew you had been our friends, he asked about you. We knew about every move you made. He said he wanted to keep you out of this, and hoped we would help him."

"Did you?"

"Well, I wanted you out, too," Nancy said. "I tried to

convince him you were—forgive me—harmless young fools. And he might have ignored you if you hadn't kept up your hunt. We saw you out our windows the day you came. We're kept in a room below this one most times. It was maddening not to be able to warn you. Bridget cried to see you."

"I don't cry now," said Bridget in a quiet, careful way. "I've got past it."

"I'm sure you have," Ann assured her.

She wanted to comfort the girl somehow. Bridget had suffered the most in this. Torn from her home to escape fear, and plunged into a worse nightmare instead. Ann wanted to tell her that her father was near, looking for her, but blocked the impulse. There was no way to be sure that someone wasn't listening in, and the less Butler knew, the better.

"You know, Bridget," she said instead, "we never would have started this without Taffy."

"Oh, poor Taffy," said the girl. "Is he safe? I made him run away when we were taken."

"He's fine," Ann told her. "Father Bonaventure has him at the abbey." She turned to Nancy. "But tell me now: why are they holding you? Just what exactly are they doing here that's so important they had to kidnap you to keep it a secret?"

"I think I'm the best one to answer that question, Mrs. Milne."

She turned in surprise to see Butler himself standing near the fire.

He had come without a sound. She had heard no turning key, no opening door. He was just quite suddenly there, smiling his warm smile at them.

As she looked at him, standing there amidst the medieval elegance, she was struck, as her husband had been, with the feeling that this was a stage carefully set for some production of his. Only this one wasn't going to be on film.

"So, how do you like my private keep, Mrs. Milne?" he asked her, stepping toward the table. "I'm very proud of it."

"It's quite a place," she told him truthfully. "I can't understand why you're risking it."

"Risking it? I've taken no risks." He sat down at the table with them. She noted that the amiable Western drawl had vanished now, replaced by the soft, rich burr of a light Irish accent. "That's the very reason why the Traherns are being held here. No one will know what great task I'm upon until I have succeeded in it."

She shook her head. "I still don't understand any of this."

"I intend to explain," he said smoothly, reassuringly. "That's why I had you and the Traherns brought here for this little reunion. I hoped that your finding them safe would convince you I don't mean harm to any of you. I want you to believe that what I'm doing is meant only to help you . . . help Ireland."

"You may say that, Mr. Butler," said Nancy Trahern in uncompromising terms, "but it's a hard task you've given yourself to make us believe you."

"Or me," said Ann. "If we'd left it all to you like you wanted us to, we'd have never found out what happened to our friends."

"No. You'd have gone safely home with some believable story about what happened to them. And when my goal was reached, they would have been set free. No harm to anyone."

"You claim," Ann retorted skeptically.

"I'm speaking the truth, Ann," he said earnestly as his piercing gaze held hers. "I think that you believe me, deep inside. I've a feeling about you. I've had it since we first met. You're a sensitive woman who understands the country. We share that spirit, you and I. It's why I believe that if I explain what I'm doing here, you'll come to understand why it's right."

"Why tell me now?" Ann challenged him. "What changed your mind? You said before you were going to wait until you had John here, too."

For the first time Butler's vast confidence faltered. His gaze slid uncomfortably away from hers.

"Because you can't get him, can you!" she crowed. "That's it. You can't find John, so you only have me."

"It's true your husband is still at large," he admitted guardedly, "but I'm really not concerned. I've even called my own people back in from the hunt. The locals have been told to keep an eye out for him. People are watching your cottage and the abbey. They'll find him or he'll show up on his own. I'm sure we'll get him here eventually. In any case, he won't go to the *Gardai*."

"Not if he thinks you might hurt me," she said pointedly.

"That can't be helped," he said more harshly. "Your own judgments created this situation. You decided I must be up to something criminal. But you don't really have any idea what that thing is. I only want to explain. I've no intent at all to harm you."

That made her angry. "Really? Is that why John is wandering alone somewhere with a wound on his head and your people hunting him?"

"Take it easy, Mrs. Milne," Butler soothed. "I'm sure he's resting in some safe place, trying to work this out."

Ann wasn't certain whether she hoped that or not. Her husband had changed so much lately—and so had she. She couldn't say now what he'd do, or even what she wanted him to do.

"Aren't you afraid the monks will call the police?" she asked him. "They know what we know."

"Which is very, very little. They don't even know where you are now. You made that happen by leaving here as you did. If you had gone straight to the abbey, I might not have been able to do anything to stop you. As it was, you gave my men a perfect chance to catch you alone once you left O'Brien's Tower."

"You saw us at the tower?" she said.

"Of course. You were followed and watched. That's how my men knew where to set the trap."

Something else occurred to her at this. "Wait a minute. Then did you have something to do with those birds? Those black ones that attacked us?"

"They were of my doing, yes," he admitted.

"And you say you don't mean to harm us?" she cried in outrage. "Those . . . whatever they were ; . . nearly chased us over the cliff!"

"That was accidental," he assured. "Their mission was simply to detain you at the tower, giving my men time to arrive and set a trap in the Burren. The birds had no real power to harm you, you see. They were purely illusions."

"Illusions," she repeated, considering him curiously. "Like some kind of special effects?"

"Simple creations compared to some spectacles I've put on film," he said. He fixed a searching look on her, and his tone became more musing. "But, tell *me* something now, Ann. Just why was it you left safety and rushed out to that tower? It was a strange thing to do. Just what were you about there?"

Ann felt a twinge of uncertainty. Did he know about Trahern? She had to be careful. She didn't want to give him anything he could use.

"We had to get away and talk." She tried to sound casual, too. As if it were of no importance. "We wanted to go someplace away from here, where we knew nobody could listen in on us. If someone was watching us, we hoped they'd just think we were sightseeing."

She wasn't sure how believable that sounded, but it seemed to satisfy Butler. She decided he hadn't been looking for an ulterior motive and had just been curious. That made her feel a little more hopeful. If he didn't know about Trahern, then she and her husband had at least one other ally who could still act freely. That was something, anyway.

"All right, then," he said. "None of that matters now. You're here. The only choice left for you is to listen to me, accept my cause, and help your husband do so, too."

"A little hard if he's not here," she said.

"But he could be," Butler said, "if you would tell me where he's most likely to be."

"And if I don't?" she said defiantly.

He leaned toward her. The blue eyes flashed a hard light, and a distinct sound of menace came into his voice.

"You're not that naïve, Ann Milne," he snapped out. "I mean to explain what I'm doing, and I hope you accept it. But if you don't, you are going to be a guest here for a very long time. Do you understand that?"

chapter
twenty-four
ᚕ

Remember all those renowned generations,
They left their bodies to fatten the wolves,
They left their homesteads to fatten the foxes,
Fled to far countries or sheltered themselves
In cavern, crevice or hole,
Defending Ireland's soul.

—W. B. YEATS: *"Three Marching Songs"*

Ann Milne looked into the hard gaze and saw the cold truth there. She nodded.

"I understand."

"Then listen," said Butler. He sat back, and his voice took on a deep, grand tone. "I have a most important mission here. It involves the future of this land and its people. Many have already come to understand it and accept."

"Like the Ryans, I suppose," said Ann.

"The Ryans have been very helpful," Butler admitted. "Like most true dwellers upon this sod, they're loyal—both to me and to their past. They and others are helping in a cause they believe to be a most important one."

"And what would that cause be?"

"To help me fulfill a great destiny," he pronounced in a noble way. "To help me bring a new glory to Ireland!"

"You're a liar!" Nancy Trahern spat out bitterly. "I can listen to no more of this." She looked to Ann. "This cursed man is in league with the IRA!"

"The IRA?" Ann repeated, aghast.

"Of course. It's how I became suspicious of Mr. Butler. Why we came to be made captive here. I saw a man I shouldn't have seen, and he led me to this place."

"Who was it?" said Ann. "Was it the man you saw at the *Teac*?"

"Yes . . . and several times taking his lorry through the town. I knew about him in the North. He was an IRA gunman and driver there, but he'd gone south into the Republic and disappeared. When I saw he was here, I worried about why."

"That was my one mistake," Butler put in. "But my dear lady, how was I to know that someone living in this town would have your insight . . . and your experience."

She ignored the compliment. "I watched him at the music house," she went on. "I saw him talk with two musicians there. Then I discovered the link Mr. Butler had with them. I saw fat envelopes changing hands far more than once. And I found other proof of his involvement soon enough. Three cold nights I waited by those old gateposts and saw that same lorry driving into these very grounds."

"It did come in through that gateway, then!" Ann exclaimed. "We followed that truck, too. We drove in on the road looking for it. And we saw that picture you painted of the posts, in your cottage."

"It was a piece I did out of a strong impulse," the older woman said. "Once I knew of this man's involvement, a sense of something dark and dangerous came on me. I felt myself in peril. I felt I must leave some kind of record. But," Nancy added ruefully, "I'm sorry I did it if it helped bring you here."

"Thank you for mentioning it, though, Mrs. Milne," Butler put in. "Paddy missed it when he checked over the cot-

tage for anything you might have left that pointed at me. I'll
have to send him back."

Ann reprimanded herself sharply for her slip. She had to
guard every word. This was no friendly conversation they
were having.

"But why is the truck so important?" she asked Butler.
"What's it for?"

"To help me fulfill the destiny I mentioned," he replied.
"One that I've awaited for many years."

"To smuggle in weapons for the IRA to hide at Dunraven
is what I say," said Nancy Trahern tersely. "He's in league
with the bloody terrorists."

Weapons! Ann thought. Well, it was certainly possible a
man like Butler could be involved. Thousands of Irish Americans supported the IRA cause in the North, and millions
more condoned the group's violent actions.

"It *would* be easy for you," she said to Butler accusingly.
"The famous filmmaker. Resources all over the world.
Money. You could probably smuggle *tanks* into this country."

"Perhaps I could," he agreed, "but you're very wrong,
Ann. I'm bringing no weapons here. You must believe that.
Why, I loathe all the modern means of waging war. They're
dishonorable and depersonalizing things. Oh, I'll admit that
I've had dealings with some radical IRA splinter groups. Yes,
I set up the *Teac an Ceoil* to use for a safe meeting place with
members of their network. And I've hired men from their
ranks to help me. Men like Paddy, one of the Black Geese."

"Black Geese?" Ann repeated.

"They're Irishmen who left the country and went seeking
their fortunes fighting in dirty little wars in countless places
about the world. Paddy's been at war somewhere since he
was sixteen. It's taught him all kinds of useful things—
mostly violent. One day he and others like him realized their
talents could be of use in the troubles back home. Some are
in the North, training men for the fighting. Paddy decided to
join my cause. Though he left most of his tact and subtlety
behind long ago, he's still a smart one. He saw and accepted

the chance to attain a higher goal and a greater glory—with me."

"You're only admitting further that you *are* in with those devils," said Mrs. Trahern, "for all of your fine talk."

"You don't understand yet, do you?" he countered. "My purpose goes far beyond theirs. I'll admit I've befriended them. And I've paid them money, too. Partly that was to gain help and materials I wished to bring secretly here, to restore this tower and do . . . other things. Partly that was to foster the radical cause and to speed the coming chaos. But not for their misguided purposes. For a much larger goal of my own: to restore the true Irish Soul."

"Irish soul?" Ann repeated, not understanding.

His eyes met hers searchingly again. His voice was emphatic, persuasive: "My only thought, my dear Ann, is for what Ireland should be; what it was before; and what it will be once again. A place of immense pride and towering heroes, of gallant deeds and bold spirits. I want to unleash the fiery heart of this land that was made hostage so long ago."

"You mean, by the British?"

"They are only part of it. Only the most recent manifestation of a plague that has infected us for a hundred generations. Civilization!"

He spat out this last word as if it were a vile thing. When he continued, his voice was tinged with both great bitterness and deep regret.

"The wasting illness came on Ireland in many ways. Oh, we missed the Romans and the first symptoms of the disease that they spread across Celtic Europe with their roads and cities and mass government. Then we became the last bastion of the older way of life. The last bit of freedom and fancy on the outmost rim of the world left untouched by the new, cold, organized view of life that had contaminated the rest.

"But the sickness crept upon us too at last. It came first on the feet of the far-wandering missionary priests, carrying the first germs abroad in the form of Christianity with its vast bureaucracy and strangling regimentation. Then came the Normans with their own laws and order, seizing any lands the church had left. The later British governments with their so-called age of reason finished the task, brutally imposing a rigid imperial control that even the Romans would have admired.

"And so the last bit of the old world we had here came to its end. Eire was left with her lands barren, her beliefs dying, and more millions of her children dead than would have been taken by any real plague." He fixed his gaze full on Nancy Trahern. "And you, lady, who are so farsighted, so aware, so truly Irish in heart, you must believe the tale I spin is true."

"I do know that it's terrible things that have been inflicted on Ireland in these hundreds of years," she admitted. "Still, there's nothing now anyone can do to change it. The past is done. The old ways are gone."

"You're wrong," Butler said fiercely. "They *can* come again. And I have the means to bring them."

"And just how is that?" Mrs. Trahern shot back. "Through more fighting? More terror? More deaths? No, no. I've grown sick of it." She put a hand upon her daughter's arm. "*We've* grown sick. And we'll have no more of it, no matter what fine names you put to your supposed cause. No more violence!"

"But none would be needed!" Butler assured her. "That's what I most want you to understand"—he looked to Ann—"and you as well. No one would be hurt if you and others accepted, believed."

"Believed in what?" said Ann. "Just exactly what plan do you have? What kind of means to make it work? If you want to convince us, tell us that."

He considered a moment, then shook his head. "I can't," he said in a tone touched by regret. "Not until I know that I have your full trust. Not until I'm certain there is no threat."

"From John, you mean," she said. "So you *do* believe he's dangerous to you. You know there's something he can do."

He ignored that. "Please, just tell me where he is or where he might go, Ann," he asked coaxingly. "Help us find him. It's for the best. Once he's here, I can reveal to you both the full extent of my secret. It would convince you. Trust me. Help me find him."

His words did sway her. The voice—so filled with certainty and power—again had that effect of drawing out a willingness to believe.

And there were the bright, penetrating eyes so close, locked unwinkingly upon hers. Within the blue glow of their twin discs she seemed to see images of her husband's form. John seemed in peril, stumbling through the rocks, falling, staggering on. He looked quite lost and alone in a barren land. He stared about wildly, panic in his face. He needed her!

The idea came that perhaps Butler was right. She was not helping John by letting him go on. She was endangering him. But she could still save him. Yes. She had only to trust Butler.

Mrs. Trahern noted her expression, saw the wavering of will reflected there. She quickly spoke.

"Be careful, Ann. It's a bard's honeyed tongue that he has, surely. But it's a serpent's fangs that he has hidden as well. We've seen them."

The cold words brought Ann back to reality. How could she trust this man? Anger at herself washed through her. John had been suspicious from the start. He warned her, but she hadn't believed. Her own hesitations had helped put her husband in jeopardy. From now on she could have no more doubts.

She sat back, looking away from Butler. His enrapturing aura was dispelled. She shook her head.

"You haven't said anything to make me believe you," she said firmly. "And I certainly won't betray John to you."

His face tightened. His voice grew icy. "Then you force me to other means, Mrs. Milne," he said in warning. He got to his feet, towering over the three women, his ominous words booming out. "Best pray that when you do see my full powers demonstrated, it will not be upon your husband!"

. . .

The dark-robed figure appeared once again upon the high rooftop. It looked out across a countryside grown gray and hazy from the overcast, misty day.

After gazing about, it moved to a roof corner. Striking a pose balanced on the roof's edge, it stretched a hand straight upward toward the sky. The mouth concealed within the hood intoned a guttural chant.

As the strange, singsong words rolled upward toward the overcast, the flat ceiling of cloud right above began to roil, like the inverted surface of a thick stew coming to a boil. Soon afterward a whole section of the gray cover a hundred yards across bulged downward, as if it were the swelling underbelly of some monstrous beast.

This circular protrusion grew darker, seeming to draw in and concentrate the overcast's force to become an angry black thunderhead thrust far downward, lights like flares of lightning flickering within its boiling mass.

It dropped yet lower, the edges of the enormous bulge now tearing free of the upper sea of clouds that closed in instantly behind it. The mass became a separate entity, flattening into a huge, slowly wheeling disc trailing sharp streamers that made it resemble a spinning buzz-saw blade.

The black disc continued to drop until it hovered only a dozen yards above the cloaked figure. A low, faint, but distinct rumbling sound came from it. But not like the sound of thunder. Like the murmuring voices of a great crowd far away.

The robed figure cried out to the swirling cloud a sharp command. It swept both arms out about it to encompass all the surrounding countryside.

"*Iarr! Faigh!*" the voice rapped out. Both outstretched hands clenched tight. "*Sgrios* John Milne!"

The black disc began to move. It swept about the rooftop in a tight circle, then began to spiral outward in increasingly wider rings.

The dark one upon the roof pivoted slowly and watched the disc grow farther away in its continuing circumnavigations. Finally the object shrank away to a small black saucer just above the far horizon, so solid in appearance at the distance that it seemed more like some alien spacecraft now.

Finally, at one point, it abruptly paused. It hung suspended for some seconds over a distant and invisible place on the ground.

Then it began slowly to shrink earthward.

John Milne felt he'd walked for miles when another village appeared ahead of him. He stopped at its outskirts and examined it from cover.

The misty weather had made the day quite cool, and he could smell the odor of peat from the cottage fires hanging in the air. It made him think of their own little cottage, their cozy vacation home, so secure and so far away.

That had been a dream, and he had been awakened from it. He had never come on a vacation. He had wandered these fields alone for a thousand years. He had died in some nameless battle for some unremembered cause and been left unburied, to roam the land for the rest of time.

He wanted badly to go into the village, go to a house, ask for help and a place to rest. But he couldn't. He was afraid of who might see him, of who might have Butler's number by their phone.

He knew he would have to work his way around the village if he wanted to go on, but he was too tired. He needed a place to sit quietly and regain his strength.

To his right the gray pile of a large ruin showed in the trees. It was an abandoned monastery, its plain, square tower thrusting its point up toward the flat ceiling of the overhanging clouds. Around it, canted and broken gravestones were scattered like the stumps of a hewn forest of trees, showing whitely with their thick coatings of mold.

In his present state of mind, the place appealed to John as a most appropriate place to rest, just as the dolmen had done. He moved through the trees toward it. He entered through one of the gaping holes in its broken outer walls and wandered through the roofless structure. He came to one of the hallways that led into the cloister, and it seemed to him that this might be a place to hide safely.

Here, now, today, that dark and overgrown space within held no terror for him. The spirits of the monks that inhabited it invited him in, whispering that he would be safe there, that he would never be found.

He walked in and lay down, almost falling, on the thick mat of dead foliage that carpeted the space. He was very weary, and he lay limply on his back, looking up through the roof of interlacing vines to the gray sky above.

Very soon he was asleep.

While he slept, the whirling disc of cloud dropped lower and lower above the monastery. As it reached a point only feet above the structure's tower, its shape began to change again. This time it assumed a concave form. Its sides dropped down until they reached the ground, enclosing all the building in a dome whose gray-black wall obscured sight of the ruin within, as if the monastery were a miniature encased in a smoked-glass dome.

Inside the dome there fell a deep silence as all sounds of the outer world were cut off. From the dark matter of the walls, shapes began coalescing, forming shadowed figures that detached themselves from the mass, stepping out to freedom, then creeping into the ruins from all sides.

A faint sound—a metallic clattering—awakened John and he roused to a semiconsciousness.

His fatigue-weighted mind fought to bring him back to full awareness, but it was too difficult. His upward gaze showed him that the sky above had become extremely dark. Had he slept until nightfall?

He propped himself up to look around. The cloister was plunged in a deeper gloom. Turning his head slowly, he saw a flickering of yet darker shadows on the stone walls of the passages into the cloister.

But it wasn't the benign spirits of the monks that now manifested themselves to him. The forms that came into view were more baleful: men wasted and white as if from long death. The shreds of long tunics and flowing cloaks fluttered about their bony frames. Teeth showing in rictus smiles gleamed in their skull-like heads, but nothing save blackness showed where their eyes had been.

The ghastly warriors poured into the cloister from all parts of the ruin, forming a solid ring about the still reclining Milne. The skeletal hands of the figures clutched round shields and swords and spears. Keen-honed blades and points glinted with malevolent light. They lifted to threaten the trapped man.

John scrambled to his feet, gazing about him. It was a dream, like before, he told himself. But this was no dream. He shook his head, and they didn't vanish. He was fully awake.

As one, the ring of beings started to move upon him.

Nearby lay an upturned, rotting wheelbarrow and a rusty scythe—the abandoned tools of some long-gone gardener. John seized the cutting implement, swinging out desperately at the attackers.

To his amazement, the curved blade slashed through the forms without harming them. The cuts opened by the wind of the whipping scythe reclosed at once.

He redoubled his efforts, wheeling around, sweeping the blade with all the speed and power he could muster.

It was for nothing. The grim warriors were not even slowed in their approach.

They were only feet from him now. A collective blast of coldness, as of the grave, welled out from them to strike him like a solid force. It took his breath. He staggered, tried to recover, but tripped across the upturned barrow, crashing heavily to the ground.

He tried to rise again, but his sore, stiffened muscles refused to obey further. He groaned and fell back, his brain whirling, his head pounding. It really didn't matter, he thought as the creatures closed in. They could just take him. What difference did it make? It had all been hopeless from the start.

The cadaverous figures loomed above him in a tight ring. Their weapons rose to strike.

CHAPTER
TWENTY-FIVE

Upon a grey old battered tombstone
In Glendalough beside the stream,
Where the O'Byrnes and Byrnes are buried,
He stretched his bones and fell in a dream
Of sun and moon that a good hour
Bellowed and pranced in the round tower;

—W. B. YEATS: *"Under the Round Tower"*

Something scraped in one of the passages beyond the tightening ring of figures. Another shadowy shape came into view.

It stopped as it came within the cloister, raising its arms. A low, sharp chanting voice issued from it.

The host of beings whirled toward it as if alarmed. As the chanting went on emphatically, they raised their arms in a gesture of defense. A collective wail as of the lost of Hell came from them. Then they began to melt.

In moments they had sunk into a ring of gauzy shadow about Milne that broke apart and fluttered upward in shreds, vanishing through the covering of vines. At the same time the gray-black dome about the place dissipated like a smoke ring shredded by a hard puff. Its fragments, with the rest, drifted up to be swallowed by the overcast.

The heavy gloom retreated from the cloister. A lighter gray sky was visible above. The figure moved forward to stand beside John Milne, peering down at him.

Realizing nothing had happened to him, John opened his eyes. He looked in bewilderment up toward a face that was only a shadow against the light above.

"Are you all right?" said a voice that at first sounded very far away.

But the voice was familiar. And it seemed to make his distress ebb away. The face moved closer as the figure stooped lower. Its features grew clearer, and suddenly he knew them.

"Mr. O'Teague!" he gasped out in surprise.

John couldn't believe that the little tinker was really there but, real or fantasy, he was a fair sight to see.

"What . . . what were those things?" he gasped out.

"Things?" said O'Teague vaguely, shaking his head. "I saw nothing but you lying here. 'Twas a dream you had, most likely."

"Dream?" said John, lifting his head up to look around the empty space.

"Mr. Milne, what's happened to you?" O'Teague asked. "Where's your wife?"

"Butler has her," he said. He struggled to a sitting position and grasped the man's arm, pulling him closer. "They're looking for me. It's not safe anywhere."

"Aye. I believe you," the tinker said gravely. "These may have been just smoke and fancy, but I've a feeling someone a bit more real is comin' soon."

"I've got to get out of here," John said urgently. "Got to go!"

He tried to rise but the effort drained him. He lay back and closed his eyes again.

From a great distance a voice, reassuring in its tones, drifted to him.

"I'll help you, Mr. Milne. You just sleep."

.   :   .

John Milne was still asleep. It was a restless sleep, interrupted by odd, unclear dreams and feelings of motion.

He was aware of awakening once and experiencing a soft, jogging sensation. His body moved up and down rhythmically and continuously. Faint thumping and jangling sounds accompanied the movement.

He opened his eyes and looked around him with vague curiosity. He seemed to be in a box, but determined it was too large for a coffin and too colorfully decorated. The roof above him was gayly painted in blues and greens, and there was furniture around him: a chair, a table, even a tiny stove.

His observations got no further than this. Assured he was still alive, he allowed himself to drift off again, lulled by the soothing motion.

When he finally awoke again, he was fairly alert. This time he found himself lying on a bed in a darkened room. Confused by the twisted web of reality and fantasy that had been spun in his mind during his flight, he sat up to try to orient himself.

There was a twinge of pain in his head as he moved, and he raised his hand to his temple. It was bandaged now, the blood cleaned away.

He looked about him more searchingly, more anxiously, expecting that the room was in Dunraven, that he had in fact been caught and taken there.

There was a certain resemblance to the place in the height and size of the room, but it lacked the plushness of Butler's manor. The bed on which he lay was little more than a cot. The only other furnishings were a washstand and a bureau.

He got to his feet, groaning as he shifted his muscles, and walked to the windows. Pulling aside the heavy draperies that closed them, he looked out.

The scene presented to him was a most pastoral one of meadows and gardens. Far off to one side he could just glimpse the corner of a building that seemed of a modern style. He shook his head, trying to puzzle out what was so familiar to him in this. Then the door opened behind him, and he wheeled about to see Father Bonaventure watching him apprehensively.

John's confusion sorted itself out. He was at Glendon Abbey.

"Are you feeling better?" asked the monk.

"Fine," John assured him. "A little dizzy and sore, but everything works. Did Mr. O'Teague bring me here?"

"Yes. In his caravan. It was well he did. He was stopped by some local lads in Adhair and asked if he had seen the likes of you on the road. It seems there's quite the hunt on hereabouts for you."

"You didn't call the police?" John asked him with concern.

"We decided against it. We had no idea what had happened. It seemed that you were hurt only slightly, and I felt it would be safe enough to wait for you to awaken. Are you well enough now to come downstairs and tell us your story?"

John told the monk he was and then followed him down through the corridors of the abbey to the common dining room. It was deserted except for Mr. O'Teague, who sat at one of the long dining tables drinking from a mug.

"Ah, it's good to see you on your feet again," the tinker said happily as John came in.

"The rest of the brothers dined some while ago," Bonaventure said. "I'll bring you some food," he promised and went out.

"What time is it?" John asked the tinker, sitting down at the table across from him.

"Nearly five in the afternoon. You've been asleep a short while."

"Five?" John repeated. Then it had been six hours since Ann had been taken. Six hours she had been in Butler's hands. He had to keep his mind from dwelling on that. "How did you find me, Mr. O'Teague?"

"Fate again, I think," the tinker said. "I was on my way from Gort to arrive here late today, as we decided yesterday.

As I came into the village, I saw you going into that old ruin. I thought it was you and I had to see. Finding you in trouble, I brought you to the only place that you'd told me you thought safe. The monks were all a help, and this Bonaventure is a wonder."

"He is, and you are, and I thank you and whatever gods are helping," said John fervently. "Are you sure nobody knows I'm here?"

"I know no one saw me bring you here. But they're surely looking. A pair of fellows in an auto stopped me to ask if I'd seen anyone on the roads."

"Father Bonaventure told me. They're not trying to hide their little conspiracy from us much anymore. They know I don't dare go to the police."

Bonaventure reentered the room. He was bearing a tray and was accompanied by a large yellow dog. With a great, bounding stride, the animal rushed to Milne, planted its forepaws on his chest, and lapped him wetly with its big tongue.

"Taffy!" said Milne with warmth. "I wasn't sure I'd see you again. What are you doing in here?"

"It's allowed," Bonaventure said laughingly as he put down the tray. "In one day's time he's gotten the run of this place. He'd come to own it surely if he stayed. He's a good dog."

"Well, he and I are in the same boat now," Milne said darkly, "and I've got to decide what I'm going to do about it."

"Here, eat first," said the monk, pushing the tray toward Milne. "It's simple food, but it will give you strength. We can talk after you eat."

John obeyed, eating with real vigor once he had started and realized how truly hungry he was.

"Boy, let me tell you, my little trip back here was really strange," he told them as he ate. He briefly described his adventures while on the run. "I still don't know how much of all that was a dream. A few wild things have happened today. You wouldn't believe."

"Just maybe I would, lad," said O'Teague most soberly. "It's a very clever and a very powerful force that's moving against you."

"What, Butler?" John said. "I don't think even his special-effects skills could pull off tricks like I saw."

"There's a great deal more than trickery and illusion to our Lord of Dunraven, young man," the tinker assured. "Be sure of that!"

Though John was somewhat intrigued by the implication in this, he had no chance to quiz the little man further at that point. Their talk was interrupted when a young monk came into the room to inform Bonaventure that yet another visitor had arrived.

He then ushered in Keith Trahern.

Taffy had started across the room in a friendly way to greet the newcomer. Now, recognizing who it was, the dog growled, circled his one time master warily, and came back to stand at John's side in a tense attitude of watchful uncertainty.

"Milne!" said Trahern, ignoring the dog. "You are here."

John was both confused and surprised by his arrival. "I am, but how did you know?"

"The Father told me. I called here only a short while ago."

"Father, why didn't you tell me?" John asked accusingly.

"I wanted you to rest and eat, not be worrying about something else. I simply told Mr. Trahern to come here and talk with you."

"Why did you call here in the first place?" John asked Trahern.

"I came straight back here this morning after our talk and began watching Dunraven as I said I would," Trahern explained. "I expected to see you and your wife return to the place. What I saw instead was your wife, driving in your car, but under the very watchful eye of a stranger.

"There was something wrong in this, I was certain. So I looked for you at the cottages and in the village. It began to distress me more that you weren't to be found, so much so that I phoned up the only other one who knew what you were doing. The rest you know."

"So, Ann really *is* there," John said.

He thought of his wife, helpless in that man's home, and his fear for her turned into anger at Butler. He had Ann's safety as a reason to act now, and this new force swept away the despair that had gripped him, leaving only a red glow of hatred at the heart.

"I want to stop that man and whatever he's doing," he said. "But Ann's got to be safe first. I'm going to have to try to get her out of there. If I can, we can call the police. If I fail, I haven't really lost anything for you. You can do what you want then."

"How will you get her out?" asked Bonaventure. "How will you even find her?"

John looked down at the yellow dog. "I think Taffy might help me with that."

"Taffy?" said Trahern. "What can the dog do?"

"We can talk about that later. Now, I think I'd better leave the abbey. They may not have seen me brought here, but they sure know about Father Bonaventure. They might be watching the place already. Is there somewhere safe around here I could hide until dark? Somewhere close to Dunraven?"

"I know a place," said the tinker with a small, strange laugh. "I can tell you that they won't think to look for you there."

"Okay. Tell me how to get there."

"No. You'd have trouble finding it yourself, and you need a way to get there without being seen. I had better take you in my wagon."

"I don't want you getting into this, Mr. O'Teague," John told him firmly.

The man brushed that aside. "I'm in it now, surely, and I'll not stand aside and watch. I'll stay with you, whether you're liking it or not."

"I'm going, too," said Bonaventure. "You'll be needing

help, and who's going to give it? She's my friend as well, and her harm is my doing for getting you into this at the start."

"And my reasons are stronger than any of yours," Trahern added grimly. "I've both a wife and a daughter in this. If Butler has taken Mrs. Milne, then it's more'n a fair chance he has my family, too."

"All right then, gentlemen," John conceded. "I can't say I mind the company. Shall we get going?"

The tinker looked over the other three men with an appraising eye.

"I'm not so sure about the lot of you," he said. "You'll be a load for my poor old wagon."

"That's no real problem," Bonaventure replied. "I've got to stay a while for evening service. I'll come down later in the car. We might need one."

"Why don't I stay here and wait for you?" Trahern suggested. "We can drive in my car. It's less known around here."

"Good idea," the monk agreed. "Now, Mr. O'Teague, tell me where you're going. I know this area well enough."

"Do you know the old mound called Cormac's Fort?" asked the tinker.

"The old mound?" The monk seemed surprised at first, but then he laughed. "I certainly do, and a perfect place it is."

"What are you talking about?" John demanded, his curiosity thoroughly aroused.

"Don't tell him, Mr. O'Teague," said the monk with a smile. "Let him be surprised."

The tinker's caravan wagon bounced and rocked its way along, and John, seated precariously upon the tiny bed within it, bounced and rocked right along with it.

He looked over the decor of the tiny room to pass the time, but there was very little to see, and he was soon reduced to thumb-twiddling. He had just begun to grow impatient when there was a sudden jerk and the wagon swung sharply around to the right, heeling over like a man-of-war caught in a crosswind.

He grabbed vainly for something solid and ended up on his back on the bed. Wondering where they were turning, he rolled on one side and took a peek out the small window just as the wagon rolled past a large stone gatepost he was surprised to find very familiar.

He had seen it and its mate twice before: once along the side of a dark road, and once in a painting done by Nancy Trahern. His curiosity about where he was going increased considerably.

The wagon rolled slowly along a way that was barely wide enough for it. He heard the branches scraping against its sides. It turned right once more at a fork in the road, went on a short distance further, and stopped with a jolt.

"We've arrived, Mr. Milne," he heard the tinker say. "Come out."

John climbed from the back of the caravan and walked around it to the front, stopping there to stare ahead.

"Well, glory be," he said.

CHAPTER
TWENTY-SIX

Blessed be this place
More blessed still this tower;
A bloody, arrogant power
Rose out of the race
Uttering, mastering it,
Rose like these walls from these
Storm-beaten cottages—
In mockery I have set
A powerful emblem up,
And sing it rhyme upon rhyme
In mockery of a time
Half dead at the top.

—W. B. YEATS: *"Blood
and the Moon"*

They had stopped at the edge of a large clearing. Ahead of them rose a high, rounded hill encircled by a shallow ditch and a low, mounded ring of earth. The mound itself was crowned by a small copse of thick brush. All the rest was covered by tall, luxuriant grass gleaming with emerald highlights in the late afternoon's slanting sunbeams.

"A glory it is surely not," said the tinker, climbing down from the caravan's box, "but this is where we'll be staying."

They walked up to the hill and circled it slowly. By its smoothness and its symmetry of shape, it was clearly not a natural feature. It was also just as clearly an ancient one. The wear of a millennium's winds and rains had eroded it badly, leaving one once-smooth cheek deeply scarred. The outer ring and ditch had nearly been erased by the scouring of time.

As the two men came around to the hill's far side, John found that close beside it stood two deserted, roofless cottages of whitewashed stone. They looked very forlorn and very saggy, and rather like miniatures carved of soap left to melt down in the shower.

"Where are we exactly?" asked John, entering the larger of the cottages through its gaping doorway.

"Well, there are some who say it was an ancient family homestead," said the tinker, following him in. "A hill fort, you know."

"Oh, sure," said John. "I've studied it some. That hill is what they called a dun. The buildings were on top. There was a wall of wooden stakes built on the lower ring."

He looked about him at the cottage's interior. Its floor plan was much the same as that of their own vacation home in Ballymurroe. He realized how very far away that seemed to him now, even though it was physically only a couple of miles distant, its coziness, its simple comforts. He saw himself and Ann seated together by its glowing peat fire, dreamily contemplating what they were going to do.

But the rather grim reality of his present situation was soon recalled by the scene about him. This poor cottage was far from cozy anymore. It had been many a year since a fire burned in that fallen fireplace. And the roofless space of the main room was empty except for a litter of fallen rafters and bits of broken furniture.

"*Some* believe it was a mortal's dun," O'Teague said with an odd lilt in his voice, "but I know better, as do some few other of the older, wiser folk. No, it's a fairy fort this was, not a mortal one. One belonging to the *Sidhe*."

"What, one of those hidden places where the Others were supposed to live?" said John with amusement. "I've read about that. An ancient superstition. It's what they used to call all of these old raths and duns before archeologists proved better."

"Maybe it's true that most were only the dwelling places of men," O'Teague agreed. "But you can believe me about this one." The little man spoke seriously. "Given to King Cormac's clan by Manannan MacLir himself it was. Very powerful they were in this place. Why, the proof's right here about you."

A puzzled John looked around him at the ruined cottage. "Why?"

"Because these fool mortal ones who just couldn't believe the old tales tried to build and live here a century ago. Too close to the fort they were. Too bold and too modern of mind for their own good. They'd trespassed upon the Others' realm, and they were cursed for it. Cows dried up, crops dried up, and at last they gave it up."

"Cursed, eh?" said John, gazing over the abject ruins. "Then, are we safe staying here?"

O'Teague gave a little smile. "I told you, I'm Their friend."

John stepped to a window, ironically still tightly closed with shutters to keep out the weather. He pushed them open. One fell outward with a rending scream as its rusted hinge parted. Revealed beyond was the pasture and forest. In the distance he could see the corner of another large structure thrusting above the trees.

He pointed to it. "What's that?"

"Dunraven," said the tinker simply, and John realized he was looking at the top of the manor's ancient main tower. It was less than a mile away.

"Right under Butler's nose," John said. "No wonder Bonaventure wanted to surprise me."

The tinker moved up close beside him, gazing out toward the tower as well.

"Over a thousand years old that tower is," he said. "A ruin for centuries past, all broken and gutted within. But it looks now just as it did then at its time of glory. A place of great strength. Just as when the earl lived there."

"That one called Feagh O'Donal?" said John. "The one who disappeared?"

"Aye. That same one. The Enchanter's what they called him. Magic powers he had, as well as great fightin' ones."

"Brother Coleman told me that, too. He said they came from some pact with the devil."

O'Teague snorted derisively. "It would be one of the church who'd say that. But it was nothing of the Christian world gave the magic skills to Earl O'Donal. No. It was those living right here. 'Twas the *Sidhe* who helped him."

John turned to the little man, intrigued by this. "The *Sidhe*? Why? I thought they stayed out of men's affairs."

"I also told you before that they did become involved in the mortal world at times," O'Teague reminded him. "When Ireland was deep in need or sorely pressed. And she was no more greatly pressed than in Earl O'Donal's time."

John looked back toward the tower. "He was pretty much fighting alone to keep Ireland free then, wasn't he?"

"That he was. A last champion of the people fighting to survive. He'd called to him all the remaining heroes still having a will to fight. Eire's greatest fighting men together, swords upraised, facing the coming darkness back to back. And that gallant stand raised the sympathies of the *Sidhe*.

"They passed to him their druid powers to use against the foe. But it was not enough. Still he was defeated in the end. The organized might of the great, new world against his remnant was overwhelming."

"So he was killed?" asked John.

O'Teague shook his head. "He used the powers to somehow vanish away. No one knew to where. And with his last light gone, the darkness fell upon the world he'd known. So black it was for those of the old ways that even the *Sidhe* fled, defeated by the new religion, the new civilization, the new way of life that took control of Eire. As that tower was abandoned, so Cormac and his people left their own mound. The Children of Danu went to their other home—back to the Isle of the Blest hidden out in the Western Sea."

"All of them?"

"Not all," the tinker said. "There were still many who loved this land they'd once ruled far too much to leave her in her time of agony. They stayed with her, scattered through the land. And when there's ever a need, I've no doubt that they will gather again to meet it."

"I'd like to believe that," John said softly, staring toward Dunraven. "Especially now." Then, more briskly, he turned away from the window and said, "Well, I can't think of a better place to plan an attack against Mr. Butler. But, the *Sidhe* aside, are you sure we're safe from more human eyes here?"

"There's no reason for anyone to come here now, save for an occasional wanderer like me," O'Teague assured. "I'll move the wagon back into the trees, and we'll be well hidden."

"I suppose so," John said thoughtfully. He was thinking about something else. "I think I'll walk back up the road a little to check, anyway."

He went back along the lane to where it forked, and there he stopped to examine the ground intently. In the still moist earth, the marks of tires showed clearly.

The tracks came up from the gateway and followed the fork to the left. Below the fork they were largely obliterated by the flat, iron wheels of the caravan wagon, but above it they were clear, and he could see the tires were large, the wheels widely spaced.

He walked back to the .cottages and found the tinker inside the larger one, heating water on a small peat fire he had built in the fireplace.

"Find anything of interest?" the man asked.

"I think so. You didn't know that there were fresh tire tracks on the road?"

"Fresh marks?" O'Teague was concerned. "Leading up here?"

"No. They go up the other fork. It leads to the manor house, doesn't it?"

"It does," the tinker said. "Why?"

John got no chance to explain just then. The sound of an engine reached them, and they went outside in time to see Trahern and Father Bonaventure arrive, accompanied by Taffy.

Trahern parked the car behind the cottage, and they all went inside to sit around the tinker's fire and sip at the tea he'd made.

"All right, Mr. Milne," said Trahern, settling himself on a fallen roof beam, "we're safe and close enough to Butler to be drinking from his glass. How do you plan to reach our women without being caught?"

"That's right, John," Bonaventure agreed. "You can't know how that building is guarded. You might never get past the main gates. And if you did, and if you found them, how would you get everyone away before Mr. Butler could stop you?"

"I've been thinking about that. A couple of nights ago, Ann and I followed a truck that we thought turned into this road. Last night we saw lights out in this direction, and I thought maybe it was that truck coming in again. We didn't find any sign of it, but I just saw fresh tracks. It *must* have come in again. If it comes in this way every night, we might have some way to use it."

"I see what you're thinking," said Trahern, "and I believe you're right. Father Bonaventure and I talked on the way here. From what he's told me about the boxes he saw in the lorry, and from what you've said, it seems certain to me that Butler is bringing some kind of contraband into his estate to hide it. It explains why that driver was so upset at the good Father here, for peepin' inside."

"And it explains why your wife had to disappear, too," said John. "She knew about the driver and about this entrance to the estate. She may have guessed what the truck was carrying, or even have found out where this stuff was being hidden."

"Most likely the lorry is moving its loads in a little at a time and at night for safety," Trahern suggested.

"Which could mean it makes a visit here every night," John finished.

"If it does, it'll give us our way in and out," Trahern said. "They'll not take special notice of their own lorry arriving, nor check to see who's inside. It might just give us time to find an entrance, find the women, and get away quickly."

"Very simple," Bonaventure said dryly. "But you'll have only minutes. Only seconds maybe. If you can get into the house, how will you find the women in that maze of rooms?"

"That's why I wanted to take Taffy with me," John explained. "I'm hoping that if Bridget is in there, he'll lead me right to her."

"I don't have any doubt that he'd go directly to her, John," Bonaventure agreed. "Still, you can't be thinking you'll not run into opposition inside the house."

John nodded grimly. "I know, Father. I'm ready to deal with it any way I have to." He knew what that implied, but he was coldly determined to accept it.

"All right, then," said Bonaventure after some consideration. "It means we're going to need a place to watch for this truck and stop it."

The monk's use of pronouns puzzled John. "We?"

"This will require more than the two of you," the monk said firmly. "My abbot may disapprove, but I can see no other way to end this thing, and I'll not be left out."

"Nor I," the tinker put in. "We're all part of it now."

John couldn't argue. He'd promised himself he wouldn't turn down any help again.

The monk clasped his hands together and said energetically, "Now, the road narrows just beyond the fork. If we block the way there, the lorry would have to stop. Once the driver is out, we can easily overpower him."

John looked at the warm pink glow that lit the monk's face. "I think you're actually looking forward to this," he said with mild accusation. "Mrs. Trahern was right, saying you were a Celt at heart."

Bonaventure's pink deepened to red with embarrassment. "It is shameful, I know. But since boyhood I've read the tales of Eire's heroes as you likely read of yours. There is a bit of me that's always dreamed of riding into battle in a great chariot-of-war, sword in hand, the battle light about my head."

John recalled the vision he'd had in the Burren of Bonaventure as a warrior and smiled. "I think I guessed that, Father," he said. "Sorry we won't be storming the battlements tonight."

"We still have to determine how to stop the lorry," Trahern put in, his sharp tone recalling them to business.

"Leave that to me," said Mr. O'Teague. "I know a trick or two that will work, not raising any suspicion in our driver's mind."

"I'll bet you do," said John. "Okay, then." He looked toward the west and the failing light. "All we have to do now is wait for the truck to come, and pray it does."

O'Teague left them, going back along the road to watch for the truck. The monk and Trahern fell into idle conversation while John, feeling restless, walked out to the mound. Daring the *Sidhe* aura there, he went up its slope to the top.

Recalling their need to stay concealed, he moved into the cover of the thicket there and sat down where he could see Dunraven while staying well hidden from sight. He stared off toward the looming tower, lost in thought.

He felt an odd kind of excitement himself. His whole body tingled, and he felt the beating of his heart. It throbbed steadily through his body, arms, and legs, as if he were vibrating from the concussion of a drum beating far away. He wondered if the warriors of darker ages had waited with the same feeling. Perhaps some chieftain or king had stood just here, looking off toward the warlord's tower, before an assault.

He had been aware of Ireland's many spirits for some time, and he felt them very strongly now, in this place.

There was something almost tangible in the scent of the air, the feel of the sod, the sound of the breeze rustling the brush and grass. Perhaps they were all generated from that ancient essence. Maybe they were part of the supernatural realm that had held sway here so long, wafting out of hidden chinks and doorways on the mound. He could almost feel the great swell of earth itself vibrating as if it were alive, making him vibrate with it, making his pulse throb to its own heartbeat.

Maybe O'Teague was right about its otherworldly connection. And if so, John's feelings only confirmed the idea. The sensations he felt were clearly telling him that the particular Ones who had occupied this mound—whoever they were—approved of what he was going to do . . . or try to do.

"Worried about Ann?" Bonaventure asked.

John turned to find that the monk had come up behind him as he dreamed.

"I suppose so, Father. I keep telling myself that Butler's just holding her and looking for me, but the fear keeps creeping in. I just want to get her out of there and stop him."

"Just be certain that the one is always before the other," Bonaventure told him, sitting down in the cover of the bushes beside the young man. "Passions are an easy acquisition in this land of mine. I know."

"Father!" said John with mild surprise. "Are you faulting your own country?"

"Only a fool never sees fault in what he loves. Remember, Butler's not the only villain in this. It seems he's having much help from my countrymen."

"But he's used them. He's used money and position and probably even fear to get loyalty from them. They think of him as a friend, and he's controlling them for reasons of his own. Men like Butler have been making this island bleed for centuries!"

"John, it's not always outsiders that have made Ireland bleed. Emotions are very strong here. They breed in this fertile earth like the grass upon it. But it isn't just in poetry and music we've expressed them. There's war, too. Anger and hatred are ancient sicknesses of the Irish. They infect everyone. Even you, I think."

"Me? Father, my wife was kidnapped. He had us chased. He even tried to kill us. Any hatred I have is justified."

"You do what you have to, John, but do it with a reasoning mind. That's been too often lacking in this land for a long, long time."

"I'm sorry, but I'm not concerned about this land, Father. I only care about my wife, just like Mr. Trahern cares about his."

Troubled by this exchange, Bonaventure wanted to argue further, but he decided to give it up. A cold humor was on John, and the monk could see that it carried everything else before it.

"You were talking with the tinker," said John. "Where did he go?"

"He's gone about getting something for tonight," said the monk. "He's a good man, but a strange one. You know, they say that the tinkers have the friendship of the fairies."

"Quite a pair you make," said John. "A monk with a yearning to be a warrior and a tinker who consorts with the *Sidhe*. With backing like that, we can't fail."

He looked away toward the rooftop of Dunraven. He wondered if Ann felt him there, so close.

In the rising shadows of evening, he noticed a large black bird, feathers glinting blue in the sunlight's last rays, sweep in and vanish behind the tower.

Ann and the Traherns looked up in surprise as a huge crow alighted in one of the high slit windows of the tower.

It sat a moment looking down at them with glittering black eyes. Then it dropped from the sill, soaring in, sweeping around the room, drawing a gasp from an alarmed Bridget.

Finally, in a great fluttering of wings, it settled to the floor by the central fire. It furled the wings about it like a cloak and stood there motionless.

"What the devil's this about?" asked Nancy Trahern.

As if in answer, the raven's form began to glow. A blue-silver light emanated from it, surrounding the form in a shimmering sheath that partly obscured it. The bird's form became only a vague shadow within the glow.

But the astonished women watching could still see it well enough to know it was altering radically. In only seconds the dark form shot upward and filled out like an inflated balloon, becoming something of a man's shape and height.

Then the glow swiftly receded, leaving the new figure revealed to the onlookers.

chapter
twenty-seven
☥

Hope that you may understand!
What can books of men that wive
In a dragon-guarded land,
Paintings of the dolphin-drawn
Sea-nymphs in their pearly wagons
Do, but awake a hope to live
That had gone
With the dragons?

— W. B. YEATS: *"The Realists"*

It was a tall figure cloaked fully in a dark hooded robe.

"Douglas Butler!" Nancy Trahern exclaimed, clearly not so taken aback by his amazing entrance as Ann. "That I should have guessed."

The figure shrugged back the hood, revealing the man's lean face. His blue eyes shone with icy light.

"Not 'Butler,'" he said to them proudly. "My name is Feagh O'Donal, Earl of Dunraven."

"You're not Douglas Butler?" said a bewildered Ann. "You're not an American?"

"I have been both—for a time," he told her. "A hundred

and fifty years perhaps. A paltry span of time for that identity. But for ten centuries it is Earl O'Donal I have always been. And as he"—he gave a little bow—"I am at your service, Lady."

"Ten centuries," said Ann. "Are you saying you're *that* earl? From so long ago? You can't be!"

"The evidence of your own eyes should help convince you that I am," he answered. He lifted the full robe up and outward in both hands, creating dark wings like those of the crow. "Why do you think I came to you this way? The time has come for me to prove to you just what power I have."

"It's some kind of trick," she said adamantly, refusing to accept. "It's more special effects. You're a master of them."

"I assure you, this is real," the man returned.

"Mrs. Trahern," said Ann, turning to the woman, "do you believe this?"

"It may be that I do," she replied gravely. "I know it's not just trickery. I've felt it in him from the very first. The energy that comes from him is of the Otherworld."

"I have the ability to transform my shape," O'Donal told them. "I can call up storms to fall upon my enemies, or create false armies out of grass and wind to confound them. More than that, I can use a special potion to sustain my life . . . almost interminably, as you see."

"Where could you get that kind of power?" Ann asked him.

"It was given to me by those who sympathized. A people of the Otherworld, as Mrs. Trahern guessed, called by many here the 'hidden ones.' They vanished from this world long, long ago."

"Do you mean the *Sidhe?*" said Ann.

"You know of them?" said Butler. Then he smiled with pleasure. "Of course. You know a great deal about our land. It's one of the reasons I wish you to understand, to know."

"Why reveal your secret now?" Ann asked. "You wouldn't do it before." She eyed him shrewdly. "It couldn't be that you aren't able to get John?"

"I will admit the young man has avoided all efforts to

find him," said Earl O'Donal grudgingly. "He seems to have rather a charmed life of his own. That's why my time is growing short. I've decided my only choice now is to gain your help. And the only way for that is to give you my proof."

"Proof of what?"

"That I can do as I say. That I can succeed in my plans for restoring the past spirit to Ireland."

"Even if these bits of magic you tell us of are real," said Mrs. Trahern, "they're surely not enough to let you carry out this great revolution of yours."

"But they're not all I have, dear lady," the earl assured her. "No. I also have a strong and willing host at my command. The finest fighting men Ireland has seen. The pick of her champions, heroes every one, gathered to me in our last, desperate days of standing together against the whole new world."

"I thought your warriors were all destroyed," said Ann.

He smiled. "As I supposedly was. But you see me before you. No. Not destroyed. When the end came, I saved them all, knowing our time would one day come again. I hadn't the power to make them all immortal, but I could do the next thing to it. I put them into a long sleep. 'Under an enchantment' they would have called it then."

"Like Sleeping Beauty?" Bridget put in.

"Very much the same. I believe the modern, scientific age would use the term 'suspended animation.'" He grimaced at the words. "A cold, unimaginative name for it, fit for the rationalist's world. Anyway, then I hid them where they might sleep in safety as long as need be."

"A thousand years ago," Ann breathed, caught up in the tale and accepting it despite her logical mind telling her it was absurd. The romantic in her was beating back the rationalist. "What did you do all that time, alone?"

"Ah, well, I lived here and there, making my way the best I could and keeping my identity and my powers secret. In the new eras of the Renaissance and the age of reason that swept upon us I would not have survived long otherwise. But the way was hard here, and when so many of my people headed for America during the famines, I went, too.

"That new land of opportunity was a boon to me. No one cared who I was or what I did. And I finally went to Texas, as I said. I was well suited to the rough Western life. Then some few decades ago, I saw the first signs that my time was coming again. I had to start getting prepared. I needed wealth to carry out my plan, reclaim my lands, and restore my men. I went to Hollywood—the Factory of Dreams they called it. Well, I had ways of creating dreams like none any had ever seen. I used my magic to help me produce films that made me rich. Then came my return here and my restoration of this place. And soon my fellows will be released from their sleep. They will finally tread the sod of Ireland again."

"And you expect this Ireland to just embrace you?" Mrs. Trahern asked. "To give up its way of life and follow yours?"

"More than you would believe already do," he said. "At the right time, it will be enough to let us establish ourselves here once again. More than sufficient for a start."

"And if others not so sympathetic come to destroy you?"

"Then I'll have the finest fighting men about me, and feel the exhilaration of charging into battle once again," he said with great vigor. "We will survive this time, I know it. And soon more and more will join with us."

He swept his gaze around the vast room with its display of Ireland's violent history. "It's what's at the very soul of this country, you know," he told them. "In her heart Eire still holds to the old ways and the old times when people thought for themselves and fought—really fought—to make what they had."

"We've made what we have now," Mrs. Trahern affirmed sharply. "A chance to finally live in peace and order and to make something better of ourselves—without your eternal fighting."

He shifted his piercing gaze to her. "Is that what your world of whining weaklings and cowards means to you?" he said disdainfully. "Then you are not so insightful as I thought. The one splendid thing that the Irish really have is the fierce, independent spirit of the Celt warrior. Without it, all they can do is lean on their fences and dream about past glories. I'm giving them a chance to bring those glories back."

He turned toward one of the displays of weapons on the wall. Looking at them, he reflected.

"War was a different thing in those times. Rifles and explosives . . . they're not really the weapons for a man. They make killing into an objective, emotionless sort of thing. Just as this modern world has made life itself."

At the mention of weapons, Ann's mind began working in a new direction—and a desperate one: toward escape.

For all that she found herself sympathizing with this man's nostalgic yearnings for the past and his great dream of regenerating it, she was convinced that he was dangerous. They had to get away. She decided they might have a chance of escape from here if they could overpower Butler and get his keys.

In the center of the table only inches from her sat the cut-glass Waterford decanter. It was squat and heavy and would make a formidable club. She looked at Butler. He still stood with his back to them, lost in reverie, his gaze fixed on the swords.

He was vulnerable.

"A great many of those films I made were Westerns, you know," he went on. "Living on the frontier, working as a cowboy myself in the early days, I learned that there was a kinship between the American West and the legends of this country. Strong men in a free, wild, self-reliant time."

Her hand began to move slowly toward the decanter.

"Even there, of course, there were the guns. More primitive ones, of course. Requiring more skill and courage to wield skillfully. Still, even they could never match the raw power in a weapon like this." He lifted a hand to the hilt of a broadsword.

Ann's own hand closed around the neck of the decanter, and she prepared herself to move.

"Mrs. Milne," he said quietly and, in a swift, whirling

movement, he swept the sword around and slammed it down on the tabletop inches from her hand.

She didn't jump. Slowly she raised her head and looked up to him with a gaze she willed to be fearless.

"I think you've distressed your table," she said evenly.

He laughed loudly at that. "Very good, Mrs. Milne. Now, sit back. You can't get out that way."

She did as she was told. He lifted the broadsword from the table and examined it critically. It was a two-handed weapon, five feet long and six inches wide, but he held it, swinging it easily in one hand. Its blade gleamed sharply in the light.

"This is a *real* weapon," he continued as if nothing had happened. "It's wholly dependent on the power and skill of the one who holds it. A true symbol, as the horse is, of the romantic's soul. Guns are for the weak and soulless. A proper symbol for the rationalist who must solve all things at once, through his science and technology." His voice grew contemptuous at these words.

He looked to them. "Well, it's *my* wish that all guns will disappear. That the time of swords should come again. And I *will* fulfill that wish."

He laughed again with a sudden exuberance, and the years faded from him. Some greater energy now coursed through him and he seemed younger, stronger, even more powerful. It resonated in his voice.

"Come with me," he said to them. "Let me show you the view from my tower."

Nancy and Ann exchanged a worried glance, then rose to follow him, herding Bridget along. Still carrying the sword, Butler led them out into the little vestibule and up the winding stair to a door that opened onto the tower's flat roof. They walked to its edge and stood looking out across the green country.

The sun was beginning to set. The last of its rays lit the fields and trees. A cool wind rose, bringing the fresh sea air to them. It blew Ann's hair out in a great, billowing mass, blazing red-gold in the sun's dying light.

"You really are perfect here," Butler said, watching her with admiration. "You could well have been the mistress of such a place. Your ancestors probably stood on towers like these. You feel the pull of it, don't you? You feel it as I do?"

She wasn't sure how to answer, a bit frightened by the sudden intensity in his voice. But he didn't await her answer. He turned to the parapet, gazing out at the countryside, which was darkening quickly as the crimson light faded behind the horizon.

"All my life I've struggled to do what I was meant to do for Ireland. All the long years of wandering. The years of labor in America, wrangling horses for a few dollars, breaking my bones doing stunts to get into films, directing my first by taking it over and, finally, gaining the wealth I'd need. Through all of that, the real purpose never lost its value. I was meant to come back here to fight my battle again, and win this time."

He looked back at the women and swept his sword around to take in the rooftop. "This tower . . . it was always the symbol of my purpose. The symbol of that warlord who had once lived here."

"But that man is gone now, with his time," Mrs. Trahern said quietly.

"He's back," the earl answered. "His time will return as well."

Ann looked down from the tower. The stream flowed against the base of the building there. The water clawed and pulled at the massive stones. They showed a deep indentation from the years of constant wear. One day the tower would fall. Nature, finally, would destroy it.

" 'The darkening flood,' " she mused.

Butler looked at her quizzically. "What?"

"I was remembering a poem. The stream reminded me. Things change, like the water flowing in a stream. They pass on and they don't come back."

"You're wrong!" he told her emphatically. "They've never really been gone here. Why, this whole country is my proof. Look at the ruins everywhere. They're *all* symbols of what was and what can still be."

"You can't use that to prove that your way will be accepted here."

"Can't I? Look at what's happened in this country over these past years. The great rising—the first sign that my time was coming again. And then the continuing troubles in the North. Even better there. Everybody swearing bloody oaths to fight, even if it means destroying their modern society. Clans forming in the cities, dividing them into little kingdoms again. They're all going back to the way of the old clans. They're even building walls. Soon enough they'll be building towers."

"It's not what they want," she said.

"It is!" he argued with force. "It's the unity and order forced on them by the 'civilized' world that's unnatural."

"And you . . . you see yourself riding through the midst of it," said Nancy Trahern, "a hero once again." Her voice grew hard. "Well, you'll never be accepted."

"You really *don't* know your own country, do you?" he said, shaking his head. "Don't you yet see how much I'm already accepted here?" He swept the sword out to take in the countryside. "The people of these villages have given me trust and loyalty for my help. When I took this tower again, the authority of it once more became mine."

A series of separate images fit into a single picture in Ann's mind at that: an abbot called a lord by villagers, people at the *Teac* paying homage to Butler, others fiercely defending him because of his help, and his own comments about "playing the lord" here. Except that Butler—or Earl O'Donal now—wasn't playing.

"For those years as a director, I created worlds for other people too stupid or too weak to make them for themselves," he went on. "Now it's finally my turn again. When the moment comes, I'll be ready to take my place the way I was meant to." He lifted the sword before him and gazed on it with satisfaction.

"The rest of the world isn't going to let Ireland tear itself apart," Ann said.

The sword was lowered and he turned to her. A smile of smug confidence overspread his face. "Really, my dear lady? Well, look at your world again. It's now disintegrating faster than even Northern Ireland is. Faster than I could ever have believed or hoped. That was the final sign to me that my time had nearly come. The chaos of the third world has spread to the more 'civilized' countries now. The Soviet state has fallen, European countries are breaking apart, sect fighting sect, clan fighting clan, fragmenting into tiny bits. Even in your own country the cracks are showing widely. Cities crumbling, order disregarded, gangs controlling the streets. From Somalia to Yugoslavia to Los Angeles it is becoming all the same. The Dark Ages will be descending on the world soon. Then it will be the time of chieftains and warlords once again."

Ann listened to this ranting speech with growing despair. She knew now. It was all madness. His fantasies, his life, and the spirit of Ireland's past had interwoven in his mind somehow. It was a dream that had gone too far.

His tirade finished, his voice again took on a calmer, coaxing tone as he moved closer to Ann. "I want you especially to believe me and to join me. You have to understand. You told me once that you wanted to be a part of this country."

She was afraid, but her own spirit brought her erect to face him and answer with determination.

"I've wished I could be a part of the life here. But only in my own way, not yours. You say you want to bring back freedom. Then set us free. We can never accept what you're doing so long as you keep us by force."

Anger darkened his features. The light, gleaming eyes grew very cold.

"You're a fool, then," he said bitterly. "You know it means I can *never* let you go. You—"

He stopped abruptly. A high, clear sound—like a bird's

call, or a baby's cry, or a dog's wail—came to them from far away.

"That cry!" he said, wheeling away from them to look out into the darkness. "I've heard that cry before!"

The cry reached four men huddled in the darkness by a crumbling ruin. They looked about them uncertainly.

"What was that?" John asked, chilled by the sound of it.

"It is a keening of the women of the *Sidhe*," O'Teague answered in hushed tones. "I've heard it often these past days." He looked around at the others grimly. "I'm afraid it means that someone will die soon."

chapter
twenty-eight

✠

You that Mitchel's prayer have heard,
'Send war in our time, O Lord!'
Know that when all words are said
And a man is fighting mad,
Something drops from eyes long blind,
He completes his partial mind,
For an instant stands at ease,
Laughs aloud, his heart at peace.
Even the wisest man grows tense
With some sort of violence
Before he can accomplish fate,
Know his work or choose his mate.

—W. B. YEATS: *"Under Ben Bulben"*

While the man now calling himself Earl O'Donal and his reluctant guests talked on atop the tower of Dunraven, a small truck turned off the road from Ballymurroe and started up the hidden lane to the manor.

The driver was half-alert, thinking of a late pint at the tavern before bed. He didn't see the obstacles in the road until he was almost upon them. He braked to a sliding halt and peered ahead at the dim, moving shapes.

"Damnable cows," he muttered.

Impatient, he got out of the truck and moved forward to chase them from the road. For some reason they seemed reluctant to budge. As he waved and shouted, they only shifted uneasily.

"What in Hades?" he cried. His temper completely lost, he brought back a leg to kick at one of them.

He went no further. A large sack was thrown over him. Taken off balance, he went down heavily. Several figures descended upon him and in moments he was thoroughly tied.

"Serves him properly," said the tinker from his seat on the captive's stomach. "Imagine, meaning to kick a poor, helpless milk cow." He got up and went to the animals. "All right, my dears . . . off the road with you now."

The animals moved away obediently and vanished into the darkness.

"Very clever, Mr. O'Teague," said John. "I wouldn't have thought of using cows."

"Some of us have a way with them," said the tinker with a wink and a sly smile.

"Well, let's see if we were right about this truck's load," John suggested. "Will our friend be safe?"

"Saint Patrick himself couldn't coax these knots loose," the tinker assured him.

They went around to the rear of the truck and Mr. Trahern pulled aside the canvas curtain to reveal the objects inside.

"That looks to be much the same as what I saw in there that night, outside the pub," Bonaventure exclaimed.

Trahern reached in and hauled one of the objects out.

It was a wooden timber, eight feet long and eight inches square.

"Why, it's not guns at all," said Bonaventure. He peered into the truck at the rest of the load. "Just more wooden posts and some kinds of metal things."

Trahern looked at the metal things. "They're jacks. For lifting heavy things, or holding them up."

"Just like they'd use for construction or restoring work on a castle," said John with chagrin.

"They don't tell us much about what Butler's doing," said the monk.

"Or why Butler would go to such lengths to protect them," added Trahern, clearly irritated. "Damn. There *must* be more to it. I *know* he's got to be stashing weapons or the like. *Something* very big!"

"It doesn't matter now," said John. "Let's just get on with it. Mr. Trahern, you drive. I'll get in back with Taffy."

"Wait, John," the monk said. "Mr. O'Teague and I have decided it might make things simpler for you going in at the back if we could draw their attention to the front of the house."

"A diversion?" John said doubtfully. "I don't know, Father. Why risk us all in this?"

"It's no risk. I merely mean to raise a fuss at the front door about where you and Ann have disappeared to. They'll have to tell me something, and while I have them occupied, you might have a better chance of getting inside unnoticed."

John saw that he wasn't going to keep the tinker or Father Bonaventure out of this. And the idea was a logical one. He agreed.

"But come right back here after," he said. "If we don't show up soon, get help!"

"Take care," Trahern cautioned. "If we do this badly, it could be a last chance for all of us."

He returned the post to the truck bed. Then he went around the vehicle and climbed behind the wheel. John took the leash from Father Bonaventure and hooked it to Taffy's collar. He lifted the dog into the back and climbed in beside him.

"Good fortune go with you," the monk said, pulling the canvas cover across the opening. "And God be with you tonight as well."

"And with you, too," John replied.

With a lurch the truck started off.

Trahern drove the truck slowly into the estate, past the old church and the ruined monastery, following the faint path around, across the stone bridge that spanned the stream and down along the manor's side to the garages at its back. He pulled up in the gravel yard and shut off the engine.

When John felt the truck stop, he climbed carefully from the back with the dog. Peering warily around the vehicle, he saw that the garage doors were open. In one bay sat the blue Volvo. In the other was their own red Escort.

"Well, well. A stowaway," said a voice.

John jerked around to find himself facing a leveled gun. It was held by one of their pursuers—the stocky one he had injured at Cashel.

The man looked him up and down. Then, without taking either eyes or gun off John, he called back over his shoulder.

"Say, Andy, you've picked up a passenger along the way."

John realized that the gunman thought their own driver was still behind the wheel. He didn't want him to find out differently.

"Glad to see you again," John said, trying to keep the man's attention focused on him. "How is the hand?"

"It's well enough, no thanks to you," the man told him irritably. "It's good to be seeing you also. We've all been thinkin' we just might. The Old Man will be happy to have you, much as I'd like you for myself."

"Too bad," said John. "I hate to disappoint people."

A figure stole up silently behind the gunman. Still, he appeared to sense its approach.

"Andy?" he said, beginning to turn. "Whaddaya mean, bringin' the—"

He got no further. Mr. Trahern hit the man once, and he dropped in a heap. It was skillfully and brutally done, and John was surprised by the seeming ease of it.

"Did you kill him?" he asked, looking down at the still form.

"No, but he'll be some time waking. We'd best tie him

anyway." Trahern picked up the man's pistol. "Then we can find a way into this ugly mass of stone."

John looked up at the manor's stark, frowning walls.

"And a way out," he added.

Father Bonaventure and Cian O'Teague got out of Trahern's car in front of the manor and eyed it speculatively.

The monk wondered for a moment if he had volunteered for this out of a Christian need to help or a personal sense of adventure. Romantic and rationalist were definitely warring factions in him as well. He told himself that it was really a foolish question, as none of them really had a choice in this. His only reason for uncertainty was the fear he felt now that his part was ready to be played. He would have to control that fear. He would have to think and act as a Finn or a Cuchulain would have.

"Best have some fine, lengthy questions to ask, Mr. O'Teague," he advised. "Once we've got them at the door, we've got to keep them there as long as we can."

"We'll manage it someway, never doubt," the tinker replied cheerfully. "But ask God for help, won't you? And any other spirits that might happen to be listening."

"I will that," Bonaventure agreed.

They walked up to the door, and the monk knocked sharply with its iron ring. Beside him Mr. O'Teague waited, as cool as ever, whistling a light air.

The large door creaked back, and Padraic O'Gadhra appeared in the opening.

"Yes, gentlemen? And how might I be helping you?"

"I'm Father Bonaventure . . . from the abbey," he said, trying to sound amiable. "I know Mr. Butler."

"Yes?" O'Gadhra was not being helpful.

"Well, our friends, the Milnes, have disappeared rather suddenly, and we understand they were last here. Do you know what happened to them?"

"I've no idea, Father," said O'Gadhra tonelessly. "The

last we saw of them they were headed for the coast. I can say for certain there was nothing wrong then."

"Did I say there was something wrong?" the monk asked.

O'Gadhra was flustered. "No . . . well . . . why else be looking for them in the dead of night, then?"

"Look here, could we speak with Mr. Butler?" said the monk, ignoring that. "It might be he knows where they were headed."

"I can't be bothering him. He's occupied now."

"You have to," Bonaventure insisted. "It's too important."

As he spoke, he and the tinker moved forward, forcing the man to give ground. They were able to get inside the door before he made a stand and blocked them again.

"I say you can't see him now," he said heatedly. "Come back when—"

"Paddy," called another young man who entered the entry hall behind him.

"What is it?" O'Gadhra snapped impatiently.

"I've been watching from the top windows," the newcomer reported. "I just saw the lorry drive up and round to the stables out back."

"What?" O'Gadhra turned toward him in astonishment. "Is Andy mad? He's never supposed to be up—" He choked this off, remembering his intruders. He turned back to them. "I'm sorry, but I've something to check. Come back later."

Bonaventure knew that the two men had made some disastrous mistake. Desperate now to delay them, he pressed forward.

"Wait! You can't push us out. We demand to see Butler!"

O'Gadhra looked closely into the monk's face, and a sudden suspicion blossomed in his mind.

"What are you about? You're part of this! Alf, hold them here!"

"You can't do this," cried Bonaventure, grabbing O'Gadhra's arm.

The second man moved forward, his hand yanking something from within his jacket.

"Be careful, Father!" the tinker shouted and leaped forward.

On top of the tower, a still arguing Feagh O'Donal was cut short in mid-sentence by the sound of a gunshot.

The explosion echoed hollowly through the manor, and all of them froze, listening, until it died away.

"Has it begun so soon?" said O'Donal, half to himself. He whirled to face his three captives. "Are they daring to come against me here?"

Ann Milne's mind was in turmoil. The ominous single shot had raised a host of dark possibilities in her own imagination.

"John," she said in a hushed voice.

The tall man heard. "Your husband! Yes, it might be him. A foolish, headstrong lad. He might well be trying to rescue his fair lady from the tower."

"But we should see," she said anxiously. "They may have killed him!"

"No," he thundered. "We stay here, hidden in my keep, where I can be sure you're safe." He looked toward the door to the roof, the sword held ready. "My men will come and report to me . . . when it's over."

Whatever, thought Ann, that "over" meant.

The sound of the shot stopped John Milne short as he wrapped the unconscious gunman's hands with rope. It had come from above them, and from the front of the house.

"What happened?" he asked in alarm.

"It's gone wrong," said Trahern simply.

"Finish tying this guy," John told him. "I've got to see."

He rose and went up the road at a run, Taffy beside him. He reached the front door without seeing anyone and found it standing open. From somewhere inside the house came a sound of clanging and thumping.

He went in cautiously, moving from one spot of cover to

another, his hand on Taffy's collar to keep the dog in check. But as they reached a massive chest against one wall, the animal pulled forward, whining excitedly and thrusting his nose around the corner of the piece.

Carefully John peered around . . . and found the tinker huddled on the floor with his back against the wall.

"Mr. O'Teague," he exclaimed in a hoarse whisper. "Are you all right?"

"I'm right enough," the tinker assured him. "One of the madmen shot me." He lifted his left arm to reveal a bloody sleeve. "But it's little to worry about. Help Bonaventure. There's two against him, inside."

John handed O'Teague his handkerchief. "Here, tie it up. But not too tight. We'll be back."

He and Taffy moved away from the fallen tinker, crossed the remainder of the entry, and boldly passed the archway into the main hall. All hope of surprise was gone, and he was fully prepared to meet the foe head-on. He wished he'd taken that guard's gun himself. He was ready to use it now.

The main hall was the scene of a pitched battle. The room was a shambles. Chairs were overturned, smashed glass and pottery were everywhere. Taffy stopped and began to bark loudly, adding to the confusion.

On the main stairs Bonaventure stood, an absurdly large broadsword swinging in his hands to hold two men at bay.

One of his attackers John recognized as the younger gunman who had chased them at Cashel. He was now armed only with a chair that he held in front of him to fend off the monk's sweeping blows. Both he and the chair were beginning to show wear.

Beside him was Padraic O'Gadhra, armed and fighting back with a long, pikelike weapon that he, like Father Bonaventure, had snatched from a wall display.

The monk seemed to be more than holding his own. Standing above the other two on the stairs, he struck out tirelessly and fiercely, timing and aiming his strokes with apparent skill and tremendous élan. His face was suffused with a ruddy glow that made John think of the Celtic heroes he'd often read about, and of the battle light that had reportedly shone from their faces in the throes of fighting. He judged that the monk was enjoying himself immensely.

At the moment of John's appearance, however, the situation changed quickly. When O'Gadhra noted his approach, he turned away from the monk to go for this new enemy. The long pike with its murderous point and sharpened edge came sweeping around to threaten John.

Unarmed himself, John lifted a small table and swung out at the weapon with blows strengthened by his anger. Taking the offensive, he forced O'Gadhra back, trying to knock the pike down, get past the point, and close.

The young Irishman realized his dilemma at once. The long weapon was too unwieldy to move quickly and too clumsy to stop an attack close in. Once John got past its cutting head, it would be worthless. He could only back away, swinging and thrusting to keep John at a distance, and look for an opening to get the advantage.

For long seconds it was a stalemate. Then O'Gadhra saw a chance. With a sudden attack he drove his adversary into a space between a wall and a broad table and, with that move, John's advantage was lost.

"You can't move behind there now, my lad," O'Gadhra said with a malicious smile. "You can't escape my reach, and you can't come closer. Give it up now, or I'll pin you like a fly!"

CHAPTER
TWENTY-NINE

✠

I climb to the tower-top and lean upon broken stone,
A mist that is like blown snow is sweeping over all,
Valley, river, and elms, under the light of a moon
That seems unlike itself, that seems unchangeable,
A glittering sword out of the east. A puff of wind
And those white glimmering fragments of the mist
    sweep by.
Frenzies bewilder, reveries perturb the mind;
Monstrous familiar images swim to the mind's eye.

—W. B. YEATS: "I See Phantoms of Hatred and of the
                Heart's Fullness and of the Coming
                                        Emptiness"

On the stairs the fighting had stopped.

Bonaventure had reduced his opponent's defense to splinters and sent him toppling down the stairs with a final, flat-bladed swipe. Now he looked across the room to his endangered comrade.

"John!" he cried, and tossed the sword hilt forward.

It was a low, easy throw, and it landed on the table, sliding down its polished length. John hurled his battered table toward O'Gadhra and grabbed at the weapon as it reached him.

In desperation, his opponent made a vicious, powerful thrust. The point of the pike went home deeply in the wall to John's right; and for that moment the weapon's slender wooden shaft lay exposed and motionless on the tabletop.

With all the strength of both arms, John brought the broadsword's edge down on the shaft. It splintered, hacked nearly through. And, as O'Gadhra hauled back on it, it parted with a snap. He fell backward onto the stone floor of the hall with some force and lay still, his wind knocked from him.

Before he could recover, John had circled the table and was on him. The young American kneeled on the downed man and raised the sword to strike.

Then reason flooded back into his conscious mind. The man was already beaten. His anger ebbed somewhat and he lowered the sword.

Grabbing O'Gadhra by his coat, John dragged him to his feet and pushed him against the table.

For the moment, the battle was over. O'Gadhra watched John, fearfully at first, but more calmly as he realized he would not be harmed.

Bonaventure went to his own opponent, now sitting up, but shaking his head, dazed. The monk helped him to his feet and led him over to stand with their other prisoner.

"This one had a gun, John," the monk said. "He lost it in the hall. I'll fetch it, if you'll watch them."

"I'll watch them," John assured. "See to O'Teague, too."

While John held the two men at swordpoint, Bonaventure went into the hall, returning in minutes with one hand holding a revolver and the other helping to support the tinker.

"I'm well enough," O'Teague complained as the monk eased him into a chair. "My wounds heal faster than you'd believe."

"I can believe it, John," the monk said. "His bleeding looks stopped already. He seems all right." He moved up beside the young American. "But what about the ladies? We must act quickly."

"Father Bonaventure is right," John told the prisoners. "We're in a hurry. Where have you got my wife and the Traherns?"

O'Gadhra smiled. He saw a chance to regain control, and with it his confidence strengthened.

"You're wasting time with us. As long as you can't find them, you've lost. If you don't want your wife to come to harm, surrender to us now."

John's temper flared again. He stepped quickly forward, grabbed O'Gadhra's throat with one hand and thrust the sword's point against his stomach with the other.

"Don't make me waste time on you, please," he said in a voice that shook with barely controlled rage.

Bonaventure moved close and took John's arm.

"Forget him, John. We have Taffy. He'll find them, remember?"

Reluctantly John released the man and stepped away from him. He looked toward the dog who stood patiently nearby.

"All right," he said at last. "We'll have to tie up these two."

They jerked down cords that held the curtains and bound the men, pushing them down in heavy chairs and tying them securely to the arms.

"There," Bonaventure declared with satisfaction. "Now, Mr. O'Teague, can you watch them alone? We have to leave you."

"We can't leave the gun with you," John added. "We might need it."

"I'll have no problem," said the tinker. He went to one of the displays of weapons and pulled down a gleaming double-bladed ax. Carrying it in his good hand, he returned to stand over the bound men. "I've got the strength to handle this, hurt arm or no," he told his captive audience. "Don't you be moving more than you have to for breathing."

"Let's go, then," said John.

"First, you take the gun," Bonaventure insisted. "I feel more comfortable without it, and I've grown used to this sword."

"All right, Father," John agreed, trading weapons.

He knelt by the dog and unhooked the leash.

"Now it's all up to you, Taffy," he said. "Go find Bridget for us."

At the sound of his beloved mistress's name the freed dog took off at a run, up the staircase and along the gallery. The two men followed. Taffy stopped a moment to sniff the air and the floor before going on, even faster now. The men ran behind, trying to keep close, afraid of losing sight of him.

The length of the gallery they ran, passing several doors and halls into the maze of rooms, then going into one corridor that turned a sharp corner. They nearly collided with the barrier that blocked the way.

It was a large opening, boarded over with heavy planks. Taffy jumped against it, clawing at the wood and whimpering deeply in his throat.

"It's here, isn't it, boy?" said John. He tried to pull down the planks, but they seemed unmovable.

Without hesitation Bonaventure lifted his sword and brought it against the thick wood, hacking at it again and again. Suddenly something gave way. With a loud click the whole thing moved outward, and the two men pulled it back.

A second door and a winding staircase faced them. Taffy made his choice without hesitation and started up the stairs.

"Check in there," John told the monk, pointing at the door. "I'm going up. Be careful." He turned and started up after the dog, taking the narrow stairs three at a time.

On the tower roof, the violent banging on the door below had erased the look of confidence from the face of the man now calling himself Feagh O'Donal, Earl of Dunraven. It had been replaced with an expression of uncertainty. But now, as footsteps sounded on the stairs, his look grew hard and defiant. He faced the doorway to the roof and dropped into a defensive stance, sword raised, as John and Taffy stormed through into view together.

"Taffy!" cried Bridget with joy, and the dog ran to her. She dropped down and hugged him close.

"You're finished, Butler," said John.

"It is the Earl of Dunraven that I am," the other declared proudly.

The sword, the man's weird getup, and now the lordly pronouncement nonplussed John for a moment. Clearly, he thought, this man was much less sane than he'd thought. But he recovered quickly.

"I don't give one damn *who* you think you are," John barked, pointing the pistol at him. "It's all over. Put down the sword."

The tall man eyed the weapon in John's hand. A new note—low, soothing, but still compelling—came into his voice.

"But John, you don't want to stop me. How could you? You're like me. I can see it, feel it in you. The spirit of most ancient Eire is strong in you. Its power over you has grown the longer you've been here."

There was something in the words and in the voice that seemed to take hold of John. There was a great truth in what this man said, he thought. He did feel the pull of this land's history. The glorious past.

Butler seemed to look different to him now. An odd aura of suffusing light seemed to have surrounded the man. Through it he appeared towering, grand, powerful. A figure of legend in gleaming chain mail and bright flowing cloak, defying all enemies with his upraised sword.

"I mean to bring that past back for us, John," the man crooned on. "For all of us. You can take a part. Just like you've dreamed. A warrior yourself. A fighting man of Eire. I can do it, John. Just believe."

He *was* beginning to believe. This man before him *was* the emodiment of that ancient past. He was magic, with the power to bring it back. Of course! He was the ever-living Enchanter, with the powers of the *Sidhe*, for whom nothing was impossible. He would make them all immortals. He would make them gods!

"Just join with me, John. That's all I ask," the voice went on, mesmerising all who heard. "You are truly a warrior. The spirit fills you. That's what's important. Together we can make this world a place of shining deeds again."

More words of W. B. Yeats came into John's mind. They were spoken about the great hero Finn MacCumhal and his own band of fighting men, the Fianna: "No thought of any life greater than that of love, and the companionship of those that have drawn their swords upon the darkness of the world, ever troubles their delight in one another."

Wasn't that what he wanted? Not to read about them. Not to teach about them to uncaring students. But to be part of such glorious company? To turn away from the soullessness of this degenerating modern world and embrace the fierce, free spirit of the old?

He began to lower the gun in his hand.

"No, John! Don't listen!" came a new voice behind him.

Groggily he turned to see. It was the tinker, wasn't it? Charging through the door onto the roof? Although a strange haze of light seemed to surround him also. He looked larger, younger, stronger. The big ax glistened in his hand and his voice resonated powerfully as he moved up to challenge their adversary.

"Who are you?" the one calling himself O'Donal demanded.

"Don't you know?" O'Teague countered.

The other eyed him intently. "You worked on the manor. On restoring some of it. You're the tinker!"

"Look again, Feagh O'Donal, Earl of Dunraven. Look beyond that face."

The icy gaze fixed longer on the smaller man. A thawing look of consternation swept suddenly into it. "No. It can't be! They're gone. They're all gone."

"They are here still," O'Teague coolly replied. "And They mean to stop you in this scheme of yours."

"But why?" the earl asked. "They wanted to help me. To help Eire. They gave me the powers for that reason."

"Power that you have turned to evil now," O'Teague said.

"How can I have done so? I only mean to regain what was. It's the same end as They should want."

O'Teague shook his head. "No longer. Your years wandering the world haven't taught you, O'Donal. But the Others have learned much by just watching that same world. It's become too vast. Too complex. The civilization mankind has created is the only chance for it now. There's no longer any place for you or your old life. You cannot go back."

"Listen to him, John!" Ann called to her husband. "He's right. Don't be fooled by that romantic's dream. I almost was. But we can't give in."

John listened and knew she was right. The spirit of the past with its strong emotions, so overwhelming in this ancient place, had nearly seized him. But to want that world was wrong. To accept its glories was also to accept its violence. It had been a time of chaos. To return to it would be to bring on a greater, new Dark Age where millions, billions would die.

"I understand," he told Ann. The gun came up to point steadily at the tall man again. John called to him: "I *won't* give in, 'Earl.' I've been a teacher too long. The only hope for mankind is to keep civilization going, by hook or by crook, and solve the problems. Not abandon it for what would be anarchy. There's no place in the world for warlords anymore."

Thwarted, the cloaked man looked darkly from the tinker to John. Then he nodded in acceptance.

"Very well. So you will oppose me. But you won't stop me. I will not stay here. My warriors await me. I will go to them."

Instantly a new, brighter aura sprang up about the man, enwrapping him in a chrysalis of blue-white glow.

"By the will of the *Sidhe*, O'Donal, you will *not* do that!" cried O'Teague.

The tinker dropped the ax and lifted his hands. They pointed toward the tall man and the fingers splayed out, vibrating as they tensed hard. O'Teague's head dropped back and his eyes closed. His tautened neck muscles quivered with strain.

The others watched with amazement as the man's odd performance seemed to create an effect. A second, ruby-hued aura arose about the first one. It seemed to literally attack the other, penetrating to intertwine with it. Like opposing currents of energy the two were instantly at war. They crackled together, creating hundreds of tiny flares of lightning, scintillating around the light-shrouded form of Feagh O'Donal. A crackling and sizzling sounded loud across the rooftop—like the lights of a whole Christmas tree shorting out, John thought.

John and the others could see the vague form of the tall man jerking spasmodically within the glow. Ann wondered if somehow the man were being electrocuted in there.

In a few moments the crimson light appeared to win. It had torn the blue light to fragments, absorbing the last shards. Then it faded too, and the glowing shell about the man vanished, revealing him again.

He looked unharmed, though winded, panting heavily. But the long cloak that he had worn was shredded, hanging about his form in scorched tatters that fluttered in the breeze.

The tinker relaxed and called out, "With the ruin of this cloak, your powers have fled. No more the Enchanter are you, Feagh O'Donal. You are but a mortal man again."

The momentary dismay in the other face was soon replaced by a look of bold defiance. "A man," he snarled, drawing himself up. "As I was before. And as such I am still more than a match for you."

In a move so sudden and swift that it took them all off guard, he moved upon Ann.

He swooped forward, threw an arm about her waist, and backed away to the very edge of the roof, raising his sword threateningly.

"Now," he grated, "you are going to drop your weapons. I would hate to harm this fine woman"—his grip on Ann tightened—"but I will be forced to do so if you don't surrender to me."

Milne lowered his gun again, but kept hold of it. "Look, Butler," he said reasoningly, "don't make this any worse. I just want my wife safe."

"*Not* 'Butler,'" the man reminded haughtily. "Earl O'Donal. And I won't be beaten by you. There's my host yet. I can still awaken them, magic or not."

"Okay . . . O'Donal," said Milne humoringly, still struggling to keep within what had become the very ephemeral bounds of reality. "Let the women go and I won't give a damn what you do. We'll go away."

"No you won't," said the earl fiercely. "I don't believe you. Your kind will never go away. You have to be defeated for me to be master of this tower again. If you want your wife safe, you must surrender to me. At once!" He gestured sharply toward Milne with the sword for emphasis.

Ann had stood quietly in his grip throughout this exchange. But now, as she felt a slight relaxation of his restraining arm, she brought her elbow up and back, slamming it into O'Donal's diaphragm while she thrust her body out against the arm.

He grunted and staggered. Ann wrenched herself away. Her husband charged forward to help, but she was already free, stepping out and away from her captor.

O'Donal's sword now lifted against John. The young man swung up his pistol in reply, muscles tensing, mind ceasing to work, motivated only by the immediate, savage need to destroy this man as quickly as he could.

Ann saw what he meant to do and screamed for him to stop, but it was a dim, meaningless sound to him. His attention was on the tall man and the great, shining sword lifting slowly . . . slowly . . . slowly to slash at him. The pistol leveled at John's hip and his finger tightened on the trigger.

Their battle never joined. Something intervened.

Taffy left Bridget and shot past John, leaping forward in a

fury of his own to protect his mistress, to strike out at her tormentor. He jumped for the big man's throat, slamming his hundred pounds of moving weight against O'Donal's chest.

It overbalanced the man. As Taffy dropped down safely to the roof, the earl was knocked backward over the roof's edge. He fought wildly for a moment to regain his balance, but failed . . . and fell.

They all rushed to the edge. A splash from below told them he had fallen into the stream, but in the darkness they could see nothing except the faint glittering of the water in the pale moonlight.

There was no further sound of splashing. No ripples of movement disturbed the stream's surface.

O'Donal was gone.

"That old man," said Ann quietly. "We should try to find him."

"He'll wash up," John answered coldly. This harsh end for his enemy suited him just fine.

But then he looked at the weapon in his hand, and it brought a sudden realization of what he'd meant to do. His rational mind recoiled from the fact. The pervasive spirit of violence had, after all, nearly won.

Repulsed by the weapon and all that it represented, he dropped it over the edge. He and Ann watched it plummet down to vanish beneath the black waters below.

CHAPTER
THIRTY

✣

I heard the old, old men say,
'Everything alters,
And one by one we drop away.'
They had hands like claws, and their knees
Were twisted like the old thorn-trees
By the waters.
I heard the old, old men say,
'All that's beautiful drifts away
Like the waters.'

—W. B. YEATS: *"The Old Men Admiring*
Themselves in the Water"

"Are you all right?" John demanded. "How are the Traherns?"

Ann assured him that they were unharmed, but she was shaken, and she could see that Bridget was badly frightened. Her first thought was to get the girl away from that place.

"I think we should get off this tower now," she said.

He agreed and led them back down the narrow stairs to meet a rather frantic Father Bonaventure coming up.

"You found them!" the monk said with relief and elation when he saw the women. "Thank our Good Lord. I searched through all the lower rooms and found no one. I'd started to despair. But what's happened to Butler?"

"He went off the top," John said flatly.

"My God!" the monk cried, aghast. "We must get help!"

"We'd never find him in the dark, Father. It wouldn't matter anyway. We're the ones who need the help now."

"What's been happening here?" Ann asked. "We heard a shot. Where are the rest of Butler's men?"

"Well in hand, I hope," said Bonaventure, eyeing the tinker.

"Quite secure when I left them," O'Teague assured.

"Then we can leave the manor?" said Ann.

"I don't think there's anybody left to stop us," John replied. "We control the whole estate, Milady Milne."

She shuddered. "Don't call me that, please. It just reminds me . . ."

He stopped and looked at her searchingly.

"Was it really rough for you?"

She shook her head. "Not so much rough as . . . as very *strange*. For a while I felt like I was a long way away from you, in space, and in time, too. That's what bothered me the most."

"I know what you mean," he said. "I've had that feeling more than once today." He slipped an arm about her waist and hugged her tight. "It's okay now. Come on. Let's get back to reality."

Once in the lower hall again, they considered their next move.

"So, does that finish it, then?" asked the monk. "Should we call the *Gardai*?"

"Not yet," John told him. "It may not be that simple anymore. We've killed a man now and damaged some others. It wasn't our own choice. Still, are the police going to believe it?"

"But he told us what he was doing," Ann said. "He kidnapped the three of us."

"And those thugs of his were likely all wanted men," added Nancy Trahern.

"That may be enough," John said. "Even so, it might be hard to convince the police that a man like Butler would be involved in kidnapping and . . . well, whatever else he was up to. Remember, the whole county loves him."

"I suppose there's some truth to what you say," said Bonaventure.

"I'd just feel better if we got some real evidence of what's been going on," John said. "Like if he has been hiding guns somewhere here."

"I thought that, too," said Nancy. "But he told us it was some kind of sleeping host."

"A what?" said O'Teague with great interest.

"He said an army of Irish warriors was in some hidden place," said Ann. "He was going to awaken them."

"Irish warriors? Hidden? Asleep?" John repeated skeptically. "What kind of crazy fantasy was he creating?"

"You might have believed him if you'd heard him," Ann said. "He was very convincing."

"I'm sure," said John, remembering his own recent encounter. "Still, he was handing you some kind of line. The great moviemaker at work again. Just a blind for what he was really up to."

"He was not all illusion and fantasy," put in O'Teague. "The earl did have something more about him, John. You saw that."

"Yeah, I guess I did," John admitted, considering the tinker's bizarre set-to with the man. "And I was going to ask you about—"

"Whatever he has hidden I'm game to search for it," said the tinker briskly. "Shall we look up or down first?"

"I don't think anything's hidden in the house," Ann said thoughtfully. "That would be too dangerous to him."

"I agree," Bonaventure said. He nodded toward the bound prisoners. "Our friends here said that the lorry was never supposed to come to the house. It was for that reason we almost came to grief."

"Of course!" John exclaimed. "We assumed these secret deliveries were being made here. That was the mistake. I should have known already that they weren't."

"What do you mean?" said Ann.

"I'll tell you, and I'll show you," he said excitedly. "I think I know where Butler's hiding spot is. Father, come with us and we'll go look now."

"In the dark?" asked the monk in confusion.

"We'll have to take the cars." John turned to the tinker. "Mr. O'Teague, would you mind the manor a little longer?"

"I think I'd rather go with you," the tinker told him. "I've a feeling you'll need me. And I do know the manor better than any of you."

"He's right there, John," said the monk.

"Okay," John agreed, nodding toward the prisoners, "but what about them?"

Nancy Trahern took the ax from the tinker, hefting it. "I can handle them well enough. With great pleasure."

"Good enough," said Milne.

"And we'll have Taffy with us, too," Bridget stoutly put in, patting her most loyal friend on his broad head. "He's quite a protector himself."

"You don't have to tell me," said John. "Okay. You two and the dog stay here. But if there's any problem while we're gone, you go ahead and call the police. Don't take chances. We'll get back as soon as we can." He looked at the rest. "Let's go."

"Good luck," Nancy Trahern and her daughter both called after the four as they started toward the front door.

Outside John pointed to the automobile the monk had parked in front.

"Father, get your car. We'll get ours from the garage and meet you back here."

O'Teague went with the monk. The young couple left them and went on at a run, around the house and down the road to the garages.

"That wasn't his car," said Ann as they ran. "Whose was it?"

"Trahern's," said John, and then remembered. "Damn, I left him at the garages! The poor man is probably going crazy with the waiting."

"He's with you? I wish we could have told his family that."

"We'll tell him they're safe when we get the car. He can go back up and see them."

They came into the graveled yard and stopped when they found no one there.

"Mr. Trahern," John called.

"I'm here," the man replied, walking out of one of the garage bays. "I wasn't certain who was coming. What's happened?"

"The castle is ours," John announced. "Your wife and daughter are safe."

"I'm grateful to hear it," he said with relief. "I hoped as much when I saw Mrs. Milne. What now?"

"Now you can go to your family, Mr. Trahern," John told him. "We're going to uncover Mr. Butler's secret here."

"Where he's stashed the weapons?"

"Or whatever it is," said Ann. "John thinks he knows where to look. We need to find out."

"That we do, after coming this far," Trahern agreed emphatically. "I'll go with you."

"Don't you want to stay with your wife and daughter?" said Ann. "They don't even know you're here."

"It's enough for now to know they're safe. Uncovering the whole secret of this place must come first. Until then it really won't be finished."

"Okay," John said. "The more help the better. We're going to need light to search. We're going to take our car."

"I'll bring the lorry and follow. Where are you bound?"

"Back down the road that we took in."

They drove the two vehicles back around the manor. In the front they met Bonaventure and O'Teague, and John took the lead of the tiny caravan.

At the fork where the two roads converged he turned,

crossed the ancient bridge, and followed the way that led toward the ruins, now invisible in the darkness.

"I should have known that truck never went up to the house," John explained to Ann as he drove. "Remember the day we walked down to the monastery to see what made the lights?"

"I thought that must have been the truck," she said, "but we couldn't find it."

"That's right," he said. "That's the point. What was the road like?"

"Muddy. It had just rained the night be—" She stopped. She knew now what he had remembered. "There weren't any tracks!"

"Right. No tracks from the manor down past the cemetery. But there *were* tracks—deep ones—on the road in from the outer gates and past the old mound."

"The truck stopped somewhere in between," she said.

"And there's only one good hiding place there," he said.

"The church!" they said together.

They were right. When they reached the tiny church, they found that the truck had come up the road that far, but no farther. The marks ended where the road passed close to the side of the abandoned structure.

To examine the area more easily, they pulled the truck and the two cars up on three sides of it. The beams of their headlamps flooded the churchyard, lighting up the church and its encircling graves, throwing the headstones into sharp relief against the black curtain of the woods behind.

The five of them left their vehicles and walked back to the road to examine the ruts more carefully.

"You can see where the truck came in," John said. "It pulled up by the church, then turned around in the pasture, there, and went back."

"Here are footprints," said the monk, examining the ground along one side of the church.

"That's where the driver unloaded," John surmised. "Let's see where he went."

They followed the prints around the church. They were a muddled trail, the prints going in both directions to indicate the route that had been used both ways, many times. They were able to trace them to the point where the cemetery began, but there the bare earth was replaced by flagstones, and the trail ended.

"Where now?" said the monk, looking at the headstones and tombs that spread around them.

"Just keep on looking," John suggested. "Something's hidden somewhere."

They wandered among the stones and examined some of them. The two Milnes noted that a few of the dates were as recent as the last century, but that most were from the twelfth to fifteenth centuries. Here and there large, coffin-shaped tombs of stone stuck up above the smaller markers. One had cracked, and a gaping hole had opened in its corner. John looked inside with morbid curiosity, but it was empty.

"For all the restoration at the manor, they didn't do much to fix this place up," he remarked. "Lots of these stones are broken. And look how scratched that one tomb is . . ."

His voice trailed off and he moved to examine the large stone tomb he had indicated more closely.

Ann watched him with curiosity. "What are you doing?" she asked.

"Look at these." He pointed out deep scratches on the sides of the tomb. "They're fresh. The mold has been scraped away and the clean stone shows. It looks black against the white mold. That has to be recent. You know how fast stone molds in this country. There are nicks and cuts all around this end."

"Something hitting it?"

"Lots of somethings. Like metal jacks, I'll bet."

They examined the thick stone lid, securely in its place. It looked quite solid and immovable, seemingly untouched for centuries. Then Ann realized something else about it.

"John, this stone—I saw it!" she exclaimed. "But not here. In the back of the manor garage where we hid."

"I remember one there. Are you sure it was the same?"

"I'm sure." She looked more closely at it. "And look here. Something else, around the edge."

He saw it, too. All about the edge, where the lid fitted closely against the sides, a line of clean, dark stone was clearly visible against the white mold that coated all the rest.

"It's been shifted, that's for certain," said Ann. "We'd never have seen it without that line showing."

"Let's shift it again," her husband suggested.

He called the others to help. Each of the four men took a corner of the lid and lifted together. It came up with amazing ease.

"That's not stone," commented Bonaventure as they set it aside.

"A duplicate," said John. "More of Butler's movie effects. Probably made of plastic."

They peered inside. The rectangular tomb was empty. A large opening showed at its bottom, going down into blackness. A modern ladder of aluminum led into the void.

"This is it," Trahern said. "Whatever Butler was hiding is down there."

"Look here," said the tinker, "I think this is where I must go first."

"You?" said Trahern.

"No need to risk us all," the other argued. "And it could be risky down there. Very old this construction looks. Remember, I've worked with such things much of my life."

"Well now," said Bonaventure, "I don't know—"

"Listen, you must do as I say in this," the little man said more adamantly. "I've a feeling there might be great danger in what we're about. It's something I have to do. So please don't question it."

The rest exchanged glances. They realized there was such force in the tinker's words that they had to accept. None could question that somehow he had taken the lead. Still, John was not going to be left out of this. Not now.

"You can go first," he said, "but not all alone. I insist on that."

The tinker eyed him hard, then gave a little smile. "Yes, all right, my lad. You've earned the right to go. But only you." He swept a commanding gaze around at the others. "The rest of you wait here, until we say it's safe. Keep a watch."

From the lorry's back and one car's glovebox the would-be explorers fetched an electric torch and lantern.

John held both, flashing the torch down the hole while O'Teague descended the ladder. Then he shoved the torch in his belt and followed.

At the hole's bottom they found an open doorway. They went through to find themselves in a long chamber. John drew the torch and shone it along the walls, showing the damp stone blocks.

"Man-made," he commented. "Looks old." He panned the torch's beam along the empty floor to the far end. It shone on a jumble of shapes there. "What's all that?"

They walked down. The torch's light played over a generator, a dozen floodlights on stands, and piles of beams and jacks. It moved upward to illuminate the row of shoring timbers and their supporting forest of jacks.

"So, this is what all the beams were for," he said, examining the ceiling. "They had a cave-in."

"Perhaps from the collapsin' of the church above," suggested O'Teague. "No wonder this entrance was never found."

He took the lantern and moved up the avenue of jacks to the metal door in the back wall. He examined the decorated and corroded bronze panel intently.

"Well, then," he pronounced, "this is surely what he was being so careful to hide."

"But that door hasn't been opened in centuries," said John. "He couldn't have been storing arms in there."

"I think it was something far more important to him. Looks like he had it all ready to be opened. We were just in time. That Fate workin' again." He looked to John. "Well, shall we be obligin' our lost earl?"

They put down the lights and threw their weight against the door. The rusted hinges held back for some moments, but then gave protestingly, screeching like something being tortured as the door moved inward.

They forced it open a foot, then squeezed through the crack. Once beyond, O'Teague held up his lantern, illuminating the new space.

"What the hell . . . ?" John breathed, staring ahead.

It was a very long, very narrow room. Down both sides of an immense table that ran its length sat over a hundred men.

They were massive figures clad in long cloaks, mail shirts, and iron helms, all of it looking like new. They sat bent forward, heads down on the table and pillowed upon their arms. Swords, shields, and spears were stacked about them, their iron still gleaming brightly, ready at any time to be wielded in battle again.

"A sleeping army," said John in astonishment. "That story was true."

He shone his torch down the length of the table's one side and up the other, the beam glinting from the burnished helmet of each warrior. It ended on a nearby pillar of stone where there hung a gracefully curved horn of brass.

"There's the Horn of Fate," O'Teague pointed out. "Ready for the Awakening."

"I heard the story," said John. "Some guy blew it once, a long time ago."

"Try it now," the tinker urged.

John thought this suggestion incredibly crazy, but found himself unable to disobey. He stepped to the pillar, took the horn down, and put it to his lips. Here he hesitated, looking to O'Teague.

"It's all right, lad," the tinker assured. "Blow it."

He puckered and blew the horn. A deep forlorn moan issued from it.

John felt the hairs on his neck rising as one of the figures stirred.

A gauntleted hand shivered, clenched, reopened. The head began to lift, the body to shift.

Then there was a dusty, crackling sound, like someone crushing a bundle of dried twigs. The warrior disintegrated before their eyes, limbs and torso grotesquely falling apart, head toppling free and rolling away to the center of the tabletop. In seconds only crumpled clothing and dust remained.

"As I thought," said the tinker. "Not on time, but far too late—for them."

He walked to the still "sleeping" warrior nearest him. He pulled up the visor of the helmeted head. John looked into the black eye sockets of a fleshless skull.

"This is his great army," O'Teague said sorrowfully. "Only a host of skeletons. So many fine heroes, sleeping their last sleep. There's no god or magic that'll awaken them now."

He lifted the lantern, lighting a long, jagged fissure in the roof above.

"The cave-in wasn't the only damage here," he remarked. "The noise and upheaval it caused must have broken the spell woven about this place. Ah well," he said, shrugging, "it's really the best way. They never even knew."

"This was Butler's secret?" said John. "Some skeletons in armor?"

"Aye, it was, in the end," O'Teague answered. "And just as well in the end that he also never knew."

They went out, John bringing along only the horn. At the tinker's insistence they pulled the bronze door closed.

They climbed the ladder to the surface. The others there had awaited them anxiously.

"Did you find it?" said Trahern with eagerness.

"We found Butler's secret, all right," the tinker said with irony. "It really is all finished now."

"Is it big, then?" Trahern wanted to know.

"It . . . well, it's unbelievable," John said truthfully. "And I think it's time we called in the police."

"I can't let you do that," said Trahern.

There was something so ominous in the soft voice that the other four at the tomb turned to face the man.

He had moved some distance away from them to stand near the edge of the lighted area. A large revolver now hung from his right hand.

Chapter
Thirty-One

✠

I see my life go drifting like a river
From change to change; I have been many things—
A green drop in the surge, a gleam of light
Upon a sword, a fir-tree on a hill,
An old slave grinding at a heavy quern,
A king sitting upon a chair of gold—
And all these things were wonderful and great;
But now I have grown nothing, knowing all.
Ah! Druid, Druid, how great webs of sorrow
Lay hidden in the small slate-coloured thing!

—W. B. YEATS: *"Fergus and the Druid"*

"Trahern?" John was bewildered. "What do you mean? What's wrong?"

"Nothing at all," the man said in his calm way. "I only mean to take whatever you've found down there away with me. And there'll be no interfering from police."

"I don't understand," said Ann. "You haven't been working with Butler all along?"

"No, Mrs. Milne. I'm with the IRA. They're the ones that really have need of Mr. Butler's cache."

"How can you be with the IRA?" said Ann. "I thought you came here to find your family. Unless . . . you're not Mr. Trahern."

"Oh, I am that," he said. "I told the truth when I said Nancy and Bridget left me because I wouldn't leave the North. I didn't say my need to stay was because of my dedication to our struggle there. My wife wanted no more to do with the cause—or with me."

"Then why did you come here?" asked Ann.

"Oh, she did write to me," he explained. "That was the truth, too. But her letter demanded to know if there was IRA activity here. She told me of a man whom I knew well. He'd been one of us some years ago. Now he was driving a mysterious lorry about Ballymurroe.

"Well, I checked. But none of my contacts knew of anything happening here. That made me suspicious. Then she disappeared. That was enough to bring me."

"Not to find her," said John.

"To see what great secret thing here might have caused her vanishing. I found much more than I'd imagined."

"What you've found is a bunch of skeletons and some antique swords," said John angrily, lifting the horn to shake toward him. "That's your big weapons cache."

"Are you trying to spin me some mad tale, too?" Trahern accused. "Save your breath. It won't help you."

"Goddammit," said John, "I am fed up with you fanatics. You used us. You used your whole family. You care more about guns than about your own daughter. You'd sacrifice anything for your damned cause, wouldn't you?"

"I do what I have to do," he said simply. "It's a war."

"A war," John repeated scornfully. "For its whole existence Ireland has been waging some bloody war or other. Wars for pride, wars for revenge, wars for ideas and beliefs, wars piled on wars, all with dim, twisted motives and ends that never come. Hasn't it gone on enough?" he asked Trahern with immense weariness. "Hasn't it destroyed you long enough?"

"It isn't finished," Trahern said, the soft voice taking on

an edge. For the first time he was really angry, and the mask of calm was wholly stripped away. In those deep black caverns of his eyes, the suppressed light of his own kind of madness now flared out brightly for them all to see. "Until we're free again as we once were, it will go on."

"You're not bringing back your dead past that way," John shot back, "you're just sleeping with it. Don't you see what that's done to you?"

"I'll not argue any longer with your likes," Trahern said tersely, bringing up the gun to point at them. "I want those weapons now. You'll bring them out of there and load them in the truck."

"I'm telling you, there *aren't* any damn guns!" John all but yelled at him. "There's nothing down there. Nothing but more dead!"

"I said I don't believe that," Trahern replied.

"Then go and look yourself!"

Trahern thumbed the gun's hammer back with an ominous click. "Don't press me further, Milne, or someone will get hurt. And who first? The Father? Your wife? You? I've no care which."

Something moved in the shadows behind Trahern, and a clattering noise broke the silence.

Startled, the man turned toward the sound, bringing the gun around to point midway between his captives and this possible new threat. All of them waited, in fear and in hope, for something to appear.

For a long moment there was nothing. Then from the void emerged the dreadful specter of a man mounted on a horse so black that it was only a glowing outline against the night.

The rider seemed a spirit from the past, one of the last champions raised from sleep by their desecration, clad in the ragged, filthy clothing it had dragged with it from its grave. Still it was a commanding figure. It sat the horse proudly, and in one hand it firmly clutched a gleaming sword.

"Butler!" said John in disbelief.

"Feagh O'Donal, Earl of Dunraven," the rider's voice boomed back.

Somehow the man had survived the fall. Somehow the immense energy that had driven him all of his long life had taken him from the river and brought him here in a desperate last defense of his great dream.

"What are you doing here?" he demanded of them. "You violate my sacred ground."

"We're taking your guns, Butler," said Trahern. "Keep out of it now."

"Guns?" The mounted man walked his horse close to Trahern and pulled up there, glaring down at the man in anger. "There are no such vile things there. It is my host. My heroes, waiting for me to lead them again, for the Glory of Eire!"

"It's only a host of the dead now, Feagh O'Donal," the tinker said. "Gone West for these hundred years or more. All you have done has been for nothing. Give it up."

"You're only a mad old man who's fooled himself," Trahern said brutally, stepping up to the mounted man. "Ireland has no need of the likes of you."

These words did more to Butler than had all his physical ordeal. It seemed as if the undauntable spirit that had always sustained him now suffered a mortal thrust. They watched him shrinking, wasting away, aging years in a single moment. He sagged forward and dropped his sword arm to his side, letting the weapon hang harmlessly from his hand.

"I thank you for your help, Butler," Trahern told him. "You've served your purpose. Let the sword fall and ride away from here with your life."

"No!" the other shouted in angry defiance.

He pulled upright upon the horse. An azure energy shone out suddenly from him, forming a glowing aura about his body. It ran in several tendrils from his hand up the sword's length, twining about the bright blade in a crackling net of power. For that moment the beaten, bedraggled figure was gone, replaced by the image of a cloaked warrior, giant and invincible upon his towering steed.

The others stared up at this apparition in astonishment. Trahern stood frozen in terror, the gun forgotten in his hand.

"I *am* Feagh O'Donal, Lord of Dunraven," the voice thundered from the figure, echoing hollowly through the black churchyard. "That will *never* be taken from me. I will not be beaten!"

With that he swung the sword out at Trahern. It was a movement so swift that the man had no time to dodge away. But in a defensive reflex he did raise his gun and fire.

The sword slash should have cut Trahern in two. But his bullet slammed hard into O'Donal's shoulder, rocking him back. That shifted the sword's blow. Instead of the weapon's keen edge, it was only the flat of the blade that caught Trahern across the chest. Still, the impact threw him back against a stone cross with tremendous force.

He hung there a moment and then toppled to the sod like something boneless.

The mounted man lifted the sword as if to strike again, but his strength seemed to fail him. The magical energy shimmering about him died away. The weapon dropped from his fingers, and he slid from the horse, holding its mane. Then he sank to his knees amongst the stones of the churchyard.

While John went to see about Trahern, Ann and Bonaventure ran to O'Donal and eased him down to rest against one of the stones. The black horse continued to stand nearby as if concerned for its fallen rider.

"Trahern's alive," said John, checking the man. He picked up the gun and came over to them. "I can't tell if he's hurt much, though. How about Butler?"

The old man seemed to be unconscious. That last outpouring of energy had had a shocking effect. His face was now ashen, his cheeks sunken, as if he had been ill for a long, long time. To John he looked like a man burned out, gutted, like the shell of an ancient, abandoned tower.

"I don't know," said Ann. "I don't think we'd better move him."

"I'll get help," said John. He handed the gun to Bona-venture. "Here, in case Trahern wakes up." He turned to go.

"Wait, John," said Ann.

He stopped and looked back to her.

"Don't say anything to the Traherns now," she said. "They've had enough. Keep them up there. After the police come, we'll work it out."

"Okay," he said. "I'll be right back."

The sound of the car leaving the churchyard seemed to rouse the wasted man. He opened his eyes and looked at Ann.

"He . . . he's going for the *Gardai,* isn't he?" he asked in a hollow voice that alarmed her with its weakness. "I've lost, haven't I? Eire . . . the tower . . . my champions . . . all lost."

"It's all right," she told him soothingly. "It doesn't matter."

"It was everything," he said with despair. "It was only this country and my destiny—they were all I had. Do you understand that?"

"Of course I do," she said. She thought of her husband, and of Trahern, and of her own feelings here, in this mystical land. Destiny seemed to have taken hold of them all.

"I meant it for the good," he said. "It wasn't just for me. I meant to help . . ."

"You did that," she assured him. "You helped the people here. And you just saved us all. You rode in here and saved us like a hero from one of the legends."

He gripped her arm tightly and his blue eyes, growing darker now, widened with concern.

"Then you know it wasn't madness, don't you?" he asked. "You believe I really was the earl."

"I believe," she assured him.

"I could have done it, couldn't I?" he demanded with more force. "I could have won my rightful place here again. I could have brought glory back to Eire."

She looked to Bonaventure and then up to O'Teague,

who stood gazing down at the fallen man with great regret. The monk and then the tinker gave a slight nod.

She understood. The Lord of Dunraven could have his dream. It had obsessed him; it had destroyed him; now it would comfort him.

"Yes," she said gently. "You could have won. You could have been a great lord again, defending Eire, ruling from your tower."

"With my warriors about me, and all the green country spread out below." He looked searchingly into her eyes. "You would have been there too, wouldn't you?"

"I would," she said. "Now, rest a while."

"A while," he said and closed his eyes.

He took a gasping breath and then released it in a long, low sigh. His body relaxed slowly, going limp.

Then another light arose about his body. It was a pale golden glow this time, shimmering around him in a soft cocoon that blurred his form a moment as it grew swiftly brighter.

Ann and the others pulled back and shielded their eyes as the gold glow intensified to a brilliant light. Then the encasing aura burst open like a shattered blown-glass vase. It splintered into myriad tiny shards that rose up in a cloud.

It seemed a vast bevy of flickering fireflies as it lifted. The scintillating points of light swiftly spread apart. They dispersed into the night and winked out, leaving only the blackness behind.

"Father!" Ann gasped in amazement, looking to the monk. "What was it?"

Bonaventure shook his head, marveling himself. "It's far beyond my poor knowledge, child."

"There was the Others' power in him still," the tinker supplied. "The last of the *Sidhe* magic that had kept him alive so long. It's only a mortal man that he is now, just as he once was. So what he said has truly come to pass . . . all of it is lost. One more piece of the old ways—for good or bad— is gone away from us forever. And maybe Ireland will be the poorer for that."

When John returned, he found Ann sitting by the old man's side, holding his hand. Beside her Bonaventure knelt and prayed quietly while the tinker looked on.

She lifted her head toward her husband as he approached, and he saw the sorrow in her eyes. He knew then what had happened. The last Lord of Dunraven was dead.

Bonaventure finished his prayer and looked up to where John stood.

"Mr. O'Teague said he'd been hearing the keening of the *Sidhe* these past days," the monk said. "Perhaps it was for him."

"They're only supposed to wail for those of pure Irish blood," John pointed out. "Butler wasn't of Ireland."

"Maybe Butler wasn't, but Feagh O'Donal was," said Ann firmly. "And I know that's who he really was. There was more of Ireland in him than in anyone."

John stepped up beside her and put a hand on her shoulder. "I guess you're right," he told her. "I feel that, too."

"Listen," said the monk, turning his head. "There's a fresh wind rising from the sea. Hear it roaring in the trees as it comes?"

"The Hosting of the *Sidhe*," said the tinker.

At the words, John was reminded of another Yeats poem. At a loss for any other fitting words, he spoke the poem aloud:

"Away, come away:
Empty your heart of its mortal dream
The winds awaken, the leaves whirl around,
Our cheeks are pale, our hair is unbound,
Our breasts are heaving, our eyes are agleam,
Our arms are waving, our lips are apart;
And if any gaze on our rushing band,
We come between him and the deed of his hand,
We come between him and the hope of his heart."*

* "The Hosting of the Sidhe"

ABOUT THE AUTHOR

Ken Flint is a lifelong resident of Omaha, Nebraska and received his Master's Degree in English literature from the University of Nebraska there. Before embarking on a full-time writing career in 1987, he taught English literature and humanities on both secondary and college levels. His researches for many of his novels have taken him on several extensive trips through the Irish Republic and the United Kingdom. Besides his novel writing he has produced short fiction and non-fiction works, including a source book of Christmas traditions, for various markets. He also enjoys working with Panorama Incorporated, an Omaha-based firm of business and writing consultants, on various writing projects. *The Darkening Flood* is his fourteenth novel for Bantam/Spectra Books.

Bantam Spectra publishes more Hugo and Nebula Award-winning novels than any other science fiction and fantasy imprint. Celebrate the Tenth Anniversary of Spectra—read them all!

HUGO WINNERS

A CANTICLE FOR LEIBOWITZ, Walter M. Miller, Jr.	____27381-7 $5.99/$6.99
THE GODS THEMSELVES, Isaac Asimov	____28810-5 $5.99/$6.99
RENDEZVOUS WITH RAMA, Arthur C. Clarke	____28789-3 $5.99/$6.99
DREAMSNAKE, Vonda N. McIntyre	____29659-0 $5.99/$7.50
THE FOUNTAINS OF PARADISE, Arthur C. Clarke	____28819-9 $5.99/$6.99
FOUNDATION'S EDGE, Isaac Asimov	____29338-9 $5.99/$6.99
STARTIDE RISING, David Brin	____27418-X $5.99/$6.99
THE UPLIFT WAR, David Brin	____27971-8 $5.99/$6.99
HYPERION, Dan Simmons	____28368-5 $5.99/$6.99
DOOMSDAY BOOK, Connie Willis	____56273-8 $5.99/$6.99
GREEN MARS, Kim Stanley Robinson	____37335-8 $12.95/$16.95

NEBULA WINNERS

THE GODS THEMSELVES, Isaac Asimov	____28810-5 $5.99/$6.99
RENDEZVOUS WITH RAMA, Arthur C. Clarke	____28789-3 $5.99/$6.99
DREAMSNAKE, Vonda N. McIntyre	____29659-0 $5.99/$7.50
THE FOUNTAINS OF PARADISE, Arthur C. Clarke	____28819-9 $5.99/$6.99
TIMESCAPE, Gregory Benford	____27709-0 $5.99/$6.99
STARTIDE RISING, David Brin	____27418-X $5.99/$6.99
TEHANU, Ursula K. Le Guin	____28873-3 $5.50/$6.99
DOOMSDAY BOOK, Connie Willis	____56273-8 $5.99/$6.99
RED MARS, Kim Stanley Robinson	____56073-5 $5.99/$7.50

Ask for these books at your local bookstore or use this page to order.

Please send me the books I have checked above. I am enclosing $____ (add $2.50 to cover postage and handling). Send check or money order, no cash or C.O.D.'s, please.

Name _____

Address _____

City/State/Zip _____

Send order to: Bantam Books, Dept. AA 2, 2451 S. Wolf Rd., Des Plaines, IL 60018
Allow four to six weeks for delivery.
Prices and availability subject to change without notice.   AA 2 2/95